THE BELOW

SCOTT T. MILLER

THE BELOW

MASCOT® BOOKS
an imprint of Amplify Publishing Group

www.mascotbooks.com

The Below

For more information, please contact:
Mascot Books, an imprint of Amplify Publishing Group
620 Herndon Parkway, Suite 220
Herndon, VA 20170
info@mascotbooks.com

Library of Congress Control Number: 2025915971
CPSIA Code: PRV0925A
ISBN-13: 979-8-89138-601-3

Printed in the United States

To my family.

Aloha 'āina

CHAPTER 1

The reprocessed rain from up top had frozen around the outside of the meat locker window, like a pond receding into the earth. Unfortunately, the temperature outside was warmer than our spot, curled up next to the hanging slabs of synthetic pork. But with the arrival of the morning's thaw, the icy frame slowly turned into rivers of water dripping onto the street. Through our partially obstructed view, the morning chaos of the island city stirred.

A bright neon flash from the club across the busy street caught our attention. It wasn't enough to distract me from the stench of recomposing meat lingering in the frozen locker. I pulled the lightweight gator over my nose to help with the temperature and smell, but it did little to relieve either.

"They said between five and nine, right?" Kamalu asked.

Bloodshot vessels tainted his eyes, and black, puffy skin surrounded the sockets.

"Yeah, but the 808s aren't known for giving precise tips," I murmured through the gator. "This is it, though; we get him, and we're done."

"The good soldier now?" The corner of his mouth curled up in a wry smile.

EO scoffed behind me, but the well-trained muscles in my face didn't betray my attention.

"Not quite. Just ready for this week to end."

"Right. Well, I need a break. Call me if you see him," Kamalu said. He climbed past the rows of meat and out onto the slightly warmer factory floor.

"He's gotta show soon, right?" EO rubbed his hands together, blowing in between them.

"Don't do that; you're not actually cold."

"I could be," he said, and glanced around the locker. "If this meat is frozen, why can't I be?"

"It's not meat." I tore my gaze away from the street outside for a moment to find EO's scrunched eyes staring back at me.

"I'm sorry, I'm just tired—"

"Don't worry about it." His face shifted, softening, yet with an undercurrent of embarrassment.

My eyes drifted to the ground. A thin layer of reconstruction fluid lacquered the concrete floors of the meat locker. Watching the remnants of imitation pork float around my boots, I tried to muster even an ounce of empathy from my drained body.

"I know—"

"Kilo, I think it's him." EO's words echoed. I followed his outstretched finger through the window and to the other side of the busy Mid-City street.

"Where?" I inched closer to the glass, watching a figure emerge from the adjacent alley and head directly for the spotlit double doors of Club Aerial. "Shit, maybe. Malu!"

I fumbled around with my personal device before materializing the grainy photo of Issac Reklov. We stared through the icy pane, trying to catch a clear glimpse of the man's face before he disappeared into the club.

Kamalu burst through the door, a little color back in his cheeks. "You see him?"

With one hand, I pointed through the window. The other hand slid behind my back with my fingers curled, with the tips pressed tightly against the top of my palm.

EO picked up the signal. "Yeah, that's definitely him."

"What do you think?" Kamalu asked.

"It's him."

I shoved through the hanging hunks of "meat" on my way to the locker's exit.

The waves of warmth from the factory floor brought feeling back to my exposed skin, but there wasn't time to bask in the temperature change. I took off through the processing warehouse. The whir of interconnected cables and conveyor belts buzzed in my ears while pre-constructed bacon fell through the slats of the massive, automated machinery, somehow leaving a worse stench in its wake. With the exit just ahead, I forced back my gag reflex through gritted teeth.

"I'll get the front. You cover the back!" I shouted before breaking through onto the street. EO exited with me, Kamalu on my heels. Indi-cycles flew past, their passengers merely a blur. I covered my eyes and gave myself a moment to adjust to the wide tapestry of neon. The stimuli faded, and my mind settled into the ostentatious normalcy of Big City.

"Got it!" Kamalu burst through the door and raced down the street toward a pedestrian bridge that crossed to Club Aerial's side of the road.

"Let me know if you pick up anything," I murmured under my breath.

"Hurry! We don't want to lose him in the club," EO responded, already a few steps into the crowd.

I pushed after him into the streams of people. We fought our way up the street, but the next pedestrian bridge curled over it at least fifty meters away.

This was too slow. I cranked my head to scan for other options, but the crowds saturated the sidewalk up and down the block.

"We can cross. I got you!" EO screamed from the edge of the nearest driving lane.

"You sure?"

"Yeah, you don't trust me?" EO laughed while he gauged the traffic. He then sprinted through the racing cycles.

"Probably too much," I muttered.

I stepped out into the street as an indi-cycle screeched past, clipping a puddle. The balancing system of the vehicle shuttered as it kept the two wheels attached to the narrow frame, upright through its hydroplane. I raised an arm to deflect the potential splash, but the water barely reached the curb. However, it still left me bathing in the feculent aroma of island city street water.

"Now!" EO yelled from halfway across the street.

I sprinted across the first few lanes, cutting through the wind left in the wake of the speeding cycles.

"Stop!" he screamed again.

Without thinking, the muscles in my legs seized at his command. A duo-cycle zipped past with its outside mirror inches from my chest.

"I think he was trying to hit you," EO said.

My face scrunched at the glimpse of EO's tensed jaw. "Probably too much!"

I jumped over the last vehicle lane onto the less congested sidewalk. With a nod, EO led me into the flow of pedestrians. We weaved halfway up the block and slipped through the spotlit double doors of Club Aerial.

The wood paneling shook with each reverberation of the throaty music roaring from the floating stage in the center of the arena. Red and black lights flashed relentlessly as hundreds of people jumped up and down, moving in a cult-like circle around the musician.

EO and I scanned the room, looking for Reklov. In the corner of the arena, surrounded by a few colorfully suited men, a long-haired man in a dirty sweater bent over, talking into a woman's ear. Reklov.

"Got him. Try to pick up anything on the way."

EO nodded and followed me through the spinning crowd of partiers. We swirled around with the music, flowing through the sea of sweaty limbs toward the far side of the floor. Finally, we forced our way through the crowd, only meters away from Reklov. His head jerked, and his wide pupils locked with mine.

"He's gonna run," EO said.

My eyes remained entangled with Reklov's for a moment before he clutched the bag at his feet and bolted for the rear of the club.

I drew the Nambu pistol from inside my coat and charged after him. Before the colorful-suited men could assess the situation, I was past them and heading for the sliver of pale light that cut into the darkness of the club. A single gunshot sounded from behind us, and the club fell into disarray.

"Is he outside?" I yelled.

"Yes! Hard left."

I dropped a shoulder into the door and crashed through into the back alley. Merchants lined the street, but I just managed to jerk my head to the left and see Reklov sprinting toward the larger adjacent alley.

I ran, leveling the Nambu toward his feet. "Stop!"

Reklov's head suddenly snapped forward as his momentum ceased. His torso folded in the center, and his legs flew into the air, sending him smashing into the ground. In the alley, standing firmly in Reklov's path, was Kamalu—his arm outstretched, with a wicked smile plastered on his face.

I stalked over to where Reklov lay, gasping for air, and holstered the Nambu. Kamalu fashioned a set of DIIP cuffs around Reklov's wrists. His bag sat next to him, tightly cinched with a drawstring.

"Let's see why I didn't get to sleep last night," I said, opening the bag and feeling around inside.

The cylindrical glass objects immediately registered. In the light, the thick tube filled with gelatin, surrounding a slim, off-gray needle, looked similar to a large syringe from a Mid-City hospital.

Kamalu hoisted Reklov to his feet, his face dropping once he saw the syringes. "Where did you get replicas?"

Reklov spat at my feet. "Just giving the people what they want."

His expression turned sinister, and a smirk wrapped around his face. Without a word, I nodded to Kamalu, who pulled Reklov down the alley.

"The DIIP doesn't want peace; it wants order. You're just as bad as the Designers!" Reklov shouted.

The words struck me, sending my heart racing for a moment.

"This is new," EO said as he watched Kamalu drag Reklov toward a duo-cycle parked at the edge of the alley.

"I guess it was only a matter of time before replicas cropped back up," I grumbled to the ground. "You think it means anything?"

EO shrugged. "Maybe."

"Hmm. Either way, this is someone else's problem." I grabbed the bag and followed the alley to Kamalu's duo-cycle. Inside, Reklov fought against the restraints and lunged toward the window when he saw me.

"Can I have a look?" Kamalu motioned for the bag and pulled out two syringes. "I've honestly only ever seen them in pictures."

"What are we going to do with them?" I asked.

"I don't know. Where the hell did he even get DPM replicas?"

My thoughts wandered to the only time I'd seen one. I still remembered the rumors spreading like wildfire that someone from the Kauaʻi Below had a replica. Everyone knew the stories of people injecting in Honolulu, but I wanted to see for myself. It only took a minute for the man's gray matter to deteriorate and congeal inside his skull, leaving only a ghostly corpse.

"You go home and get some rest. I'll take care of this. Then I'm gonna do the same," Kamalu said. For the first time in a week, I let my shoulders relax and released the tension in my chest. "You sure?"

"Yeah. I got this."

The crunch of powder sent soothing waves and painful constrictions through my body. It was never the same feeling twice, watching the fine pink dust demolished and then constructed into round, imprinted pills. The only constant was the nameless woman who concocted the drug I needed but could live without. It never quite managed to quell the shard of agony.

"How many?" The question brought me back from the trance of the process. Exhaustion overrode my consciousness, more so than usual.

"Twenty's fine."

The thickset woman scooped a handful of pills into a clear bag and sealed the edge. "Well?"

"Right." I pulled out my personal device and transferred the payment. "One hundred credits. Transfer."

Before I could give the woman a courteous nod, she turned and disappeared back into the eclectic shop.

The bag of pills slipped easily into my coat pocket before EO and I exited onto the street. The brutalist shop soon faded behind us, replaced with inextricably interwoven concrete high rises. With each step, the slight crackle from the pill bag made sure my attention didn't drift too far away.

"You all right?" EO asked.

"I think I'll feel better once I get some sleep." Even though the rumbling of cycles, buzzing fluorescent lights, and muddled conversations made it unlikely anyone would hear us, I maintained my hushed tone.

"It's weird, though, right? The replica DPMs?"

"I don't have the energy to think about it right now, so I don't know."

"All right, but they exploded before Honolulu fell and then after—nothing. For ten years, I could count on one hand how many replicas we'd heard about. And now . . ." His voice trailed off, losing himself in connections that didn't matter to me.

We walked in silence for a few minutes before finally making it to our apartment building. As I entered the drab double doors at the stocky base of the high-rise, I reached into my coat and pulled out a single pink pill.

"I'm sorry," EO said.

The pill melted on my tongue within moments, but the chalky aftertaste lingered in my throat.

"You don't have to apologize every time."

His eyes searched the ground. "I know, but somehow it makes me feel better . . . at least a bit."

I pushed open my apartment door with my back. The dim light flicked on after recognizing my entrance. The apartment was a "sleek one-bedroom with fantastic Mid-City views," or so the ad had said when I signed the lease, sight unseen. While calling this room sleek now seemed like a gross misrepresentation, the view lived up to expectations.

"Still living like a king, I see." Kamalu's voice sent a shot through my body, and I reflexively reached for the Nambu.

"What the hell. I almost shot you," I breathed. My fingers relaxed around the rough, cold steel of the Nambu's handle. With another breath, I placed it atop the dresser and pulled off my jacket. "I'm sorry, but I just spent 118 hours of my week with you tracking down a bunch of lowlifes from Maui—you're the last person I want to see right now."

"Believe me, I'm not thrilled about spending the rest of my day with you either, but I need to give you a heads-up about tomorrow's meeting."

An empty glass rested on the coffee table, something that hadn't been there yesterday morning. I shot a quick glance at EO, who nodded at my assessment.

"Malu, this could've been a call. Why are you in my apartment?"

He played with his fingers as I waited for an answer. "I didn't tell them about the DPMs."

EO balked in the corner, but I held my composure and waited a moment for any follow-up. Kamalu provided none. Instead, he paced on the other side of the slide-bed, his free hand playing with the sheets.

"Why didn't you tell them we found replica DPMs?"

"I don't know . . . Reklov wouldn't shut up in the cycle about how normal people deserve DPMs." His voice quickened. "I mean, I know no one talks about it, but DPMs were created for us, right? Not just Designers?"

"Slow down, Malu. I get it, but I also understand what happens to people who pick that fight."

"He has one with him," EO said, stepping closer to Kamalu. "Back pocket."

Kamalu's eyes never left the bedsheets.

I gave EO a sly nod and shifted until I saw Kamalu's other hand clenched around it. "Kamalu, did you keep any?"

His eyes shot up. Dissonance raged there for a moment before he produced the syringe.

"Believe me when I say I'm with you," I said, "but replicas are fifty-fifty at best, man. It's not worth it."

EO twitched hearing the words but forced a half smile across his face. Kamalu surveyed the city through the window, his face wrinkling at the implications.

"You're right. We can turn them in tomorrow." He slumped back down into the chair and threw the syringe onto the bed. "I think this week broke me, and then this meeting tomorrow—it doesn't feel like just another meeting. It was called by a Director."

"It'll be all right," I lied. "I'm sure it's nothing."

A pained smile broke onto his face.

"You need to go home and get some sleep," I said.

"But—"

"Go. Home."

"Okay." He stood shakily and hobbled toward the door. "You're a good friend, Kilo."

Kamalu's limp arms wrapped around me. I patted his back lightly and watched EO fight back a smile as he imitated the hug behind us.

"Screw you," I mouthed.

"I'll see you tomorrow," Kamalu said.

"Sleep it off, Malu; you'll be fine." The door closed behind him, and I latched the crank lock.

"That's the last time I leave the door unlocked."

"It only took eight years, but you made a friend. I'm proud of you." EO's smile consumed his face.

"Shut up." I brushed past him, closing the blinds and hiding the effervescent city outside. "I'm going to sleep and enjoy some much-earned time away from you and Kamalu."

My body melted into the mattress. Any remnants of the aches in my muscles quickly faded into comfort, but my mind kept racing.

It's not worth it. My words cut like a knife in my mind. They'd just slipped out, but I knew EO's half smile had been anything but authentic.

"You know I didn't mean it, right, about it not being worth it?"

"Yes," EO said, kicking his legs up over the side of the chair into a comfortable position. "I also know you're worried about tomorrow. Whatever it is, we got this."

I nodded and let out a deep breath. A part of me wanted to talk more, to make sure he knew, but the pill had taken full effect, and the light faded to darkness.

CHAPTER 2

A muffled beeping shocked me awake. I gasped for air, inhaling a mouthful of freezing shower water. I hacked out what I could through labored coughs that burned the back of my throat.

Again? Three mornings in a row, I'd been unable to keep myself present. Contemplative daydreams consumed my consciousness, ones that tried to make sense of everything while still withholding any answers. I hoped it was nothing more than the past week catching up with me, but Reklov and the discovery of the replicas crystallized doubt in the back of my mind.

I wiped the hair off my forehead and cleared the water from my eyes before grabbing the circular temperature gauge on the wall and dialing it all the way to HOT.

"Alarm off!" After a moment, the ringing ceased. I stood there, letting the water run down my shoulders for another half minute. It scalded my body and enveloped everything in a burning mist until I could no longer stand the pulsating.

I dried off and cinched a towel around my waist before shuffling my way out of the cramped bathroom. Steam billowed off my skin as heat clashed with the chilly air.

"You know there are better ways to wake up, right?" EO said from the other side of the slide-bed. His eyes didn't break from the lettering projected from another one of his books. "I would hazard a guess that coffee will do just as well as burning yourself awake," he said.

"You'd be surprised." My gaze drifted to the sliding window, where the vibrant neon lights of Mid-City lined the Inter-District Highway below. For whatever reason, this view of the Hakkuin District drew me in morning after morning—an alluring, unfinished puzzle of something I could never quite piece together.

The Inter-District Highway pointed straight out toward the center of Big City, disappearing in the distance, and was engulfed among a blurred cluster of brake lights and buildings. The sixteen-lane street bustled under the concrete canopy of the interconnected superstructure of the island city. Along the street, the bright lights reflected off windows of apartments, restaurants, and shopping stations, making it impossible to look directly at many of the imposing buildings. The radiance of the city never dimmed or failed.

Far below, an indi-cycle screeched to a halt at the stoplight and sat idly as rows of the indi-, duo-, family-, and transit-cycles filed in behind it. In the distance, the cycles looked much like grains of sand flowing through the minimized gaps between the monoliths lining the highway. It often made me question whether there was a separation between the buildings at all.

The city's life started to take form among the pedestrian walkways that created unnatural levels crossing above the highway. Hundreds of people strolled along them with business on the other side, seemingly unfazed by the odd magnetism of it all.

The longer I watched, the faster chilled air outside the window overcame my body's heat. Peripherals of my vision clouded with the straight Inter-District and the countless buildings reaching up toward Mid-City's next level—the only things remaining. I tried to discern the pattern of colored specks through the condensation, but the harder I tried, the cloudier the puzzle became.

"Kilo!" EO shouted.

"What?" I turned to face him, confusion driving my response.

He stood partially obstructed by the book that floated in front of him. His curled hair, wrapped tightly in a bun, shook as he motioned to me. His brow furrowed.

I couldn't help but think of yesterday's slip of the tongue. Although I wanted to attribute it to sleep deprivation, I could only convince myself of so much. In some ways, it wasn't my frustration, but envy. EO lived in my twenty-one-year-old body forever while I aged, grew, and decayed. *Maybe he envies me, too?*

"Are you okay?" EO asked. "I know it's been rough with your rotation in Hilo, but it seems like you're not here."

"I'm fine. I just got lost watching the Inter-District."

"Really? Because your personal device rang twice since you've been up, and you haven't noticed."

My senses rushed back. The same loud beeps from the shower now emanated from my personal device on the coffee table. I lunged for the table, but my towel knot gave way. Before I could make it across the room, my personal device went silent.

"That was my PD?"

"Yeah," EO said.

"Shit, I thought it was the alarm."

I grabbed it from the table and brought the device to life. A message illuminated in sparkling green projected above the PD. MISSED CALL FROM DIIP DIRECTOR: UNKNOWN.

"A Director is calling *you*?" The concerned tone in EO's voice sent a frigid rush through my veins.

"Better ways to wake up, huh?" I asked. I knew Kamalu said we had a meeting with a Director today, but a personal call was anything but a good sign.

"Any idea why he would be calling us?" I showed EO the name displayed: Director Hula. "You know anything about him?"

"Not really." His gaze drifted as he thought about the name.

"I guess we're going to find out."

I headed over to the closet, throwing on some wrinkled pants and a long-sleeved shirt. "We can head to work like normal. If there's a problem, they will let us know."

"Door?" EO said.

"Yeah, I'm coming. Give me a second."

I propped the door fully open, latching its magnetic handle onto the adjacent wall. EO strolled out into the apartment's complex hallway, a well-lit yet garish corridor with red flowery wallpaper running its length.

"Let's go. If you were my DPM, you would never have to wait," he said with a straight face.

"I'm coming!"

It frustrated me when he was impatient, but I'd tried my best to cut him some slack. I couldn't imagine what it was truly like being a DPM. He resided between worlds, able to interact with me and the environment around him while remaining invisible and imperceptible to everyone else. My heart dropped whenever he reached for a door handle. We both knew he could touch it, feel it, but no matter how hard he turned, the knob never budged.

"You're going to be late!" he shouted from down the hallway.

I headed after EO, but yesterday's burned coffee sitting on the table taunted me. The swig left its usual motor oil aftertaste and painful tingling in my throat. Slinging my shadowy peacoat around my shoulders with my other hand, I slammed the door behind me. Time to figure out what kind of problem we needed to deal with now.

The wind rushed past, blocked by the full helmet that only left a sliver of my neck exposed to the frosty morning air. I cranked the handle of the jet-black Series Seven motorcycle, increasing our speed to make it through the six-way intersection. EO sat behind me, his arms clasped around my waist.

"Why didn't you tell me about the calls earlier?"

"I don't know," he paused, the whistling of the wind filling the silence before he spoke again. "I'm worried about you. I feel like the last month or so has been turbulent."

I weaved through the heavy traffic of the Inter-District. EO constricted each time we made a tight pass, seemingly to challenge the integrity of my ribcage. The old-school motorcycle I piloted blew by the heavy indi- and duo-cycles. Occasionally, a family-cycle would congest two lanes of highway, forcing us to mount the outside curb to race by. Anything with a heavy balancing system wasn't a match for us.

"I went out and had drinks with Kamalu and those other guys a couple of times," I shouted above the sounds of traffic.

"I know, but . . ."

"Today, we should only be worried about avoiding Directors," I yelled back at him.

He patted me on the back, bringing back memories of how he used to congratulate me after winning a fight. Rather than misinterpret the gesture, I took it as a compliment and refocused my attention on interlacing through the traffic.

The city lights were blinding even through my tinted visor, so with each pass, I kept my head down and focused on the passing lines of the road. Out of the corner of my eye, second-level Mid-City flashed by. Every few seconds, an alley would shoot off from the slow lane of the highway, perpendicular into the stacks of buildings. For moments, I glimpsed down the endless roads, which were alive with street vendors, pickup fights, and outdoor gatherings.

On the fast lane side of the road, a gaping divide separated oncoming and going traffic. Fast-moving elevators pulled people up and down between levels. I knew if I edged close enough to the barrier, I could look over and see the first level of Mid-City, about 150 meters down, and EO would lose it.

The height from the second level to the first didn't bother me, but the thoughts of each subsequent descent never failed to churn my stomach. The city was broken into three sub-levels, and the further down you went, the less comfortable it was. I tried to keep my mind in Mid-City, not the Below.

It wasn't long before we reached the exit, which headed toward the Department of Inter-Island Peace in Mid-City's third level. We left the Inter-District and made our way onto the much smaller and less crowded Kilauea Road. The tires of the Series Seven slipped every few seconds on the black ice camouflaged on the street, but we continued to shoot up toward the height of the island city.

Concrete towers lined the road, and pedestrian walkways zigzagged overhead, but the immense overture of the conglomerate wasn't quite as imposing as along the Inter-District. About 150 meters above us, the cross section between the second and third level of Mid-City closed on us as the chill intensified with each meter of elevation.

The small opening at the end of the road leading to Mid-City's third level only left us a meter or two from decapitation. I ducked for good measure through the terse tunnel before we popped out into the upper sector. Although Mid-City here looked much like the first and second levels, a saturation of ego and id always lingered in the air. I slowed as we approached the DIIP building.

From behind a parked cycle, a man crossed the street, oblivious to traffic. I slammed on the brakes, narrowly sparing him from a few broken bones, and in return was left with an obscene gesture. The change in people's demeanor within Upper Mid-City never failed to amuse me. They walked the streets with their heads held a little higher, not clutching their briefcases so tightly, and looked at you with just enough contempt. They were so close to the exaltation they believed accompanied a life in Design City, yet so far away.

I eyed a spot near the entrance of the nearly four-block-long building and parked. The face of the towering cream-colored skyscraper extended a few meters higher than the other more traditional buildings beside and above it, generating a natural magnetism that made it stand out.

I took a breath, allowing my apprehension to dissipate and simmer the best I could before heading up the marble staircase. We took the steps two at a time while EO spoke encouragingly, but I didn't hear a word.

What could possibly make a Director want to speak with me? As much as I tried to convince myself and EO that it was probably nothing, there was little chance it was true.

We finally reached the top of the stairs and stood before the massive glass door, which could have admitted ten people at a time if needed. The doors slid up into the walls along an oblique axis below the inescapable "THE DEPARTMENT OF INTER-ISLAND PEACE: A COURTESY TO THE PEOPLE OF HAWAI'I CITY" sign.

Even though I'd seen it a thousand times, each time I came to work, the sign challenged my composure.

"Your benevolence," EO said, bowing contemptuously.

I watched him gracefully pop back up, and a weakly masked smile grew across his face as he waited for commendation. My eyes rolled toward the back of my head. We both entered the building to the intense sounds of office work and indistinct conversations bouncing throughout the auditorium, only bound by the eighth floor above. The voices represented just a fraction of the hundreds of people that filled the vast central hall.

We walked through the main section and weaved through the countless fully enclosed cubicles that were stacked in helix-like structures. A few agents I recognized climbed the staircases that wrapped around the cubicles to the elevated office spaces.

I gave brusque nods to those I recognized but tried to keep my head down on our way toward the larger glass offices at the back of the central hall. I had barely set foot into my fishbowl office before a rapping on the outside window startled me. Kamalu anxiously sought my attention, the glass wall vibrating with each hit.

"Where have you been? We have our meeting with the Director in ten minutes," he shouted. His voice barely penetrated the office. Regardless, I got the message.

I turned and left the way I'd come, shooting EO a look of concern before rounding the fishbowl to meet with Kamalu. He was uncharacteristically withdrawn; his eyebrows were furrowed, his lips dry and cracked, and his hands shook in his pockets. Without a word, he started through the maze of cubicle towers.

"Kamalu, what's going on? Why are we meeting with a Director?"

His face remained scrunched, and I nearly had to jog to keep pace. We entered one of the elevators that splintered the side wall of the central hall, and EO slid in behind us. Kamalu tapped a button, and the elevator shot up toward the Director levels.

He whispered, "We aren't just meeting a Director. We're meeting with the Director of DIIP Operations and the Big City Deputy Designer for DIIP."

The words brought with them an uncomfortable silence. We both stared out the glass doors and watched the giant workspace recede below us until the clear view turned into the metal structure of the building's upper levels. The air stagnated. The discomfort of our situation was palpable, until a soft ring from the elevator announced our arrival. Kamalu and I simultaneously let out held, strained breaths as we stepped onto level fifteen.

My heart rate had steadily increased ever since Kamalu said the word "Designer," and now it was trying to burst straight through my chest. DPMs weren't designed to read the host's mind, but there were times I wish they could. I caught EO's eye as we stepped down the desolate corridor and pressed together my index and ring fingers with my middle finger resting on top.

It had taken us years to develop a way of communicating around others. We'd finally settled on hand contortions. The silent language was noticeable enough for EO but kept it discrete that I was communicating with a DPM.

EO immediately recognized my hand signal and responded, "I know. This isn't good. I'll do what I can during the meeting."

Kamalu's head didn't turn, and his ears didn't pique at the sound of EO's voice. He just continued to trudge straight through the heavy wooden doors sealed at the end of the hallway.

In times like this, my communication with EO needed to be flawless. It was always dangerous, the prospect of someone discovering I had a DPM, but in the presence of high-ranking DIIP officials, let alone a Designer, it would be disastrous.

The spacious conference room was empty, presumably because the other members wouldn't arrive until they knew we were already there. Kamalu and I sat at the large conference table made of a cherry wood that would have been unthinkably expensive in any of the island cities.

In the middle of the table, surrounded by the arching patterns that told the tree's life story, was the DIIP emblem. Each of the island cities' skylines crossed and met in the middle, their summits touching in a poorly designed star. On the surface, it was a nice symbol of inter-island community between the cities, but it was just that: a symbol. Since the fall of Honolulu, we'd been given front row seats to the growing discontent between each of the island cities' Designers and then between their peoples. The emblem on the table was nothing more than a false hope.

I peered out beyond the symbol into the real world. The windows of the conference room offered a striking panoramic view of Kilauea Road, but just above us, the next level of Big City loomed. The thick concrete divider only meters above us separated Mid-City from Design City. I could almost feel its strength, the impenetrable nature of the forty-meter divide.

Forty meters were the closest I would ever be to stepping foot back in Design City. Most people on any given island would kill their loved ones to become a Designer. It was insanity. People from every island city knew, without a shred of doubt, that ascension was impossible but still admired, served, and fought for the Designers. If only they understood—even descension was more of a blessing.

I was content with my work at DIIP and could go five lifetimes without shedding a tear for the time lost in that pretentious, theatrical bubble. It was a place where people seemed to grow into something else entirely, unconcerned with the fundamentals of being human. But somehow, in a city impervious to the masses below them, people reveled in the love and adornment for their creation of the island cities. Even as I thought about the careless people above us, my heart flickered, the memories of Design City never failing to trigger unwanted feelings deep within me.

A few minutes passed while Kamalu and I sat in silence in the conference room. He filled the time by reading something on his personal device. I waited patiently, tapping my finger against the hardwood of the table, enduring EO, who droned on about some story he'd read, clearly trying to lighten the mood. If Kamalu hadn't been there, I'd have told EO I preferred the quiet. But without that option, I was forced to stomach his rambling.

EO's story was cut off when the door swung open and cracked against the doorstop. Three men entered the room in the middle of serious conversation. The first—a tall, thin Asian man—was the Director of DIIP Operations, Jackson Hula. I'd never actually met him, but I'd seen him on occasion. His dark eyes buried into his skull were unmistakable.

Second through the door was a shorter man, balding and wearing glasses. Director Hula's assistant, or so I presumed. He stumbled around the table and placed digital files down, covering the space in front of the chair Hula pulled out for himself.

Finally, the third man strutted into the room. His long, white shawl billowed, as if caught by air coming in through the window. His face was clean and his beard well manicured. The office light sheened off the man's near-perfect, light-brown skin. The colors of his suit refracted with every step, like a rainbow through mist.

Both Director Hula and his assistant sat across the conference table from Kamalu and me, while the Designer positioned himself at the table's head.

"Hello, everyone. As you may know, I am Shasha Decambra, one of the Deputy Designers for the Department of Inter-Island Peace." He spoke through pursed lips as if he was delivering oratory rations to a grateful, starving citizenry. "Director Hula has informed me that both of you are excellent choices to help with our current needs."

He pulled apart his personal device, splitting it like a banana down the middle and opening the digital screen a few centimeters above. In a fluid motion, he grasped at the air just over the PD and threw a clenched fist toward the center of the table to expand it. A three-dimensional, interactive display of what shone on the Designer's personal device appeared. I found myself staring at a green and blue diagram of Kaua'i City, specifically highlighting the Nāpali and Ludo Districts.

"Jesus Christ," EO said.

Decambra repeated the motion and threw up a two-dimensional picture with my profile, which detailed my experience and history in the DIIP.

"Kilohana Ressler, agent with the DIIP for eight years. The first and only member of Big City DIIP to have been born and resided in Kaua'i City. Served eighty-six tours on the Continent and reached the rank of sergeant major in the Continental Security Forces. That's more than most, Mr. Ressler. You must have lost—"

Decambra cut himself off as an invisible force pulled his attention over his shoulder. After a few seconds of intense concentration, he turned back and continued.

"It seems as though you have lost nearly twenty years during your service on the Continent. Only a man who understands his usefulness or hopes to find himself in an early grave would stay in service of his island city for that long. Wouldn't you agree?" Decambra's eyes pierced mine as he waited for an answer.

"I suppose I would qualify as the first, sir."

"Good, good. I need someone with your . . . experience."

From the corner of my eye, I saw EO's jaw clench and his eyes light with fire. I felt it, too, but I needed to keep mine buried deep, not allowing even a whiff of dissatisfaction to cross my face. Designers were not well known for their compassion.

"What experience would that be?" I asked.

"Well, you were no longer excavating raw materials once you joined the Security Forces, were you?"

"I did what they told me to do to protect the island cities."

"Right you are, Mr. Ressler, and your file makes it very clear what you were willing to do and what you were not." Decambra made his way around the conference table, speaking to no one in particular. "Everyone in this room is to be made aware of a sensitive situation currently evolving between the diplomatic groups of both Big City and Kaua'i City. The details of the situation are unimportant, but what *is* important is that information be found that allows Big City's diplomatic corps to call a special emergency session between the two cities. Believe it or not, this is Designer Makrumbi's top priority, and he is heavily invested in its success."

"What exactly are Kilo and I being asked to do?" Kamalu interrupted Decambra bravely.

"*You* aren't being asked to do much—Kilo, on the other hand . . . nothing as challenging as what you did on the Continent."

I started, "I'm not a—"

Decambra stopped me with a casual wave of his hand and continued onto his next question. "You're both aware of the casualty regulations agreed upon by all under the Century Island Cities Agreement?"

We nodded, but Decambra frowned with a raised eyebrow and answered his question anyway.

"Each island is allowed no more than 10 percent casualties on the Continent directly related to Carbon Sytride exposure in their service companies. We have reason to believe that Kaua'i City has exceeded that number for several years now. If this is the case, there is immediate cause to call an island citywide diplomatic meeting, where any issue can be brought up and voted on. The Designers need *you*, Mr. Ressler, to spend forty-eight hours at the Kaua'i Department of Inter-Island Peace building to find any information that may substantiate our claim . . ." Decambra paused, again listening intently with his head tilted to the left.

"Right, of course. Mr. Ressler, with your previous experience in Kaua'i City, it will be easier for us to convince their Directors and Designers to allow you in their facility. Although we have every legal right, the Kaua'i City Designers have become increasingly unreceptive to our agents traveling there. I expect you will be ready to leave tonight. I have already informed Kaua'i DIIP that you will be arriving sometime in the early morning. That will be all."

I kept the dry, obedient look plastered to my face. As soon as I saw my bio, it wasn't a matter of whether I wanted to accept this assignment, but rather how to get through it.

Kamalu spoke up, halting Decambra's move toward the door. "With respect, Designer Decambra, is Kilo really the most appropriate person to send on an inter-island assignment? He's only had assignments in—"

Hula almost leapt out of his chair at Kamalu's lack of decorum. He spoke through gritted teeth, "Kilo has already been chosen for this assignment, and that decision is final. We are not having a debate about this with Designer Decambra. He is well informed, and I expect you to trust his judgment. That will be all. Thank you both."

He motioned to his assistant, speaking faster now, "Makana will have all the information and access passes you will need, Kilo. See him before you leave."

Both Hula and Makana stood up from their seats and followed Decambra out of the room. I sat quietly, contemplating what had just happened. Kamalu merely looked stunned. As if on cue, the lights dimmed with the exit of the other parties. I debated asking whether Kamalu was all right. His face was racked with the confusion and fear that accompanied meeting a Designer.

"Kilo, what are you going to do?" EO asked.

I didn't have a chance to respond with a hand signal before Kamalu spoke, "Are you good for this, Kilo?"

My thoughts raced with what Decambra expected me to find in Kaua'i City and what I hoped I wouldn't find if I went back. Kaua'i had defined my life for so long and was somehow drawing me back in again. In a matter of minutes, I'd been blindfolded, turned around, and kicked off a bridge into the freezing water below.

"Honestly, I don't know. But it doesn't sound like I have a choice."

A thin, reassured smile crept across Kamalu's lips. "You'll figure it out." His eyes lit up. "Did you see the way Decambra talked to his DPM? That was incredible. I've never seen anyone talk to one in person. I heard the Designers have daily medical treatments just to ensure their hippocampus doesn't fail."

I couldn't help the laugh that worked its way up from my gut. He wasn't wrong. People said that, but it wasn't true, at least not entirely. A hint of endorphins rushed through my head until I remembered what I'd just been asked to do. The weight of it was too heavy. I looked at EO, my eyes fighting back even the faintest appearance of fear. I knew this would not be like before, and that's what made it terrifying.

CHAPTER 3

My knuckles burned white hot as I clenched my stuffed duffle bag. The thoughts of who Decambra believed me to be had plagued my drive from the DIIP to the train station. I wasn't interested in reliving my life in Kaua'i or on the Continent, but when a Designer asked you to do something, you didn't have much choice. A soft caress of EO's hand along my shoulder helped relax my muscles ever so slightly.

"We just need to get some information and come back. No big deal, all right?"

"Yeah," I replied.

Another bullet train whizzed past with a roar, and a tornado of wind almost knocked me off balance. I glanced down at my personal device and compared the time on the station clock to my ticket for the eleven p.m. direct line to Kaua'i City.

Pins of cold pierced my torso, courtesy of my holstered 9mm Nambu pistol, a staple of the DIIP. I hoped for a smooth transit to Kaua'i and back, but you never knew.

EO and I had been waiting for the past half hour on the south platform, staring down the countless magnetic rail lines where trains periodically entered and left the station. After the meeting at the DIIP with Decambra and Hula, I'd gone home, packed a small bag with a few essentials and a change of clothes. Then I traveled from the Hakkuin District to the Inter-Island Rail Station on the edge of the Mahukona District.

"ELEVEN O'CLOCK TRAIN TO KAUA'I CITY, NĀPALI DISTRICT, NOW ARRIVING. PLEASE STEP BACK FROM THE PLATFORM." The mechanical, feminine-sounding voice reverberated down from the speakers above, followed shortly by our train.

The enormous metal railcars screeched to a halt, the sheer weight of the train fighting against the magnetic stop mechanisms. I stared up at the behemoth and quickly completed the calculations in my head. Even considering the massive dips in travel over the past decade, the number of passengers that passed through here each day boggled the mind.

"I'm going to sit right side so I can see Maui City," EO said, and with a whoosh, the doors slid open. EO made his way toward the entrance. I nodded and trailed him into the train, relieved I could rely on him as a guide for the moment.

EO selected an empty row on the bottom floor near the middle of the railcar and crawled into the window seat. I followed, sitting next to him and leaving the two remaining seats closest to the aisle vacant. I dropped my personal device onto the flimsy tray table and turned to EO.

"When we arrive, let's go straight to the DIIP building. We can eat there and work through the night and hopefully leave by tomorrow afternoon."

"Fine with me. You want to walk or grab a transit-cycle?"

"Walk. The only thing worse than being there will be having to explain what a DIIP agent from Big City is doing in Kaua'i."

The doors closed on either side of the railcar. I relaxed into the leather seat and allowed the heat from the warmer to penetrate my peacoat. We would be heading straight to the DIIP once we reached Kaua'i, so this would be my only chance for some shut-eye tonight. A glossy blackness crested over my eyes. As I felt the weight on my shoulders lift, the nebulous, porcelain dots on the interior of my eyelids clashed together all at once.

Kilo? Kilo, are you listening to me? A voice echoed for a moment along a sound continuum before settling into the soft, recognizable melody of my mother.

Her lips curved up in a wide smile, but her muscles strained around her eyes in a veiled effort to present a happy face. I didn't care. I softened into her enveloping embrace and allowed its warmth to accumulate until it was all that existed.

"I need you to listen carefully, sweet boy. I know—" A hand pulled on her shoulder, breaking our connection. The whipping winds along the platform smacked my small frame. More aggressively now, the man whose hand pulled at my mother forced her back.

"It's time. We're going down." His eyes turned, a deep darkness peering down at me. "Let's go, Kilo." My father's grasp burned around my arm. I fought back, pulling toward my mother, but every attempt failed."Noah, please! Just give him one! That's all I'll ask." An outstretched hand cradled a transparent syringe. Inside, a thin gray orb floated, waiting to be injected.

"Fine." My father grabbed the syringe and yanked me down the platform.

The tears welling in my mother's eyes soon faded. Again, I pulled against the forces dragging me away, but to no avail. A screeching sound ripped through the fabric of reality and sent ripples through the frozen air.

"Mom!"

A high-pitched voice startled me awake. "Excuse me, is the window seat taken?" The voice belonged to a middle-aged woman with graying hair and a bright yellow outfit made of several layers of opaque material."Sorry, my wife is in the bathroom," I said.

"Oh, that's all right. I just like to pray as we pass over Honolulu City."

"I think Honolulu will actually be on the left."

"Oh, you're right! It's been a long day. I hope it's still all right I sit here."

"Mm-hmm." I produced a disarming grin, attempting to hide the vomit itching to wretch its way from my stomach. EO let out a laugh as he watched the scene unfold.

After what seemed like an eternity of bathing in the woman's citrus-scented perfume, the train finally started to accelerate, bringing with it the automated air conditioning's clean breeze. A hologram of a small woman appeared above the tray table between me and my new neighbor, thwarting any unwanted conversations she may have been plotting. I wasn't prepared for the volume that outmatched the personal information guide's tiny design as she shouted.

"THANK YOU FOR TRAVELING WITH US ON INTER-ISLAND RAIL. WE APPRECIATE THAT YOU ARE ONE OF THE MILLIONS OF PEOPLE WHO RIDE OUR TRAINS EACH YEAR, AND IT IS OUR PLEASURE TO GET YOU BETWEEN THE ISLAND CITIES SAFELY AND LEGALLY."

As she finished, the train shot out from the island city station and arched upward into the stormy night, hundreds of meters above the darkened ocean. The artificially lit cabin valiantly held back the darkness outside. The train cut through the rain as the lit pyramidal outline of Big City faded into the distance.

It had been a while since either of us had seen the true depth of the outside world. When you live under the concrete sky for so long, it's natural to forget what a true midnight is. The deep, eerie shade of black tunneled into nothingness. My pupils widened as I strained to peer into it.

Droplets of water on the windows raced toward the rear, with the train's speed and altitude increasing. I slumped into my seat, tilted my head back, and closed my eyes to resume what little rest I could get.

But it wasn't long before EO pulled me from my intermission of consciousness. Outside the window, Maui City waded toward us in the depths of the sea. The glistening lights pouring from the monolithic metropolis reminded me of the pre-fall castles I'd seen in pictures. However, the bastillion that was Maui City was, in reality, a conglomerate of hundreds of thousands of interconnected and codependent buildings, only distinguishable the closer we came to the city. I watched EO gape at the architectural feat looming still above our elevated railway.

Surrounding Maui City stood the twin island cities of Molokai ʻokina and Lānaʻi. They were unimpressive compared to the former, smaller and less magnificent, but I'd always been partial to their connective design. An arched bridge far above the ocean connected the two cities, the light inside emanated from the thousands of residences. These days, they were a rare example of cooperation, but maybe it was an illusion; maybe the twin cities were nothing more than a consolidation of habitable, buildable land. I'd never spent enough time there to find out.

"I overheard a conversation in the Hilo District claiming the Designers in Maui have completely withdrawn their plans to rebuild Honolulu," EO said, his eyes still glued to the passing city.

"I'm not buying second-rate gossip from Hilo."

"But it makes sense, doesn't it? They've always had a terrible time importing metals from the Continent. Their food supply is fantastic, but I don't think their bids could ever realistically compete with Big City or Kaua'i City."

"Maybe, but why? It's not like it matters. Until someone figures out what to do with the survivors, it's all talk and blueprints."

"I guess you're—"

"I'm sorry, were you talking to me?" The yellow-suited woman interjected with no less self-importance than before and a furrowed brow.

I motioned to my personal device, still lying on the tray table. "I'm speaking with my supervisor."

"Oh, where do you work? I was in Big City for business with Capital."

I could sense EO itching to offer something witty. Before he could, I lifted my erect index finger above the armrest where my hand sat. I didn't hear a laugh or commentary from EO, so I assumed he'd received the message to keep his joke to himself.

"I work in construction."

"Oh, wonderful! Such a powerful profession." She moved eagerly to the seat closest to me and grabbed my left hand. A wide smile ripped across her face. "You are one of the most important tools the Designers have to create a more perfect world."

"Thank you," I said, my eyes glazing over. "Just trying to do my part."

She nodded and moved back to her original seat, where she flicked through some complicated documents floating above her personal device. This was my opportunity to make a break for it. The clothes, the tone of her voice, and even the perfume screamed she was a member of the Children of the Designers. I needed to take any shot I had at avoiding more conversations with this sycophant.

I tapped EO's hand to make sure he knew I was leaving and then headed up-train. I figured I could reach the Designer railcar by the time we pulled into Kaua'i City Station. Maybe that would be far enough away from my new "friend."

The cabin shook with each wind gust that swiped against the island side of the train. Most of the seats were filled with well-dressed men, women, and the occasional child. My ears perked up at the various conversations along the way. A family squabbled with animated faces, and a couple of scientists hurling jargon at each other answered energy depletion questions.

After passing through several railcars, the bustle among the train's passengers abruptly died down to a wave of silence. Outside the left-hand-side windows, a shadowy landmass approached, the cracks of its broken exterior growing more visible, even in the darkened night. I bracketed myself between two free seats as a chill meandered down my spine. The remains of the large superstructure atop the island soon came into focus.

Sporadic buildings reached up into the sky among rubble and vegetation, like proverbial needles wishing to be found among the haystacks. Some buildings were in better shape than others, somehow surviving the collapse that had occurred above them. Faint lights littered the remains of the city—a subtle reminder of the 5 percent. Official survivor counts after the fall had never been released, but whenever we passed, I couldn't shake the thought: How many more lives could have been saved if it weren't for the vainglory of each of the island cities' Designers?

They were eerie, really, the silent gazes from a loaded, passing train. All of it was hard to stomach, but it was the abandoned rail line only a few hundred meters away that never failed to grasp at my heart.

Honolulu City had been one of the five major island city arcologies, but now it was reduced to something else, something more significant to all the other island cities.

The train door opened, and a gust of wind tousled my tamed, short hair. EO found me after I'd taken my journey up-train, and we stepped onto the platform in stride. The head of the train was nestled into the forward-most area of the station, with the platforms rising toward the main hall. People streamed out the doors ahead of us and merged into a clustered mass of bopping heads pushing up to the exit.

My fingers went numb at the sight of Kaua'i City's Grand Station. The ceiling arched high above, taking inspiration from the ancient transport hubs of the Old World. Ionic columns steadied the ceiling. Although mostly decorative, the thick circular pillars dwarfed any passersby. The curved walls of the station boasted colorful and intricate murals telling the ageless stories of the city's past.

The customs control station was crowded with document-wielding residents frustrated by the wait. I took EO and squeezed through to a barren station with a sign that read, "For Designers and official personnel only."

"Big City, huh?" the brutish guard asked. He scanned over my digital papers. "Don't get many like you."

Before I could respond with something witty, he motioned to my coat, an eyebrow raised in suspicion. I pulled the Nambu out of the holster and placed it on the scratched surface of the security desk, adding a couple more scuffs to its surface. The man eyed the weapon, turned it around in his fingers, and peered in through the gashed openings of the air diffusion chambers on the barrel.

"Anything in here I need to know about?" he said without looking up.

"Standard, except the tracer rounds."

He nodded, slid the weapon back across the desk, and waved his hand along an open holographic screen. "Admit one: Ressler."

I let a heavy breath flow through my nostrils as we passed through the turnstile.

The deafening street-level noise of the city resumed beyond the black iron gates. I took the first few steps outside onto Halloway Street, entranced by the familiarity of it. A mental roadmap materialized in my mind. If I closed my eyes, I firmly believed I'd still be able to navigate straight to the Kauaʻi City DIIP building. Everything around me seemed so similar. I wasn't sure how much I'd really expected this city to change in eight years, but oddly, it felt like I was stepping back into a well-worn pair of shoes. EO touched my shoulder and nodded before we headed toward our destination.

The city levels hung high above my head, supported by the buildings, much like the ionic columns in the station. Pedestrian walkways paralleled the crowded Inter-District roads with sporadic staircases that allowed for access to free-space levels connected by the buildings.

Among the growling noises of the cycles, hissing of neon lights, and rumbling of footsteps and conversations, there was a clear absence of a specific noise—large, gas engines. It took a moment to adjust to the difference. I could still hear the complaints in my head from people here, begging for changes to the infrastructure, making it more like Big City. *Still as likely as when we lived here,* I thought.

We crossed over the bridge that arched beyond Halloway Street. Up ahead, I finally saw the DIIP building nestled along the first-level Mid-City block.

"Do you really think there's anything to this death limit breach?" EO asked the question that had lingered in the back of my mind since we reached Kauaʻi.

"That's what I don't get—I didn't even know it was possible to crack the limit. Ten percent of the people working on the Continent? No one has ever seen anything close to that," I whispered. "What if we don't find anything?"

"I don't think that's an option."

EO's perception was often spot on, and there was no reason to believe otherwise regarding my meeting with Decambra. I didn't know if it worked the same for all DPMs, but he'd harnessed a sensitivity to the world around us. Although he experienced stimuli through me, somehow he'd developed an awareness just beyond my consciousness. I never knew if EO's ability had something to do with being free from normal interactions or the flexibility of his perspective, but it worked.

"Did you notice anything else?"

"I don't know. It felt weird how Decambra spoke about the *need* to call a diplomatic meeting with the other cities."

The pause in EO's voice halted me in my tracks, the gears in my mind turning as fast as they could.

"He seemed impatient . . . or pressured?" he finished.

"There have been a hundred more egregious violations, so why is this one so important?"

EO's puzzled look matched mine, making me more apprehensive about spending the next twenty-four hours at the Kaua'i City DIIP. I didn't anticipate any particular danger within the walls. After all, Kaua'i City and Big City were supposed to be working together to develop more peace among the cities. But I couldn't shake the sinking feeling.

The Kaua'i DIIP building's facade was markedly less ornate than the one in Big City. It was a two-block, brick-faced, windowless building with much less pretentious double wooden doors than the Big City entrance. However, the inside was magnificent. Instead of a huge auditorium-style layout, the entire building was broken up vertically by department.

I couldn't help but look around as we were greeted by an arrival attaché—a fancy title for the short man in an ill-fitting suit whose only job was to watch me. Each of the departments seemed to be leveled with continuous, doorless elevators running vertically within the sectioned area. The departments—highly complicated yet well-oiled machines—stretched the length of the building. Inter-Island Transit, Inter-Island Law, and Inter-Island Investigations, to name but a few, were lined up along the main corridor.

My arrival attaché led us along the busy hall until he stopped and showed us to a rather antiseptic-looking investigation room. The spotless white tabletops, blank digital screens, and stiff chairs made it appear as though the office hadn't existed before today. The attaché ushered us into the room with a courteous gesture of his hand, then closed the door. EO and I settled into the stale-aired room at a horseshoe table.

We stared for hours at the blurry screens, searching for any sign of malfeasance effectuated by Kaua'i City. We found out the hard way that every conceivable piece of information about people working on the Continent lay dormant in these devices. An agonizing headache slowly developed after sifting through the countless statistics, reports, and surveys.

If there was anything here, we would have found it already. "How could someone hide thousands of deaths? That's impossible on the Continent," I said. The headache fought with my fingers as I rubbed my temples. "I need a break. Let's see if the attaché will let me use the toilet."

"Good luck. There's a trash can in the corner if he says no."

I glanced over and indeed found a pristine miniature wastebasket. Like the rest of the room, it looked like it had been purchased minutes before we arrived. I gave EO a courtesy laugh and swung the investigation room door open.

I propped it ajar for EO, out of habit. A quick glimpse back showed me he was still examining the automatically rotating set of digital files as quickly as possible. He wouldn't be able to read anything new, but it wouldn't hurt to review the files he'd already seen.

"I need to use the toilet."

The attaché shook awake in his seat across the hall. The solitary chair pressed up against the wall sat strikingly out of place, but then again, Kauaʻi probably didn't get many visitors like me.

He stood up, a cheesy smile appearing at my request to use the facilities, and motioned for me to follow him down the hallway. "Sure. What are you looking for in those files?"

The question caught me off guard.

"Uh—I don't really know."

"Hmm. Must be something important to get sent across island cities."

I nodded, not sure whether his innocent, inquisitive nature was a well-crafted act or genuine naivete. Either way, I planned to keep my findings to myself.

"Kilohana?" A woman's voice came from somewhere behind me. My heartbeat quickened, and my muscles seized. I recognized the voice. It was light and exciting, and my brain translated the sound waves into something melodic that seemed to transcend speech and language. I tried to piece the voice together with a face.

Alessia. My heart stopped, and a numbness overcame me. My eyes were the only part of my body that felt capable of responding, but somehow, I still found myself walking toward her. Five or six other people dressed in mismatched, colorful suits surrounded her. One of them attempted to block my path, but Alessia waved him off.

"Kilo, what are you doing here?" She gave me a brief hug, the warmth bringing a tingling sensation back to my extremities. Locks of hair brushed across her face and then flowed back down into their natural state along her shoulders. My eyes attempted to make sense of the collage of pastel colors so vibrant that I believed for a second it must be a trick of the lights. Her soft lips curved up below a short nose, and her long eyelashes covered deep green eyes.

"I'm here on a special assignment." I managed to mutter the words through my limp lips. "I work as an agent at the DIIP in Big City." The clouds in my mind were breaking, her face beginning to resemble the small, plump face of my childhood friend.

"Really? That's great! Congratulations."

"Thanks, what are you—"

"Oh, I'm the Designer liaison for the DIIP here in Kaua'i City."

"A Designer liaison position—I didn't think you'd ever do that." I heard the judgment as soon as the words left my mouth and tried to steer the subject. "What Design Department do you work for?"

She swallowed and looked away briefly. "Protection and Endurance."

My heartbeat spiked, and the veins along my skull pounded, attempting to rip through my skin.

"You work for *him*?" I stammered.

Red flushed her face, a mix of embarrassment and defensiveness in her voice. "It's not like that, Kilo. I make a difference here. I chose this post to work in Mid-City to live in the real world. Everything has changed up top. I don't even recognize it anymore."

"I don't understand. You know who he is? What he did?"

"It's complicated, but I'm here for the right reasons."

The words echoed those of the little brown-haired girl from years ago, running in the grass, chasing me until we could hardly breathe. *Trust me, we will make people happy someday.*

"It's just good to see you," I said.

"It's been so long, Kilo. I've thought about you a lot—ever since you left." She clasped her hands around mine, gently squeezing. "Part of me wanted to find you and talk to you so many times, but I didn't know how. I'm so sorry . . ."

Although she didn't say it, I also lived with the same regretful feelings of longing, a spinning ball of *what-ifs*? And *how comes*? There wasn't any action or thought that I was remorseful for, but the suffocating weight of seeing her now filled me with endless regrets.

"It's okay. I—"

"No. I'm . . . sorry about your mom. I never had the courage to find you and be there for you."

Whatever small part of me was hanging on to consciousness broke with reality. My mind departed from my body. An agonizing feeling of emptiness was all that remained.

She drew back, batting away a hint of tears from her eyes.

"I—"

Alessia cut me off with a casual wave of her hand. "Speaking of, I have a meeting I was supposed to be at five minutes ago. Come see me before you go back. I'd like to make up for lost time."

"Of course."

"Bye, Kilo." A flash of a smile and she was gone.

The space around me warped, and I couldn't help but question whether the interaction had taken place at all.

"I can take you back to the investigation room now," the attaché said.

I'd forgotten he was standing next to me. "I'm okay. Need to step outside for a minute."

Without waiting for his approval, I started down the main corridor to the exit. But with every step, the corridor elongated and pushed the double doors further away, like light fleeing at the end of a tunnel. Suddenly, out of the blur, I found myself outside, on one of the alley roads adjacent to Halloway Street. I slammed my back against the brick wall and slumped down to the ground.

My jaw tightened, and the muscles in my neck fully contracted amid my attempt to hold on to consciousness. Thoughts raced uncontrollably, spitting out memories and feelings: my mother's grasp, darkened buildings and unfamiliar alleyways, the sounds of my failures. The onslaught continued, and I grimaced, clenching both of my fists. I did everything I could to bore my fingers through my palm. The words pounded my head: "Sad. Stupid. Worthless. Angry. Scared."

"EO, please help me. EO, please," I whispered through gritted teeth, hoping he could hear me. The street began to spin. I tried to speak, but my mouth locked up. The best I could muster were slight moans. My eyes slammed shut, leaving me in the desolate black box of my mind. My body stopped fighting as I went under.

"Kilo! I'm here; you're okay. Listen to my voice and focus on my touch." EO's words quickly went from panicked to calming. I felt his fingers wrap around my forearm, and I weakly grasped him back. The time that passed while we held each other was hard to discern. At points, it was imperceptible, and at others, it felt as if I was running on a moving carpet.

"Are you with me?" EO said.

"Yeah, I think so. I'm not sure what happened."

"You haven't had one of these in years."

"It felt like before . . . I saw Alessia."

EO gaped. "You saw Alessia? How? Where?"

"She's one of the Designers that works with DIIP. I just saw her, and she—"

"Did you talk to her?"

"I think so. It felt like it wasn't me, though."

We sat in silence for a minute. EO didn't need to ask anything else. His experience of my childhood, his memories, were close enough to understand.

"I found something," he said.

"The Continent?"

"Yeah. Something that doesn't make sense."

"Are you gonna tell me, or do I have to guess?"

EO paused for a second, chewing on his lip. "We could go back to Big City and tell them we came up empty-handed."

"What did you find?"

"It's Maurice; he was one of the casualties."

Needles poked at my heart and repeated, persistently trying to empty it of blood. A memory of Maurice passed through my mind. His wide smile puffing up his cheeks as we posed for a photo. I didn't know whether it was the shock or just hearing the words that hurt more, but the pain was deeper than I thought it would be.

"There's more. The numbers—there's something way off about them. The Below is sending guys to the Continent like crazy."

"No. I'm not going down there. Not the Below."

EO relaxed against the wall, still holding my hand, but his face hardened. "You asked what I found."

"I want to revise my answer to your offer to go back to Big City."

He snorted. "*You* are the one with a body. You know what I'd give to make a difference here?"

I picked a small blemish in the building's structure across the street and tried to immerse myself in it. We'd agreed to come to Kaua'i City because there was no choice, but I could just as easily hop a train, head back to Big City, and feed Decambra some numbers. *I earned that life. I shouldn't have to go to the Below again.*

"I won't let you go back to Big City, not yet," EO whispered.

Cracks in the concrete appeared, and the phantom sounds of gunfire and screaming people intensified in my mind. Invisible bullets ripped into the wall, tearing the synthetic concrete to shreds. I forced my eyes closed and focused on the cold air that burned my lungs, tethering myself to the present.

"Okay, we'll stay—forty-eight hours—and then we go home." I opened my eyes and looked at him. "For Maurice. He didn't deserve this."

"So, where do we start?" EO asked.

"We need to see Bless."

He let out a deep breath and stared into Mid-City. "Fine."

CHAPTER 4

Red, black, and blue lights flashed from the multistory club across the crowded street. The prisms of tear-shaped water droplets reflected and blurred our view. We stood, shrouded in the shadows of the dilapidated Nāpali District apartment buildings, watching through the cycle traffic. Usos Gym drew the attention of everything on the block, like a wood fire in a deep cave. The smell of the murky puddles around my boots hinted at the stale water's journey from the top of the island city, down through Mid-City, and to the Below.

Buildings along the block looked mostly the same as a decade ago, save for a few paint jobs and minor construction add-ons. The only change was Bless' gym. Although it was still called Usos, it looked nothing like the one-level fight club that had been owned by his father.

A line of hopeful people stretched down the street to the entrance, one by one facing the judgment of three gigantic Samoans with stone-cold faces. These people were nothing short of fanatical, with bloodstained boxing gloves tied around their fists, belts cinching their gis tightly around their waists, or the names of their favorite fighters tattooed across various body parts. One man's face was even black and blue with intensely realistic gashes along his cheeks. The excited banter among the fans was contagious and sparked memories of the many fights I'd watched here as a kid.

"Let's try the underground entrance," I said.

A man-sized hatch lay hidden under an arching footbridge leading to Usos' side of the street. I ripped the latch off, revealing a desolate tunnel that led underneath the city. The stale stench that poured out from the tunnel was laced with a trace of earthiness.

It was easy to get lost in the maze of passages of the underground, as they were never designed to be navigable. However, if you spent enough time there, the tunnels soon turned into a world outside of the given structure of the island city.

I tightened the hood of my peacoat to conceal most of my face and climbed inside. My lungs burned as I inhaled some of the smoke from a group of delirious kids huddled around a small fire. Few knew of the elaborate tunnel network on the underside of the Below, just beneath true ground level, but those who did took care to keep it that way.

The deeper we went into the tunnels, the more I needed to rely on EO for guidance. Petite glow orbs had been placed along the ground long before I lived here, but only a handful remained lit. Using a Mid-City personal device in the underground would end exactly as one would expect: being beaten and robbed. So, we walked along in scarcely lit darkness.

After a few minutes of shuffling through the dimly lit corridors, I noticed and felt for the worn metal handle of an entrance. An inconspicuous black door that barely distinguished itself from the rest of the metal wall stood before us, a circular symbol etched into its face. I rapped several times and waited. A slit in the middle of the door suddenly slid open, and dim light attacked my pupils.

"Hand," the gruff voice said from the other side of the door.

I rolled up my sleeve and put my hand through the opening. The person on the other side grabbed it and rotated.

"Fuck off," he said, pushing my hand back and violently closing the slit.

I gave EO an annoyed look, letting out a sigh, and rapped again on the door. This time, the larger door flung open, and I found myself staring down the barrel of a fully automatic pistol. The scarred hand gripping the gun belonged to a muscular man with tattoos covering most of his shirtless torso. His face was only visible up to a crooked nose, but I didn't recognize him. Although he seemed like someone Bless would hire.

"I said fuck off. No band. No entrance."

"Band?"

"What don't you get about this situation?" He pushed the gun within a few centimeters of my head, his finger playing with the trigger.

"Tell Bless that Kilo is here."

"Who the hell do you—"

I took a step closer, now touching my forehead to the cool metal of the barrel's opening.

"I don't know who you are, and I don't really care, but you're gonna want to talk to Blessman and tell him Kilo's here."

His bravado broke momentarily, and the muscles in the man's square jaw hardened. I couldn't see his eyes, but I imagined the debate raging behind them.

"Okay. If he doesn't know you, I'm putting one through your knee." He pulled the gun back inside and slammed the slide shut.

"Feels like right where we left off," EO said.

I grunted, acknowledging his observation, but refused to start a conversation about the Kilo from eight years ago, who might have slipped into my body for a moment. A minute later, the door opened to reveal the face of a woman with long, black hair and visible scars along her shoulders and neck. Behind her stood the first man with his arms crossed and fists clenched.

"Kilo," the woman said, giving my body a once-over, "do you remember me?"

I took a second to scan her face and body for something recognizable, but I came up with nothing. There was a good chance EO knew, but he didn't volunteer the information, and I wasn't about to make my DPM obvious.

"Should I?"

"Guess not. Come on, let's go."

I followed them up a tight set of stairs into a small makeshift office space. Three women in bulky coats sat at card tables sifting through screens and counting digital credits. The scarred woman scaled another staircase on the far side of the room. At the top, there was a door she struggled to open. She eventually succeeded with a muffled grunt, and a stream of light poured through.

The door opened to a spacious office on the street level of Usos. Floor-to-ceiling windows offered a view inside the club, where people streamed into the vaulted stadium seats surrounding a sand-covered ring. I touched my finger to the glass, and a forked reflection stared back at me. It was one-way, painted with some kind of acrylic that obstructed sight into the office but allowed clear views to the other side.

The room itself seemed more like a hookah lounge than a business office, with a large gathering area of couches, relaxation swings, tables, fighting equipment, and weights. But in the corner sat a heavy wooden desk, and behind it, a steel safe guarded by a dual crank mechanism.

"Bruddah, is that you?" The voice boomed from outside the office. A mammoth-sized Samoan man bounced in through the door. His ponytailed hair was loosely held together with a hair tie, and his muscular, albeit soft, arms rippled through the oversized T-shirt.

"Bless!" I threw my right arm around his shoulder and my left arm under his armpit, hitting him on the back with closed fists. "It's so good to hear your voice."

His accent was thick, a deep, soft caressing of words. He bubbled the O's and A's from his lips and pronounced my full name as close to perfect as I had heard in a long time. "Kilohana. It is *good* to see you." Bless ushered out the scarred woman and took a seat on one of the gaudy couches.

"What are you doin' here?" He motioned for me to sit on the couch across from him. "I thought once you left for Big City, that was it."

"I did, too, but it's a small world. I guess I was bound to end up back here eventually." I watched the door close behind the woman. "Who's the girl? She seemed to know me?"

"You don't remember Mirella? That's Mo's girl."

"That's Mirella? She must have started fighting. I didn't even recognize her."

Bless' laugh erupted from his throat, and a deep, infectious smile broke across his face. I couldn't stop my lips from curling up in response.

"So . . ." His eyes searched the empty space next to me. "Is EO here?"

"Over here," EO said from across the room. His voice hummed with annoyance.

I responded for him, "Yeah, he's sitting on the swing over there." I motioned to a complicated-looking swing, which was putting EO in a compromising position, struggling to get comfortable.

"Is he still mad?"

"Go screw yourself, Bless," EO responded.

"You could say that."

Bless delivered an encore to the earlier laugh and relaxed back into his seat.

"All right, Kilo, I love seeing you, man, but we got a fight in fifteen, so you gonna tell me why you're here, or what?"

"Why can't I just come to see an old friend?"

Bless' eyebrows rose. "I assume that doesn't mean Sandra?"

The mention of her name caught me off guard and cut through my chest like a saber. I quelled the resentment swelling in me for letting EO talk me into coming to the Below. How could I expect to navigate this place when everything wanted to take a bite out of my soul?

My face must have betrayed the turmoil inside since Bless' voice took on a serious tone. "It's all right. Tell me why you're here, Bruddah."

"DIIP sent me to investigate the Kaua'i City's Continent death rate." I paused, and the muscles in my face dropped. "EO found something."

"Okay. What?" A hint of curiosity flickered on his jovial face.

"There's been an abnormal number of deaths on the Continent from two specific districts, Ludo and Nāpali. I'm not sure what it means yet, but it's unsettling."

Bless stood up and searched the ground with his eyes before heading to the wall on the closest side of the room, where he opened a safe, pulling hard on both crank levers. He removed a personal device backup from the safe and placed it on a table in the middle of the room. His eyes glazed over as he stared at it for a few seconds before he looked at me.

"A lot of my guys go to the Continent. You know how it is."

I nodded.

"If my guys are dying while Lualila District kids come back, I want to know."

"That's why I'm here." I walked over to Bless and leaned on the table with both hands, the wood almost cracking from the pressure. "There's something else. It's Maurice . . . Mo. According to DIIP records, he didn't make it back."

Bless grabbed the personal device backup from the table and squeezed, looking like he would crush it into a thousand pieces. The frown that spread across his face was one of despair. EO saw it, too—yet not a hint of surprise crossed his face.

"I think I might be able to help, but I want something in return, Bruddah."

"You seriously gonna ask me to fight?"

"You've been gone for too long. Information isn't free down here."

I thought about it for a few seconds and checked with EO.

"You're considering it?"

I shrugged.

He had climbed down from the swing and now paced alongside Bless. "He uses people. I know you've got a soft spot, but we had a very different time here with him. You don't owe him anything."

"Yes or no?" I asked pointedly.

He shook his head.

"What did he say?" Bless asked.

I turned my gaze back to Bless and nodded. "If that's what you want, I'll fight, but it has to be tonight. I'm only legal for forty-eight hours."

"I'll set it up. But since you work for the DIIP now, I just want to make sure you're still cool with Near Death."

"Are you serious, Kilo?" EO scoffed.

My jaw clenched at the words, "Yeah, we're good."

"They're tight enough."

The blood in my right hand returned to its normal flow as I loosened the boxing wraps. I had wrapped and unwrapped my fists five or six times now, never quite feeling like they were right. EO and I sat on a bed in a drab, windowless room waiting for the fight. Photos of Bless' crew hung on the wall, outlined by the yellow stains of where our childhood pictures used to live. If I thought hard enough, I probably could have named the relics that had once hung in each of the faded yellow outlines.

But one photo of us remained above the dresser. It framed Maurice and me, in our Continent tox suits, assault weapons slung around our shoulders. The cold wind whipped around my head, and my fingertips went numb. I saw the evidence of a smile under the mask, and Maurice's arms flexed around my shoulder. I could still feel the Continent as if I was standing there with him. We'd spent so much time on the Continent that I always thought it was where we'd die. I guess Maurice did, too.

"Yeah, all right," I said, wrapping my hand for the last time.

"It's been a long time since you fought with ND. Try not to go too deep," EO warned. I could hardly remember the last time. But the memories of the feeling never went away.

"Small price to pay. Plus, maybe I still got it."

"Maybe if you still looked like me, you'd have it. But now . . . you look like you." EO gave my body a once-over. Although most of the muscle was still there, my training wasn't what it once was. My abs were soft, if I was being generous, and none of my muscles had the endurance of EO's version of my body.

"I thought you were supposed to build me up?"

A laugh caught in EO's throat.

"Proud of yourself?" A smile broke through on my face, and he failed to hold back his own chuckle any longer. I was thankful for the levity, as it kept the strain of revisiting this place at bay.

"Hey, I worked hard for this body," he said.

"Shut up. You didn't do anything."

A knock on the door interrupted the conversation. EO stood up and put both of his fists out.

"We're in this together; nothing breaks that," I said, and pounded them.

He gave me a brief nod. "You got this. One fight and then we can get out of here and find out what's going on in this city."

The arena in no way resembled what I remembered. We stood on the street level of the three-tier fighting stadium. Staggered seating was attached to each of the four walls, creating a cylindrical space in the middle for the fighters to battle. In the center of the floor sat a circle of sand, which was being curated by two of Bless' men. Blood-infused sand was removed and replaced with buckets of clean sand, washing away the memories of what had happened minutes before.

"That's new."

Bless looked pleased with himself. "A lot has changed since you left, Bruddah." He pulled something out of his pocket and handed it to me. The two-capsuled Near Death nasal injector contained a greenish transparent liquid. The color was more of an ocean green compared to the dark green that was common in Big City, but I had no doubt the effects would be the same.

The ND tangoed with air bubbles in the cartridges. I watched the liquid fight for a chokehold on the air. But every time it brought an air bubble close to extinction, the bubble shifted, escaping and reforming before the liquid's next attempt. If I could just buy some time and come back stronger, I would have a chance.

The sand crunched beneath my bare feet, irritating my toes as I walked into the fight circle. My ears rang from the deafening screams, 5,000 people all on their feet, begging Bless to start the exhibition. In the early days, we would have maybe gotten a few hundred people to show, but nothing like this. Bless stood on the second level, pressed up shoulder to shoulder with a couple of his people.

Nearby, EO balanced against the railing. I shifted the fingers on my hand opposite the way I had before the meeting with Decambra and gave him a nod. Now my middle finger lay atop my index and ring fingers, which, in turn, were on top of my pinky and thumb. He clapped his hands together and yelled some words of encouragement that were lost among the swell of voices.

"Ladies, gentlemen, and all of you other disgusting people of the Below, welcome to the Blessed fight!"

A little much, I thought as I watched Bless spin toward the various corners of the stadium. But who was I to judge?

"Tonight, we have a special feature for you." The timbre of Bless' voice turned low and seductive.

"We have an old friend of mine, someone who decided he would rather live in Big City and work for the Department of Inter-Island Peace than fight for your affection."

The crowd groaned. A few fans hurled pieces of their costumes down to where I stood, narrowly missing me. I didn't expect a warm welcome, but the animosity from the crowd was more intense than I remembered.

"Come on, now. Come on, now! Some of you may remember him—he's the kid who took down Jack Duecy with pure rage. Kilohana Ressler!"

A few cheers broke through among the ocean of boos, but my goal wasn't to make friends; it was to make it through the fight and get some information as a reward. I ripped my long-sleeved shirt over my head and reached down to grab some of the sand. The coarse grains rolled through my hands.

It absorbed most of the sweat, knowing I would produce more.

"But I know who you all came to see tonight. Our very own club fighter and the baddest motherfucker I've ever allowed in this house. Von Cammon!"

Without skipping a beat, a tall man in his twenties, covered in scars, sprinted out from behind the floor-level crowd toward the ring. Cammon could only be described as a monstrosity of muscle, dwarfing my thinner frame. Once he reached his mark, he lurched back and let out a terrifying scream that drove the crowd into a frenzy. Between his lips was a wild smile that matched the intensity in his black eyes. And without breaking his glare, he rubbed sand along his arms and between his hands before throwing what was left into the air.

Without warning, the ground below us rapidly elevated. My balance faltered, and I dropped to a knee as the rectangular platform rose through the air, steadying after a few moments once it was even with the second level. Some of the sand had fallen away to reveal the clear platform beneath. Steel chains clamped to its four corners attached the ring to the arena walls and created a small but noticeable bounce.

A moment after the platform reached equilibrium, Cammon stuck an inhaler in his nose and drained the chambers of their green liquid. I pulled out the inhaler Bless had given me and stared at it for a second.

This is fine. I've done this before, I thought, but I was less than convincing. Regardless, I jammed the two prongs of the inhaler into my nostrils and pressed the buttons on either side. The chemical rushed through my body like ice through my veins, leaving a burning sensation in its wake. After a couple of seconds, my body acclimated to the drug, leaving only a slight stimulation in my brain and a thick coat of sweat on my skin.

"Now, let's watch these boys try to kill each other!"

Bless' voice shook the arena, but Cammon got the jump. He was already hurtling toward me at full speed. As he got within swinging distance, I slid to the left and dropped my right shoulder forward, dodging his first right hook. In a spin, I managed to take a few steps back and regain my balance.

By then, Cammon had already bounced back, charging again like an angry bull. I absorbed two quick punches aimed at my chest and swung a right jab in retaliation toward his core. The punch connected but didn't slow Cammon's determined onslaught. He leapt off his back foot, kicking upward at my head again, failing to connect beyond my forearms.

His kick left a slight opening there hadn't been with his punches. I took it. But just as I put my full weight behind a cross, the sand beneath my planted foot rolled. My fist never connected. Cammon's did.

I fell hard on my left side and tried to roll into a defensive stance, but it was too late. Cammon had already grabbed hold of my leg and torso and lifted me into the air. I lost all control as he tossed me a full three meters off the ground. My head thudded to the platform as I fell, and Cammon circled my prone figure, flexing to the crowd in a victory lap.

"Make me feel something!" Cammon shouted.

I felt the ND pulse through the muscles in my back where I had landed. The incredible feeling rushed through my body and launched me straight back to my feet. I was nowhere near death, but the ND kicked in like a mix of adrenaline and jet fuel being shot through my synapses. The fight required a change of strategy. As long as Cammon didn't knock me off my feet, I could use the ND to push myself further, faster, and stronger.

I lunged toward Cammon and threw a flurry of punches that still didn't put a dent in the goliath. The speed threw him off, though, and his hands started moving slower between combos.

I finally landed a strong uppercut, and Cammon's jaw cracked, the blow echoing throughout the arena, knocking him backward. He regained his footing and tested his jaw before using his palm to force the protruding bone back into place. His reformed jaw shifted around several times as if he was working each of the organic mechanisms back into place.

His eyes narrowed. "Now we can have some real fun." He spat a mouthful of blood over the side of the platform.

Shit. I wasn't the only one feeling the ND. He lunged at me, connecting a few punches to my head and body before I could fight back. I dropped to my knees and spun my leg, sweeping his out from under him. He tried to recover but took a dropkick straight to his shoulder. The crowd let out shocked expletives as he crumbled to the ground.

I drove my fists into his body as fast and hard as I could. His defensive position on the ground blocked some of the blows, but not all. The ND drove the punches as if propellant blasted from my elbows. I sat on top of him, relentlessly trying to finish this here and now, when suddenly, he opened his chest and clamped his hands together against my ears.

The intense ringing threw off my balance. I tried to regain my footing, but only managed to stumble to my knees. Cammon pushed himself to his feet, blood dripping from every orifice in his head, and smiled, red lining the gaps between his teeth. We both stood for a second, absorbing the ND. The crowd's roar was deadened by the ringing in my ears.

I made out a blurry EO. His arms were folded anxiously, his eyes wide. *God, how did I ever do this several times a month, sometimes even twice a week?* The ND alone kept me upright. I hoped Cammon needed a few seconds so I could breathe, but when I looked back, I saw his torn knuckles headed toward my nose. His blow connected, and I staggered back before righting myself and unleashing everything into a burst of punches.

The fight turned into a fully offensive match, each of us trying to hit as hard and as fast as we could. Any blocking became incidental. Cammon finally landed a clean blow that knocked me off my feet. I rolled toward the edge of the ring.

My body was shutting down. The burning from the accumulating gashes in my face intensified, while the ND convinced my heart to keep the blood pumping. My body became numb. The pain dissipated, but the ability to control my appendages remained. The effects of the ND unleashed my body as a cold, forged tool. But I didn't have time to bask in the ecstatic rush swirling around my head.

Before I could harness the full functionality of the ND coursing through my veins, a hand grabbed my hair and pulled me up. I stood there, momentarily limp, which gave Cammon time to shift his weight to his back foot and kick, connecting with my chest.

The platform receded as I fell toward the arena floor. Cammon disappeared, obscured by the ledge as my head cracked against the ground. The thud resounded through the arena.

Someone rushed over amid the cheers of, "Cammon . . . Cammon . . . Cammon!" They crouched above me, wrapping white cloths around my arms and head before several hands lifted my body off the ground. But the world around me seemed to unfold on a delay, challenging my ability to correlate their actions with time.

My mind attempted to make sense of my reality. I saw Bless' mouth moving out of the corner of my eye, but whatever he said came out garbled in my ears. My temples started to burn, and the bones in my skull felt as though they were cracking in some cruel lobotomy gone wrong.

The excruciating pain endured for several moments before I shot up, my senses at full alert, the fighting platform only a few meters away.

"Welcome back, Bruddah. You got a bit messed up. Bet that felt good."

The throbbing from the maroon-colored bruises that covered my body felt like I had been in a motorcycle accident, but from a week ago.

"What did you give me? How long has it been?"

"Revive salts from Ludo. This is the good stuff, so just be happy I wasted some on you."

"I forgot what it feels like after one of these fights." My head continued to throb in my hands.

"When he's good, will you bring him to my office?" Bless said to one of the attending nurses. "Take a second, Kilo; you'll be all right."

When I was able to walk over to Bless' office with help, EO met me along the path.

I locked eyes with him and shook my head ruefully.

"I told you," he said.

Bless ushered us into his office and closed the door after sending the nurse back to the arena. Mirella sat at a table reviewing some paper documents I hoped were the ones he had promised me.

"Paper, huh?" EO said.

"We found a couple of things for you, Kilo." Bless motioned to Mirella for one of the documents. As he did, Bless pulled a pin-shaped object with a diminutive hook from his neck. The thin metal line slid out, coated in his blood, and at its head sat a black, diamond-encrusted tip—an ND pin. Judging by the languid look that came over his face, he had used one of the ND inhalers and then the pin to release the euphoria. He produced a hefty cotton compress, which he held tightly against his neck before speaking again. "Mirella went through some of the deployment records on the drive, but all we could find were these—recruitment data that show most guys from Nāpali went to Outposts 370 through 380."

"Why do those sound familiar?"

"They were run by Shipley until a year or two ago. You knew him pretty well, right?"

"You could say that," I said, darting a look over to EO, who glared back with lips pressed in a tight line.

"Well, if someone knows what's going on out there, it's him."

"And where am I supposed to find him?"

"No idea. I don't have anything after he left the Security Forces on the Continent."

"Okay. What else?"

"Not much. But I talk to a lot of the boys when they come back. Contraband being snuck into Kaua'i City has skyrocketed."

"You're kidding me. I almost die in a fight for you, and you tell me to find the Doctor? Jesus, Bless! That's nothing."

"This is all I got, Bruddah. I'm sorry."

"Well, shit. Playing the chances, can you give me anything else on Shipley?"

"I got a file on him and the Doctor, but both are pretty thin. They're all yours."

I thumbed through each of them. Pictures, deployment reports, and recruitment data. *This isn't enough, but maybe someone else could help me make sense of it.*

"You need a place to stay, Bruddah?"

"No. I need to go to Ludo."

"Fine. At least take a couple of these; you might need them." I didn't need to look inside the bag that he slid toward my feet. I averted my gaze from EO. I didn't like it either, but ND was worth something down here.

CHAPTER 5

The golden glow of the artificially lit city flashed by as we bumped along the Inter-District Line between Nāpali and the Ludo District. Throughout the short ride, Shipley's words rattled around in my wandering mind. *I forged you, so I decide when you break!*

The hot steel from the AAP 445 assault rifle still burned in my hands, dredging up a memory I'd long hoped to forget. He'd wanted to turn us from protectors to mercenaries, but as the years dragged on and he pushed us closer to the edge, my fervorous trust in him waned. Shipley had refused to accept that.

The train came to a stop, jerking the few passengers forward in their hard plastic seats. The emptiness of the station was surprising for the week before a deployment, but I wouldn't want to be here either if I didn't need to be.

We stepped off and made our way along the elevated receiving platform, descending onto the thin sidewalk of the busy streets of Ludo. Among the fluorescent lights shining from the row of buildings, a strand of sunlight peeked through the overarching barrier wall. The air filled with a salty, sulfurous smell, one of the many downsides of the district, but I didn't mind it. It tripped some neurons and brought back memories of my departure days in Ludo, a few drunk friends and I stumbling our way to the gates.

Across the street, a dilapidated four-story building sat at the base of an unused apartment complex. Its sign hung prominently, displaying the Continental Services emblem, but beyond that, it wasn't anything special. We crossed the street between screaming cycles and ended up at the entrance to the Ludo District Official Continental Services Station. It looked a lot like the other stations I'd been to, but clearly less appreciated.

"Focus on the station leader. Anything you can get, all right?"

"Got it," EO said, and followed me through the door.

The cramped foyer was crowded with young men flipping through documents on their personal devices. I rolled back my shoulders and puffed out my chest before walking past the potential new recruits.

A check-in booth manned by a brown-uniformed official sat between me and the metal-clad door that led deeper into the facility. In the time it took me to walk from the entrance to the desk, I'd completed as much of a profile on the official as I could.

He wore thick glasses, which likely meant he'd had recent facial exposure in a high-density area on deployment, something that would embitter even the most loyal Continent workers. Scars peeked out from below his collar and, based on the angle, presumably ran deeper under his shirt.

I hardly noticed his personal device, set to one of the softest voice control settings available, indicating he'd maybe worked in security on the Continent and was used to the quiet, clandestine work. Finally, a deep brown patch was stitched to the inside of his open coat—the Designer Symbol. *A patriot.*

I walked right past the desk and headed for the door behind the official, my eyes pinned forward.

"Hey, what are you doing?"

I shot back, "I'm here to see your boss' boss. Through the door at the back on the left, correct?" It was a total guess, but chances were that anyone behind that door could be considered this man's boss. The heads of the potential new recruits snapped up, eyes wide, waiting for his response.

"No one is allowed back there without authorization from a colonel. Who did you say you were?"

"I didn't. But if that's protocol, then get a colonel out here to escort me back."

The official picked up his personal device and made the request, his voice barely whispering through the transmission. EO leaned in against the door, listening for anything valuable from behind the wall.

"I think it's him." EO straightened and backed up from the door just as it opened. A tall, pale man wearing a decorated uniform came through. He threw a brown standard Continent cap on before making his way toward me.

"I'm not sure how you think the Continental Forces works, but you don't just demand an audience with the station leader. I want your name and who you work for. I'll be filing a report." The man's voice grew gruffer and more agitated with each word. "Charles. Don't call me anymore for no-names."

"You misunderstand. You are an official, yes? A colonel?"

His facial muscles morphed into a snarl at my words. "You work for me for the next hour. I would like to speak with the station leader of this site immediately. I'm here from the Department of Inter-Island Peace, sent here specifically by Designer Decambra and Designer Owyang on special assignment to investigate this station. Now, unless you care to have my report to the Designer's Joint Committee include a refusal to comply by Colonel . . ." I paused for a moment to read the badge that sat under the Colonel's Kaua'i Design emblem. "Anderson, I suggest you take me to the station leader. Now."

If the room had been quiet before, my words turned it into a vacuum where sound no longer existed. Any movement from the potential new recruits ceased, and all eyes were locked on Colonel Anderson.

"Not bad." EO's voice broke the silence for me. All he would have to do is dig into current joint commissions to learn mine was exaggerated, but I gambled on the pressure.

The man's muscles tensed, and his eyes flashed as we waited for his decision. Without a word, the colonel turned on his heel and walked back through the door. I maintained my manufactured confidence and followed him into the corridor. The dim lights hung every meter or so, giving the impression of an ND lab, but more stifling.

Worn doors lined the corridor walls, each with a placard holding the name of the official working inside. As the end of the hallway approached, Colonel Anderson pushed on the wall to reveal a handle that beeped after he grabbed hold of it. The door opened to a spiral staircase that led up. We climbed it and exited on the third level.

The colonel led me down the hallway the way we'd come two floors below and motioned with a limp hand to a door on the right.

"Knock twice," he said, and left.

I gave EO a directive look. He leaned toward the door.

"I can't hear anything. We'll have to go inside."

I knocked twice. Within a few seconds, the door swung open, exposing a large office inconsistent with the hallways that had led us here. An overweight man, younger than the colonel, ushered me into the room and motioned for me to take a seat on the available chair facing a wooden desk. Atop the desk, several PDs whined, each running different programs.

The rest of the room was littered with oil and acrylic paintings that appeared as if they had been smuggled in from the Continent. One, in particular, caught my eye. Pink splashes that covered the canvas were cut down the middle by a winding river of blue. Its oddity captivated me. I'd rarely seen brushstrokes so attentive.

"So, you're Agent . . . ?"

"Ressler."

"To what do I owe the pleasure, Mr. Ressler?"

"I need to ask you some questions about recruitment for the Continent."

The man continued to scan a floating screen above one of the personal devices. I waited, inspecting the framed photographs the man displayed behind his desk.

"Nice, aren't they?" he asked.

"Wonderful."

"This one was my favorite." He spun and grabbed a lavishly framed photo from the shelf. Smudged oil trailed along the faces, but I still recognized the men shaking hands.

"Our greatest Designers, wouldn't you say? I was there that day," he said.

"Well appreciated, to be sure." The two men in the photo grinned with their arms clasped together. They both wore quiet, restrained shawls and suits for Designers, but were unmistakable: Designer Akashi and Designer Wahama, the late Co-Designers for the Department of Original Design and Architecture.

"How far we've come. Symbols for the everlasting Design." He gave one last longing look at the photo before replacing it. "Now, I must say, I'm partial to Designer Forsythe of Agriculture and Food Production. Fantastic work in the past few decades, and a true delight."

"I've heard great things about Designer Forsythe, but—"

"I like to know who I'm meeting with, Mr. Ressler, and I can often tell a lot about a man by how he perceives the Design and the Designers. For instance, a man without a favorite Designer is someone uninformed or uninterested in our society. After all, if he took the time, there's no doubt he would find appreciation in them, and surely in one above all others." Although not a question, his facial expression told me he was waiting for a response.

I matched his patience for a few moments before he balked.

"Who and what do you admire, Mr. Ressler?"

"I would say . . . my appreciation resides in its development, in their development. To pick a single Designer or iteration of the Design of our society is a discredit to its journey. My appreciation lies with the eternal growth of the Design, its scope and service, and the ever-changing Designers who serve our city. I'm not entirely sure what type of person that makes me, but I'm sure you will enlighten me."

I stretched a placatory smile on my face, but the words left a spoiled taste in my mouth. Whatever bullshit this guy needed to hear.

"Interesting . . . " He trailed off and allowed his gaze to drift behind me, clearly puzzling over my response.

"Enough foreplay," EO said.

"The Continent, I'd like to ask you a few questions about recruitment."

The words brought him back. "Of course, although I'm sure no one notified me to expect you. It was a Designer Joint Commission?"

"Sit closer to the desk," EO said from behind the man. His eyes darted along the screen from over the station leader's shoulder.

I shifted in my seat, fixing my posture slightly and scooting forward in the chair. I looked around at the framed paintings—some were encapsulated in glass, presumably the treasured ones. In the corner of the office, a particular painting offered a slight reflection of the official's screens. The reflection was unclear, but EO had spent a lifetime harnessing his gift, pooling his connection to my senses into an extrapolated vision. I took a deep breath and allowed my concentration to narrow for just a moment and provided EO with as much sensitivity to the stimuli as I could muster.

He nodded.

"I'm sorry. They should have spoken with all recruitment sites before I arrived. Would you like me to get Designer Decambra to confirm this for you?"

I'd finally been able to make eye contact with the man but was having trouble reading him. His greasy skin puffed around his eyes, dampening any facial movement. Regardless, what I said wasn't entirely false. Decambra had sent me to Kaua'i City to investigate death rates on the Continent, just not technically to Ludo.

"I don't think that will be necessary. We don't need to bother a Designer at this hour." He sat back in his chair. "What can I do for you?"

I jerked my eyes toward the ground and then back up above the man's shoulder, trying to solicit an update from EO.

"Nothing," he said.

"I spent some time reviewing Continent records from the past few years at the DIIP, and there were some uncomfortable numbers. I'm hoping you might be able to shed light on these." I slid my open personal device toward him. "As you can see, there's been a steady increase in recruitment for the past five years."

A bead of sweat materialized at his hairline, and he shifted forward to take a better look at the data. His perspiration was possibly caused by the humidity in the room, possibly by something more.

"Mm-hmm. These seem right. I can't speak for other districts, but Ludo has definitely seen some more guys signing up."

"And what about how many guys come back?" I asked pointedly.

The man pushed my personal device back across the table. "You know as well as I do, not everyone comes back, but they serve the greater Design."

"Do you keep track of how many return?"

"Well, we do, but those numbers are sent directly to the Designers. I don't keep them here."

"You don't have access to them?" I asked. But a shift back in his chair and his crossed arms gave me the feeling he wasn't interested in describing the exact mechanisms of death counting, so I didn't give him a chance to answer. "Do you know what percentage of service members from Ludo died on the Continent last year?"

He hesitated. "The Designers have those numbers. Why do you need them from me?"

"What about the name Shipley? Anything I should know about him?"

"Agent Ressler, where are these questions coming from?"

"I don't question the directives of the Designers. I'm just here to get some information." My grip over the interrogation was weakening. If I pushed too far, I risked Ludo District tightening around me. "You know what, I'm sure I can get those numbers from the Designers, and I will. Station leaders are busy, and I wouldn't want to waste any more of your time."

I stood up, fixed my coat, and returned my personal device to my pocket. "Last thing. Have there been any changes of note on the Continent?"

"None that I've heard of. Looks the same as when you were there, Agent Ressler," he said with a watery smile.

"I appreciate you giving me your time. I'll make sure the Designers are well aware of the great work you are doing down here."

I let myself out through the door and headed straight for the exit, EO at my hip.

"As soon as you said Shipley, his leg started shaking like he was having a seizure," EO said. "He knew a lot more than he was giving up."

He was right. The station leader had been like an iceberg, but I didn't expect any other officials in the district to be any different. They weren't the only people in this district with information, though. I just needed to find who I was looking for as soon as possible.

Water sprayed across my face, courtesy of a speeding indi-cycle too close to the curb. I wiped the dirty mixture of recycled water, cycle fluid, and mud from my eyes. The frigid remains dripped down the rough cotton of my peacoat. The same revolting street water smell from Big City blanketed me once again.

EO placed the back of his hand against his nostrils discreetly, like he was wiping something from his skin.

"Don't even," I said with a glare.

With the palms of my hands, I whisked away what moisture I could and slammed the crosswalk button attached to the streetlamp. We'd made it several blocks since leaving the Recruitment Station, and we now stood at one of the five major Ludo intersections. A plan was formulating in my mind. The cavalier indi-cycle driver had interrupted that.

I hadn't figured out exactly how I was going to get us in, but I knew our best chance for information was going to be the fight rings across the district, more than a few blocks away from the Recruitment Station. After crossing the massive intersection, we jumped into a packed pedestrian elevator.

The door to the elevator opened on the second level of the Below at one of the mid-level platforms, where a sea of people clogged the walkways. I'd expected some mixture of leisure groups or merchants, but not this. It was crowded with countless people stretching from either side of the buildings; without the guardrails, no doubt more than a few would have fallen into the streets below.

I weaved through the chanting people, signs bobbing above their heads like pistons. As I was trying to make out the scribbled writing, one protester pushed me, throwing me off balance. Then I heard it. The piercing voice of a Designer shook through the platform, weaving its way through the crowd.

"The Design is all of us. We are the Design!"

A makeshift screen stretched between the buildings, hung tight by fiber cables. On it, a shaking face looked down at the crowd, the true power of his oratory uncapturable in two dimensions. Along the buildings on either side of the walkway hung massive banners with the speaker's augmented, strong-jawed face angled up and to the left in a mechanical art style, splashed with monochrome colors. Crudely drawn letters were scrawled above and below the face, somehow diminishing his authority.

BRING
IT
DOWN

The face, the voice, the words of conviction—they all belonged to my father.

Spit flew from his mouth as he lectured the ungrateful citizens of the Below. "The discontent in some of our districts is nothing but a lack of education, an unwillingness of those around you to watch as we continue to build our great city!"

With each syllable, his words faded into the wave of growing screams and chants, struck back by the fierce protest.

"We won't be Designed! People can't be Designed!" The woman who shoved me now shouted next to my ear. "DPMs were made for us! DPMs were made for us!" I no longer needed to see the signs to understand.

"Come on, we have to get to street level," EO said.

But my father's face seemed to watch me. My heart raced, and as hard as I tried, I couldn't pull my eyes from him. The tingling in my fingers crept up my arms, slowly fading the control of my body.

"Kilo, look at me. You're okay. He's not here!"

EO grabbed me and forcefully massaged the veins up and down my arm. The blood flow responded, bringing feeling back to my hands.

"We need to go! This is about to break."

"Okay," I said weakly before focusing on his face. "Okay!"

In EO's footsteps, I pushed through the molecular structure of the crowd. Moments later, murderous screams broke out in front of us. The signs that bobbed above the crowd rolled down like a tsunami headed toward the center of the platform. My father's speech continued in the background, unaffected by the destruction in its wake.

The screaming grew steadily, and dark figures suddenly emerged: Night Sticks. Electricity crackled off their truncheons, swinging above the horizon of heads before smashing down on the protesters.

"Run!" I yelled back to EO. I drove my legs into the ground, pushing through the crowd. It was a free-for-all of sweaty bodies racing for their lives. My father's eyes, perched on the fluttering banner, appeared to watch us fight back toward the elevator.

Although his eyes didn't move from their place above, soundless words mouthed from his pursed lips, much different from those screaming from the screen beside us. His resolute face didn't resemble the man I remembered, but his aura hadn't changed.

Visions of my descension jolted through my mind: my small hand slipping from my mother's grasp, the men screaming as they loaded me into the truck, tears rolling down my face, watching my mother's face disappear for the last time. The fears of coming to Kaua'i City—to the Below—from the moment I met Decambra had been realized.

I started to lose the battle against the other fleeing people. The density of the crowd only became thicker as protesters funneled into the staircases at the end of the platform. My flailing mind only made it more challenging to keep up.

"Kilo, you gotta move; they're right on you."

Even without EO's warning, the sound of skulls cracking under the power of truncheons signaled they were closing in. I wasn't going to make it. *Only one option.* I stared up at the man's gray face. A fire now burned up the banner, engulfing his neck and chin in its blazing path. *Fuck you.*

EO must have seen the decision matrix running in my face and looked around for another option.

"Stairs, end of the block."

I turned amid the flow of people, now seeing fifteen or twenty brutish Night Sticks only a few meters away, cutting down protesters effortlessly with powerful swings of their namesake weapons.

They were frightening, even for someone who'd encountered them countless times, with their black, full-body armor covered in silver stenciling. Their helmets completely hid the human being inside with crossed slits running diagonally down the front, angled toward the middle. Breath streamed from the dark openings. Someone was in there, but you could never truly be certain if it was human or monster.

There stood only a few people between them and me. The mouths of protesters producing the blood-curdling cries were now visible. I tensed my already beaten body, regretting the fight at Usos, and focused on the elite guards closing in. Using artificial help from the ND inhalers Bless had given me crossed my mind, but there wasn't enough time.

The last of the protesters pushed past me. I stood staring at three Night Sticks while several others on either side continued to plow forward through the crowd. One of the Night Sticks smashed his weapon against his thigh, sending electricity flying. A single hit and you went down; they knew it, and they wanted to make sure I knew it, too. But there wasn't much of a choice.

I rushed toward the center Night Stick. His comrades immediately flanked him on either side. All three cocked their weapons, angling an attack at my upper body.

Instead of letting them take a shot, I bolted straight ahead and ducked slightly to avoid the middle Night Stick's swing. I barreled into him. His truncheon fell and rolled away, just out of reach, as he crashed to the ground.

The second my shoulder hit the platform, the rest of my body screamed with pain. Burning sensations flared from the healing bruises and cuts.

Still, I jumped to my feet just in time to see one of the Night Sticks rushing toward me, followed by the other. I reached down and ripped the helmet off the dazed man below me. As he tried to get back to his feet, I wound up and bashed it against his head, sending him right back to the ground.

In the time it took to make the fight two-on-one, the other Night Sticks closed the gap. I took a defensive position and blocked the first swing of the Night Stick with the helmet. He swung again. This time, I deflected and pushed through the swing, shouldering the man and dropping him to the ground. I tensed for the next onslaught, blood pumping through my muscles. I reconsidered my decision to use ND, but my unadulterated body needed to make do.

"Behind you!"

EO's cry came from my six o'clock. Without thinking, I threw the helmet behind my head and hoped for a high swing. Reverberations from the truncheon ripped through the helmet into my hands. I turned in time to see the Night Stick winding up again.

Pieces of the reinforced synthetic helmet crumbled in my hands. I looked around for anything else I could use but came up empty. I braced for impact, flexing my crossed arms in front of my face, hoping to withstand one shot and maybe be able to gain an advantage.

The truncheon never connected. Through my limited vision, the Night Stick fell face-first to the ground. His body convulsed atop his truncheon. At his feet, a protester lay bloody and weak with her hands wrapped around the Night Stick's ankle.

"Thank you," I said.

The woman nodded before her head drooped to the ground in a puddle of her own blood. As I walked past her, I didn't allow myself to think of what she might have just sacrificed for me. I needed to get to the stairs.

EO was already in a full sprint across the body-riddled wasteland. Some of the other Night Sticks stopped their frontal assault on the protesters, seeing what had happened to the rest of their squad. I broke into a run and headed toward EO, the opening to the twisting stairs only twenty meters away. While the Night Sticks were tough and menacing, they were hindered by their body armor.

I hit the entrance before any of them could clear the halfway point of the mid-level. We descended two, sometimes three steps at a time. The staircase zigzagged back and forth over the busy street below, and I glanced up to see the massive "BRING IT DOWN" banner gliding down toward the cycles zipping through traffic, half of my father's face clouded in ashes. With each corner we turned, the screams of people from above dampened until only faint whispers lingered.

I pushed through the gate onto street level. The Night Sticks were no longer in pursuit. But there was no telling what that meant for the rest of the protesters I left behind. Using both hands, I waved down the first transit-cycle I saw and jumped inside.

CHAPTER 6

We sat with two other passengers in the cramped, rigidly framed transit-cycle. The staggered seats, although cushioned, provided little comfort for any of us. I watched countless cycles pass by in the Ludo morning rush.

EO's elbows jabbed into my chest with each bump, an uncomfortable thanks for letting him sit on my lap.

"Seat three, stop arriving in three . . . two . . . one. Seat three, please exit the vehicle and have a nice day." I paid for the ride and got out. The transit-cycle left us on the busy sidewalk under the entrance to the Ludo fighting sub-district.

"Let's go somewhere loud," EO said, and started up the alley, which bottle-necked at the entrance, and then opened into a wide street rivaling that of the Inter-District Highways. Crowds formed in circles and cheered around makeshift fight rings. They were slightly elevated on wooden crates. They lacked the distinctive sand feature of Bless' fight club but were no less exciting. Among the vertical shops and restaurants along the crowded street, a pulsing neon sign caught my eye a few stories up.

"There. They may have a private viewing deck."

We made our way through the roaring crowds and up to the third level, where we were greeted by a hostess waiting patiently under the words *It's*

About Time carved into the wood frame above her.

"Welcome to the fighting rings. Can I help you?"

"You have any privates?" I practically screamed the question through the music that oscillated around us.

"No. I can sit you in the corner, though, if you're all right with not being able to see the Muay Thai or Mixed Hawaiian?"

"That's fine," I said, but before we could move past her, she stopped me. "Where you from?"

I hesitated. "Mid-City."

Her eyes surveyed my body, then she nodded. "Okay. Forgive me for asking. We've been getting a lot of people from the Below trying to get a free meal. I can see you haven't been caught up in the Ludo shortages. Right this way."

At our table, the view of a few fights was partially obstructed by the staggered stilts of the building, but the Samoan Sumo and Hawai'i Lua fights were both visible, so I didn't mind. The woman bowed, her breasts nearly falling out of her shirt as she did, then left.

"I didn't know food was that scarce down here," I said.

"I've heard rumors of some of the districts in Big City, too."

"Yeah? What the hell are they doing with all the processing plants? There should be enough food for ten island cities."

"I don't know. Supposedly, the problems are with the real stuff. It's causing issues at the plants."

"How does that even happen?" I scoffed and paused before answering it myself. "The fuckin' Design."

The fights below roared, and I glanced out over the rail to see a trainer trying to reattach a kid's dislocated jaw. EO's eyes didn't leave me.

"You all right?" he asked.

"Fine."

He watched me survey the other tables. I wasn't interested in talking about my father—about any of it.

"Kilo, that's the first time you've seen him like that in . . . twenty years."

"I said I'm fine." The words came out punitively. EO let the silence linger until I could feel the effect. "I'm sorry. I just don't want to think about him right now. I'm still having dreams about it—about Mom."

"It's okay. I have them, too," he said with a disarming smile.

"You do?"

"Yeah, all the time." I picked up on the hint of loss in his voice, carefully masked by his stoic face. "Kilo, we don't talk the way we used to. We can't help each other if there is a trench between us."

"It's not a trench."

He stared back at me.

"Okay, you're right, but it's not like there is a manual on how to live a life with a DPM."

"Fair enough. Maybe when you're on your deathbed, I'll write one."

I chuckled and, with his blessing, changed the subject. "What did you make of the station leader?"

"I don't know what's going on, but I have the feeling none of this is as innocuous as Decambra made it sound."

"I'm beginning to believe you." I waved over one of the waitresses. "Did you notice anything I didn't?" I asked as we waited.

"Nothing on any of his devices. The guy had three open, and they were all just testing data."

"Figures, but he knew something about the elevated death rates, even if it was just that they existed."

"And he knew Shipley. That tells me the numbers aren't bullshit."

"But we still don't know anything." Out of the corner of my eye, I saw the waitress close in on our table.

"Single Nāpali, please," I said.

"Anything to eat? I must warn you, we're no longer serving poultry due to the shortage."

"Just the drink. Thank you."

The woman smiled, bowed, and headed back to the bar.

"I told you," EO said.

"Yeah, yeah. The fuckin' Design."

The crowd went wild for a split second, giving me an excuse to look away. Below, one sumo hurled his opponent from the ring. The fighter rolled off the stage and over a couple of supporters in imitation sumo attire. I thought of how much fun it would have been visiting these fights with EO and Bless. As terrible as Ludo was, it hadn't always been so bad. Maybe a different life would have unfolded if I'd been sent here instead of Nāpali—one only limited by the boundaries of my imagination.

We sat for a few minutes, watching some of the other fights. I focused primarily on the lightning-fast Hawai'i Lua fighters. The cracks from breaking bones were audible even through the bar's music as each of the fighters attempted to strike first, preempting any counteroffensives. It was a thrilling sport, made even more entertaining by the canoe paddles, leiomanos, and vicious strikes aimed at the other fighters' weak points.

A minute later, I received my drink. The dirty amber liquid inside the shot glass waited with placid patience.

"So, the Ludo Company runs this?" I asked.

"I remember that being the word fifteen years ago, but who knows anymore?" EO watched me as I poured the liquid down my throat and winced at the bitter flavor.

I looked over EO's shoulder and waved at the hostess, who'd just finished sitting a couple. She approached and leaned in. "Something else? A bet, perhaps?"

"A question." I shifted closer to meet her. "You know anything about the Company?"

She stiffened and shifted the personal device in her hands nervously before answering. "What do you wanna know?"

"Somewhere I can find an Elder." The Company held a strict hierarchy. If someone was going to know anything about the deaths going on in the district, it would probably be one of them.

"Care to buy anything else?" the hostess asked with a bit more confidence, placing her personal device on the table in front of me.

I tapped my PD to hers. "Two hundred credits." She looked down at the device to ensure the transaction had been authenticated.

"One of them runs the Hawai'i Lua ring. Anything else?"

"No, thanks."

I scanned the exterior of the Lua ring, my experiences with the gangs in Big City swirling around in my head. The largest Big City gang, the Kuhio 808s, was always a challenge as a DIIP agent. They were scrappy and had built a well-developed, durable network throughout the city. The Continent dealers from Maui City I'd busted the week before were working with the 808s.

But from what EO had told me, the Company was different. Their members cared more about the district than the island city and even had a reputation for mixing with anarchists from Honolulu prior to the fall. If the Designers were taking advantage of people in Ludo, the Company would know, and they would want to do something about it.

We didn't stay much longer at the club, being more concerned with trying to contact the Company.

Down in the alley, the crowd around me let out a cheer as one fighter jumped into a sweeping high kick, knocking his opponent out cold. We pressed forward until we made it between the Hawai'i Lua fighting ring and the Muay Thai ring. People bounced around shoulder to shoulder, attempting to see every punch, kick, and blood splat.

Although the hostess had made it seem like someone from the Company would be easy to find near the Hawai'i Lua fight, she was either lying or expected us to know what we were looking for. Usually, EO and I could spot someone ganged up the instant we saw them. EO could pick up conversations that may have otherwise been muddled, and I'd spent enough time with gang members on the Continent to know most of the signs.

"Black spikes, the far side of the ring."

I followed EO's gaze, seeing a few people lining the opposite side of the fight ring. *Bingo.* A smaller Asian man leaned against the ropes with tar-colored black spikes erupting from his head. Even from this far, his confident demeanor stood out. He was flanked by two much larger Samoans, further confirming EO's hunch. His torn jacket reeked of the Company; black and yellow vertical stripes covered the chest and arms, while red lettering was splattered across the front. I was disappointed that I hadn't spotted it earlier.

"Got him." I pushed my way through the crowd. "Can you make out anything?"

"Just talking about a bet on the fight. The guy in the red shorts is his."

"Fine. I'll see what I can do."

It took a few minutes to circumvent the ring as the closer I got to the fight, the more people stood their ground. These fights were sometimes all people in the Below could look forward to in a day, so if you were fortunate enough to get a spot toward the front, you held on to it with everything you had.

I finally made it shoulder to shoulder with one of the men guarding the spiky-haired man.

"Name?" I asked EO, dropping my head slightly.

"Fuka? I think—worth a shot."

"Fuka, can I talk to you a minute?" I leaned over the ring and past the Samoan to make eye contact with Fuka. He glanced back at me for a moment.

"What do you want?" he said, and returned his focus to his fighter.

"I need a meet with someone in the Company." The Samoan between Fuka and me took a powerful step, pushing me further from the ring. "I hear you're a man that can set that up?" I screamed over the noise of the crowded street. I had no idea how the leadership structure of the Company worked beyond the Elders at the top, and the word of a hostess wasn't the strongest branch to crawl out on, but I needed to try.

"Who are you, man? What makes you think you can ask me that?" For the first time, his gaze locked with mine.

"You guys wanna know more about how the Designers target the Below, how they target Ludo? I can help you if you help me."

His eyes now gleamed with interest.

"Okay. Give me a taste."

"Yesterday, I spent time inside DIIP looking at Kaua'i City Continent Force records. I can tell you, the Company's onto something."

Fuka refocused his attention on the fight as his guy took a huge hit from a canoe paddle and nodded his head.

"Mal, give this guy a card." The Samoan, still blocking any kind of close contact with him, pulled out a blank silver card and handed it to me.

"Kamehameha Building Seven. If you don't have anything, imma have him beat the shit out of you." Fuka pointed at the man in red shorts, who now grabbed a leiomano and swung the shark-toothed club at his opponent, opening a sizable gash in the man's arm. I thought for a moment about my fight with Cammon and understood what it meant if I didn't come through. I nodded to Fuka and slipped away, back into the crowd.

The inside of the Kamehameha Building was unlike anything I'd seen in Big City. It was a true homage to the history of the Hawaiian Islands before the fall of the Continents. Vibrant murals swept throughout the building center, with statues of the Lost Company and Queens standing prominently at the entrance, greeting residents. Painted seas of blood soaked the walls around brown figures at odds in the forests and beaches of the old islands.

This was much different from the history taught in my Nāpali all-level school. Each of the walls of the building center was themed with the experience of a different major island, all except Kaua'i. The four murals were complex but blended seamlessly together as they met at each intersection. I couldn't fathom the trauma this painter must have endured to tell these stories. The feeling of ignorance the murals left in me was hard to shake. I'd lived at all levels of this world, in these cities, but only ever seen what I'd been allowed to see.

A tap on the glass from someone outside refocused my attention on the present. EO and I sat in the café and watched people parade through the hallways of the Kamehameha Building Center. It was enormous, with three levels reserved for food, water, education, communication, and numerous other services for residents.

A pungent odor wafted in from the conveyor belt along our table, which roared to life and dropped a plate of Nāpali-style eggs into the middle of our cramped booth. The mush of food smelled somewhat inedible, but deep down, my stomach growled, eagerly waiting to be satiated. The mix of egg whites and shell spread over a coagulated protein bar made it worth coming back to the Kauaʻi Below.

"Your all-time favorite," EO said.

"Hardly, but it has an unfair reputation." I spooned a combination of the eggs and protein, a contented murmur coming from my mouth. "What makes processed bacon better than this? If there is a shortage, I'm going to enjoy the real thing until it's gone." I gave a couple more jovial stabs at the eggs before stuffing my face.

"I don't agree with Bless a lot, but you're insane if you think that slop is better than bacon," EO said.

"I broke the addiction a long time ago. I'm not letting Designer-run meat processing plants dictate my life. If I wanted an addiction, I'd huff everything Bless gave us."

"A synth-salt addiction is a small price to pay. We both remember what it tasted like for you." Saliva was almost dripping from EO's mouth now. "Besides, it won't kill you any faster than the Continent."

"You have to have a *body* to have an opinion." The words came out unexpectedly.

He looked down at the table, and the smile dropped from his face.

Why did I say that? God, you're such an idiot. It wasn't the first time we'd joked about this, but the words clearly cut through him, as if his body were made of flesh and bone.

"I'm sorry, I shouldn't have said it like that. On the bright side, you don't have to experience what a meal like this does to your intestines, so it's not all bad."

His cheek pulled up into a half smile. "If Bless knew this was your first real meal here, he would take back his files, and I'd support him."

"Not much to take back, EO. Shipley could be in any of the Below Districts. The stuff he has on him was surface level at best."

"You really think the Company will know more?"

"I think they care more. Bless only cares about his guys, but the Company is ideological."

I just hope they aren't too far gone, I thought. I'd never felt this kind of apprehension meeting with members of the 808, but here, the knot in my stomach grew. Connections with the Honolulu anarchists always stimulated this feeling. The Company held some strong ideological beliefs about the Designers and the island cities, but the anarchists were on a whole other level. *If the Designers really are systematically targeting certain districts in the Below, would the Company go that far?* Unfortunately, I wouldn't know until the meet.

I searched the café for an indication of the time. A digital clock perched above the bar read 6:30 p.m.

EO and I had walked some of the Kamehameha Building before coming to the diner and figured the place where Fuka wanted us to meet was on the thirty-seventh level, the top floor of the building. It was the most isolated, which meant the Night Sticks would have a tough time accessing it.

We still had time before we needed to be on thirty-seven, but EO passed it talking about a story he'd heard about how the Company had formed during the initial building period of the island cities. I'd heard it before. The laborers had amended some of the original Designs of Ludo and created secret places for dissentients to meet. Who knew how much of it was true? I'd never actually heard of the places existing, but if it had happened anywhere, it would have been Ludo. As he told the colorful story, I examined the Kamehameha

Building Center again, noting more than just the murals this time.

There was something different about the people in Ludo. I couldn't pinpoint it, but it was evident in their freedom of movement. They had an air of liberalism that didn't exist in any of the other Below districts.

"Do you notice anything about the locals?" I asked, still trying to express it in words myself. The people dressed similarly to everyone else in the Below, with lots of dark coats and pants, completely unlike the colorful dress you might see in Mid-City or near the Architecture Buildings. Nothing stood out about their wild hairstyles or the interactions, but their movements were unique—the slightest curvature of their folded arms or relaxation in their abdomen combined with confident steps.

"I don't know. What do you see?"

"I think this building, or this district, is different somehow." And then I saw it. A man's shoes step-in-step with a woman's, her shoes the same. The soles of their shoes were worn, but not in the same way as others in the Below. These shoes were scuffed with something I hadn't seen in a long time: sand.

"Let's go see the Company."

We joined the flow of Kamehameha residents toward the central elevators and stepped inside. Part of me wished I could spend more time here, visit some of the local shops, and maybe have a Ludo beer. There was a warm feeling of constriction in the building, akin to being swaddled like a baby. Then the doors closed, and the elevator glided up toward the thirty-seventh floor.

Most of the other passengers exited on lower floors, but a few remained in the large octagonal space until the doors reopened on thirty-seven.

The thirty-seventh level of the Kamehameha Building was strikingly different from its other levels. The floor was covered with garbage and dirt, like a forgotten city during the initial fall of the Continents. Wooden boxes, broken furniture, and dead insect carcasses lined the dilapidated hallways. Each of the occupied apartments had water damage running down the walls and splintered doors, revealing the interiors. *Clever*, I thought. *Who'd want to go poking through this mess?*

After a few minutes of investigating the maze of hallways, we came across a door that was different from the others. Its iron metal could have only been reformed here, not transported in a solid slate from the street level. The hinges had started to rust on the edges, but the door had a strong metallic shine in its middle, where a circular emblem was carved. The Company's emblem was subtle, yet curated to catch the eye—a circle with an M and a horizontal line scratched across it. I knocked on the door. "I got this."

EO nodded, but pressed his tongue against the inside of his cheek. "It'll be fine."

After a few moments, the door opened and revealed Fuka.

"You found it. Maybe what you have *is* worth a shit," he said, and ushered me inside.

Surprisingly, the interior echoed the state of the top floor. A few school tables were positioned in a disjointed circle resembling a hexagon. The walls that still stood were bare, and those that might have previously separated bedrooms or bathrooms lay shattered and torn. Each of the tables, except one, was occupied by two individuals. Fuka pulled out one of the two empty seats, scraping the metal chair legs against the concrete floor.

"Sit."

I did as I was told. The voice belonged to a man directly opposite where I sat. The unmistakable, but also illegible, character tattoos covering his shoulders and neck spoke of his connections to a Japanese family. I didn't need to scan the rest of the room to know each of these Elders belonged to the first family.

"Kilohana Ressler. Pretty bold for a DIIP agent to come to our building this far out of your jurisdiction."

I resisted the urge to look at EO as my heart pounded. "How do you know my name?"

"You bought a drink and a meal in Ludo, so I know everything about you."

Not everything, I thought.

"Fuka said you may have some new information about how the Designers have decided to rape our district. You have five minutes to tell me something I don't know, or when you step out of this building, it will be on stumps." Some of the other Company Elders present let out a burst of harsh laughter, a few fiddling with knives that sat atop their tables.

I started slowly. "Ludo and Nāpali are being targeted for Continent recruitment. I'm not entirely sure how, but they are manipulating the numbers so that more of your guys—"

"Something I *don't* know, Ressler."

The Elders in the room stared at me, a few tapping their fingers against the desks or shifting anxiously in their seats, clearly waiting for my response.

"There is a tunnel to the beachhead in Ludo, which I figure is something only the Company is privy to. That's probably how you have so much control of the district. And I'm guessing if anyone has an inkling about what's happening with the deaths on the Continent, it's you. I want to know what I'm missing."

The room froze, and the gazes of the first family split between me and the man in charge.

"So, you don't have anything for us. Instead, you want information from us?"

"No. I want to do something about whatever's going on, and unlike you, I can walk freely in Mid-City. I might even have a shot at taking an elevator to Design City, so let me help you."

I guessed what the Elder was thinking: *Is this DIIP agent from Big City worth the risk*? I was willing to bet I was. The Company didn't run a business and didn't calculate risk like the 808s. But they wanted change, and a slim shot sat in front of them.

"What are the numbers from DIIP?"

EO let out a sigh of relief behind me.

"Thirty-five percent from Ludo and 27 percent from Nāpali. I've never seen numbers that high. I asked the Ludo station leader today if he knew about them, and he suddenly wanted to ensure we followed correct procedures before disclosing any information."

"Hmm. Doesn't surprise me. They're all scum down there. Most of the time, they work hand in hand with the Night Sticks. What did you learn in Nāpali?"

"Not much. Shipley, an old CO of mine from the Continent, is supposedly the person to talk to, but he's not easy to track down. Maybe you can help with that?"

"Shipley, huh?" The Elder aimed his rhetorical question at the woman adjacent to him.

"He hasn't made much noise since he retired," the woman responded.

Her long hair almost touched her seat, and she sported similar Japanese character tattoos on her hands. These I recognized. They were the symbols of the Elite crew on the Continent, people not to be messed with. She looked at me. "We think he's in Nāpali Central."

"That's a wide net," I said.

She shrugged her shoulders.

"What about what he was doing on the Continent before he retired?"

The woman leaned in to confer with the Elder before answering, "The past few years, most of our people that come back either don't or can't talk about what is happening over there."

"What do you mean, *can't?*"

"A few of our people have been coming back without tongues."

"Tongues?" I was finally able to steal a look at EO, who only shook his head. "Is that from Carbon Sytride exposure?"

"That's what they say, but you know how it is . . ." Her mouth twisted. "The ones that end up talking think it has something to do with replica DPMs."

"Replicas on the Continent?" I asked cautiously.

The Elder interjected. "We're not sure, but if there are, they didn't come from Honolulu, and they aren't from before the fall."

The thought of Reklov's replicas pulled at my mind. I wanted to chase the rabbit and figure out how he could be so sure, but decided against it. It wasn't worth testing their patience.

"So how does Shipley fit into this?" I asked.

He stood up and walked over to the far wall. A long, cylindrical object hung horizontally from the ceiling. He pulled a cord at the end and unraveled a world map dating from before the contamination of the Continents.

"Nāpali and Ludo recruits are typically stationed here, right?" He pointed to the middle of the South American Continent. A few red circles already highlighted various regions in the area. "Word is, their mining operations have been moving north consistently for the past decade—"

"Toward Maui City territory," I finished for him.

"Yeah. Standard response is that new deposits have been found there, but we're not buying it."

"Hmm." I examined the map, orienting myself and attempting to picture where I'd been stationed. With my eyes, I followed the ground our team had covered under Shipley.

"And guess who was in charge of the stations right here . . ." The leader traced one of the northernmost circles with his finger. "Shipley."

"So, Shipley *is* the key. There is no way he wouldn't know what's going on."

The Elder sat back in his chair and casually threw up his hands. "You tell me, Ressler. You're the one who knew him."

"When I met with a Designer in Big City, it seemed like there was a real urgency to produce some information about the deaths on the Continent. Shipley never struck me as the kind to go underground after his service. I think he knows something the Kaua'i City Designers would very much like to keep to themselves."

The leader's eyes shifted to the woman again. "Anything from Honolulu?"

"No."

He turned back. "We want Shipley, or at the very least, the information he has about the Continent. If you learn anything, I expect we'll be the first to know."

"Of course."

"People are losing their will to fight, Mr. Ressler, but with *him,* we could start a real revolution."

I'd become so focused on learning what the Company knew that I'd entirely forgotten about who I was dealing with: the friends of anarchists. *A revolution?* The images of Honolulu from the train appeared in my mind. I knew part of me would enjoy watching Kaua'i City burn, but what would be left then?

"I'll leave for Nāpali in the morning. Anything I find, I'll pass on to the Company."

"Good luck. We'll be watching you."

I stood and stole a look at EO. His furrowed brow made me guess he was thinking the same thing. *The Company likely wouldn't offer a bargain so easily.*

CHAPTER 7

Bumps in the road shook the vehicle. *My mind felt its way into the dark surroundings of the truck. It was almost impossible to distinguish anything, save a blur of male faces covered in black and muffled words back and forth. As some of the darkness faded, I could make out the heavy automatic weapons slung across the men's shoulders and the irritating clicking of their fingers fiddling with the safety mechanisms.*

The man closest to the cockpit banged on the metal divider. "Find a place here."

Fear overwhelmed my senses. The back of the cargo truck slowly became visible, as if some omnipotent being had turned up the lights. We jolted to a halt.

I waited patiently, following the lead of those around me. The tail of the vehicle cracked open and fell to the ground. Weak streetlights poured in. My heart palpitated with stress-induced panic. A salt-and-pepper-haired man with a strong jaw looked up at me.

"Get out!" his voice echoed savagely throughout the cabin.

Then the man's nose elongated, his eyes changed colors, and his cheekbones shifted from sharp to flat as his chin softened. In a snap, each feature changed again. My mind fought to place the man, the memory of his face eluding construction in my mind. Though his eyes changed color and shape, the man's gaze never wavered.

"Get out!" he screamed at me.

My heart pounded in my throat. I tried desperately to work out where we'd stopped, but nothing familiar presented itself. Blue-and-yellow fog distorted my long-range vision until all I saw was the beginnings of a run-down alley.

A hand gripped my arm and thrusted me up, leading me toward the open door, then pushed me out of the vehicle. I fell, landing on my shoulder, and rolled into a fetal position. The face-shifting man now stood clearly in the open hatch. My father's face had assumed its final shape, forming a contorted, angry scowl.

"Give him this, and then we leave." Something clanked to the ground next to me, rolling out of sight. Another man, maybe the one who'd thrown me from the hatch, stalked toward me. He grabbed the object and opened it before kneeling next to me.

My body shook. My heart lurched, and I lunged toward my father as he disappeared into the vehicle. I raised a hand toward him before feeling a painful pinch at the back of my skull. Then all I could see was my hand, a child's hand, dropping slowly from my blurred vision. The vehicle's engine roared to life and rolled away. I thought I could hear him faintly speaking, and I forced words from my mouth with everything I had: "Wait, Dad! Wait!"

"Kilo. Kilo, wake up."

The voice ripped me from my dream, but it was impossible to tell from which reality it echoed. My eyes opened to see EO silhouetted and standing over me.

"Kilo, you need to get up now." The panic in his voice jolted my nerves, demanding instant brain function, but the effects of the pink pills I'd taken to fall asleep fought back. The sedative was powerful, but I'd never experienced it mid-REM cycle. My muscles felt distant from my mind, and my body moved slowly, as if it took an extra second for my commands to reach my limbs."Someone's in the room."

The words sent a final shock through me and brought back strict control of my physical faculties. I shot up in the uneven bed and followed EO's next command, standing against the wall perpendicular to the hallway entrance. I threw out my hands in a questioning gesture, hoping for any indication of what was going on. He waited near me, staring into the shadows at the entrance to our hotel room.

"Hallway."

I tensed my muscles, waiting for further instructions. My eyes had already acclimated to the dark room thanks to a few hours of sleep, but it still wasn't enough to make out anything down the hall, apart from the remnants of last night's work scattered across the far desk. Some of the folders Bless had provided lay open with documents arranged chaotically to make some sense of Shipley's life.

A bright red light, belonging to a second-level butcher across the avenue, flashed from outside my window, blinding me for a split second. The burst hadn't bothered us much before, but with dilated pupils, the flares of light attacked my brain with frustrating intensity.

EO relayed what he could see. "Woman, 170 centimeters maybe, and a long knife in her right hand. Can't make out any other weapons." EO must have been able to catch a clearer image of the woman thanks to the flash from the butcher's sign. "Three seconds to the corner."

The dark returned. I counted in my head, *Three . . . two . . . one*. I whipped around the corner and brought my right arm across my body with as much force as I could muster. My triceps connected with the woman's chest, knocking her into the wall. I continued through with the force and pinned her against a framed painting, crushing the wood exterior. In an instant, I grasped her wrists and locked them above her head. Her hand barely clutched the knife, but I used my body weight to plaster her to the wall.

"Who are you?" I said, but before I could get an answer, she dropped the knife and kicked up, pinning it sidelong between her knee and my leg. I groaned and looked down to see the knife had sliced through muscle tissue.

A vicious pain burned through my thigh, and my grip weakened for only a moment, but she wasted no time in taking advantage. Her hands slipped through my grasp, and she pivoted her body, using the momentum to force me back against the opposite wall. My head thudded against the unyielding surface, sending blurry waves through my vision.

Before I could react, the woman lunged for the knife, grabbing the hilt.

She's fast. I followed her, grabbing hold of her legs and bringing her to the ground. We both hit the carpeted floor of the hotel room. She twisted and swung the knife. The wind from the blade made the hairs on my arms stand up as it narrowly missed my curled hands. Again she lunged at me, forcing me to the ground. This time I caught her arm, the tip of the blade only centimeters away from my neck.

"Kilo, get off your back or you're done!" EO kneeled in my peripheral vision, close enough to offer advice and also see the trajectory of the situation.

The woman grabbed her arm with her other hand and forced the blade closer to my face. Her teeth gritted, and she let out a strained moan, pressuring the blade with every ounce of force. Blood pulsed through my arms, and my brain fought with everything it had to give my muscles a chance.

The blinding red light blasted through the window again but had little effect other than to shimmer against the blade that was now piercing my skin.

"Kilo! Small knife, left ankle!" EO shouted at me just as the knife dug toward my carotid.

I released my grip from her arm and forced my other hand across my body to push the blade away, but not quite hard enough. It opened my neck on its way to the ground, mere centimeters from my jugular. I reached for her leg, feeling the penknife latched to her ankle. I ripped the blade from her holster and drove it into her throat.

The woman's cry pierced the walls as I pulled the blade back out. A spray of blood erupted across my face. She winced and tried to crawl, clasping a hand against the spewing wound. Her body dropped to the floor, unconscious, one leg still draped over my waist.

I relaxed, falling backward and lying open-armed on the floor.

"You okay?" EO asked as he inspected the woman.

"Well, I'm not the dead one, so . . ."

"She's not technically dead, but it won't be long."

I used the back of my hand to wipe away some of the blood from my mouth. But it didn't help lessen the overwhelming taste of iron. "You should have let me go back to Big City. Might have been better for my health."

EO watched me for a moment before his gaze lowered, and his shoulders slumped.

"I also wouldn't have had to kill someone," I lamented.

"Kilo, this woman just broke into your hotel, and not in a fun way." He stood up and looked at the body lying in a growing pool of blood. "You didn't do anything wrong."

Without warning, a memory of Shipley's words attacked my mind. *Shoot her! Do what you're told! You signed up to protect every person in Kaua'i City, and you will do what it takes!*

Blood continued to pour from the woman's neck. "What happens when the person isn't trying to kill me?"

"I know you, Kilo. You aren't a murderer. That's not what this is. That's not what the Continent was."

Kaua'i City, the Continent, the Below, it doesn't matter. You become as you were Designed.

I sat up and pushed the woman's leg off me. "We're not even in Nāpali. What the fuck is going on?" I padded over to the bathroom to clean off the blood and treat the gash on my neck.

"Someone thinks we know something, but we don't," EO said.

"You think this was Shipley?"

"Don't you?" He turned to look at the files in the room.

"We spent hours poring through this stuff, and we don't even know where to find the man who *might* know something about it?"

"You're right. But the sheer fact that there's a dead assassin on our floor means he has something worth protecting, even if it leads to a trail of bodies."

With most of the blood washed away, I could finally see my face again in the mirror. But no matter how hard I tried, the viscera coagulated in my eyebrows, lingered in the two days' worth of stubble along my jaw, and discolored my lips. I'd stood in front of a mirror more times than I wanted to admit, looking back at my face like this, with just enough blood smeared on it to remind me of what I'd done.

You're not a murderer. However, the eyes that stared back at me weren't so sure.

My deep breath fogged the mirror for an instant before disappearing. With my cut hand, I applied some healing ointment to the gash on my face that stung the side of my neck. It bubbled instantly upon contact with the tissue, and even with the treatment, I realized it would probably leave a nasty scar.

The red light from the butcher pulsed again, this time with almost zero impact through the overhead lights of the studio hotel room.

"We should at least buy the guy a beer and tell him we like his sign," I said, pointing.

But EO was distracted by the documents, flipping between assorted pictures, letters, notes, and public records.

At least he could forget, I thought.

"I'm going to contact Kamalu—we're burned here," I said, but he didn't react.

On the bedside table sat my personal device, undisturbed by the fight. I put through the call to Kamalu using an inter-island DIIP code. Seconds later, the only words that could make this situation worse filled the screen. CONNECTION SUSPENDED.

"Damn it." I tried the call again, and this time, Kamalu's blurry, round face crackled to life.

"Kilo, what the hell? Where are you? I've been trying to contact you."

"I'm in Ludo. There's more—"

"Jesus. Please tell me you aren't in the Below. You were supposed to stay at DIIP and then come straight back!" It was tough to hear him through the broken connection, but his concern was obvious.

"I found something. The trail led to the Below, but it's not worth it. I'm coming back today."

"No, you're not."

"What do you mean, no?"

"Kauaʻi City reduced your inter-island diplomatic residency to twenty-four hours."

I looked at the time in the corner of the projection. 4:37 a.m.

"You became an unverified traveler five hours ago," he said.

I dropped to the bed and wrestled the inside of my mouth with my tongue.

"So, what am I supposed to do?"

"I'll see if I can get a temporary residency, just enough for you to get on a train and come back, but it might take a while," Kamalu said.

"Fine, do it."

He paused. For a moment, I thought the connection had frozen with his pixelated face staring at me. But then his eyes moved slightly, showing a flicker of life. "What did you find?" His voice changed, barely, but EO heard it, too.

I looked above the projection. EO watched intently, waiting for Kamalu to speak again.

"Kilo, what did you find?" The question felt dry and demanding—someone else was in the room with him.

"I don't know yet. I'll contact you when I know more."

"Kilo—" Kamalu started, but I cut the line before he could finish.

I watched the CONNECTION SUSPENDED notification blink a few times. *Fuck.*

"We're not going anywhere. I don't think they're telling us everything," I said.

"You sure?"

"No, but I have a feeling the Designers are playing a different game up top. We're on our own for now."

"It's Kamalu, though?"

I thought about it. I trusted Kamalu. It wasn't that, but Kamalu worked for the Designers just like everyone else. "It just . . . something felt wrong."

"Well, maybe it's good I found a sign of Shipley then." EO crouched down onto the balls of his feet and pointed at something.

"Look at this." The curiosity in his voice drew me to him. "You see it?"

"See what?" I asked.

"That's an officer's photo, right? But these guys weren't with us on the Continent . . . so they worked with him after your last deployment."

"Okay. So what? We try to find out who they are instead?" I still wasn't seeing the line EO was drawing. "Even if they know, they'd probably kill me or die before telling us where Shipley is."

"Right. Who cares about them? Look at the background." I leaned in closer to see the grainy edges of the photo. "You see that right there?" He pointed at the corner of the picture. "They're at the Wharf."

I finally saw it: a sign framed in blue and white on the inside of the building where the picture had been taken, the words cut off.

-NTINENT, HAVE A FREE WHARFMASTER FISH BURGER ON US.

My mind raced to catch up to EO's trail of thought. *But if they were at the Wharf, that means Shipley probably—*

"No. Hell no!" I took a few steps back, realizing what he'd actually discovered. "I'm not doing that. I can face some of the stuff from this place, but I'm not going there."

"You don't need to visit that one, but there are thirty clubs in the Alley, and this tells me Shipley probably visited at least one."

"NO! You know how hard it was to leave her!" My hands shook with the intensity of my scream. I looked back to see the soft patience in EO's eyes. My bottom lip quivered just thinking about what it would be like to go back to the Alley. The question of what I might find there attacked my soul and pierced its way into my mind. "What if it's too much? What if she's still there?"

"I will be there with you like I've always been." EO moved closer. I turned my head to hide the evidence of blood flushing my face. "I know it's hard, but maybe this is the one you need to face."

I stared back at the picture on the ground, Shipley's wry smile as taunting as ever.

"Something is happening here, Kilo, and I know it would be easier to let everything go. I know that's what you want, but you can't escape it in Big City. Maurice died on the Continent, and at the very least, you owe *him* some answers."

"Fine, let's go to the Alley."

CHAPTER 8

The salvaged water from the rain up top pounded the hood of my peacoat. We walked along Laniloa Street and finally crossed into the Nāpali district. A huge storm would have had to hit up top hours ago for us to receive this type of runoff.

We were only a few blocks from Aloha Alley, and my feet burned from the Inter-District journey. EO had suggested we stick to the back alleys, rather than something more public after the attempt on my life last night, and I agreed.

I tried to stop reliving the attack but couldn't. The woman's blood had been hard to contain, and she was heavier than she looked, so bagging her up was physically exhausting. But after seeing her lifeless eyes every time I rolled her over, it was thinking of who this person had once been that took the real toll. I forced EO's words to the forefront of my mind, trying my best to believe them. *You're not a murderer.*

When we left, I broke off the handle to the hotel room, hoping that would buy us some time before whoever had sent the assassin realized they needed to double their efforts. But we couldn't know for sure how much it would slow them down, if at all. Right now, I just needed to focus on navigating the Alley.

Like most of the other roads in the Below, Laniloa was crowded with transit-cycles and pedestrians. It was impossible to take ten steps without bumping into people selling something or the occasional suit visiting from Mid-City. Even though we weren't technically in the Ludo District anymore, I couldn't shake the insecurity that set in thanks to our time there.

We were welcomed to the bustling industrial zone of Nāpali by the lights glaring unapologetically on streets that never slept. The neighborhoods here were distinct, though; even in Nāpali, the buildings were ancient. We passed an apartment building with immense cracks in the concrete that had exposed some of the steel foundation, and others made from synthetic materials, long obsolete within the city superstructure.

Although strictly prohibited, a few kids crawled along the fifteen-meter-wide, synthetic, tungsten beam that traversed the encapsulated city. It pierced one of the buildings that lined Laniloa near street level, maybe eight meters above traffic, extending across the street toward the center of the island. On my side of Laniloa, the beam tilted upward into a building above, gouging through an apartment complex like the wall had been built around a thousand-year-old tree.

Something about it was different from when I'd spent time here, but I couldn't figure out what.

"You okay?" EO asked.

Just before my focus drew back to him, I noticed the thin black lines crudely drawn along the length of the beam. The drawings seemingly elongated the beam as we walked past, also appearing to shrink in width as it moved further into the city. An optical illusion that probably meant something to the people here.

"Yeah," I said. "We can start at Hope's House and make our way down." Once we crossed under the massive Nāpali District structural beam, the air grew saturated with the scent of body fluids from the Alley. We rounded the corner and were met with a neon-pink sign covering the rainbow-shaped entrance.

ALOHA ALLEY

Down the pedestrian-only street, half-clothed people walked between the different clubs. Men and women latched to their arms. Directly behind us, a few stories up, stood the Wharf. Maybe a few years ago, we might have just bumped into Shipley there.

As I turned back, the lights of the Aloha Alley sign flickered and turned into a rainbow, each letter flashing, then turning to the next bright color. I couldn't count how many times I'd watched the colors dance, waiting here for Sandra. It seemed impossible at first, but somehow, we'd both managed to leave behind everything we were in the Alley when we stepped outside the sign. We'd found a way to not only to survive but to *live* in the Below.

"I'm here with you," EO said. "You okay?"

His question snapped me back from the captivity of the sign. "Yeah," I answered.

I scanned the Alley, and a few familiar clubs caught my eye—Rockabye, The Zoo, Hope's House—*there it is*. Hope's House sat a few doors down on the left. It had been repurposed, with two domestic viewing decks built onto the second floor. From outside the bow windows, I watched one of the scantily clad women clean the sills while another vacuumed the floor. Somehow, their efforts managed to enhance the club's oedipal draw.

Blue light dripped along the facade of the club, mimicking an entrance to a Design party, but the endeavor was aspirational at best. Cartoonish paneling framed the door and created a sensual yet warm and inviting aura. The club had once been considered a bit niche, among other things, but it always seemed like Shipley's type of place.

Through the door, a woman dressed like a young schoolgirl peeked out from behind a satin curtain and greeted us. Her pigtails and uniformed outfit would have likely fit in at any of the Engage Schools in Kaua'i City.

"Hello, sir. Can I help you?" the woman asked in a high-pitched voice. "You look like you could use a home-cooked meal."

"Just the viewing deck, thank you." I tried to look around for any familiar faces, but *this* was not one of the clubs I had frequented years ago, so no luck.

"Are you sure?" She caressed my arm, maintaining forceful eye contact. "You could spend some time with me instead?"

"Just the deck." I pulled my personal device out and presented it to her. "Credits."

The woman accepted the payment and whipped around back behind the curtain. With her bouncing pigtails out of sight, we preceded into the heart of the club.

From the small door and entrance to Hope's House, you wouldn't have expected the inside to feel so large, but the long floor of the room, coupled with the mirrors placed strategically throughout the club, made it seem endless.

A tall, solid wood divider split the club in half. On either side were cushioned seats where many people sat or reclined, some moaning uncontrollably. Most of the patrons were fully nude, but a few, presumably newer to the clubs in Aloha Alley, sat uncomfortably with their pants around their ankles.

Thankfully, the linguistic pop music that played in the background drowned out the reverberant moans. The artist's quick changes between languages helped to keep my mind from wandering too far.

People lining the divider were masturbating or pleasuring each other to the scenes taking place inside clear cubic stages along the walls. Most of them were open viewing, but several near the back were blacked-out. I decided those must have been the VIP boxes, which wouldn't have been affordable for people from the Below. In my experience, though, the cheaper boxes sold better. Being on display gave an extra level of exhilaration to the experience.

I sat down on the bench. Next to me, a man and a woman sat side by side, holding hands while they pleasured themselves to the activities within the windowed box before us. Positioned front and center inside the box was a middle-aged man having anal sex with a woman dressed like the girl who'd taken my payment. He let out a primal scream and tightened his belt around her neck. Around him, women who had had their makeup done to seem like school-aged girls danced with only corsets covering their midriffs.

The man lost control and started screaming with pleasure. The couple next to me moaned in sync. I slid my foot away from them, knowing what would happen in a few moments.

"Oh, fuck!" They both screamed in unison, ejaculating their money's worth all around them. Within a few seconds, a woman in a tight dress and collared blouse hurried over to the couple.

"Let me clean that up for you." She bent down to her hands and knees and began to clean the couple, who relaxed back into their seats. I watched her wipe and scrub the seating area, and after a thorough job, she stood up to leave. Through it all, she kept a sensual smile carved into her face.

I jumped up and followed her. "Hey, can I ask you a question? I'm new here."

"Oh yes, of course, sir." She was much shyer than the hostess at the entrance, but still proceeded to grab my arm and caress it. "We're primarily an Augmented-Reality club. In our viewable boxes, you'll be given Hope's House contact lenses to intensify pleasure, but if you pay for a black room, you can—"

"No, thank you. I'm looking for someone, an old friend. Do you think you can help me?" I pulled out a couple Near Death inhalers Bless had given me after the fight. "They are yours if you can point me in the right direction."

The woman's expression changed swiftly from faux erotica to fear as her eyes narrowed. "We're never supposed to talk about clients."

"I know. But we served together on the Continent, and I just want to track him down to let him know a friend of ours passed."

"I'm sorry to hear that." Her voice lowered. She seemed genuinely innocent, but it was hard to tell in places like this.

"It's all right; the person I'm looking for is named Shipley." I pulled out my PD and produced a picture of him, me, and a few other guys during my twenty-sixth tour. "Do you know him?"

She scanned the picture, scrunching her face in thought. "Yeah. He used to come in here when I first started, but I haven't seen him since the club became AR."

"Do you know which clubs he visits now?" My voice wavered. I secretly hoped she didn't know.

"One of the girls here did privates for him on the side, and he paid extra. When she left the district, she recommended some girls from the clubs down at the end of the Alley that still do Mixed-Reality." She paused and pursed her lips, still subconsciously putting on the young girl routine. "I think she sent him to the Palm Frond."

"Mm-hmm." I turned my head slightly as if I was looking at something else in the room and locked eyes with EO.

"I know," he said sympathetically.

"Thank you." I handed the ND inhalers over to the woman and headed for the exit. Outside, the gravity of the girl's answer pressed down on my shoulders. I'd tried to convince myself earlier that I wouldn't have to go to the Frond, so there was no point in worrying about it. I no longer had that luxury.

"Take a deep breath, Kilo. If she's in there, you have the chance to atone for what happened; otherwise, you can forgive yourself and move on."

It likely wouldn't be that easy.

The club door loomed in front of us. I didn't need to look at the etchings around the dimly lit entrance, as I could still picture them clearly in my mind. The trademark mechanical palm fronds still swung above the entrance. The weathering on the black door showed some of the deep red that lay underneath. I let a few people enter ahead of me before I convinced myself to grab the latch and pull the heavy door open.

The Frond was designed like the older, standard clubs, with a long hallway that branched off filled with private rooms no more affordable than any of the ones in the AR clubs. Cloth curtains, each a unique color with varying designs, covered the doors to the private rooms but failed to provide full discretion for the patrons inside.

"A usual or dealer's choice?" The raspy voice came from a man above. I'd forgotten about the unique concierge that helped make a name for the Frond. A naked, hairy man hung, suspended horizontally, in a transparent box attached to the ceiling, his arms and legs held taut by chains. Just above my head, his abnormally large penis bowed down against the glass in presentation.

"Dealer's choice, please."

"Amethyst room," he said.

I nodded and made my way down the hall, the faint noises from within each of the rooms bringing back memories. As I continued, the corridors grew darker, and it became harder to distinguish many of the curtain colors.

"Over here." EO motioned from one of the branched hallways. "Amethyst room."

"You gonna come in with me?" I asked out of habit, assuming I already had the answer.

After a moment, I realized he hadn't responded and looked to see his head angled toward the floor.

"I think you need to go in on your own."

The words left a stinging in my chest, a throbbing feeling of distress interwoven with betrayal. My response reflected my disconcertion. "What do you mean? I can't do this without you."

"I don't want to go in there, Kilo." His face hardened, but I noticed squirming fingers in his pockets. "I'm here in the Alley with you, but Sandra . . . Sandra is something you need to do alone."

"What? You said you'd help me!"

His tone jumped, but he continued to avoid eye contact. "There are some things you have to do without me. That's how this works."

"Bullshit. You only help when you want to."

"That's not true!" he yelled back. Finally, his gaze met mine, his eyes burning amid his crumpled, frustrated face. "Some things I can't do *for* you."

"Whatever. Thanks for the help," I said under my breath, turning back to the Amethyst room door.

I heard him slide his back down the wall and slump to the floor behind me.

Fine, I'll do it myself. I grabbed the handle and turned. As I stepped inside, I heard EO let out a soft, pained gasp. A part of me wanted to step back, to not leave things like that, but he'd made his choice and could deal with the consequences himself.

Inside, a scantily clad blonde woman lounged, smoking in the single chair among the floor-to-ceiling light fixtures. A puff of smoke drifted toward me through the maze of light columns.

"Hi, sweetheart, what are you looking—"

"Do you know Sandra?"

The woman's half-cocked smile faded, replaced with a practiced glare. Before I could speak again, she brushed past me and left the room, slamming the door behind her. I helped myself to the seat, not knowing what or who to expect when the door reopened. I waited patiently for a minute before someone else came in.

"Kilo?" The voice was familiar but too deep to be Sandra's. "I heard you're looking for someone. Maybe I will do?"

A tall, dark-skinned woman leaned in, staring at me with a lipsticked smile on her face. Her hair was braided and laced with platinum and blonde streaks. Her breasts were barely contained in the skintight dress that only reached mid-thigh. But the flash of red-dye tattoos on her arms belonged singularly to her.

"Ade?" I asked.

"Hi, Kilo. I thought one day we might spend some time together in a room." Ade circled behind me and pressed a few buttons on the wall.

The room transformed. At first, I couldn't discern my surroundings with the light penetrating from a thousand angles, but figures soon materialized around me. Men in suits, coupled with women in revealing cocktail dresses, stood arm in arm, swaying to the jazz music playing around us. Their conversations were imperceptible in the suddenly large party that unfolded.

Ade shifted around the chair, pushing her body close to mine before she dropped to her knees, her lips pursed as she stared up into my eyes. Her hands grabbed my belt and began to unbuckle it before reaching for the zipper.

"Ade, please. I want to talk to Sandra." I could feel the blood beginning to pulse through my pelvis. "I . . . I need to . . . Ade, stop!" I grabbed both of her hands, which were now wrapped around me. The animal inside begged her to continue.

I stood up and adjusted my pants. One of the female partygoers turned to me, revealing her breasts. "You enjoying the party?"

I stumbled to the back wall and shut down the Mixed-Reality simulation. In a flash of light, the room returned to its natural blank state. "I'm looking for someone, and this is where I was told I could find him. I'm not here for MR."

"What happened to the fun, Kilo? Only for Sandy?" Her words were playful but cracking with the act. "At least you said goodbye to her when you left."

"I can't do this right now." I only had the emotional capacity to address one painful relationship today, and it wasn't with Ade. "I'm looking for a man named Shipley. I have a cosmic feeling she might know him."

Ade started laughing almost uncontrollably. "Shipley? I know Shipley."

I waited patiently for her explanation.

"You're right. If you were standing here about a year ago, you would've seen him knee-deep in Sandra."

The image of the sweaty, middle-aged man thrusting churned my stomach. "Can you tell me where either of them are?"

"Shipley? No. Sandra? Well . . ." Ade took a seat in the chair. Her amusement faded. "She's one of the Children of the Designers now."

"She's what?" My face burned, and my fists clinched reflexively.

"She worships at the Architecture Building uptown." Ade looked at me now with softened cheeks and sympathetic eyes that said she knew the words would shatter my world. "You know where to find me if you need to talk to someone." With that, she left, closing the door gently behind her.

How could she do this? I grabbed the chair and threw it against the wall, shattering some of the light fixtures. Blood from my hands trailed behind me as I left the room. I didn't wait for EO.

"Kilo. What happened?"

We left the Frond before I even acknowledged him. The Alley felt different now. Any comfort had dissolved through black-tinted glasses. The mock Designer clothes, the Mid-City men stepping out on their families, and residents of the Below high out of their minds—it all infuriated me.

I tried to keep my eyes forward, not focused on anything in particular. But people here always wanted you to buy something, join them in something, or confide in you about something. It was always the same shit you could never quite wash off.

About halfway down the Alley, I stopped cold. EO caught up and brushed against my side before he saw it. His eyes shrunk into his head, and his breath quickened. He understood before I did. My gaze drifted toward the object that had caught my eye. It was a small mailbox, worn, a prop for one of the clubs.

"Kilo, don't. If there's anything in there, it won't fix it."

His words passed through my ears, and I opened the bottom of the box where Sandra and I had hidden notes for so many years. A piece of paper floated wistfully to the ground. The words scribbled in Sandra's handwriting crushed what little hope was left.

KILO, IF YOU EVER SEE THIS, I HOPE YOU UNDERSTAND I FORGAVE YOU A LONG TIME AGO. YOU DID WHAT YOU HAD TO DO, AND I DON'T BLAME YOU. I HOPE YOU CAN FORGIVE ME FOR WHAT I NEEDED TO DO. YOU WILL ALWAYS BE WITH ME.

CHAPTER 9

The shot of Nāpali Vodka slid down my throat. But the alcohol didn't relieve the discomfort of the uneven bar bench or the thought of Sandra. Above me, a projected screen with a talking head occupied my gaze. I wasn't really watching it, but in a way, still absorbed the vitriol spewing from the program. On-screen, two colorfully clothed men talked about the upcoming Design Show. Flashes of the obligatory tournament from the previous year appeared before the commentators argued the odds for this year's contestants. It baffled the mind that in a week or two, thousands of Designers would gather for little more than pleasure while the rest of us ached.

The men were diametrically opposed to whatever aspect of the show they were covering. Their cheeks grew red, and spit flew as each failed to win the other over but succeeded in winning an audience. There wasn't a pair of eyes in the bar not glued to the screen. I swallowed the last remnants of my vodka, and as if by some cruel joke, the talking head shouted my father's name. "He'll answer to Designer Arasi!"

I need another drink.

I tapped the table with the edges of my fingernails until an exhausted-looking bartender refilled the glass. The bag of pink pills I always kept near rested in my palm. I thought about it for a moment before sticking them back in my pocket—*just another drink.*

An hour had passed since we left Aloha Alley, since I learned about Sandra and read the note. Yet it felt much longer. Thoughts pounded my brain relentlessly. *How could I have just given up on her? How could she have given up on me?*

Across the street, the Nāpali Architecture Building taunted me. The ethereal house of Designers was more ornate than others I'd seen in Big City or Kaua'i City, a projectile vomit of colors and soulless tapestry. Among the gaudiness, sculptures of faceless Designers guarded the entrance, and etchings of the original Design of Kaua'i City covered the facade of the building. Although it was no larger than the surrounding buildings, its distinct design and long stretch of stairs leading to the sidewalk gave it an air of unrivaled dominance. I didn't need to look inside to know what to expect.

"Why didn't you come in with me?"

"I don't know," EO responded. "I thought you needed to go on your own."

I forced down the lump growing in my throat. "You told me you'd be there for me in the Alley."

"I'm sorry, Kilo. I didn't know it would turn out like that."

"Really?" I asked.

"Of course not. How could you even . . ."

I downed what was left of my vodka and stood up. "Whatever. It won't hurt any less just sitting here."

I knew I should keep my voice lower, more clandestine, but I lacked the energy. A few people at the bar looked our way with confused glances. I hoped they just thought it was the liquor.

"Service starts at two. I want a good seat," I said.

Concern grew in EO's eyes. I'd come so far, consigned so much pain to the past, but now here we were in the Below. *Does any of this matter? Maurice is already dead. I can just go back to Big City and forget all of it. Let the Designers destroy whatever they want! That's how it works, anyway.*

EO's strong hand pinched my shoulder as we left the bar. Once we were alone in the back alley, I turned and wrapped my arms around him. The tears begged to flow, but I held everything inside and squeezed.

"I know. It'll be okay," he said.

Through the arched doors of the Architecture Building, the air turned uncomfortably dense. Several people streamed into the building with me and immediately dropped to the floor on both knees before mechanically raising themselves back to a standing position, then repeating the motion. The staple practice of the Children of the Designers looked ridiculous, but it wasn't going away anytime soon. I brushed past them, hoping I might accidentally interrupt the ritual.

Inside, I grabbed a fistful of the bread pieces placed in a standing chalice and looked for a seat. A few of the Children followed my lead and stuffed some pieces of bread into their coat pockets. I'd never seen such irreverence—an unholy act against the benevolence of the Designers and the Design. But even if they refused to acknowledge it, I could: When you're starving, it doesn't matter.

I found it disgusting to watch these people who'd turned their whole lives into an identity associated with something they didn't understand for nothing—no credits, no ascension, no love. All they had to show for it were scraps of bread and the promise of a future they'd never see.

The quiet conversations among the Children carried throughout the chapel along the countless rows of wooden benches. The foyer and the chapel displayed the painstaking attention to detail the architects of this building must have taken to ensure it was something worthy, and not merely an evolution of the old churches. Parables from the original Designers were etched into the carefully curated raw stone walls, ensuring the manicured masquerade remained intact.

I recognized a few of them, but one caught my eye. The abridged version on the wall told of a man holding a hammer and working until the wooden handle turned red. His other hand relaxed at his side. The sculptor had drawn the old man facing away from the sunset with a look of stoic pride. However, it was missing the most important detail, the first fully functioning Designed Psychological Manifestation (DPM).

"Never thought I'd see the Helvik story in one of these." I nodded in its direction. "Do you think any of it's real?"

"Other than he built DPMs, probably not," EO said. "I believe the Helvik Theory more than these stories."

I scoffed. "Funny to think he's immortalized in a building ordained to the Designers who banned his life's work from the people it was created for."

"It's insane, how many people didn't question it or think about it. It's just fear disguised as protection."

"Hmm." I could only imagine how many had passed through these doors and looked at stories like the one of Jacob Helvik, wondering what it would be like to possess a DPM, even for a day.

Suddenly, the doors behind us closed with a boom, and a calm, far-reaching voice filled the chapel.

"Welcome, Children of the Designers."

The room erupted in applause. Everyone looked at the other members, smiles flaring and eyes wide as if they were congratulating themselves on raising a new building. I scoffed at their self-assigned level of importance.

It sparked memories from when I'd visited various Architecture Buildings as a child. The smiles were always so intense that it was hard to believe they were real. I was reminded of the fervorous beliefs in the Designers and the island cities. Thankfully, I sat in a half-full pew and strategically positioned myself far enough back to avoid engaging in their traditions. I stuffed my face with the bread and watched the proceedings.

"We have a special guest for you today." The orator was dressed in eclectic and nauseating clothing, similar to the woman I'd sat with on the train from Big City. "We will be hearing from one of the seventy district Designers; please welcome, Designer Kamusaki."

A tall, sun-kissed man walked out and was greeted with a handshake from the orator and a flurry of excited gasps throughout the auditorium. I was pretty sure I'd never seen or met this Designer, but there was something familiar about him.

Designer Weatherford dressed much like Decambra but didn't seem to have the same unearned confidence. His checkered shawl remained tame during his appearance.

As the man spoke, launching into a profound monologue about the divinity of the Design, I could only focus on his face. The stubble on his cheeks shifted with every encore of emotion. Somehow, all the Designers' faces looked alike, with varying shades of the same color.

Again, my thoughts drifted back to the time I'd spent in buildings just like this, my mother's soft hand guiding me to our prominent seat. The space around Weatherford warped as I felt my grasp on reality submit to my memories. *Remember, Kilo, don't call him Dad down here, okay? He is Designer Arasi, and we are his guests.* My father's gray face from the banner in Ludo replaced Weatherford's, and his words now spouted from my father's lips. The feelings of excitement and pride I'd felt as a child twisted into ones of despair and hatred.

I stared, the horror within me growing. My body fought to keep me from the pain, but his intensity burned around me. *How could you kill her?*

"Kilo, hey, you all right?" EO asked.

The question removed my father's face from Weatherford's, and the Designer's authentic voice returned.

"It is truly a great honor to serve the greater Design and to see our city live for a thousand years!"

The room erupted in applause, and some of the more fragile Children of the Designers wept. It was nothing more than a recruitment meeting with potential donors and unwitting parents.

Then a scream burst out from across the pews. "We won't be Designed! You don't deserve DPMs!" A scarred man ripped off his luminous shirt, revealing words etched in blood along his torso. Designer security swarmed the man and dragged him away. A moment later, a wave of composure flowed throughout the auditorium once more. Concerned looks on the faces of the Designed soon turned to resolute smiles.

The two men on the stage finally took their leave, allowing for a more informal discussion among the crowd to ensue. I panned the room again, looking for Sandra. The poofs of varied, multicolored hair made it challenging to identify any one person, but we would find her if she was here.

"Can you take a lap and see if she showed?" I asked.

EO nodded and headed toward the mix of parishioners now gathered in front of the Jacob Helvik story.

Fuck. What am I doing here? I thought, relaxing back into the pew. I didn't fully understand all those years ago, but these people were willfully blind. Each and every one of them knew our world but made a conscious decision to live in an alternate one. They would never be Designers, no matter how much of their lives they dedicated to the *Immaculate* Design. As a child, I had been curious about them, but now it was maddening.

"Hey." The whisper blew into my ear along with a soft touch on my shoulder. I turned reactively to see Ade. Her cheeks softened and lips relaxed. She appeared like the friend I used to know, making it odd to see her still in the debauched outfit she'd been wearing at the Frond. But her pupils consumed the whites of her eyes, and sweat glistened across her arms.

"What are you doing here?" I asked.

"She's gone." The quiver in her voice shook my empathy loose.

"Sandra?"

"Yes. Kilo, I'm sorry about the routine at the club, but I was just shocked to see you . . ." She trailed off, falling into the past.

"Ade. What do you mean she's gone?"

"After you left, I figured I'd go by her place and at least give her a heads-up that you were here . . . maybe find a better way to see you than at an Architecture Building, but her place was destroyed. It looked like a hurricane blew through. I think someone took her."

"Where does she live?"

Ade's face contorted in response to my words, which came out more fiercely than I had intended. "She lives in the Coffins."

I didn't waste any time grabbing Ade and pushing my way through the line of people exiting through the wide doors. These people took so damn long strolling their way outside. I let out a loud whistle to part the crowd and grab EO's attention. Ade's soft hands clasped within mine, and I pulled her through the door.

"Fastest way to the Coffins?" I asked, already heading in the general direction.

"Cut across Maile Street and use the alleys until you reach the Inter-District."

We sprinted across Maile, dodging cycles that whizzed by. Ade's hand crunched the bones in mine as our feet pounded the pavement. By the time we made it to the other side of the street, EO had caught up. The sounds and lights of the city dulled, much like when I listened to the speech from Designer Weatherford, but now I was focused instead of lost. The dead assassin, my parents, all of it was gone.

"Keep up." I knew the Coffins were only a few blocks away, but I didn't want to let the apartment scene go cold. There was no way of knowing how long she'd been missing. I dropped Ade's hand and picked up speed.

We finally cut into the alley that opened to the Inter-District. The street buzzed far in front of us like nebulous organic machinery.

"Which apartment?" I screamed back at Ade, hoping she was still in earshot.

The response was muffled, but loud enough to comprehend.

"1305. The entrance is on the alley side."

I didn't need to shoot a look at EO, who matched my stride.

The Inter-District road became clearer as we approached, no longer a mess of lights and buildings, and finally, the checkered exterior of the Coffins came into focus. They lined the Inter-District and stretched forty or fifty meters deep into the city block. I approached the building, which looked like another of the monoliths that stood in Big City. From the side, there were no windows, no distinguishing marks, just a blank concrete canvas.

I didn't wait to see how far Ade had fallen behind. I pushed through sunken-eyed, confused children of large families crowding the alley side entrance. The foyer of the Coffins was cramped, with low ceilings, multiple segregated entrances, and too many people for the two elevators that offered vertical transportation.

Before I could scan the area, EO sprinted toward the far corner of the room, where there was an uninviting metal door.

"Stairs!" he yelled back.

I followed, smashing through the door, and ascended as quickly as my legs allowed. Rust and mold filled the stairwell, progressively deteriorating with each level we rounded. Once we reached the ninth level, my footsteps sloshed in a light current of water running down the staircase from the upper levels, a feature of a few unlucky buildings in Kaua'i City. Once we finally reached the thirteenth floor, we burst into the Coffins hallway.

"1301." I glanced briefly at the digits that hung above the door closest to the exit from the stairwell. The hallway extended, seemingly indefinitely, with what I could only presume was a wall at the end of a hundred or so Coffin apartments. Each door stood only a meter apart from the next, creating a symmetrical pattern that played games with my eyes. Wallpaper further decorated the hallway and provided an optical illusion of space through its woven lines over every centimeter of the walls. I couldn't view the apartment floor as anything but a cattle car, inside a density ratio unlike any other in the island cities.

The door to 1305 looked exactly like every other door we passed. It was gray, but its uneven texture made me second-guess the metal material. With a sharp rap at the door, a metallic echo rang through the level and proved its authenticity.

"I'm going in." I grabbed the doorknob and turned, opening it slowly. The fingers on my free hand lightly cradled the Nambu and pulled it from the holster under my coat. The room was small, exactly what you would expect from what they called a "Coffin." I bowed my head to ensure it didn't connect with the water-stained ceiling. A single light hung from the center of the room, emitting a dim, yellow glow. I assumed Ade had left it on when she came to find me, but my fingers twitched on the Nambu's trigger in case she hadn't.

Her description of a hurricane was dead-on. It looked as though someone had taken everything in the apartment, put it into a container, shaken it up, and then dumped it back wildly into the space. I waded through the assortment of Sandra's belongings, every step squishing the wet carpet underneath my boots.

A side table further into the room caught my attention. A lamp hung, suspended over the table's side by a cord attached to the wall, and something else lay face down next to the table's leg. I put the Nambu away and picked up the rectangular frame.

A well of emotion flooded my chest as I stared at a candid picture of Sandra, her smile beaming as she stood against a window somewhere in the upper levels of the Below. It was hard to tell when the photo was taken, but it had to have been after I left for Big City. The flowing blonde hair I knew had been chopped off into a bob cut.

The more I stared at the photo, the more I felt her with me. The smell of her lavender perfume clogged my nostrils, and the soft skin of her cheek tickled the back of my hand. A decade of time flashed before my eyes. I remembered waking up to a smothering hug in our apartment on the outskirts of Nāpali and running down the block trying to escape the rain.

EO came up behind me as I continued to lose myself in the photo.

"I didn't think someone living in the Coffins would be able to afford a printed photograph," he said.

I didn't respond, but I also wondered how she'd been able to pay for something like this. Footsteps grew louder in the hallway until Ade appeared in the door, bracing herself against the doorframe. I placed the picture upright on the table and turned my attention back to the apartment.

"Kilo." Ade gulped for breath. "Anything?"

"I've only been here a minute. I thought it would take you longer to catch up."

Ade let out a painful laugh, twisted with a wheeze.

It only took five or six strides to reach the back wall. I saw nothing of note. I'd only ever been in a few apartments like this and thought back to the horrific days spent there.

"Basement or attic?" EO asked, seemingly recalling the same experiences.

I nodded and ran my hand along the ceiling, coming close to the wall until I felt a small indent cave under my fingers. I pushed softly with an open palm and moved a step to the left. A collapsible ladder came screeching down, its legs landing right next to my feet.

"You haven't been up here, right?" I looked at Ade, who frowned at me.

"No."

I scaled until the darkness surrounded my head. A scarcely visible string dangled in front of me, and a pull caused a series of bulbs to illuminate with a dim glow. The attic was almost empty. Only a few boxes had been shoved toward the end of the space. *Nothing.* I flicked the string once again and started to descend.

"Kilo, wait."

I tilted my head down to see EO standing below me with his head cocked.

"There is something behind the boxes. It's small," he said.

No way. If there was something there, I would have noticed it. But as much as I wanted to be right, EO was rarely wrong. I took the ladder steps back up into the attic and crawled along the condensed space. The lights from the string of bulbs didn't do much to help me see past the boxes.

I pushed the first box aside easily. Then the next, but it didn't move. Sighing, I repositioned myself to gain some leverage and pushed harder. It moved a few centimeters and then jolted a further half a meter before desisting again. I sat up and opened the box. As I pried it open, something lunged past me and scratched my face.

What little light there was in the room went dark as the thing pulled the string while rushing to the ladder. The surprise only lasted a second before I reacted and jumped after it, grabbing what I could only hope was a foot.

"Let go of me!" A high-pitched, feminine-sounding voice screamed back.

A kid? I let go of the foot and watched her scamper down the ladder.

"Incoming, Ade."

"I got her." Ade's confused voice quickly took on a soothing tone. "You're all right, sweetheart. We just want to talk to you."

I made my way down the ladder again, hoping there wasn't another surprise reason I would have to go back up. In the middle of the chaotic room, a small girl clutched her arms around Ade's waist. Her blonde hair was matted and her face dirty, which wasn't surprising after spending some time in a Coffin crawlspace. She turned her head slowly to look at me, tears filling her eyes.

"It's okay. He's a friend of mine and Sandra's. Do you know Sandra?"

The girl nodded.

"Is Sandra your mom?" Ade asked.

She nodded again, with her head buried in Ade's stomach. Ade looked at me, eyes wide, mouthing a question, but I didn't have the answer. I didn't have the slightest idea Sandra had a kid. She looked to be five or six, so she definitely wasn't mine, but it seemed like Ade hadn't known her either.

"Do you know where your mom is?" I asked shakily.

"They took her," she sobbed.

"Who took her? When? Did you see them?" Ade shot me a look as I machine-gunned the questions at the girl.

"What's your name, sweetheart?" Ade cooed and stroked her hair.

"Abegail."

Ade crouched down to Abegail's level. "Abegail, sweetie. Can you tell us what happened to your mom?"

"She came home after lunch like she always does to bring me a sandwich, but she didn't have one. She came in and told me I needed to go into the attic and to not ask any questions. While I was up there, I heard knocking at the door, and then I heard voices. Mom screamed, and there were a bunch of loud noises. After that, I covered my ears and got into one of the boxes. I was in there until . . ." She trailed off, looking in my direction before welling up with tears.

"Why would someone want to take Sandra?" Ade mouthed at me.

I glanced to the side where EO stood watching as an innocent bystander. "It couldn't have been more than a few hours ago," EO said, gesturing to a half-filled coffee cup that sat on the counter. I walked over and stuck my finger in—warm, barely.

"I don't know." I placed my personal device on the counter in what little space there was and opened the search function. My last search popped up, but when I swiped to clear it in favor of a search for Sandra, Abegail stopped me.

"I know him." Her voice bore a hint of excitement, and for a moment, it seemed she could at least focus on something else.

Shipley's face stared back at us. The last search on my device. "You know this man? Are you sure?" I asked.

Abegail leaned closer to the picture, squinting to focus on the somewhat grainy image of Shipley I'd shown the woman at Hope's House.

"Yes. Mom took me to see him sometimes."

My thoughts ran through my brain a mile a minute, racing to be the first for consideration. A bewildered expression must have coated my face. Ade's cheeks dropped. *If Shipley has Sandra, I need to find him. Now!*

CHAPTER 10

Our trip to the Coffins had shaken me to the core. In the space of a few hours, I'd learned that Sandra had joined the Children of the Designers, she had a daughter, and Shipley could have something to do with her disappearance. It seemed like every time we got close to an answer, more questions appeared. Chief among them: What did Sandra have to do with Shipley? There was only one way to find out.

On our way down through the Coffins to street level, Abegail told us more about when she'd gone to see Shipley. She talked about how much she enjoyed spending time with him because she rarely had the chance to visit the upper levels of the Below. I couldn't blame her. I remembered how excited Maurice and Bless would get when we snuck into the upper levels.

We now stood between the Inter-District and the Coffins building. It must have been raining up top again because pellets of water sprinkled down around us. The warmth of the droplets surprised me, but sometimes, the water flowed along the corroded heating vents of the superstructure and created hot rain. It didn't matter, though; it could have been snowing up top, and we wouldn't know the difference in the Below.

I'd wondered about the water when I was a kid, the first couple of years living in the Below. A raindrop from hundreds of meters above made its way down the maze of the island city, eventually landing on my shoulder.

Something so common, so natural, could traverse every level of the city without harassment; then add other organic matter to it, and it became more complicated.

A light tug from a miniature hand brought me back to the Inter-District crosswalk. Abegail's wide blue eyes stared back up at me.

"You sure you can remember the building you visited?" I asked.

"Mm-hmm." Abegail had warmed up to me since I chased her out of hiding. Now, she clung to my arm like a sloth, her feet barely touching the ground as we walked.

"Okay. We'll head to the third level using the service elevators. It won't be hard to blend in there."

I hailed a transit-cycle with a couple of fingers, and the next cycle came to a screeching stop. We piled into the cramped three-person vehicle.

"Destination, please." Abegail shrank back at the sound of the automated voice from the cycle. It dawned on me that this could likely be the first time she'd actually ridden in a transit-cycle.

"Corner of Station and West," I said toward the front of the cycle. "It's all right, kiddo. They do whatever we say." I forced a smile across my face, and Abegail's expression lightened, opening with wonder.

The transit-cycle raced through traffic, following the Inter-District for only a few minutes before taking us through some residential streets that were free of the hustle and bustle of the main drags. Each of the buildings looked nicer than the Coffins or the Kamehameha Building, but not by much.

Thanks to the narrow street, makeshift walkways connected the adjacent apartment buildings several stories above. Some were fortified with suspension wires and looked as if they were communal dining areas. I could hardly imagine what it would be like for a child eating dinner with multiple families, but then again, you could throw a rock in these areas and hit a relative. I looked at EO, his eyes wide with curiosity, considering the passing buildings, but it didn't seem like he was drawing on the same memories. *Good.*

"Please exit to the right. Thank you for riding with us today."

The transit-cycle stopped a block away from the service elevators. Dirt and rust covered the entrance to the elevators, pinched between two buildings. I watched a couple of young men huddled at the edge of the entrance. Their clean haircuts and heavy workers' outfits didn't match the lighthearted conversation.

Maybe they could fool elevator operators, but I knew exactly what they were up to. Bless, Mo, EO, and I had stood in the same spot, waiting for an opening to slip into the elevator and move freely among the levels.

"Let's go." I started walking with Abegail sandwiched between Ade and me. EO followed closely behind. In front of us, about halfway up the block, a worn sign stuck out from the building lining the street.

BELOW SERVICE ELEVATOR ENTRANCE
LEVELS 1, 2, AND 3

Right where I left it. A host of people dressed in dark, heavy work attire streamed out in a line from under the sign and extended parallel to the street. Most were construction workers, but some looked like transport workers or food processors, giving us a few options. Thankfully, there were only thirty or forty people queued, so we might get lucky and be able to squeeze in on the first ride.

A couple waited in front of us, their bulky work suits covered in remnants of black soot. The uneven coating showed they'd feverishly attempted to clean the suits after their last shift, but a thick layer of dirt remained. I looked closer to see that the suits were designed to work in the transit tunnels, cleaning out any dangerous and unwanted debris from train rails, elevators, or any other passenger or cargo carrier that linked the city. The poor couple must have been getting ready to start another fourteen-hour shift. I couldn't help them, but they could help me.

A shrill buzz blasted from the entrance to the elevator shaft, sending a wake-up call through the line and causing the queue to caterpillar forward.

"Hey, everything's going to be okay. Just hold my hand." Ade triaged Abegail's reaction to the buzzer. The whites of Abegail's eyes glistened. I wanted to help, but realized it'd be better to leave it to Ade. My only responsibility now was to make sure everyone got into the elevator. I took my coat and wrapped it around Ade, and then, with a few steps, I bumped into the couple in front of us, my hands grasping their suits.

"Excuse me. I'm so sorry."

The couple glanced at us with dull eyes, barely acknowledging our presence, but a coarse black coating of soot covered my palms.

"All right, I'm gonna touch your faces. Don't move," I said to Ade and Abegail. I lightly brushed my hands diagonally across their faces, creating a striped dusting of black reaching from their temples to their jaws.

"Not bad. Take a look."

They both turned to peer into one of the thin windows that lined the building. Ade hoisted Abegail up to chest level, enough for the girl to see the black and white camouflaged face staring back in the reflection. Abegail's smile broke through, attached to an innocent laugh.

"I look like an animal."

"A little bit, yeah, but when we get inside, I'm going to tell them we all work for Nāpali Buildings, all right?"

"Okay," Abegail responded meekly, still admiring her new face paint.

People paced forward, and the line moved quicker. EO stood on his toes at the curve of the line, watching each worker pass through into the elevator. Once we reached him, without losing his focus, he gripped my arm.

"You might have to flash a badge."

I looked around the corner, trying to see what he was seeing.

"They want credentials," he said.

I shot him an incredulous look that said: "What the fuck?" *These elevators never needed credentials before; that's why service workers use them.*

There were only a few people ahead of us now. Two elevator attendants in reflective, nylon-laced jumpsuits ushered workers into the elevator. Every few seconds, the attendants outstretched a firm, open hand to a new worker and requested work credentials.

"Next, step up." One of the attendants gestured brusquely for me to step forward. I complied only with the command given.

"Credentials?" The pitch in his voice shifted; clearly, he was unamused by the literal interpretation of his request.

"Since when do we need credentials to go up to three?"

"Just show me yours and get on the elevator."

EO held his breath as the few people behind us crowded the area, muttering about the delay. Ade and Abegail hid behind me while the attendant scanned their faces.

"You want on or not? Credentials."

I only had my DIIP ID, but the minute I showed that, it would ping a location to whoever wanted me dead.

The man's eyes narrowed with impatience. Chatting about old policies wasn't going to change his mind. *The other option then.*

The palm of my hand drove through the man's nose, sending the cartilage bursting through the skin. His head flew back, and blood sprayed from his nose as he stumbled and fell to the ground. The workers already loaded huddled together at the back of the elevator. With two quick steps, I lunged at the second attendant and caught his stomach with a strong punch. He keeled over, groaning in pain. I drove my knee up into his head, the crack of breaking bones trumping the nose strike I landed on his companion.

"Inside!" I yelled through a single breath. Ade and Abegail ran inside the elevator. I followed and pulled the grated doors closed. I didn't dare look at Abegail's face. The fear that must have been billowing in her mind hurt. I hoped at least Ade understood; after all, she knew who I used to be.

"Everything is okay. I'm not going to hurt you," I said to the workers. Their arms remained constricted around their friends, and they avoided eye contact. I could tell my words didn't ease their fear, but soon it wouldn't matter. I pulled the lever in front of me, and the metal box rocketed upward.

The elevator shook as it rose toward the top of the Below. The air sat still and silent. It didn't surprise me. Most of these people probably went to work every day using this elevator with nothing of note happening. But eternal monotony wasn't something you could count on in the Below. They learned that lesson quickly.

In the corner of the elevator, Abegail cowered behind Ade, her tiny face hardly visible. A single eye poked out, watching me like a wild creature. I bent down to a crouch, my knees feeling the pain from the past day, and I extended a hand to her. As only a child could, she slunk out from behind Ade, placed her tiny palm in mine, and squeezed. The apprehension that swirled in her eyes dissipated. I let out a sigh, fueled with optimism for the first time in a while.

Once the doors opened, there wasn't time to wander around an entire district until this little girl saw something she remembered. I hoped she could follow through. Abegail had said she knew where to find Shipley and could recognize the building once she saw it, but there would be more eyes on us on Level Three and more chances to have someone question what we were doing. I stared into her eyes and forced myself to trust, pushing back my natural concerns.

"Level Three." The metal box came to a jarring halt, and the passengers pushed their way out.

"Abegail, can you remember how to get to the building?" I asked.

"Yes. Follow me." The little girl stepped out of the elevator, dragging Ade and me behind her. Surprisingly, she seemed more eager after that ordeal than she had before. *She might be more like Sandra than I thought.*

The little girl's hand barely wrapped around my fingers, but her squeeze was tight. I'd never really considered what Sandra would be like as a mother, but I could see her in the resilience, the light in Abegail's eyes. I couldn't help but feel the warmth from her, the same warmth I'd felt from Sandra. A flicker of hope lit in me, surrounded by the darkness of the Below. *I'll find her.*

We walked at pace, winding through alleys and district roads. Once in a while, Abegail would stop and point something out to us, reciting what her mother had told her about the buildings, streets, or shops. EO smiled every time she did.

Sometimes, during moments like this, I wondered what would be different if EO was the one on the outside and I was his DPM. What secrets would I have to carry for him for the price of ease? Did I sometimes feel bouts of jealousy about something I didn't understand?

"There it is." Abegail stopped at the corner of the congested road as if she was waiting for a crosswalk signal. She pointed up at a brick building that rose clear to the bottom of Nāpali's Mid-City. The other buildings on the block were cut several times by mid-level walkways or plazas. But the building Abegail pointed to stood disconnected from the other structures around it, a wide conspicuous tower unaffected by the island city around it.

"Are you sure?" Ade asked.

"It looks like a building Shipley would live in—"

EO's words were interrupted by Abegail. "Yes."

"Good. Thank you, Abegail. I am going to go find your mom, okay?" I reassured her without taking my eyes off the building.

"Shouldn't we wait here? What if you find her and need our help?" Ade asked.

"No. Take Abegail back to your apartment and keep her safe. I'll find Sandra and bring her back. She isn't the only thing I need to talk to him about."

EO nodded his head in approval. I looked at Ade and Abegail, ensuring they followed my directive. They did. With only a hug goodbye, both made their way down the street to the transit station. They would be safer without me.

To be fair, I hadn't only sent them away for their safety. I didn't expect the meeting between Shipley and me to be pleasant. Considering Sandra, the Continent death toll, and sending an assassin after me—he would be lucky if he wasn't eating from a tube when I was done.

CHAPTER 11

Having EO with me removed much of the challenge of getting into the building. It turned out the place Sandra had taken Abegail to all those times was a stand-alone luxury hospital, resembling the ones in Mid-City. Only the most prominent residents of the Below could dream of such treatment, and it wasn't unheard of either for lower-Mid-City locals to prefer traveling down to places like this.

Wide, cushioned seats outside furnished waiting rooms lined the inside of the building. The smiling, nonchalant faces of families waiting for good news told us everything we needed to know about this place. It wouldn't be like the hospitals in the lower levels.

At the entrance, I spoke with a weathered woman from reception who looked old enough to have helped build the island cities herself. Although she refused to disclose any information on a patient with the last name Shipley when I inquired, EO managed to see his full medical record thanks to a slight reflection in the tinted medicine cabinets behind her.

"He's on the third floor," EO said.

Once there, EO deciphered the convoluted sign, which held the names of several departments and wings, and compared them to what he'd seen on the chart.

"Long-term patient care. East Wing."

If the entire hospital resembled anything like the third floor and the lobby, it wasn't a bad place to end up, depending on your reason for admission. The hallways were clean and decorated with flowers, and the pristine baseboards shined with a noticeable absence of water damage.

Through an open door, I saw an empty mechanical bed in the middle of a spacious room filled with unnecessary furnishings. If I lost a limb on the Continent, I'd rather be shipped here than a Nāpali common hospital. Chances were if you went in for treatment at Level One of the Below, you'd lose more leaving than you came in with. I wondered how many kids from the Continent would have survived if they'd been received here for injuries after their tour of duty.

"East Wing is right here." EO had led the way until now, but he paused in front of the door. "Sandra or the Continent first?"

"Sandra."

I pushed through the doors, only to find myself barred from entering by another set of double doors. In place of a handle, there was a single finger-sized button. I pushed it, triggering a low buzz in the room beyond. The mechanism clicked, and the door swung ajar.

"I always hoped you would visit." The strained, weak voice came from a man lying in a mechanical bed among unused living room furniture. This room seemed to be the entirety of the East Wing. It looked as though it had been remodeled to be a single suite for one individual patient. Pictures, paintings, artifacts, and a liquor bar personalized the room. I stepped closer to the bed, and an old, dying husk of the man I once knew as Shipley gazed at me, waiting with a crooked smile.

"I hoped you'd die more painfully than this."

Shipley laughed until his gasps turned into deep, scratchy coughs.

"Fair enough, Kilo."

"You know why I'm here?"

Shipley was hard to look at. Maybe because of the illness eating away at him or maybe because I didn't recognize the person before me. Either way, the foreign, wrinkled face and bloodshot veins crossing his forehead only gave him a cursory resemblance to the Continent-renowned security leader.

Shipley had always taken care of me on the Continent. It was he who'd brought me into security training and promoted me, but he was also the man who broke my leg when I missed an outpost pickup. In his natural disposition, he sat before me, an embodiment of dissonance.

A fire burned inside, while a knot clogged my throat. Regardless of who he'd been when I knew him, the instant his clouded black eyes looked me over, I knew this was no longer the commanding, fearsome man I'd served with for years.

"The nurse told me you were here," he said.

"Hmm." I tried to keep eye contact with him. *Bullshit.* "Right. Well, you're a hard person to track down nowadays. What happened?"

The room's south-facing windows were partially uncovered, allowing light from the city to fill the room. Flashes of signs from the opposite buildings flushed Shipley's face with neon colors. I considered what it must have taken to construct a stand-alone building like this. I figured Shipley enjoyed more than tangible luxury. He'd clearly made some powerful friends.

"Just retirement. Didn't need much after I left," Shipley said with a weak smile.

I didn't care for any more of the small talk. "Was Sandra a part of your retirement?"

"There is an alarm somewhere in the building." EO's words took me by surprise. Without moving my head, my eyes darted toward him as he searched the street below.

"Sandra," I continued. "She was taken, and her daughter identified you, Shipley. I've spent enough time with you to know it's not a coincidence."

"You always spoke so highly of her. I figured I'd see what was so special."

"Where is she?"

"No idea. Is that why you're here? A girl you left eight years ago?"

"She came here, I know she—"

"Of course, she came here. I bent the whore over twice a week for the past four years, and when I got sick, I made it worth her while to visit me here. What is this, Kilo? You were never this soft on the Continent. You don't deal with the real shit anymore?"

Heated blood flooded my cheeks. I stashed a hand under my coat and produced the Nambu.

He didn't flinch. "You gonna shoot me because I fucked some girl?"

The hammer of the Nambu pulled back with a click. I took a couple of steps toward him and leveled the long barrel of the gun at his temple.

"I saw so much in you, Kilo, so much fire, but you could never sacrifice yourself to pull the trigger. You always thought if you could hold on to the small remaining part of the innocent boy, you could live with yourself." Shipley grabbed the wide barrel of the Nambu and pushed it up against his forehead. "This world needed better from you."

"Tell me where Sandra is. I've been all around Nāpali and Ludo for the past two days looking for *you* to tell me about the deaths on the Continent, but now Sandra is missing, and it *still* led me to you. Tell me where she fuckin' is, you prick!"

"What did you say?" His face dropped, and the coy smile that had been on his face as he toyed with me faded. "What do you mean you've been looking for me about the deaths?"

His question turned me on my heels. I tried to piece the puzzle together. Shipley was at the center of all this, but what was *this*? An assassin? Sandra missing? The Ludo Company targeting Shipley?

"Kilo, the alarm isn't an evacuation; it's a lockdown," EO said.

"Why is the building being locked down?" I lowered the gun, but my tone remained impatient.

"What have you done? I was happy here. It was a place to die peacefully," Shipley spat.

"Does this have to do with the Continent?"

"It has everything to do with the Continent. You and I are already dead if we're having this conversation." For the first time, Shipley tried to lift himself out of bed. He looked like a malnourished dog that could hardly muster the energy to stand.

"Don't move. We're not done here!" I screamed.

EO paced between the window and the door, his head jerking each time something sounded in the hallway. The situation was getting out of hand.

"I'm here because of what I did for them on the Continent. They put me here to die peacefully, but you—"

"What happened on the Continent, Shipley? Why did so many people from Ludo and Nāpali die?"

"Why don't you ask your DPM? Do you even know what he's hiding from you?" Shipley croaked as he failed to stand, dropping back down to the bed.

My DPM? EO? Although I heard him perfectly, I couldn't understand the question. There were maybe two handfuls of people alive who knew about EO, and Shipley definitely wasn't one of them.

EO came to a standstill, and we both stared at Shipley.

"Where is he?" Shipley looked around the room. "Your DPM. He must be here, right?" A long, bony finger pointed close enough to EO to send a chill down my spine.

"How do you know? What—" I asked.

"I—" Just as the word left his mouth, a spray of bullets blasted through the window. Glass crashed to the floor, breaking into a million pieces. I instinctively jumped to the side of the bed and ducked for cover. The vibrations from the bullets tearing through the machinery and metal frame rippled along my back.

"Kilo! Three shooters across the street, fourth level!"

"What about the door?" I screamed back.

EO ran across the room into my line of sight and huddled up next to the door. Another burst of fire drilled into the bed.

"Five, maybe six outside."

"And Shipley?"

EO shook his head.

"Fuck!"

Shipley had been an easy target, but I wouldn't be.

The shooting paused briefly as I remained hidden behind the bed. Shipley's blood flowed in a stream along the curvature of the sheets and dripped into a pool beside me. Screams from other patients, nurses, and doctors pierced the wall, but it was impossible to tell whether they were survivors or screaming with their last breath.

I popped my head just above the blankets atop Shipley's newly minted resting place. His dead body lay contorted, with his legs still hanging off the side and open holes in his head and chest. Blood had stained the bedsheets crimson. I peeked over the body of my former mentor and caught a glimpse of the buildings across the street.

Since the hospital stood isolated from the rest of the third-level buildings on the block, it was hard to pinpoint the shots. From my vantage point, three buildings, all attached like the ones in Mid-City, fit the trajectory needed to connect shots inside the room.

"I don't see them," I said through another flurry of bullets that rattled the East Wing. I ducked just in time to see some of the stray shots explode the bottles on the bar.

"Middle building." EO now stood at my side, looking through the window. Bullets continued to whiz by, ripping into the wall. "Has to be mid-range weapons. Three shooters cycling—when two are reloading, another covers."

"Do I have a clean exit?"

"No, but your best chance is probably while the other two are reloading. More are coming from inside the building."

What options do I have? The scenarios ran through my mind, one by one deemed unviable. The only real move was the window, but even if I made it down to street level and commandeered a cycle, I would still be an easy target.

"Make a decision, Kilo. If you stay in this room, we're dead."

I peered down at the Nambu clenched in my right hand. It wasn't much against several shooters, but it would have to do. "I'll take my chances with the window. Once the two shooters reload, I'll make a break for it."

"Got it. I'll tell you when."

I took a deep breath and stood up, barely peeking my head over Shipley's body. As soon as my head cleared the bed, the hail of fire resumed. I dropped back into a squat and stared up at EO, waiting for the signal. The bullets stopped.

"Go!" EO yelled.

I jumped up and darted around the corner of the bed before dropping to a slide toward the shattered window. As my feet connected with the wall, I absorbed the impact with my knees and vaulted through the window. Bullets whizzed over my head as I cleared the ledge. Bricks from the building's exterior exploded around me as the ground rose to meet me. I smashed into a first-floor awning covering the windows and rolled off, landing in the street. Horns blared from cycles, swerving to spare my life.

There wasn't much time. The bullets stopped, but maybe only a few seconds remained before the other two shooters were back up and loaded.

I fired a single shot into the air and pointed my gun at the first indi-cycle that came into view. The cycle screeched to a stop. The bewildered man inside stared at me wide-eyed, then reached for the glove box. I had no way of knowing what he was reaching for, but I didn't take a chance.

My second bullet drove through the front window of the cycle, narrowly missing the driver, who shuddered and threw his bare arms up to cover his face.

"Out," I said.

I barely made it around the side of the cycle before the other shooters reloaded. Their bullets rained down from above, drilling into the cycle.

"This way," I shouted at the driver as I forced the door open. The glass on the side windows and top shield shattered as I switched places with him.

Litters of food containers juxtaposed with a clean briefcase inside the indi-cycle marked the man as one of the many faceless people of the city. His scalding coffee spilled from its holder onto the seat, burning through my pants as I slammed on the pedal, but the adrenaline helped dull the sensation. The wheels spun, and I jerked the fluff-covered steering wheel to the left. The cycle slid in a 180-degree motion before the tires caught the pavement and squealed forward.

From the rearview mirror, which somehow remained intact, I saw EO sitting in the back seat, watching the mayhem left in our wake. This wasn't a simple assassination anymore, but something else entirely. These people had attacked in coordination to take out the target at all costs. It wouldn't be long before the crew from inside the hospital regrouped and attempted to run us down in something more effective than a pedestrian indi-cycle.

"Any ideas?"

"I don't know. We could—" EO began.

"No," I said coldly. He was answering the wrong question. "What was Shipley talking about? How did he know about you?" I shouted.

The sounds of the city were deeper through the broken windows, and the lights of the buildings flashed brighter. The wind rustled my hair as it circled throughout the cycle. My adrenaline was dissipating with each meter gained away from the hospital. However, the question hung in the air as if none of that mattered, as if we were in a one-square-meter vacuum.

"I don't—"

Again, I refused to let him finish. "There are things you remember about before that are black for me." The speedometer now hit its maximum, flickering between eighty-four and eighty-five kilometers per hour. "Trust has been something you've had since the day you joined me, a trust that you would tell me what I needed to know and hold on to what I didn't. What aren't you telling me?"

EO dropped his head, allowing me to see clearly through the rear window. "I swear, Kilo, I don't know how he knew about me. Anything I've held on to, I did because I thought it was best for you." There was no need to see his face to know he was riddled with pain, the pain of a life he hadn't lived but had been subjected to carrying.

I looked at him in the rearview mirror. "I don't believe you."

The pain in his eyes bled into agony. "You have no idea what it's like to be me, Kilo!"

"You are my—"

"Don't you fuckin' say it!" Tears streamed down his cheeks. "You have always been more to me than that, and I'd like to think I'm more to you, so don't fucking say it."

As much as I wanted to interrogate and look him in the eyes, now wasn't the time. Being in a half-crumbling indi-cycle warranted a stopgap of trust.

"Fine. I'm going to head for the cycle transit center. Whatever this is, we'll finish it later." It was a long shot, but maybe if we could get to the center in time, we could lose our pursuers in one of the vertical transit pods.

"I'm not sure we have that kind of time." He wiped away a wayward tear.

"Shit." In the reflection of the rearview, two motorcycles far behind us weaved through traffic, gaining ground. These bikes weren't like indi-cycles, and worse for us, they were built for something exactly like this. Even from a distance, it was easy to make out the gas-powered motors like my Series Seven in Big City, but faster, leaner, and easier to handle. I would have given every credit I had to be on my bike instead of this indi-clunker.

"Can we make the bridge?" EO said.

I didn't respond and instead jammed the brake and drifted the cycle toward a shadowy, canyon-like alley, bouncing the machine against the wall of the entrance. The cycle crunched against the building and screeched as the metal exterior slid along the wall before we broke away. We gradually sped up, just enough to dodge the bullets that pounded the concrete of the building behind us.

"Tell me when they're fifty meters," I shouted.

The semi-detached buildings of the alley dashed by as I tried to avoid the few people who inhabited the area. It would have been exhilarating if it were under different circumstances.

Through it, the alley opened up, flooding light into the cycle. I tried to drift the vehicle into the oncoming traffic on Seminole Street, which ended better than my previous attempt. But making it here was only the first step.

Fewer cycles clogged the Inter-District road than expected, paying off my gamble to get to the bridge. The Montefair bridge was probably ten or twelve kilometers from here. As long as we could make it to the bottleneck and the long concrete straight, we'd have a chance.

"One hundred meters."

"Come on. I need you closer," I whispered.

"Seventy-five."

The cycle shook as it pushed to eighty-seven kilometers per hour. Through the front window, a massive, neon-yellow sign above the Inter-District came into view.

NĀPALI DISTRICT LINE—7 KILOMETERS
MONTEFAIR BRIDGE—8 KILOMETERS

"Fifty, Kilo!" EO shouted.

The timing hadn't worked out. I'd hoped we would be at least within a kilometer of the bridge before they made it so close. I stole a glance in the mirror to see the sterling bikes, piloted by wide single riders, continue to gain on us. I needed more time.

I glided the cycle across two lanes, into the fast lane bordering the divide between incoming and outgoing traffic. I hoped EO was too busy to be shaken by the gaping divide that reached down to the Below.

"Cruise Pilot." The demand forced the indi-cycle's steering wheel to lock and decelerate slightly to what manufacturers argued was "the acceptably safe top speed."

Designed to only store personal items beyond the driver's area, the cramped cabin of the indi-cycle made it difficult for me to maneuver, but I managed to climb my way behind the driver's seat. Through the back window, the riders were close enough now for me to see the bloodshot whites of their eyes through their clear visors.

"All right, go up front and let me know what voice commands you need," I said to EO. I pulled up the Nambu to eye level and aimed at the nearest bike. "I'm going to slow them down."

Two bullets hissed past our cycle, narrowly missing the exterior. I fired back. The blast from the Nambu deadened the excess noise around me. One rider swerved. I discharged three more quick rounds. Two missed, ripping into the road in front of the motorcycles, but I landed the third in the front grill of the lead bike. Even with a sizable hole, the shot failed to slow him down.

The riders split up and weaved into the mass of cycles. I picked the one already hit, switched the Nambu to fully automatic, and delivered a hail of bullets toward the bike. Several bullets tore through the motorcycle and forced it to swerve. The wheel of the bike turned hard to a 90-degree angle and lurched, sending the bike and the rider flying into a duo-cycle two lanes over.

"We need to pass. Right two lanes and back two lanes," EO said.

Multiple cycles in front of us had slowed down now, but EO shouted out what he needed.

I repeated his directions as I reloaded the Nambu. "Cruise, two lanes right followed by two lanes left, accelerate to max speed."

The cycle's Cruise Pilot followed the request and took us around two slower cycles.

"Do you see the second bike?" While I was focused on taking out the motorcycle in our lane and directing the Cruise Pilot, I had lost sight of the second rider.

"I don't see him." EO's head swiveled, looking through the driver's windows as we passed cycles on both sides. "I got him. Fourth—" Bullets riddled the cycle door, which would have torn EO's body in half if his integrity hadn't resided entirely in my frontal cortex.

EO didn't flinch. "Three lanes over, moving toward us."

The closer the motorcycle got, the better chance I had at a clear shot. The rider must have had the same thought because he pressed closer to our cycle. He continued to fire across the lanes, and a few more bullets pierced our metal hull closer to the rear. I took a chance and peered through one of the freshly melted circles just in time to see the man on the bike shift into the lane directly next to us. His eyes locked with mine, and he unloaded on the cycle.

My scream caused EO to turn sharply from his focus on the road in front of us.

"Damn it!" I winced. A single bullet blew open a pit in my bicep. Blood oozed onto the floor of the cycle. My hand released the Nambu, no longer able to properly control my limb. The blood pulsed through my veins toward the open wound like a spigot for a water pump.

"Kilo! Shoot here." I hadn't noticed EO make his way back, but now he kneeled right next to me with his pointer finger on the interior of the cycle, moving gradually toward the front. I growled through the blinding pain, pulled up the Nambu with my functioning hand, and put the end of the barrel up against the tip of EO's finger.

The shot cracked through the metal, blind to the outside world.

After a second, I heard screeching from behind us and turned my head to see a driverless motorcycle veering toward the open valley between highways. I slumped back toward the rear of the cycle and let out a small laugh, matched by EO.

"I can see the bridge up—" I never finished the sentence. The cycle crunched in its middle, folding inward. My body flew against the metal interior. There was no way to know for sure, but I thought I felt the cycle leave the ground before slamming into the safety barrier for the Inter-District.

The cycle flipped and launched into a vertical spin, gaining speed as it dropped. During the second oscillation, the force of the spin threw me through the jagged front windshield and away from the cycle. For a split second, I saw my trajectory, but it was too late.

My head slammed against the frame of the cycle as my body ejected. I saw EO's outstretched hand grasping desperately for mine from the vehicle before blackness consumed my vision. His hand didn't connect.

CHAPTER 12

The darkness in the periphery *of my vision started to clear. But the throbbing in my head continued, making it all but impossible to hear.*

The surroundings were unfamiliar but resembled a lower city district. Exposed pipes and worn siding of numerous buildings on the street alluded to the dilapidated nature of the Below. It felt eerily familiar but also as though I was staring through the dimensions of an abstract painting.

I shook my head, trying to remove the "cobwebs," like my mother had always said, but it didn't help much. My hearing finally returned, but only registered water drops falling from above, splashing into the meager puddles around me.

"Hello?" At first, I thought the voice came from inside my head, but once I turned, I saw the speaker sitting on the alley ground among the overflowing rubbish bins. His face contorted as he strained to pull himself up.

"Hi," I said cautiously. Although unfamiliarity remained, the dark alleys, crisp air, and coarse buildings gradually felt less threatening. "Do you know where we are?"

The man examined his hands with a furrowed brow. "I'm not entirely—" He paused and looked at me, seeing my face for the first time. "I know you."

"You do?"

"Yes, of course." He stepped closer, showing his face and body more clearly

under a dimly lit streetlamp. As he walked toward me, his long hair caught some of the water drops, and his lips etched up into a toothy smile. His long arms wrapped around me and squeezed me tightly from above. "It's nice to meet you, Kilo. I am your Designed Psychological Manifestation."

EO scanned the alleyway and seemed to catch a glimpse of himself in a nearby window.

"I see your unconscious manifested me as an older version of yourself. I'm sure one day we will look like twins," he said. "I hope you know you're safe with—"

I squeezed around his waist with all the force in my scrawny muscles. Amid the hug, memories flooded back—the truck, my father, the other Designers, and the shot in the neck. I'd been descended to the Below.

My memory raced, attempting to reach further back into the past and relive the journey down. I fought to glimpse my mother on the platform waving goodbye, but it was like reaching into a muddy hole, searching for something swirling around below, but feeling it slip against the outside of my hand, never able to grasp it. Finally, I caught a brief glance of a soft, long-haired woman whose features had forever lived in my memory.

The harder I fought to stay, the more my body pressed in upon itself, fighting to come back to where it thought I belonged. My chest convulsed and shook me back to the street where I was wrapped in the DPM's embrace.

"EO!" I shouted, like I had just woken up from a nightmare.

He pulled back from the hug and looked down at me, compassion filling his deep brown eyes. "If you like. You can call me whatever you want." The tears streamed down my face, and I tried to nestle into his chest, but before my head could make contact, I convulsed once again, and my body was ripped back into darkness.

I gasped for air as I sat up in the padded bed. Thick leather straps encased my wrists and ankles. I tried to wrestle free, only burning the skin around my wrists in the process. The hole in my arm had been sutured shut, along with a few other large cuts I must have received during the fall.

Where am I? How am I alive? The thoughts crept through my foggy brain and unleashed a burning wake of adrenaline through my system.

"He's awake." A couple of figures in white coats rushed over to the bedside with frantic looks in their uncovered eyes. "We need him under, now."

I noticed the medical equipment rolling toward me out of the corner of my eye. Almost all at once, every fiber of my being beckoned for escape from the pristine, mirrored room. The newly mended carvings across my body stretched, nearly reopening, and a sharp pain erupted from my bicep. I let out an animalistic cry at the pain wreathing my arm.

The floors and ceiling resembled the natural tiling you would see in any halfway decent building in Mid-City, but the wall-to-wall mirrors reflected my bloody and beaten face.

"You need to calm down, Kilo." The whisper came from behind me as several doctors held down my legs and arms. Through the struggle, a quiet moaning pierced my ears. I stopped fighting long enough to hear a retching sound in the corner of the room. EO lay curled up, only visible through the reflection of two mirrors.

"EO." I fought against my instincts, remaining still and keeping him in my line of sight. There he was, his eyes barely staying open, fighting for his life.

"Please don't let them sever the stem," he whimpered. Blood dripped from his eyes, mixing with the tears running down his cheeks. "I'm scared, Kilo."

"All right, Kilohana, we're going to put you back under so we can sever your brain stem." I wrenched at my restraints, this time lifting the left side slightly off the ground, yet still failing to break free. Next to me, the doctor inspected an oversized needle filled with a thick, coagulated fluid. "It's okay. This is a normal procedure for body trauma victims, especially someone who fell an entire level. We can fix you in a matter of a half hour, but we need to sever your brain stem to ensure you don't feel any pain. Do you understand?"

"No! No! Do it without," I said in a breathy voice. "I can take it. Just don't sever the stem."

The doctor looked around at the other doctors and nurses restraining me and scoffed. "I'm sorry, but I don't think you understand how this works. Reconstruction surgery is your only option, and it is quite literally impossible to withstand the pain. There is a 98 percent chance of you dying without severing the brain stem. I wouldn't be doing my job if I didn't."

I looked at EO. My tears matched his, blurring the mirrored picture of him. I'd never really considered what would happen if a DPM was left to die inside your mind. Now, the thought petrified me.

"Nurse, if you please," the doctor said, now out of sight. A sharp sting pierced my neck.

"Please, no," I objected softly as the feeling in my upper body deteriorated before taking over my legs.

"Kilo, you *will* be okay. I promise," the voice again whispered in my ear.

I fought the overwhelming nothingness that crept up my neck, but it was useless. I succumbed.

Regaining consciousness was never easy after body trauma reconstruction. The toll the procedure took on your mechanisms was unlike any other. A stabbing pain throughout your skeletal system greeted you as life reentered the body.

In the minutes after the doctors disconnect the brain stem from your body, your organs shut down. The shock of reconnection afterward sends the body into a frenzy. It causes what is ominously termed on the Continent as organ realignment, where most of the body's vital organs readjust from the process of dying to reviving in a matter of seconds. This leaves the newly reanimated patient with unbearable burning, piercing, and shooting pain throughout their body.

I woke with a convulsed gasp for air.

Although the realignment left me in intense visceral, nociceptive pain, the psychological agony ripped me apart. EO's lifeless body lay in the same niche of the room where he'd begged for his life before the surgery. I tried to close my eyes and cry, to expunge some of the pain, but tears refused to flow. Part of me wanted to be thankful he still existed at all, but it wouldn't shrink the hole he left in my soul. The other part wanted to stick a scalpel through my eye and rip out chunks of my brain until the sight of EO disappeared. It was a sick joke that even with him gone, somehow my mind forced me to watch what was left of him waste away.

The words I'd said to him played in my mind. *I don't believe you.* Those angry, confused words left every part of me in anguish. I would never have the chance to rescind them, to make sure he knew I trusted him, only him.

"You're awake. That's good." The familiar voice spoke from out of view—it was the woman who had whispered in my ear before going under. "Although body trauma surgery has a fairly high survival rate, some people still die from it." I tried to turn my head to get a complete look at the woman, but the surgery's lasting effects had left me almost paralyzed, save for the slight ability to wiggle my index fingers.

After a moment, a bronze-skinned woman walked into my eyeline and stood in front of the bed. She administered a variety of liquids into an IV connected to my arm. Her surgical mask was pulled down to reveal a beautiful, albeit crooked, smile.

"I wish I died," I said as the sensation in my toes, arms, and face returned, along with the indescribable pain of organ realignment.

"I don't blame you. A DPM is like a part of you. It lives, breathes, and grows beside you; it was created to be a perfect companion. To lose that, even for a moment, must be more excruciating than losing a child." The words flowed from her mouth without caution, like she knew for certain that we were the only two people in the room.

I must be hallucinating, reliving the moment I learned Shipley knew of EO and projecting the memory. My face betrayed the thought.

"Yes, I know about EO, too," she said casually, and loosened the restraints.

"How? What do you mean, too?"

She responded slowly, as if vetting every word. "There are a number of people who have been watching you, or at least trying to, since you arrived in Kaua'i City. Your secret is not as well kept as you believe."

"If you knew, how could you let them sever me?" I snapped, the anger boiling over. It felt like a piece had been ripped from my brain, my body.

"If there was another way, I wouldn't have. But you need to be alive."

"What's that supposed to mean?"

The crooked smile again broke onto her face. "Good question, but right now, we're leaving before the doctors come back."

She grabbed both my legs and threw them over the bed, sending a fire tearing through my body. I crunched the enamel of my teeth together just to bear it.

"I know it hurts, but we have to leave, Kilo."

"I'm not going anywhere with you. I'm staying right fucking here, with EO." My body screamed for the opportunity to cry, but there was nothing left.

Her eyes narrowed, and deep brown irises stared into mine. "You and EO are coming with me because I'm the only one who can help him." She leaned over the bed to pull my arm up, her chest pressing against mine for a moment, sending a mix of painful and libidinous signals through my reawakening synapses. I didn't need to be a doctor to know my organs were still realigning and not yet corresponding with their correct functions.

"You're full of shit. Once a DPM's severed, they can't be reconnected."

"You study DPMs a lot, do you? I'm guessing some things have changed since you learned about them in Design City."

"EO isn't some concocted DPM replica; he's the real thing. You can't save him!"

"You don't understand a thing about DPMs, Kilo."

"And you do? Who the fuck *are* you?"

"I don't have time to explain. You know there's only one choice here, so make it."

I contemplated the offer for a moment. I wanted to fight it, but in no world could I say no if there was even a microscopic chance of saving EO. He deserved whatever I had left to give him.

"Fine." I stood up shakily. An uncomfortable compression in my muscles surged with each step. It felt like my skeletal frame was collapsing in on itself. "I'll get EO."

I walked a few paces to his fetal body, the emotional pain again drowning out any pain from the surgery. His hair had turned white, and dried blood covered his bleached skin. His death couldn't have been anything less than excruciating. I picked up his ethereal body with both arms and followed the nurse to the door. The mirrors taunted me as we left, screaming at me in my voice that I had failed the only thing that mattered. *I will fix it.*

It must have looked awkward, a person walking through the emergency room, arms outstretched and carrying nothing, attached to a body that looked like it should be in the morgue. But people were too busy with their own problems or their patients to care.

The lobby could have been a war zone—screaming families trying to scrape the blood from the floor and transfuse it back into their loved ones. Frantic doctors tended to patients who were still breathing, while the families of the dead were forced toward the exit. None of it phased me. The horror was simply a part of existing in the Below. Their lives were at the mercy of fortune.

EO's life, though, might still be in my hands. I possessed a control these people could only pray for. The nurse led me out of the hospital and onto the street to an inconspicuous duo-cycle parked in the alley alongside numerous others. I gently laid EO in the cycle at the foot of the second chair and sat. His body continued to deteriorate before my eyes, his fingernails falling from his hand, leaving tumultuous yellow skin exposed.

"How do you know he won't die before we get there?"

"As long as we don't run into any problems on the way, he has plenty of time."

"Doesn't look like it."

The city passed by, lights flickering, wind rushing against the cycle, but it didn't feel like it did in Ludo or Mid-City. The emptiness reflected in the streets. Each alley seemed darker, each building more worn, and each person less human.

The silence lingered for several minutes before either of us spoke. "What's your name?"

"Kilah."

"Funny," I said dryly.

"We're here." Kilah pulled into a small tunnel that bore through conjoined buildings with a unique architectural style. Whereas most of the buildings in the island cities were rectangular, these curved with arches and were rounded along the edges. The tunnel opened several times to reveal vast areas within the buildings, like courtyards of the administration buildings in Design City.

"The Below University?"

"Yes," she said matter-of-factly.

The answer seemed so obvious to Kilah, but undercut all my expectations. The Universities of the Below, within any of the island cities, were less than prestigious. As Bless used to say, "The University only tells people what shitty jobs the Designers want them to do." I'd been here once, as a teenager. Some friends had invited us to a fight nearby, and I'd walked through the campus briefly, only to find it less than inspiring.

We pulled off the road into one of the courtyards and parked near a soft blue building decorated with pictures of countless half-naked people fighting with ancient weaponry.

"Let's go," Kilah said.

I hoisted EO out of the cycle and followed Kilah into the building.

Windows lined the halls, revealing classrooms inside full of young people from the Below. In some, there were interactive presentations with students conversing with people dressed in styles that were anything but contemporary.

Inside one of the windows, the students read physical books whose pages were filled with ink from another time. I stopped and stared in disbelief.

"Never seen that many physical books in one place before?" Kilah asked.

"It's not like they print them every day," I responded, my eyes focused on one of the books. It had a deep red cover with white lettering and was thinner than I expected. The student reading from the book looked through the window for a moment. His eyes lit with fire, and his hands clutched the book feverishly.

"What are they reading?" I asked.

"I don't know. Come on, we're up here."

The student's gaze broke away, and I followed Kilah further down the halls. At the end of the building, she stopped and opened a wooden door. Inside, we descended a steep, poorly lit staircase, then emerged into a central room with a few doors. In the middle of the room, a young woman sat at an antique desk that hid the lower half of her body. Although she presented as a meek, helpful student, her muscles tensed at the sight of us, and one hand disappeared behind the desk.

Kilah walked up, leaned down halfway across the table, and murmured something to the girl. The room was empty, but not like an empty room that could benefit from additional furniture or decorations. Absolutely nothing except for the table guarded by the girl lived in this concrete box.

"That door. I don't need to go in with you." Kilah motioned to the corner of the room.

"What about EO? You said you'd help him."

She motioned for me to place EO at her feet. I did so, gently relaxing his body to the ground, and watched Kilah disappear into another room, leaving EO lying there—a forgotten corpse.

"I'll take care of him," Kilah said as she reemerged a few moments later with a personal device connected to some other gadget I didn't recognize.

From the corner of my eye, I caught the girl at the desk repositioning her hidden hand. A flexed forearm muscle along the elbow joint gave her away.

"Relax. I was clinically dead twenty minutes ago. You have nothing to fear from me."

The girl eased her grip on the gun stashed underneath. I shook my head and headed toward the door in the corner of the room. As I grabbed the handle, a stenciled placard on the door stared at me.

DR. AMELIA MANUMA, PhD

Realization hit. *A university? No one on earth could be that lucky.* With Shipley dead, only one other person could have answers about the deaths on the Continent or why they'd taken Sandra, and I'd stumbled right to their door.

CHAPTER 13

Dr. Amelia Manuma's office in no way resembled the barren foyer outside. Her space was lived-in and felt alive. Statues of marble and gold covered the room, their bodies muscular and heads adorned with unrecognizable leadership headdresses from a lost era. A decaying odor stemming from a large wooden carving permeated the air. It shimmered under the fluorescent lights with a hint of amber hidden in the rustic wood, standing ominously behind a drab executive desk.

The woman sat behind the desk, quietly writing on an already cluttered paper, among a scattering of books and other trinkets. Her skin broke through the slits of her pre-cut blouse, and brown bangs splintered with gray hairs covered her forehead.

The room was a task to take in after the sparse nature of the foyer, and the woman—somewhere in her late fifties probably—only added to the challenge of piecing together what I was doing here. Dr. Manuma removed her glasses and stood at the sight of me with a welcoming smile, much like the one from Kilah.

"Hello, Kilo. I'm glad you decided to meet with me."

"Are you—"

"Yes, I am. Are you surprised I'm from the Below, or that you found me *here*?"

I could hardly get the words out of my mouth. "Just surprised the infamous Doctor exists."

The Doctor's smile deepened. "Well, good. That's what I hope people feel when they meet me." She motioned to a flower-printed couch between two marble statues with cushions torn from overuse.

I sank into the couch, still feeling the remnants of my trauma surgery, and appreciated not having to stand on needles any longer.

"I'm sure you recognize the one to your right?"

I studied the stone man, his outstretched arm pointing toward something infinite. "Yeah, of course, but . . . there are hundreds of statues commemorating the original Designers. Why keep this one?"

"Because this is the first. It was thought lost in the commotion of building a city and society from scratch. It was found a few decades ago on the Continent of all places. I suppose he would have been happy there, watching his architectural innovations coming to life. Now, he will live the rest of his days in my dungeon."

"Right." Although the marble was noticeably decayed, its elegance still captured me, a fable of blood and beauty.

"And the one on your left is . . . well, he's someone not so well celebrated, from the Old World."

The man in question wore a leafy crown atop a pudgy face, and lavish clothes covered his obese body. The artistry was remarkable, incorporating unfathomable detail and producing a feeling of life. It was as if the man stood high above his people, the architectural achievements of a past age beneath his feet.

"I didn't know works like this existed."

"The Continents still hide treasures of the Old World. In the desert rests art, architecture, and infrastructure vastly different from that of the island cities. True megalomania was but a dream in the Old World."

"So, you really are the Doctor?" I stuttered, slowly allowing myself to believe. "The stories make it sound like you were a medical doctor from

Mid-City or even Design City, not a basement dweller at a university."

"Do not mistake humility for ineptitude, Kilo. But you're right; my father was a doctor at Nāpali Hospital in Mid-City. Although I did take a lifelong interest in his clandestine hobby, I never cared much for medicine. *This* is what I care about." She swept her arms around at the many valuables in her possession.

"Okay, you're a collector. What do you want with me?"

She leaned over her desk, shuffling papers around until she grasped what she was looking for with an eager smile.

"This is what I need from you." She handed me a paper, damaged around the edges as if it had traveled around the world in someone's pocket. Thankfully, the inked writing was still clearly visible.

I perused the title, not recognizing it.

"Read it," she said.

MEMO:
THE SPEER PROJECT

SITE LOCATION: LUDO/NĀPALI MINING TERRITORIES SECTOR 7, OUTPOST 378. CONTINENT OF SOUTH AMERICA.

PERSONNEL: REQUIRED RECRUITMENT FOR THE PROJECT WILL NOT EXCEED 150,000 OVER THE COURSE OF 10 YEARS AND IS SUBJECT TO REEVALUATION UPON DEADLINE REVIEWS.

RESOURCES: 5% OF ALL RESOURCES BOUND FOR KAUA'I CITY WILL BE DIVERTED TO THE PROJECT. 6% CURRENTLY STANDS AS AN ACCEPTABLE LOSS OF RESOURCES AS A RESULT OF APPROVED CIRCUMSTANCES.

SITE MANAGER AND RECRUITMENT SUPERVISOR PER DESIGNER KAMI: ANTHONY SHIPLEY.
FILE ACCESS TYPE: TOP SECRET. DESIGN AND SITE MANAGER EYES ONLY.

IN SERVICE OF THE DESIGN,
NOAH ARASI

"The Speer Project? Am I supposed to know what this is?" I handed the memo back to the Doctor.

"The bottom, Kilo."

My eyes drifted to the bottom of the page, the words hitting me like a shot through the throat.

Blood rushed to my head, leaving my vision of the surrounding room swirling. The numbness in my fingers returned, and the paper slipped from my grasp.

"I know what your father did to you, to your mother, but—"

"What does my father have to do with this?" I asked slowly. "What is this?"

"We've been trying to find out for a very long time, but I think there are only a few people in the island cities that know; chief among them is your father."

"I was sent here to investigate disproportionate numbers of deaths of Ludo and Nāpali service members on the Continent, not some witch hunt for Designers, let alone him."

"They are all the same, Kilo: your father and the rest of them. They would burn the world down for an inch of progress. We aren't dealing with architects any longer." She turned to face the original Designer statue. "They no longer build, Kilo; they develop, maintain, and aggregate. You think you know the Designers, but you don't."

As much as I wanted to agree, the absolutism of it didn't escape me. "He's different. They aren't all irredeemable, or even bad, no matter how much we want them to be."

Her back stiffened. Her surprise at my rebuff mirrored my own. After all, I should have been the first to unilaterally categorize the Designers this way, but something about this woman evoked resistance. Antagonism.

The Doctor toyed with the inside of her lip along her bottom row of teeth. "You think your childhood friend is good because you knew her as a kid? You think she's above reproach?"

I didn't have a response—not a logical one, at least.

"Kilo, do you know who's in line to be the next Head Designer for Island City Protection and Endurance?"

"I assume you're going to tell me."

"Alessia Landrum."

"So what? That doesn't mean she's like my father. It doesn't mean they are all like my father." I took a breath. "What's any of this supposed to mean? Why am I here?"

"Kilo, what if they're connected?" She softened as she stood and began pacing the room, a look of consternation covering her face as if she were trying to jump-start her brain and solve the mysteries of the memo in an instant. "You started looking for deaths but found something more, didn't you?"

Her question caught me off guard. "I don't know."

"The truth is *we* don't know. We thought, for a long time, that the deaths were completely unrelated to the Speer Project, but when we found a DIIP agent from Big City investigating deaths on behalf of the Big City Designers, it became much easier to believe in a connection."

My mind raced, trying to rewind the past two days and recall the meeting with Decambra at the DIIP office. "This is Designer Makrumbi's top priority, and he is heavily invested in its success," Decambra had said.

EO had been convinced, even before the attempts on my life, that there was more to this assignment than Decambra disclosed. I thought the

Designers in Big City knew nothing of the deaths on the Continent. They were simply grasping for anything to trigger a diplomatic meeting between the two island cities, but maybe they knew. Maybe they knew exactly what was happening on the Continent, and I'd been a patsy in their effort to stop it.

"So what? Your nurse made it sound like you needed me to help you. Let me guess: Design City? I can't get in. I can't help you if this goes up as far as the Designers."

"I think you underestimate yourself. You were born there."

Her intimation of what she thought she knew of my childhood curdled my blood. The memory of my father tossing me from the truck was at the forefront of my mind. I tensed my arms only to feel my sewed-up holes scream with pain.

"It doesn't mean shit when you aren't wanted there."

As the Doctor chewed on the idea, contemplating the leverage she thought I had with Design City, I seized the opportunity to learn more.

"How do you know so much about me? I mean EO, Design City, it all seems a bit more intrusive than I'd expect from a smuggler."

A half smile cocked her lips as the two competing trains of thought swirled around between us.

"When I say *this*"—she made a presentational motion to the artifacts around the room—"I mean people, history, societies. At first, I cared about the items as treasures, something that enjoyed value because no one else possessed them, but as I learned about what they were and who they represented . . ." She trailed off, staring at the statue that appeared to be guarding me.

"People are terrible to each other, and those in power seize the opportunity to wield that terror. I'm not an anarchist, Kilo—don't misunderstand me—but if a world is solely focused on preserving posterity, then the structures you build may bring about the end of that very goal."

The thought was nice—perpetual endurance leading to the importance of structures over people—but that didn't explain why she was so invested. Ideologues had come and gone in the cities, Fabian Maraku from Maui City,

Gestal from Big City, and Lolian Franchesca from Honolulu City, all dead now with their ideas turned to ash in their urns.

"Fine, you're an academic, an idealist, but what does that have to do with me?" I asked.

"Much like you, my family struggled once and was affected by the absolutes of the Designers. You are the greatest-kept secret in the island cities. Naturally, I was intrigued."

"Not as well kept as I thought. I've almost doubled the people that knew about EO and my father in a single—"

"Speaking of, I hope you know EO will be fine. In six to eight days, he should reanimate."

EO. I mentioned him as if he were standing next to me, forgetting he was in the other room fighting for his life. I'd allowed distrust and contempt for him to infect me and believed his imaginary betrayal with Shipley. In reality, the secret I'd guarded so diligently seemed to be more renowned than I thought.

"How can you bring him back?" I asked.

"It's really quite easy if you have the resources." The Doctor shuffled some papers away from her desk to reveal her personal device, which blinked to life. The image that appeared in shades of blue and green a half meter above the desk showed EO's curled-up body, lifeless and unrecognizable.

"Kilah has started working on him. The device in your head can be remotely accessed through brain matter retrieved from your prefrontal cortex."

"I assume she took some during the procedure?"

"Yes. I hope you don't mind. Anyway, EO can be recreated, so to speak, by using brain matter developed while he was with you."

Throughout her explanation, she directed me to the images of EO as if she were attempting to transfuse knowledge for practice. I tried to keep a straight face, but the thought of bringing back my friend brought me close to tears.

"As I said, in six to eight days, once Kilah is through, EO should reappear to you the same as before he died."

"Okay," I said, the word trembling between my lips. "I'll wait here for a week until he's back, and then we can do whatever you want."

Her PD powered down, returning EO's body to its dark penitentiary.

"I'm afraid we can't wait that long. You leave tomorrow out of Ludo."

"No way. I'm not going anywhere without EO." I stood and edged toward the door.

"That's the deal. Either you go, or EO can find help elsewhere." Her expression turned stone-cold. Her face cemented, revealing a second side to the Doctor, a ruthless persona that had been missing from the lore since I entered the room. A persona I assumed would accompany someone as infamous as her.

I dared to entertain the thought of tearing the woman limb from limb, leaving just enough life in her to ensure she knew not to fuck with EO. The blood that pumped through my veins prepared me for war. I couldn't risk it, though. Not with EO in the condition he was.

"Why Ludo? It's impossible to get into Design City from there."

"You still misunderstand. You're not going to Design City. You're going to the Continent."

Along with a sigh of relief, a new set of problems took shape. The trip to Design City made sense, but I hadn't considered she might want someone to see things with their own eyes. *But they could send almost anyone to work on the Continent. Why me?*

"Why the Continent? Why me?" I asked, repeating my thoughts out loud. The words came out savagely—a question of the mission and the rationale—but honestly, it was a relief. The Continent was tread territory for me, a place I could slip back into. Unlike Design City, which constantly changed. I much preferred to navigate the work sites of the Continent than the sociopolitical dynamics of even one square meter up top.

"Why you? This isn't about *you*." She then paused for a moment, released some of the tension in her brow, and produced a thin, forced smile. "Speak with Hanna. She has all the appropriate information for you and can answer any questions you have." The civility returned to her voice. She sat down behind her desk and resumed work on the papers she'd been examining upon my arrival.

"So, I go to the Continent, come back, tell you what I found, and we're done?"

She spoke without looking up. "See what you find, and you can let me know if you're done."

I grunted in compliance. "One more thing."

"Yes?" she inquired.

"I need you to take care of some people for me. I want a woman and a girl kept safe while I'm gone, and I want you to find someone for me before I get back. You do that and help EO, and I'll get you what you need."

"A list of demands. Fine. You'll meet your contact at the docks."

"Contact? What are you talking about?"

"I believe you spoke with them in Ludo. They're sending someone to help on the Continent."

The Company? That alliance wasn't in the stories.

I left the room, closing the door behind me with some force to show the woman I wasn't entirely overjoyed by our meeting. It probably wasn't needed.

The same girl guarded the solitary desk in the foyer. Hanna, I presumed.

"I want to see EO before I leave."

Her compassionless eyes pierced mine. For a moment, our gaze remained locked. But behind her hardened face, I could sense the uncertainty, the doubt in her effectiveness as a gatekeeper. From the moment she'd gripped the gun under the table, I knew she was just a girl caught up in an organization that made her feel as close to power as a young girl from the Below ever could.

I released the tension and threw my hands in the air, surrendering. "I'm going to talk to Kilah for a minute, and I'll come back for my documents." I turned and walked toward the door Kilah had taken EO through earlier. I figured I'd convinced her, but it was never entirely comforting walking away from someone whose finger was locked on a trigger.

Kilah's office was much larger than the Doctor's and filled with computing equipment that rivaled the DIIP. Each of the gray walls had been fitted with portable monitors, which at first seemed discontinuous but indeed were connected through complex patterns. Kilah stood in front of several of the monitors, utilizing both hands to rapidly sequence numbers and letters. The symbols would appear on the screen adjacent to each other before combining and producing an interconnected web of particles, resembling narrow, curving streams of water. EO's body lay on a vaulted, tall slab situated squarely in the center of the room.

His pale-white hair matched his ivory body like one of the Doctor's statues. As I moved closer, I noticed his deteriorated skin was infused with gentle specks of aqua.

"It's going well." Kilah looked briefly at EO before turning her attention back to the screens.

"This aqua in his skin, did you . . . can you see him?"

She turned once again, this time pulling away from the screens completely.

"Yes." Her hand rode gently along his hair. "I assume this is what you looked like as a younger man?"

"Not exactly."

It was stunning. I'd never conceived that anyone could reanimate a DPM, let alone create a holographic image that was visible to someone other than the companion.

I touched his shoulder only to feel the ice-cold temperature of his body. With it, the vision of EO's outstretched hand grasping for me as I fell from the indi-cycle flashed in my mind. My hand recoiled.

"She said six to eight days."

"Mm-hmm. Maybe sooner if I work fast."

"How is any of this possible? Can the Designers even—?"

"Like I said, it will be faster if you let me work."

I tried to leave, to take a step, but what sat before me beckoned. I wanted to believe it was EO begging me to stay, but it wasn't him alone. The transformative knowledge in this room pulled me in.

I stood there for a minute, quietly, as Kilah worked, entranced by the body before me. EO had become more than a figment. Although not animate, he no longer fully resided in the manifestation. A prickling sensation covered my skin at the thought. He'd always been real to me. DPMs had always been real to their companions, but now he was *real.*

I bent down and touched my forehead to his, whispering a soft "I'm sorry" before exiting the room. Kilah wasted no time seeing me out before typing furiously away on the monitors. Her determination, whether out of a sense of altruism or service, didn't matter to me, as long as she brought back my friend.

CHAPTER 14

An hour had passed since leaving the University, and it took the same time to make my way to the Nāpali outer graveyard. It wasn't much of a final resting place, at least not compared to the Old World. It had never mattered to me, though, as long as there was a place I could talk to her.

I liked to imagine the water hammering down on my head as real rain pouring from a stone cloud far above in a dark sky. In reality, it was the same water that fell in Nāpali, standing outside Bless' fight club and in Ludo, where the Night Sticks had rampaged through the protesting crowd. It was nothing more than a dirty, recycled version of the pure rain showers outside the island city superstructure. However, this was the one place I allowed myself to believe the lie, to live in the fantasy.

"Hey, Mom." I dropped to the cold, saturated, dying grass and crossed my legs in front of the miniature stone pyramid.

Similar pyramids littered the large, circular patch of grass, forming something like a worship circle around the base of the smaller foundational cylinder of the superstructure. When I'd first seen this place as a child, the graveyard was not a graveyard at all and had only served as the foot of the cylinder—nothing more.

The story went: One day, a woman had put a green and blue pyramid covered in stenciled flowers next to the cylinder. When someone asked, she told them it was for her son, whom she'd never met. Every day she visited, sobbing for her son until she managed to drag herself away. A few weeks later, a handful more pyramids appeared, accompanied by grieving mothers and fathers. A year later, almost one hundred pyramids encircled the cylinder, a new family created from loss and bound by love. Sometime later, a small obsidian pyramid with crude white carvings of a beautiful woman was placed in the grass circle. That pyramid belonged to my mother.

The Nāpali Below provided a monument where a son could grieve, even without a body. I tried to remember her voice, but all I could muster were the same two words as always: "Sweet boy."

"It's just me today, Mom. EO was in an accident, but I'm trying to help him."

A file from my personal device glowed under the shadow of the foundation cylinder. I leafed through the files of information the Doctor had provided for my trip to the Continent. With only soft hums from the buildings around us, the graveyard offered me as close to pure silence as I could ask for in the Below. It somehow felt more manageable here than it did in the eclectic office at the University.

The documents showed detailed plans for a departure from Ludo at six a.m. Apparently, I'd been signed up for service under the name Kilo Walker. I cursorily flicked through the documents that described Walker as a fan of the fights who'd fallen on hard times because of some reckless bets.

"Widowed. Educated at Nāpali Cont-School. Member, Children of the Designers. Basic combat training. Construction experience. Yeah, yeah. I get it." I muttered the qualifications and facts of my falsified life out loud, as if my mother might laugh at the implications. Everything seemed to be solid, but I also didn't have the energy to deep dive into Walker's life, so I trusted this wasn't the Doctor's first time creating a new identity.

I let out a deep breath that had built in my lungs and closed the file. "I don't know how to do this without him, Mom. It's not like I would rather go to Design City, but I had him with me every day for all eight years I served."

I looked around at some of the other pyramids that ranged in colors, sizes, and exterior designs.

"You think any of their families know what happened to them?"

An empty response filled the air. It was one thing to lose someone, but it was entirely different not to know how or why they were gone. "Maybe some," I answered for her.

My PD lit up, flashing the clock at me. Time to go. But the secrecy of this mission gnawed at me. It wasn't until I reviewed the bio for Kilo Walker that I realized the problem. The island cities had been relatively peaceful for so long, but ever since Honolulu City fell, the world had changed. The deterioration had been felt for years now—drops in inter-island travel, increased propaganda, Night Sticks hacking their way through the Below, and Continent disputes.

So, what was so precious on the Continent that the Designers would sacrifice tens of thousands of people for it, employ assassins to protect it? And what was so important that the legendary Doctor would, without hesitation, save my DPM for a glimpse of it? New deposits? Priceless historical foundations? Something biological? No. The only project worth risking an inter-island breakdown for was a weapon, something that would change the game up top. A weapon that would make the world all the more dangerous.

I peered down the street from a pedestrian bridge at an archaic building that took up half the block. The school looked more like a prison than a child-friendly learning center. It resembled the boys' school Bless, Mo, and I'd attended a couple of decades earlier. If it was indeed similar, I commiserated for Abegail.

I watched for a while, hoping to spot her through the mesh windows. Kids as young as three years old passed through the school hallways, obscured by the screen, but there was enough visibility to see a little blonde head bobbing up and down past the window. The gravity weighing my shoulders down suddenly lightened—even if it was in a Nāpali school, at least she was safe.

On the far side of the building, at the end of the block, Ade sat hunched over on a street bench. Her previously manicured braids now flowed along her shoulders in broken curls, the assortment of colors mismatched in a confusing tapestry. Even from afar, her pain and angst consumed the air. I still had a couple of hours before Kilo Walker's departure, and although I didn't have much emotional capacity left, I needed to muster whatever there was and get Ade and Abegail to safety in Ludo.

I crossed the bridge and walked down the block to see her.

"Abegail inside?"

"Kilo!" Ade lunged off the bench and threw her arms around me. "There was so much commotion on the third level after we left, I didn't know what to think."

"I'm okay, but Shipley didn't turn out to be the life-changing find I thought he'd be."

"Anything on Sandra?"

I shook my head. "An acquaintance is looking for her, though."

"Okay . . . well, I'm glad you're all right."

"How's she been?"

Ade looked over toward the windows of the school. "She's fine. She asked about you. I wasn't sure what to say, so I told her you're riding the elevators."

I let out a chortle, picturing the conversation. "Perfect."

"What do we do now?"

I didn't have the slightest clue how to tell her, but I tried. "I need to go away for a few days."

"What do you mean, go away? For what?"

"The Continent."

"Kilo! If you're in danger in the city, they could just as easily kill you on the Continent, and no one would care, not even the DIIP."

"I know, but I have to go. It's the only way."

Ade shook her head, giving me a dirty look somewhere between disbelief and disappointment. "The only way—"

I spoke before she could finish. "I need you and Abegail to go to Ludo for a few days."

"Ludo? Kilo, you're fucking with me, right? Go to the Continent if you want, but we are *not* going to Ludo." Anger stirred; the confusion and pain of the past day masked with red. "Sandra is missing, and her daughter witnessed her kidnapping from the attic. Now you want me to take her to the Ludo District, a place she's never been? Are you insane?" she shouted.

I moved closer to her and put my hands on her shoulders. "I need you to trust me. What's going on is a lot bigger than we thought, and as *insane* as it sounds, Ludo is probably the safest place in the city for both of you."

"I don't—" She yelled back before I grabbed her with both my arms and pulled her in, cradling her for a second before she reciprocated the gesture.

A tumbling feeling in the pit of my stomach rocked my core. Losing EO and knowing someone held Sandra against her will, or worse, was tough. I needed to be sure Ade and Abegail were safe.

I pulled back from our embrace enough for Ade to look at me. Thunderclouds of emotion swirled behind her eyes. I'd known her for a long time, and I'd seen the emotion before. As much as it pained me, she could handle it.

"Someone gave me an address in Ludo where I can guarantee your safety."

The anger hadn't fully dissipated, but she nodded her head in agreement. "If it has to be Ludo, then we're going somewhere I trust."

"Ade—"

"No. I will bring her, but we go where I say, all right?"

I nodded.

Her chest decompressed, and the color in her face faded with the cool wind. The glint of green in her eyes flashed as her gaze drifted down the street. "Fuck, Kilo, what did you get me into?"

"Honestly, I don't know."

"The Continent, huh?"

I showed her the documents for Kilo Walker, and she leafed through the projected pages.

"You're serious? Kilo, these may get you onto the boat, but the officials on the Continent won't buy this is you."

"What do you mean? They seemed fine to me."

"Did you even look at them?"

"Yes . . . sort of."

"This Walker guy doesn't make any fuckin' sense—they're going to flag you in a heartbeat."

"Since when have you been an expert in forged recruitment docs?"

"Giving Mid-City pricks a good time doesn't pay as much as you'd think."

I took back my personal device and looked closer at the profile for Kilo Walker. She was right. I should have looked at it more closely. There was something off, but I couldn't pinpoint it.

"Okay, so what's wrong with it?"

"You need to make him a person, not an amalgamation of attributes. It's different down here now; they care who they're sending out there."

"My boat leaves in two hours, Ade. It'll have to do."

Ade squinted to see the time on my PD and then gazed down the street toward Ludo. "I think we have enough time. Come with me."

Concrete dust saturated the air with each step. You couldn't tell from the outside of the building, but inside, a state-of-the-art construction facility operated autonomously. Through the clouds of byproducts, the massive Nāpali Construction machines delivered raw materials along interconnected, speeding conveyor belts along interconnected pathways. Like roaches into the grinder, the stone was ripped to shreds until only the base fabric for synthetic concrete remained.

I covered my mouth, but a worrying amount of dust still broke through to my lungs. Through coughs, I checked the time on my personal device—an hour and a half until departure.

"We almost there?" I asked.

"Patience," Ade responded through a cough of her own. "In here."

She ducked into a doorway under one of the grinding machines and down a less polluted, narrow hallway. She grabbed a couple of worker masks off the wall and threw one back to me. The elastic strap fastened easily around my head and hissed as I exhaled.

"My guy is up here," Ade said.

A few meters in front of her, a light blinked above a reinforced door. "In there?"

"You didn't think I brought you to Nāpali Construction to see the sights, did you?"

I grunted through the mask.

Ade knocked three times on the door, sending an uncomfortable vibration through the hallway. Nothing. She knocked again with the same cadence. As her fist rapped a third time, the metal latch cracked open, and the door swung inward.

"What are you doing here, Ade?" A short man stuck his head out the door and peered down the hall at me. "Who's this?"

"Someone from Mid-City with Mid-City cash. He needs docs that'll pass. I told him I knew someone."

He rubbed his shaved head. "This isn't how we do this."

"Shut the fuck up, June. We're partners; sometimes you have to do what I say."

His face pinched into a snarl, but he relented and waved us in. Under his breath, he muttered, "When are we not doing what you say?"

Synthetic concrete dust covered the floor, leaving footprints around the cramped office. June collapsed into a worn chair behind an uneven desk and started rifling through documents on his personal device. Suddenly, the room shook. I braced myself against the wall and stashed my free hand in my jacket.

"Easy, guy. It's just the machines. Sometimes Continent materials mess with the grinder, but it sorts itself out." After a second, the rumbling ceased. "See, nothing to worry about."

Ade laughed as June continued working.

"Where'd you meet this guy?" I asked.

"She's a bitch. Just walked in one day and told me we were makin' docs together. Now she won't leave me alone."

"That's one way to tell it."

His thin eyes drifted up and fixated on Ade. "What do you need?"

"Kilo Walker—first tour, gambling, divorced."

"First tour?" he asked, turning and inspecting me.

Ade followed and gave me a once-over. "I know, but it's all about the story, and you're the best."

I threw my hands up at her indignantly.

"Sorry, but you don't exactly look twenty anymore," she said before turning back to June. "And he's gone in an hour, so this is a rush job."

June's head dropped before he stretched it back as far as he could. "You're a terrible person."

I smiled for the first time in a day or so. I couldn't help but admire her elasticity. Ade had been put through the wringer the past twenty-four hours and turned into who she needed to be every step of the way. As much as I tried, I couldn't think of anyone I'd ever met who could adapt to the moment so well. She gave me a quick nod, and we waited for June to finish his work.

Twenty minutes later, he tossed his personal device over to me. "Sync and you're good. It will auto-withdraw a thousand."

I did as he said. "That's it?"

"Yeah, you're now Kilo Walker—sad deadbeat who only has one option left."

I brought my device to life and reviewed the changes to Kilo Walker's profile. "These are good."

"To be fair, whoever set this up for you did a lot right; they just couldn't story tell," he said with an air of pride.

"Thanks, June," Ade said, standing.

"Anything for you, Ade. But I hope I don't see you for a while."

She gave him a charming smile and left. I nodded to June, who reciprocated, and I followed her out. As I stepped through the door, a glint caught my eye from a half-covered compact box near the corner of the room. I only saw it for a moment, but the gray liquid marred in the syringe was unmistakable.

I waited until the door closed behind me before grabbing Ade. "What are you doing? You guys have replica DPMs? Where the hell did you get them?"

"I don't know," she replied, her eyes opening wide at their mention. "I only do the docs, I swear."

"What do you mean you don't know? They used to string people up in the Below for replicas, Ade . . ."

She peeled my hand from her arm. "I'm not going to do anything to put Abegail in danger. I promise."

An uneasiness in my chest grew as the cracks continued to grow in my assumptions. The Designers made it a priority to reel in replicas after Honolulu fell, and for years, they'd been rare to the point that some questioned if they still existed. But Reklov, the Company's whispers, and now some guy tucked away in a construction factory—where were these replicas coming from?

I waited for EO's touch to help me through the scare, but it never came. Instead, I took a breath. "Okay. I trust you, but you should tell June to get rid of them."

With that, she led me back through the Nāpali Construction factory and outside into the adjacent alley. We looked down the street to see a couple of cycles coming toward the factory, but Ade slid in front of me before I could signal for a ride.

"Kilo, if I go to Ludo, you need to promise me you'll come back."

"I don't know if—"

"Promise. Whatever you have to do out there, you'll come back. We might have lost Sandra, and I can't do this alone."

"I'll come back. You just get Abegail to Ludo." I wrapped my arms around her and squeezed. It was hard to tell if the lie was convincing or not, but it was the best I could do under the circumstances.

CHAPTER 15

Sirens warbled in the distance, mixed with the buzzing undertone of the Ludo district, a sound from the Below I'd long tried to forget.

Young men and women filled the streets. Unrefined groups of recruits formed outside the administration building that EO and I had visited earlier that week. A number of Continent officials beat back the potential recruits and tried their best to keep the crowds orderly. The threat of the station leader recognizing me loomed, but I didn't spot him as I approached.

I pushed my way into the crowd of anxious recruits. Above, the island city wall stood immovable. Its concrete structure encased us, an unmatched designed containment. The top of the wall bled into one of the second-level buildings far above, creating a semi-dome over our heads. Outside belonged to another world—an older world. The restless people fought for a spot on the Continent and a glimpse of escape.

"First tour? Line here." The official's words were muffled even from only a few meters away.

Between the jumbled conversations and the horns signaling each ship's departure, the circus of potential workers moved in a chaotic yet mechanical fashion, the oxymoron of the Below.

A hoard of people crowded next to the base of the Kaua'i City Wall, forming a crude single-file line. The few recruits in front of me pulled out their personal devices and hastily reviewed their deployment documents. I did the same, staring back at Kilo Walker's profile.

It felt uncomfortable to play another version of myself. There was a mixture of familiarity and disturbing appropriation. What I thought of were incomprehensible images of the cold, dreary night of my first deployment sweeping through my mind, but they were feelings rather than memories. Vertigo toiled with my brain. It was as if my cerebellum had taken over, sparing me from reliving my deployments.

These were the moments EO had been designed for all those years ago: a constant companion who could help me weather the storms in my own mind. I didn't know exactly how he would calm me if he were here, but it didn't matter. His voice was what I needed, a melody tuned specifically for me. I didn't want to do this alone.

The line crawled forward regardless, and one by one the recruits' digital credentials were inspected. Upon approval, they were directed to follow the wall into the darkness of the blockaded street beyond.

Only a handful of kids now stood between the official and me, the first hurdle in getting EO back on his feet.

"I'm sorry, uh, I have it somewhere here." The boy just in front of me fumbled through files on his personal device, looking frantically as the official's face turned sour.

"How do you expect to make it on the Continent if you can't even find your documents?"

Sweat grabbed hold of the long, curly hair along his neck. "It's right here I—"

From over his shoulder, I watched him speed-scroll past a work certification. I knew the official would let the kid through if it'd been any other document, but he wasn't going anywhere without a work cert.

"I think I saw your work cert a few files back." I pointed at the device. He glanced at me and then back at the floating screen. The items scrolled in reverse for a few seconds before I saw it.

"There it is," I said.

The kid showed the official, who waved him down the street.

"Documents?" the official asked, now glaring at me, clearly unimpressed with the help I'd given.

I didn't say anything and showed him the credentials June created for me. Maybe they were sufficient, or maybe my savior act had had an internal effect on him; either way, he waved me through.

A few poorly lit lampposts guided recruits toward the entrance to the docks. As if chained together, they hugged the wall and marched toward the unknown. I fell in line.

"Hey."

I tensed and fought back the rush of adrenaline from the unknown stimuli. The voice came from a darkened alley between two brick-exposed factory buildings. The inlet wasn't very large but provided a cloak for anyone who needed it.

"Sorry, I didn't mean to scare you. I wanted to thank you for what you did back there." The shadowy figure emerged, revealing the curly hair of the kid I'd just helped. He was tall and slender, with a bony nose and an optimistic smile. The tribal forearm tattoos and worn shoes tipped me off. He was of Ludo Below heritage, a local kid.

"No problem."

He couldn't have been older than eighteen or nineteen and didn't seem to fully grasp what he had signed up for. As I continued to follow the wall, he glided up next to me. If he'd been slightly darker, it could have been EO walking with me.

"Have you been?" he asked.

"Been where?"

"To the Continent. You seemed like you'd done the intake before."

I responded without hesitation, "No, this is my first time. I've just seen people do it."

"Nice. I can actually see people believing you."

"I'm sorry?" I responded, hoping I misunderstood the subtext.

"I can't believe you found me first. They said you were good, but that's next level."

This kid? You've gotta be kidding me!

"You're my contact?"

He nodded, his hair bouncing as he did. "I'm with the Ludo Company. This is my first assignment."

"Tell me that's not true." I slowed my speed a bit, hoping he might just walk ahead, chattering away.

"Nope. I'm supposed to help you find out what Outpost 378 is," he whispered.

My hand jetted up to his mouth, covering it forcefully. "First thing, talk less. Second thing, act like you've done this before."

He stared back at me with solemn eyes.

"Got it?" I seethed. He nodded, and I released my hand.

The boy continued to trail shortly behind me like a shamed dog until we saw the opening to the docks. The golden light grew with every meter. As we made our way through the gated doorway, the light from an orange sunrise stopped the kid in his tracks. His remorse dissipated.

"Woah," he gasped.

I could remember the feeling, if not the memory. I always thought it would've been smart to allow for more viewing areas of the outside to make the people of the Below happy, but the Designers didn't see it that way.

The sun rose over massive concrete platforms jettisoning out from the rocky beach. Several of the platforms housed ships that buoyed above the water, rivaling the size of Mid-City buildings. Trails of recruits led onto each of the boats, like ants marching under a door. The kid's astonishment didn't cease as a few more people pushed past us, heading for the closest line.

"They say each one can fit 30,000, but I heard they cram thirty-five in there," he said.

“Come on, let’s go.”

He followed me down the ramp into the snaking line that led to our ship, KI 2767. Thankfully, it didn’t take too long before we reached the entrance of the vessel. The retractable platform engulfed several people at a time into the hull of the massive, silver-plated boat.

We approached a pair of officials reviewing work certs. They waved the kid up first.

“Matagi Edden, construction specialist,” he said.

Quicker than before, the official passed him through.

“Kilo Walker, construction specialist.” The official shifted between eye contact and the work certificate.

“Little old for your first deployment?”

“I wouldn’t be here if I didn’t have to be.”

He grunted and passed me through.

The magnificence of the ship’s external features didn’t translate to its inner construction. Engineers had designed these ships for three things: carrying as many people as possible, hauling as much material from the Continent as possible, and not sinking. I knew from experience that the last one was the least concerning to the Designers. There were always more ships.

The tight corridor forced me to duck and twist slightly when crossing the thresholds that divided the main sections of the ship. They dragged on, stretching the length of the stern to the bow, making it a portable version of an island city. Once I reached Section C, I grabbed a seat among the sea of metal chairs that were bolted crudely to the floor. It was packed with recruits, shoulder to shoulder, under the rusty linings of the hull. An accurate first impression of the Continent.

The young eyes in the room gravitated in my direction and inspected me the same way June had. But soon, the recruits’ wide eyes nervously swept the hull. The excitement that had consumed the registration line had now clearly turned to a combination of anxiety and panic. The Continent’s ships had a way of doing that to people, especially tour-ones.

How the hell am I supposed to fit in? I scanned the room, looking for an answer. Among the crowd of heads, I saw thick, curly hair bouncing toward the starboard side. *Fine.* I stood up and followed Matagi to a seat almost touching the interior wall of the ship. Matagi welcomed me with a wide smile.

I sat with him throughout the thirteen-hour trip until we reached the Continent. He told me several stories about his family, their fall from Mid-City to the Below a couple of generations back, and his decision to sign up for the Continent. It was a shame he didn't understand the gravity of working a tour on the Continent, although he tried to convince me he did.

I didn't have the heart to tell him what life on the Continent could do to a person, compounded by the pressure of working for the Company. He was genuinely excited for the Continent, almost as if he wasn't here for the Company at all, but just as a kid getting a fresh start. I knew if EO had been there, he would've tried to convince me of the resemblance.

With no windows in the interior of the behemoth transport, we only realized our arrival after the metal exterior screeched against something immovable outside, jolting everyone in the hull. I checked my personal device, which confirmed the right amount of time had passed for us to make landfall. An intercom came to life with the crackling voice of an official welcoming us to the Continent.

"Each recruit will report to their command post based on the following sections: Section A: Post thirteen, Section B: Post fifty-six . . ." I tuned out the rest of the announcement, already knowing we were heading to Outpost 101.

Everyone from Section C filed pensively through the corridors until we were ushered to the platform, the sealed exit just ahead. The wondering, laughing, and smiling faces had turned stiff. During your first tour, everything was an exciting prospect until you crossed the final threshold.

This time, the officials wore full tox suits, which insulated them from the Carbon Sytride air on the Continent. The thick, mustard-green, poly-fabric suits covered everything except the tox masks firmly fitted in the small hole of the suit. The officials handed each of the recruits less impressive, basic face masks before pushing them through the seal toward the barren wasteland. But no suits.

It had been their suits that had shocked me on my first tour. The ships, the travel, and the barren desert all made some sense to me, but the suits made me realize this was something entirely different. The oblong shape and the tox mask, with its breathing hose wrapped around the back, and only the small eye slits making the human inside visible, haunted me for months. It was a helpless feeling, looking at someone in a tox suit for the first time, wondering exactly what was happening. Years later, being the one in a suit, watching kids try them on for the first time, stayed with me.

Matagi grabbed his mask and secured it tightly, as instructed. It saddened me watching him, knowing the only reason we weren't offered tox suits was because it was a logistical nightmare. Officials could fill the ship with suits, but they'd lose a quarter of their labor per voyage. The suits could alternatively be delivered to the port from outposts scattered around the Continent. However, that would double the amount of transports needed. I could only guess some Designer made the call that people's lives didn't outweigh the resources needed to keep them safe.

Instead, recruits ended up losing more years of their life expectancy on average during the time they stepped off the ship, to when they got to the outpost, than any other single activity during their tour. Since that wasn't widespread knowledge, I wasn't about to show my hand by asking for a tox suit. I secured the mask around my chin and nose and exited through the seal.

We huddled together in our sections, creating small pockets of people among the sea of recruits. Once outside the docks, everyone stood along unpaved paths worn into hard-packed dirt roads. Mid-Sized Continent Vehicles loaded 200 to 300 recruits at a time before speeding away. Each MCV seemed to head in the same direction, then veer to its unique path near the end of our eyeline.

"Section C, this is you," a security official shouted through his tox mask, waving at the MCV for those who couldn't hear. Slung around his back was an AAP 445 assault rifle, something with which I was all too familiar.

I tried to see through his mask, but the hazy visor obstructed his face. Even so, I knew underneath was someone who would shoot any of us if he needed to. It wasn't until I joined the Security Forces that I realized their job was twofold: Protect the territory from the other island cities, and protect it from us.

Hundreds of the Section C recruits pushed toward the vehicle that pulled up. I followed Matagi as he slunk through the crowd, making it to the front where we boarded. Walking up a short staircase past the two-meter-high, all-terrain tires led us into a spacious, but soon-to-be cramped, transport cabin.

"Stand here," I said, positioning myself near the front of the transport. "It'll get crazy once everyone tries to get off."

Matagi nodded. He stood quietly, watching people funnel into the area, eventually cramming us against the wall. Matagi's eyes widened, and he flinched each time another recruit pushed him closer to the wall. Maybe the masks affected him the way they had me, or maybe he'd begun to feel the weight of it all; regardless, his face betrayed his mounting fear and uncertainty.

"Hey, I heard the food isn't too bad at the outposts," I whispered in his ear. It was a lie, but if he'd spent the last nineteen years in Ludo, it wouldn't be much of a step down.

"Yeah? I could tear through some Nāpali eggs right now."

A smile broke through on my face. "I don't know if they have Nāpali eggs, but I'm sure they'll feed us once we get there."

The MCV roared out of its idle and lurched forward, throwing everyone in the cabin backward. Thankfully, the section we'd taken up had thin windows lining its sides. I didn't know whether I could take another hour or two in a metal vault.

After a while, the road outside disappeared, and we switched to a rougher path. It wasn't long before the white specks of light in the distance grew larger.

The recruits in the MCV buzzed with nerves and excitement. Twenty or thirty dome-shaped buildings connected by narrow corridors passed by as the MCV circled around to the loading bay.

As soon as we stopped, security officials loaded us off the transport. Many of the restless kids pushed their way toward the door, trying to get priority for the next step in onboarding.

I led Matagi out after most of the recruits had already exited. Some of his lightheartedness returned upon arrival as he patted me on the back in anticipation, bouncing with each step. Outpost officials wearing tox suits guided people one by one to the decontamination lock.

"Once inside, have your work certs ready, and you'll be directed to your building assignment." The outpost official repeated that phrase every minute or so as new batches of recruits passed him by. I made out a bit of the strained undertone in his voice, but much like the other officials, it was barely comprehensible through the tox mask.

As I entered the large metal-framed doorway of the decontamination lock, several spigots on each side spurted a clear liquid violently toward each other, creating a torso-level crossfire. A few of the recruits ahead lost their balance once they entered, but I was ready, planting my left foot slightly ahead of my right before the chemical attack initiated. Matagi followed, imitating the foot placement I'd taken, and maintained his posture. Just barely.

Once inside, we both continued to follow the flow of people into the Rotunda of the primary section of the outpost. Outpost officials waited dressed in their traditional Continent uniforms, flanked by security officials who guided recruits toward the different hallways that jetted out, connecting the other outpost buildings.

The outpost officials' suits looked much like the officials I'd encountered at the Ludo Recruitment Office, sporting medallions and badges detailing their service outside the island cities. A frail foundation of authority. The security officials didn't suffer from the same issue. Their bastardized version of the Night Sticks' uniforms drew the eyes of the new recruits. If they didn't understand before, they did now.

"Work cert?" an outpost official asked robotically.

"Kilo Walker, construction," I said, and showed him the digital file.

The man stared at my photo, short list of qualifications, and job tasks before looking up again. "You'll be with me, building A4. Follow the hallways this way until you reach the last building; A4 dormitories are there." He pointed over my shoulder to a relatively empty hallway that led into another of the domed buildings.

I sidestepped, waiting to see where Matagi would be assigned.

"A3. You can follow him, but you'll be the building before."

Matagi thanked the official and hurried over toward me.

"You all right?" I asked.

He gave an excited nod that was too quick to be genuine. A minute later, we passed through the first domed section of the outpost. It looked similar to the outpost compounds I'd been stationed at a decade ago, tall arching walls with mazes of rooms, offices, and work areas branching off from the large corridor that cut straight through its center.

"Are they all like this?"

"Mostly. Not what you expected?" I asked.

"I guess I shouldn't have expected anything. It's so . . . mechanical."

I sneered. EO always said the outposts on the Continents were full of robotic people driving robotic cattle. The first time he said it, he had to explain what cattle were, but once I understood, it was hard to argue.

"Just keep your head down and do your job. I'll find you if I need anything."

He nodded but remained quiet until we said our goodbyes at building A3. It wasn't too much further to A4, and I knew what to expect by the time I reached it. The buildings were identical. At least with some of the other outposts, construction changed from building to building, but these were copied and pasted.

In the dormitory, thirty bunks on each side of the room were stacked four tall, with a narrow walkway in between. Thin sheets and wool blankets rested atop the uninviting single mattresses.

How generous, I thought as I picked up one of the pillows to find a second underneath. I climbed to the top bunks and selected one near the back of the room. I figured it was as good a place as any to lie low while at the outpost.

As I settled, an ear-splitting crack sounded from the entrance. I instinctively reached for the Nambu that was no longer there before turning to see the outpost official who had checked us in standing by the doorway.

"Welcome to the Continent. Your shift starts tomorrow at eight a.m. Since this is everyone's first time to the Continent, we'll be taking you to the Amazon Gorge."

Shit.

"You can collect your suits before deployment to the site tomorrow. If you have any questions, you'll find out tomorrow. Personal devices stay at the outpost. Don't be late."

Once he was out of sight, the chatter among the recruits erupted. *What's the Amazon Gorge? Are we digging with shovels? Why didn't we have suits today?*

I tried to tune it all out. It was time to focus. I had one goal. I peered down at my PD, pulling up the skeleton file on Outpost 378. Get to 378 and find out what was going on. Get EO back. That was it.

CHAPTER 16

The MCV screeched to a stop, and the violent shaking of the Continent Road ceased. Yet the incessant shifting of the recruits in their tox suits only worsened. Throughout the two-hour journey, I had also fidgeted in the thick synthetic tox suit, even complaining to a few of the recruits nearby. But my "tox suit dancing" was all for show.

Unlike most of the people in the MCV, I had developed a tolerance to the sticky, skin-pulling suits long ago. But if Kilo Walker's skin would have crawled in the suits, mine needed to as well.

The vacuum pressure released from the doors before they opened to reveal the outer lands of the Continent—more desolate remains of the earth that we'd been welcomed to the day before. I stepped out onto the solid, scarred surface and remembered the toughness of the earth in these parts.

In school, everyone in the island cities learned about the death of the Old World and the transformation of a once vibrant and alive planet into a stone-cold rock. A place where every living creature fought for survival, but you didn't really understand until you saw it with your own eyes.

I rounded the transport vehicle, where a clump of recruits blocked my path. Pushing my way through, the cause for the unexpected break in protocol soon grew visible past the motionless kids. A wide ravine curled down below, snaking east toward the far side of the Continent beyond the range of human sight. Next to our feet, small snow drifts plunged over the canyon wall into the hundred-meter-deep Amazon Gorge.

For many, the mechanical contraptions that lined each of its enormous sides, penetrating the earth like metal spiders drilling for the most valuable resources available, were equally as impressive. Mustard-green tox suits and the colossal drilling machines littered the base of the gorge, creating a yellow-stringed tapestry of labor.

"All right. Thirty in the elevators at a time. Keep it moving." The outpost official assigned to our workforce was the same man who'd used a shovel as an attention-getter. He pushed workers into the elevator before slamming the black button to the side of the contraption and sending those inside plummeting down.

"Let's go, Walker. You're in on this one!"

I squeezed into the elevator, failing to secure my footing before the doors shut, and I slipped as gravity suspended. We barreled downward, this morning's meager bread and oats fighting to escape from my stomach. To my relief, the elevator slowed to a stop at the base of the gorge, and the doors opened to the wild commotion of recruits being sent in ten different directions to their work sites.

Makeshift walkways crisscrossed along the kilometer-wide base leading to workstations, medical tents, and, most importantly, the drilling machines. Although I'd come across all sorts of drilling machines during my tours on the Continent, the feeling of awe that arose in me upon seeing these behemoths was genuine.

"Workers from Outpost 101, you're on the south side today. Make your way to Drill Five for a briefing on the next month of your life," an official yelled, perched above the ocean of recruits.

Without question, the group of us who'd traveled down the elevator together headed toward the south side of the gorge, eventually ending up underneath one of the spider-like drills. Here, there was no tent or building for recruits to take shelter in during the briefing, just the howling winds rushing over the curvature of the gorge and direct exposure to Carbon Sytride.

Two men in slightly discolored tox suits (that now seemed more straight mustard than mustard-green) talked between themselves atop a wooden platform, preparing for their introduction. On the far side of the platform, two security officials lurked, poised to unleash hell on any threat to operations.

"Outpost 101, we're glad you are here on the Continent helping to fulfill the Designs of the island cities. Each of you is vital to the continued survival of the human race for millennia to come." The speaker leaned over to the other mustard-suited man, speaking indistinctly before straightening up. "Now that I've read the official welcome from the Designers, I am going to tell you how things work here."

I wondered how this info brief would deviate from the twenty or thirty I'd heard before or even the few I'd given. It was the statement on the percentage of Carbon Sytride transference through the tox suits that gave away where your loyalties lay.

In the island cities, they told us the Carbon Sytride transference percentage was 0.5 percent, meaning that your lifespan was shortened by five months for every month spent on the Continent. As I'd learned after spending several years here, and later, after joining the Security Forces, it was more like 1.25 percent, or six months of your life for every month exposed.

"Our goal here for the next month is to withdraw as much composite metal as possible. You all know what composite metal is used for, so it should be clear how valuable it is to Kaua'i City for maintaining and growing its infrastructure. The tox suits we are wearing are the safest possible design and only allow for 0.4 percent transference of Carbon Sytride, meaning you're trading only a fraction of your life for the greater well-being of Kaua'i City."

Designer shill. No wonder he's got two security guys. No one claimed below 0.5 percent unless they really wanted to impress someone.

"Since all of you have been selected for this posting based on your various construction and specialty backgrounds, you'll be well suited to working on the structures that support the drills. Your immediate supervisors will provide you with specifics on the areas where you will be working and will answer any questions you may have."

The mustard-suited man gestured to the synthetic concrete scaffolding. It wrapped around the drill like a milky web that cradled the engine, while its arms split through and attached to the gorge wall. With my moderate construction knowledge, I knew what the scaffolding did for the drill, and so did my alias, so I didn't need to act the part of a tour-one.

"Lastly, I need to reiterate one thing. *Do not,* under any circumstances, remove your tox suit outside of your outpost buildings. If you do, you will lose three months of your life every sixty seconds."

Muttered chatter grew among the crowd of neophytes, stunned by the transparent warning. EO said Carbon Sytride was the world's poison; everyone knew about it but didn't truly understand.

"To work!"

These were the last words offered before we ascended the jagged staircases that led partway up the gorge wall to our work section on the scaffold. The winds intensified as we climbed, forcing each of us against the side of the stairs, grasping the railing. From the ground, security officials watched with AAP 445s at the ready.

Once we reached the top, several men presented us with hefty work bags full of tools and raw materials, then pointed us to our section. Along with three other workers, I climbed across a metal beam thirty meters above the ground to an elbow in the scaffold. The frigid air and snow from the drifts blew down around us as a man lit up a blowtorch.

"I can start replacing the grafting inside the elbow if I can get someone to help with the extraction," he said.

It took a few moments to understand what the man was talking about. Apparently, we'd been tasked with replacing some of the metal inside the structure, which had cracked from the powerful movements of the drill.

I pushed through the tools in the bag until I found a clamp.

"I'll help you," I wheezed through the tox mask.

"Good. Now you two need to solder the edges of the pieces they gave us so we can replace it once it's out."

The other two men searched through the bag and pulled out square metal sheets, each about half a square meter in size. They followed the instructions and used a smaller blowtorch to melt away the edges of the metal.

As if he'd done it a hundred times, the man directing us cracked open a pre-cut slab of the mix-concrete exterior. Inside, I saw the complex structure that the scaffold was built with, a hybrid of synthetic metals, plastics, and other materials I didn't recognize. He felt around the welds with his hands before applying the fire of the blowtorch. Looking at the crude connections between materials, it was hard to believe these were some of the strongest bonds ever created. It baffled my mind to think anything could crack them.

"You been out here before?" I asked genuinely, as if I didn't know the answer.

"Third tour. Your first, right?"

"Yeah, but I'm sure it won't be my last."

He squinted through his tox mask, examining my face.

"You look a little older than most tour-ones."

"Long story," I said. "Had a brother that came over here, though, so I felt more prepared than most."

My best guess was the other two guys were actually tour-ones. Subtle mannerisms, like looking out into the gorge and fogging inside their tox masks, showed their novice status. The tour-three was the one I needed to question.

The first shift lasted six hours before the officials recalled us for food, a toilet break, and medical attention. Inside the dining hall, which looked more like a school cafeteria, hundreds of recruits sat mostly quiet after their first real experience on the Continent. I could almost see their thoughts—the dread mounting before their next shift.

I tried to connect with my crew and learn their names. Ben and Mataio from Ludo were, in fact, tour-ones. Their stories might have been interesting at another time, but Solomon was my focus right now; it only made sense to focus on developing a relationship with someone who'd been here. He was from Nāpali, which would have been an easy way to connect if I wasn't Kilo Walker. I needed to try my luck, anyway.

"How many tours you plan on serving?"

"As many as I need to," Solomon replied with a full mouth and eyes focused on his food.

"Any advice?" I asked.

"Don't get married."

Ben and Mataio laughed, and I forced out a chuckle. It would have been nice to have EO here reading Solomon's facial expressions and seeing if there was any crack that could lead to a connection.

"Yeah, I tried that. Good advice," I said.

Walker's profile alluded to him having been married at one point, so leaning into it might not be a bad strategy.

I continued, "I said it was a long story why I'm older than most tour-ones, but I guess it's not that long. I need the money."

"You got that shit right. Ben and Mataio, you two don't want to end up like us." Solomon jabbed a finger at himself and then in my direction.

"You know of any transfers that could make some good money quick?" I asked.

"Obviously not. I'm working with you three."

"My brother told me there are some new projects in the Ludo/Nāpali zones. You guys heard anything about that?" I directed the question at Ben and Mataio. They both shook their heads. I looked over to Solomon, my gaze questioning.

"Rumors around the outpost say officials recruit a handful of people selected for special work each tour, but I'm not sure how real it is."

"What do you mean by 'selected'?" Mataio chimed in, doing the work for me.

"Well, on my second tour, two guys in my group were convinced they could get selected to work on a special project. Some veteran recruit told 'em if they made a splash, they could get assigned to a special project at some other outpost. Small pay increase, but more importantly, connections that could help back in the island cities."

"That sounds like exactly what I need," Ben said.

"What happened?" I asked.

"I don't know. They told me they were going to speak with their outpost official at the end of the tour, but I didn't see them on the transport back to Kaua'i City."

The tour-ones sat quietly, finishing their food and staring aimlessly at the mush in their bowls, clearly more concerned with what a "special project" might mean.

"How do you get to be one of those? I'm sure they don't eat this slop," Ben groused, watching the food drip off his spoon.

In each corner of the mess hall, security officials guarded the doors. They seemed relaxed. Their gloved hands gently gripped their rifles, and their masked faces swiveled, surveying, but I knew that no matter how calm they presented, any perceived threat to Kaua'i City would trigger a vicious response.

Without thinking, I responded, "They eat the same shit."

Several pairs of eyes turned to me, and Solomon asked, "How do you know that?"

Idiot. Walker wouldn't have known that. "It's what I heard from a friend who served as a security official."

"Shit, you know someone who made it into security?" Mataio asked.

I nodded and tried to focus on the inevitable questions. To keep my cover intact, Walker could know some things about the Security Forces, but too much would seem suspicious. *Get ahead of it.*

Just as Ben opened his mouth, I spoke. "He said it was hell. Got offered the post after a few tours on the Continent and joined up. When he made it back, he told me at first it was exciting, powerful, but then he realized it was something else altogether. Once these guys finish a couple of tours guarding work sites, they go to the border outposts. They turn us from security guards to mercenaries. They try to break us any way they can."

"Us?" Ben asked.

"Us?" I repeated, confused. Then my mind caught up with my slip of words. "I mean, that's how he told it."

"Sounds rough," Mataio said, turning to look at the security officials. However, his wide eyes told a different story.

"My friend told me if they ever ask you to join, leave. Leave the Continent and don't come back."

"Would you do it, Walker, leave if they asked?" Ben probed.

The photo of Mo and I in my old room at Bless' came to life. The ruckus of a few new security recruits reveling in the joy of their first successful mission with dirt and blood covering their suits. I watched myself take the picture, smiling, arms around Mo and another recruit whose name I couldn't remember. Once the group broke, the smile faded from my face. Although I couldn't see him, I felt the warm presence of EO standing just behind me.

What a fool I'd been—searching to fill the emptiness inside with power and domination, but all it had ever brought me was hurt and regret. The cold crept up my fingers, and my hand forced itself around the AAP 445. It had been a descent into exactly what EO had believed: We'd become cruel, unforgiving, selfish people who craved the feeling of power. A soft warmth battled with my frostbitten hand. I allowed it to consume me and relieve the pressure in my fingers. So many years of growing emptiness and not acknowledging the dark pain ripping through my flesh and organs until it consumed everything.

"I'd run until my feet bled," I said, snapping from my reverie.

The table fell quiet. Thankfully, it wasn't much longer before a raspy voice informed us over an overpowered intercom that it was time for med checks.

Med officials seemed to speed-run the checks, almost as if they weren't looking for anything. That was good. If they'd done a full tox screen, I would have had to answer some awkward questions about my body's level of exposure to Carbon Sytride. After a few minutes, our team was released and sent back to the scaffold.

A few more hours passed as we made slow progress on the replacements. Solomon was deliberate in his grafting, which often left Ben and Mataio waiting with freshly soldered sheets of metal. After the mid-shift break, the drill powered up for a few minutes, shaking the entire scaffolding and sending debris falling around us from the gorge wall. That danger must have accounted for part of the 10 percent acceptable casualties written in the Century Island Cities Agreement.

I couldn't help but wonder whether the living Designers had even been to the Continent, let alone stepped foot on a work site. I couldn't recall ever hearing of one coming during the eight years I'd toured here.

They were the Designers, after all. Their hands didn't get dirty. They just created the plan and allowed others to execute it, even if it meant a rock fell on someone's head from thirty meters above. The materials inside the earth were worth it.

Stop getting distracted! Stop wasting time! You're here to do a job! I scolded myself inwardly.

"What's our Section Supervisor like?" I practically screamed the words through the tox mask so Solomon could hear them over the blowtorch.

Solomon paused for a second before resuming. "Pretty much a son of a bitch. He lives for the Continent and wants everyone who works for him to feel the same."

"Jesus."

"Yeah. This is supposedly his twelfth tour."

"Holy shit, twelve?" Mataio yelled from behind us.

My brow furrowed, creating a fake, astonished expression in case Solomon looked through my tox mask. I'd served seven-fold that over eight years. The guys who weren't even in the teens had done our shit work.

"So, I guess we just need to show some enthusiasm to get on his good side," I said.

"He's fucking crazy. He likes it when people get hurt here. Says it's proof they would do anything for the Design."

Get hurt, huh? That wouldn't be too hard in this Death Valley.

The work continued. Every hour, or so it seemed, the drill activated for a few minutes. Other workers crawled around on the part of the drill that looked like the spider's head. Mechanical engineers.

I guessed they were testing it. Maybe it malfunctioned, or part of the drill broke, and they could only turn it on for minutes at a time for diagnostics. Either way, I didn't envy them. Although I never worked directly with the drills during my other tours, I knew engineers often caught the heat if materials production failed to meet expectations.

The sight of the engineers triggered something in me. Those atop the drill slowly faded into dust, the haunting memory canopying around me in a cloud of ash and dirt.

A quick jerk from EO caught my attention from the other side of the exit threshold.

"There's someone else here."

Among the wreckage of the drill's control room, EO pointed to a conspicuous panel beneath the primary control station. I opened it, my short-barreled AAP 445 crunched tight against my ribcage, and my finger locked against the trigger.

As the door swung open, a woman fell out, desperately grasping at a handful of personal devices that skidded across the floor.

"Hands!" I yelled through the tox mask.

The stocky woman froze. Underneath the thick engineering tox suit, her hands shook. And behind the mask, she stared back at me, wild-eyed. I caught her looking at one of the devices that had activated in the commotion.

"Please, I'm just an engineer." The woman's panicked words cut through, muffled by her tox mask.

"Shipley, I have a situation in the control room." I released the pressure from my fingers against my forearm and waited for Shipley's voice to crackle back through my PD.

"They're going to kill me," she whispered.

I took my finger off the trigger and lowered my weapon slightly. "No, it doesn't matter where you're from. We don't kill unarmed engineers."

Behind us, the door cracked open. Shipley only took two steps before he saw it—the open personal device showing rotating plans for every projected outpost in the Kaua'i territory. In a moment, his face turned sour, and his nose snarled up. He unsheathed his knife and rushed toward the woman.

"What the fuck!" I jumped toward him, just barely wrapping my arms around his shoulders and pulling him away from the woman as she covered her face and cowered. EO watched as my world shifted, then shattered. The work I had been doing for the better part of four years changed in an instant.

"Shoot her." Shipley's bony finger scratched through the Carbon Sytride-filled air toward the woman.

"No. She's unarmed. She's an engineer, not Maui Security."

"I don't care. Every person who came within a hundred meters of this drill killed themselves when they found those."

"What are you talking—"

"Do what you're told. You signed up to protect everyone in Kaua'i City, and you will do what it takes."

"No, I'm not going to shoot a—"

Shipley raised his weapon level to my chest. "Shoot her!"

"Kilo, what the hell?" Solomon shouted. "I'm about to lose my hand here; you wanna do your job?"

I snapped back to reality just as the blowtorch reached Solomon's pinky finger.

"Sorry." I firmed my grip on the sheet of metal and rotated it, allowing Solomon to redirect the torch away from his finger and complete the solder.

"You guys all right?" either Ben or Mataio shouted.

"We're good. Kilo just needs to stay focused," Solomon said, melding the replacement metal with the internal structure of the scaffolding. "I think we're done for the day. Ben, you can keep that sheet for tomorrow."

I handed the sheet of metal back to Ben, and after some cleanup, we made for the stairs.

On the way down, I thought about how close I'd come to cutting off Solomon's fingers and what he'd said earlier about our supervising official. *Maybe an injury could curry some favor?*

Lines of workers shuffled across the gorge toward the elevators on the far side, passing the hordes of incoming workers reporting for the next shift. Looking at their broken, weary faces, I could only imagine what they'd done to earn themselves the night shift. The elevators took us back to the top of the gorge, where officials loaded us onto the transport vehicles.

All the while, I couldn't stop thinking about how our official might respond to a minor injury while I was working on the scaffolding. It needed to be something to make him feel as though I was a prospective worker who didn't mind making sacrifices for the Design, but it couldn't be an injury that landed me in a med tent indefinitely. The gashes left in the earth's crust by machines passed by as I puzzled over the question. Out of nowhere, a sharp pain shot up my arm. I looked down to see the razored edge of a tox mask rim piercing into my forearm. The recruit was totally oblivious. The point of his mask had slid out easily, leaving only a small cut, but a thin line of blood ran down to my fingers and then dripped onto the floor. Thankfully, my tox suit was wrapped around my waist, so I wouldn't need to go to an outpost official for a new one.

A hole! I flexed my arm to feel the healed bullet wound from the cycle chase back in Kaua'i City. Open wounds, like bullet holes or deep gashes, were easily fixed with medical suture technology. What would be even easier, though, was a blowtorch hole through the hand.

If I could create an accident whereby my hand ended up getting hit by the torch, that could be enough to get recognized by the official. Even better if I orchestrated it to save Solomon from harm. The official would fucking love me.

CHAPTER 17

There was still no hole in my hand two days after my introduction to the Amazon Gorge work site, and my eagerness to make something happen grew with each passing hour. Although the officials had charged our site team with replacing the same set of metal pieces inside the drill scaffolding, it proved difficult to find an organic way to insert myself into the replacement process during dangerous steps.

Sure, I could just accidentally bump into Solomon and then artificially create a situation where someone might get hurt, but I couldn't risk being the villain of an accident. I needed to be the hero. What I needed was a spit amplifier.

The food on my plate, much like the momentum of my plan, sat stale. Bread and oats had been the winning dish over the past couple of days, making me that much more of a liar when I tried to comfort Matagi with the prospect of decent food. Normally, some banter with EO would've made it more digestible, but I tried not to think about him. Too many issues back in Kaua'i City needed to be solved. Spiraling out about EO and some dry bread wouldn't help.

The only positive during our disappointing dinners was the opportunity to watch the officials. After two days, I knew their preparation routines down to the minute. Although I'd spent years around them as they navigated the logistical nightmare of coordinating equipment to and from the work sites, I'd never paid much attention to how they did it. The tox suits, tools, medical supplies, and anything else we ever needed just appeared on demand.

Now that I was watching, patterns of preparation emerged. Tox suits had to go through a decontamination process every night. Two officials from each section of the outpost collected the suits and took them to an adjoining room to the Rotunda, where they were put into some kind of decontamination machine. After a few minutes, they were taken out and placed in supply boxes near the exit of the outpost.

There was only one problem. All worksite items seemed to be loaded based on their perceived importance by the officials, or maybe the Designers. Officials organized each set of supply boxes in the order they would be loaded, and clearly the tox suits were the most closely guarded. Each time an official filled a box with clean tox suits, at least a few others stood by watching. Made sense, but this process helped me ascertain how to get something onto the transport vehicles.

I considered using medical equipment to hold the spit amplifier, but such equipment was replenished, sterilized, and then loaded first. Since it was the least important, it would be unloaded last from the MCV, and I'd already be halfway to the scaffold by that point.

Tools were also a nonstarter. There was no way to know if the spit amplifier would end up in our tool bag, and a one in 2,000 chance wouldn't cut it. Tox suits remained the only possibility. It was still early in the evening, so the officials had only recently finished the decontamination process and were taking inventory of the tools that would be used during the next shift.

I didn't have a brilliant plan yet, but one was formulating. I just needed to eat slowly and keep an eye on how fast the inventory went. Fortunately, that wouldn't be hard, seeing as eating anything here was as close as you could get to choking yourself.

"Kilo. Hey, I've been trying to find you for the past couple of days." The voice came from behind me, before someone lifted their leg over the cafeteria table bench and sat down next to me. The Rotunda dining hall droned with murmurs from the hungry recruits, but my mind had lingered elsewhere until now.

"I've mostly been in my sector trying to get some sleep," I said, eyeing Matagi. "Guys, this is Matagi. We met during recruitment."

Ben and Mataio nodded from across the table at him before turning back to their food.

"Where you from, Matagi?" Solomon's voice carried as he leaned over the table to get a look at Matagi.

"Ludo. How 'bout you guys?"

"I'm from Nāpali. Ben and Mataio are from Ludo."

"Nice to meet you all. Where are you from in—"

"How have your shifts been so far?" I cut off Matagi, ensuring the conversation didn't turn into a deep exploration of everyone's origins.

"They've been good. Took me some time to get accustomed to it, but I think I'm finding my groove."

"What team are you working with?" Solomon asked.

"I'm on the north side of the gorge, working with drill two."

"Isn't that the only one functioning on the north wall?"

I didn't hear Matagi's answer. My attention drew back to the officials on the far side of the room, shutting boxes. *Shit.* The window was closing if I wanted to get some time with one of the toolboxes.

Before I could even think about how to get something into a tox suit, I needed to get my hands on an amplifier. I could wait until tomorrow and maybe get a better window, but there was no guarantee I'd ever get a good look.

"Matagi, come with me for a second. I need your help with something."

The kid looked through his bulky fringe with a frown pulling at his lips. "Can I eat first?"

"I'll give you what's left of mine if you come."

The lines of distress on his face softened. "You guys can watch my food?"

The other three chimed in with a muffled yes. Matagi followed as I made my way through the checkerboard of tables toward the outpost exit. A few steps before we reached the piles of boxes, I clued him in on the plan.

"I just need to ask her a question. Follow my lead."

He opened his mouth to speak, but before he could ask me anything, I shouted at one of the outpost officials standing over the toolbox.

"Hey, we were promised a relocation this week out of the gorge, but I was just told our assignments were extended. What the hell?"

A flash of surprise covered the woman's face before she regained her equilibrium. "I'm not the right person to talk to. Go see your sector supervisor."

"Sector supervisor. Section official. Site official. Team leader. How many people do I have to talk to for a transfer? Anyway, we aren't even in the same sector."

"Well then, go talk to each of your sector supervisors individually."

"I want to talk to you. They don't care what happens to us out there."

"Look, you are recruits. You do what you're told. If they change their minds, it's up to them. Now go back to your table."

The woman's face pulled into a shape I'd become all too familiar with from EO. A long face mixed with furrowed eyebrows—the sweet spot of frustration and fatigue from dealing with me.

"Matagi, tell her what you said about wanting to work at different sites. Who knows how many tours you'll serve, and you deserve a chance to help the cause all over the Continent before you're shipped back."

The woman shifted slightly, glancing over at Matagi as he stared back at me, confused.

"Well?" she asked.

"I did say that to him, but I'm not sure I need to work other places. The gorge has been great." He stumbled across his words a bit before finding his pace. "I actually really like working in the Amazon Gorge. It's amazing. The amount of material we extract daily makes me feel like I'm literally helping the Designers build Kaua'i City."

There he was: the hard-to-hate chatterbox who'd consumed our trip from Kaua'i City to the Continent only a couple days prior. The official rolled her eyes as Matagi took her on a roller coaster ride of excitement and passion.

I stole a look at the open box that sat next to the official and me. Inside, a myriad of tools were lazily stacked on top of each other. A second or two was all I needed to confirm what I hoped was in the box: a spit amplifier. I'd only seen one used a few times, but enough to know what the small hexagonal tool could do to a blowtorch.

Matagi continued, trying to please the glowering official. I pulled out my personal device and dropped it to the floor conspicuously. The official glanced at me, her cheekbones bulging, courtesy of her clenched jaw.

"Sorry. I'm going to show you the confirmation I got from my supervisor," I said. As I bent down, the woman focused her attention back on Matagi. Lifting slowly off the ground, my head stayed bent, looking forward, and I felt around in the box for the small piece of metal. Sharp edges of other tools passed through my grip before I registered a hexagonal shape between my fingers.

"What are you doing?" The official stared straight at me.

Pulling up quickly, I showed her my personal device clenched between my palm and fingers, extending out of my hand like a pen. "I lost my balance."

"Okay, that's enough. I'm done listening to you both. Either you go sit down now, or I'll sit you down myself." She motioned over to the nearest security official. "You need to know your place on the Continent. Now leave, or he will make you."

"We'll find a section supervisor," I said. I grabbed Matagi's arm and pulled him away.

Halfway back to our table, I checked over my shoulder to ensure the situation had diffused. When we finally sat back down, I peered over a final time to see the growl had disappeared from the official's face.

Only Ben remained with our food, sitting leisurely over an empty plate. "I made sure no one ate your food, but not without some effort."

We both nodded as he stood up and started toward the Section A corridor.

"What was all that about?" Matagi asked.

"Sorry, didn't have time to tell you. There are special project recruitments that take place each tour. I need to find a way to get picked, and something I needed was inside that box."

"What?"

I readjusted my fingers under the table. Behind the personal device, a small hexagonal piece of metal rolled around in my hand. He squinted his eyes to get a better look at the spit amplifier.

"Don't worry about it. I have a plan," I said.

It was true. I'd almost figured it out, but getting the amplifier into my specific tox suit remained a bit of an issue.

"Meet me out here at 1:30 a.m. I might need your help again."

He nodded. I pushed my half-finished plate over to him. Without another word, I stood and headed back to the dormitory.

A blanket of darkness descended on Outpost 101. I stared at the stains on the ceiling while my mind puzzled over the questions of Outpost 378. My body begged for the pink pills I'd left behind in Kaua'i City to fall asleep and leave this all behind for a time, but I knew I didn't have that luxury. The clock on my personal device ticked over to 1:30 a.m. *It's time.*

After dinner, I'd gone straight to the dormitories and played around on my personal device, trying to find anything on Outpost 378 we might have missed. After a couple fruitless hours, I shifted my attention to thinking how to get the spit amplifier into my specific tox suit. It would've been easier if we could take our personal devices along—maybe create some trickery with the spit amplifier—but the officials had ruled that out a few days ago.

My mind drifted away from the challenges, shifting to what the security officials would do if they caught me. During my time in the security services, the officials had hammered into us that monitoring our workers was just as important as overseeing the Continental borders. "Monitoring" ended up being a lot more brutal than I'd ever imagined.

I tried to forget the jobs we'd done here, the pain we'd caused people like Matagi, but being back made that impossible. The blood we'd spilled manifested itself in the stains on the ceiling above me. *You're not a murderer. You're not a murderer. You're trying to save people.*

My forearm seized up, and the muscles in my arm pulled inward. The darkness of the dormitory fought to overpower my vision. *EO, help me!* I pleaded in my mind, but no one came. *I'm sorry! I'm so sorry!* I fought back against the episode and focused every ounce of energy on slowing my breathing. Deep breaths, followed by long exhales, deflating my chest.

Soon, the black in my periphery faded, and the muscles in my arms loosened. I tried to picture EO sitting next to me, his arms around my shoulders. But he wasn't here, and all because of me. I was in control of my body, and he was at my mercy. I didn't even deserve to imagine him.

I tried to calm my mind, picturing myself sitting on a black box in a black room, my tranquil silhouette the only image I allowed in my mind. My heartbeat slowed, and I managed to redirect my thoughts to the tox suits and the spit amplifier. Most of the memories flowed away, with only a specific collection of integral remnants left behind.

You can do this—focus.

Despite my lack of control over the transport vehicle loading, my most valuable asset remained: experience. Outpost 101 was different from others, but each of the outposts shared a few intrinsic structural and procedural qualities. The gears turned in my mind. There might be a better way to get the spit amplifier into a tox suit, and if so, I knew where to find it.

I slid off the blanket and crawled to the outside of the bunk and down the ladder. Once outside the snore-filled room, dim lights illuminated the corridor that led back to the Rotunda. There wasn't much movement in any of the A Sections, only a few outpost officials passed out in lounges, and some night staff prepping meals or laundry for the morning. I crept by unnoticed.

At the end of the A corridor, the Rotunda, which had been swamped with hungry workers a few hours ago, now stood deserted. The absence of hallway lights left a black hole waiting to release its morning, dreary-eyed workers into the frozen abyss once again.

I called out in a low voice for Matagi. No reply. I waited a minute before losing patience. *Just as he was starting to grow on me*, I thought. The darkness made it difficult to see which corridors led to which sections. Usually, I would use EO to guide me through, but all I could do now was tread carefully and hope for the best.

I navigated through the room by feel, using the dining tables as a guide. To my relief, I was able to make out the faint etching of the section numbers labeled at the opening of each corridor. The scratched letters and numbers slid under my finger like Braille. Without exploring each of the sections, it was hard to know which ones housed the official offices. Usually, it had been either C or D at other outposts, so I started with those. Here, the corridors were lit like Section A, allowing me to search unencumbered throughout the buildings.

I made my way past each of the engineering quarters in Section C, which yielded nothing. Several officials were stationed inside the quarters, but there were no official offices there either.

In the Section D4 cul-de-sac of offices, I found what I was looking for. Official seals marked the doors with a set of construction tools bound together with a composite metal string. A clouded gray tint covered the windows on the door, making it impossible to see anything inside. I remembered from other outposts that each official office should have a numerical insignia on it that identified what section worked inside. However, after scouring every door, I found nothing. Evidently, my experience wasn't as valuable as I'd hoped.

The chilled handles of the doors didn't move under pressure. Locked. All of them. *Shit.* I pulled my personal device out, opening the interactive screen, which produced a green aura in the shadowy corridor. As I flipped through the archives of my time working on the Continent, a code sheet popped up and captured my attention. A single line of numbers spread across the documents page. Supposedly, there was a master code for all official workspaces, or at least there had been ten years ago. I tried the code on the door, only to hear a sharp beep, accompanied by a small red light.

"Fuck." *How the hell am I supposed to get into these rooms?* The frame of the door slid along my back as I slumped to the ground. *You can figure this out, just think. How would EO do it? Admin codes? Maybe . . . no.*

For the first time, I was forced to contemplate what life could be like without EO. The small things I'd taken for granted, no longer available. Ever since I descended, I'd heard people talk about the amazing ways DPMs could help a person thrive: cognitive capacity, peripheral senses, or even as an educator. It had been so long since people outside Design City had experienced a DPM, they always forgot what mattered most. What Jacob Helvik had wanted for us: someone to be there.

I cycled through the limited options, but something caught my eye. The low glow of my personal device showed just bright enough for me to make out the seal on the door directly opposite me. A small detail in the official's seal distinguished itself from the others, an additional object among the common tools etched within the insignia: a blade. It could have easily been written off by the uninitiated as just another tool, signifying some bullshit about the different types of people needed to complete the Design, but it was much more.

Shipley's voice rang in my head. *You see the blade, Kilo; that is you and I now. We're not like the other workers here. We are the sword of the Designers, meant to ensure the future of Kaua'i City by all means necessary.* Those were words he spoke during my first mission on the special task force. For once, I was happy to hear his voice in my head.

I grabbed my PD and flicked through more records until I found a redacted document with Shipley's face on it. *Thanks, asshole.* The document was crowded with codes, names, locations, and other blacked-out information.

ADMIN KEY. The words ripped a smile across my face. I bounced up and moved across the corridor to the door marked with the security official seal. After I punched in the final number of the short code, a click sounded, accompanied by a green light. I looked around before slipping inside and gently closing the door behind me.

Digital maps of the various work sites throughout the Ludo and Nāpali Continental region covered the walls. Each map intensified the closer I stood to it, glowing bright blue and white when in touching distance. Some of them had notes scribbled on certain sites, referring to a myriad of needs, from drill capacities to weather patterns.

The most detailed maps appeared on the far wall and covered a number of work sites that bordered the Maui Continental region. Security Force numbers had been written in red, then scratched out with black and replaced with another number below. When I squinted, I could read the scribbled-out troop counts, which were considerably lower than what existed now.

The room itself wasn't anything impressive: a desk with a few chairs surrounding it and a small bar in the corner with several half-filled liquor bottles. I sat in the chair behind the desk and placed my personal device on the wooden surface.

It instantly linked to the data processor embedded within, and a large screen spanning the sizable length of the desk replaced the modest interface. The glow of the digital maps around the office adjusted with the introduction of the PD, their visibility growing to peak strength and giving off an uncomfortable brightness in the empty room. Hopefully, the blurred glass of the door's window concealed most of the light inside. Either way, I needed to work fast.

It took a minute to familiarize myself with the system and the plethora of information available. I craved to dig into countless questions that remained unanswered from the past decade, but I forced myself to stay on task: finding a way to get the spit amplifier into a tox suit.

8,390 workers were scheduled for the next day in the Amazon Gorge, and 8,490 tox suits would be sent along with them. I couldn't believe a hundred tox suits would rupture in a single day, but maybe that was naive. *How about we add five workers to tomorrow's shift?*

As the number of workers jumped up by five, the tox suit count increased correspondingly. Although promising, if the officials responsible for adding the additional tox suits woke up to a notification of a personnel change, they might question its legitimacy and send it up the food chain.

If there was a way to have the tox suits ready to go next to the supply boxes, there might be a better chance of them taking the change at face value. After all, it was natural for officials not to question their leaders—I just needed to make the decision easy for them. It didn't matter if the change was questioned later, just as long as I could create enough pressure on a couple of cogs in the machine to act without hesitation.

I submitted the change using the credentials already loaded into the computer. Just as my finger hovered over TERMINATE SESSION, the realization that I might be able to cut this mission short dawned on me. *It can't be that easy, right?* Using the system-wide search function, I typed in "Outpost 378." An error function flashed back at me. A second attempt yielded the same result. *What the hell?*

"Outpost 377" immediately retrieved several documents and maps, all of which seemed to be relatively standard.

"Voice function," I whispered.

"HOW CAN I HELP YOU?" a robotic voice whispered back at the same decibel.

"Overlay Outpost 377 Alpha map on this map," I said, pointing to the map of the border work sites on the wall.

The computer's voice function didn't respond, but the Outpost 377 Alpha map materialized from digital particles over the border map before settling in and creating a convoluted singular map. I ran my finger across the map, looking at the outposts near 377. Both 376 and 379 were in the general vicinity, but no 378. The distances between outposts seemed random, but the more outposts I considered, the easier it was to determine where a missing outpost might be.

"Historical records of Outpost 378."

"NO HISTORICAL RECORDS OF OUTPOST 378 EXIST. HOWEVER, A CHARTER TO COMPLETE OUTPOST 379 DOES MENTION AN OUTPOST 378. WOULD YOU LIKE TO VIEW THE CHARTER?"

"Yes. Alongside the map, please."

The document materialized, quickly filling in the gaps of data to create what looked like a formal document from Continent officials addressed to the Designers. About halfway down the document, a single paragraph mentioned "Outpost 378," relating to an overflow of work and a need to expand operations in the area. It read like a construction contract, but between the lines hid evidence of much more: special building materials, higher-than-usual recruitment requests, and specialty supervision.

Pieces were falling into place, but the overall picture remained elusive. A weapon still seemed the most plausible, but what would it even look like? How could they have destroyed any record of it?

"Terminate session."

I exited the office, the lights fading behind me, and returned to the Rotunda. The dining tables led me through the dark until I found the cold metal of the supply boxes. Hoping my luck hadn't run out, I felt my way over to the decontamination chambers and stuck my arms inside, searching until my hand grasped the gritty plastic.

I folded the tox suits in the dark as best I could so they would match the others and placed them atop the last supply box. The spit amplifier slid easily into the opening of the top tox suit and rested in a crevice below the hood.

Now I needed to ensure I was the first one off the transport. There were a lot of eager recruits here willing to prove themselves at any turn, but tomorrow, there would be someone else stepping on the transport first—whatever it took.

CHAPTER 18

I didn't sleep much the rest of the night. The outpost beds weren't made for tossing and turning, but I couldn't help worrying about the spit amplifier hidden within the tox suit. It was impossible to keep myself from fiddling with the imaginary pieces of my plan, trying to ensure they fitted into place. Finally, I decided it wasn't worth fighting for sleep and headed over early to the mess hall.

There were a few other early risers by the time I got there, but I ate quickly and lined up at the outpost exit. A skinny, eager tour-one kid tried, and failed, to shove his way past me. The line steadily grew, and we waited to be loaded onto the MCVs. A brief look around for Matagi revealed nothing. If everything went well today, I might not see him again—but that was probably for the better.

Outpost officials handed out the tox suits as workers stepped up the staircase toward the exit. My heart skipped a few beats as I felt along the inside of my suit's hood. After fumbling around, the spit amplifier landed in my hand, and I quickly stretched the suit over my body before stepping outside and boarding the MCV.

An uncomfortable silence marred the trip to the gorge. It was likely just the toll from the work, but my eyes darted around the MCV in search of any indication that someone knew what was hidden in my suit. We followed the same route we'd driven for a week, yet today, it seemed longer.

Once at the site, the doors hissed, releasing the recruits back into the hell that'd become their life. It had only been a few days, but their sunken eyes burrowed deep into limp faces made it seem like they'd spent a lifetime on the Continent. The wonderment of the Amazon Gorge had obviously worn off for most of them, and what would have been a sight to behold a few days ago was now routine unloading and descent into the gorge.

The amplifier rested inside the pocket of my pants underneath the tox suit. As we descended, I surreptitiously felt for it through the thick lining of the tox suit.

Good . . . still there.

I continued to fidget in my gloves. It was hard to tell if the anxiety was a result of being alone, worrying about the people back in Kaua'i City, or because deep-cover espionage made my stomach churn. Regardless, there was no room to feel, not today. Today, I needed to be robotic. Precise.

The elevator shook as it reached the ground of the gorge. Everyone exited and made their way to their assigned workstations, each step calculated as if they'd been doing it for years. For all the bloated adoration the officials spewed about the Designers and the Continent, even I had to admit this was one of the most efficient work sites I'd seen. All the work equipment was delivered on time, and most recruits followed the schedule to the letter.

It had taken a couple of days to notice, but I realized there were more officials here than at other work sites. Fifteen or twenty of them oversaw each sector, facilitating the projects, and a few security officials paced along the base of the drill. But without knowing the death toll, I reserved my commendation of the site's efficiency.

The work on the scaffolding was routine. Ben and Mataio cut sheet metal for the repair and stacked it in a pile. I supported Solomon with the interior replacements. A few opportunities presented themselves to secure the spit amplifier to Solomon's blowtorch, but there would only be one chance, and I didn't plan on letting a security official with an itchy trigger finger ruin it.

Since the first day at the gorge, drill testing had commenced at a regular time in the afternoon following the break for lunch and medical treatment. Because I'd clocked the exact times, it would be easy to make sure Solomon didn't fire up his blowtorch during a drill test.

The last thing I needed was some kind of disruption to make Solomon check his equipment before the amplifier could work. However, if he'd already used the blowtorch throughout the day, he might be less likely to inspect it before igniting it. After mulling it over while we worked, I decided the only option was to attach the amplifier after our break.

About a half hour after our normal schedule, the site manager signaled for us to head down to break. I managed to slip the spit amplifier onto the blowtorch without noticeably lagging.

The break flew by thanks to the officials releasing us late and foregoing medical exams due to a "crunched schedule." Once we got back to the scaffolding, everyone grabbed their tools and prepped to resume work. Solomon didn't give the blowtorch so much as a glance before holstering it in the loop of his tool belt.

Thirty seconds passed, then a minute, before Solomon was ready to start again. The full minute felt like an eternity, each second providing ample opportunity for him to check the equipment.

Finally, he grabbed the torch from his belt and bent down, positioning the nose above the replacement metal inside the scaffold. At first, nothing happened, as if the torch was compromised altogether.

What the hell? Did I attach it wrong? I thought.

Solomon tried again, and this time, a cone of fire erupted from the blowtorch before centralizing into a powerful stream of fire that illuminated the inside of the scaffold.

I didn't waste any time, grabbing the hot metal where the torch melted open a hole, growing wider every second. The flame incinerated my glove, intensifying rapidly as it burned through my hand. I gritted my teeth through the blood-curdling pain and watched the flame turn blue as it reached peak amplification.

"Shit!" Solomon leapt backward and, after a couple of seconds, released the blowtorch, extinguishing the fire that had left a sizable, cauterized hole in my hand. Ben and Mataio had taken defensive positions and were now frozen, looking unsure of what to do.

Just as the situation seemed to calm, the drill beneath the scaffolding suddenly started shaking. Our scaffolding platform began to move in unison with the drill. Ben and Mataio dropped into position and attempted to brace themselves with their hands and knees.

"Kilo!" Solomon screamed, muffled through the mask. I jerked my head to see him teetering between the scaffold and the thirty-meter drop below.

The skin on my hand had already begun to cool and fuse with the synthetic material of the tox suit and the metal replacement piece. Instinctively, I yanked my hand away and lunged toward Solomon, feeling the skin rip. He narrowly grasped my wrist as he lost his battle with gravity. His clutch sent a shockwave of agony through my hand, like the blowtorch had somehow been reignited.

"I got you. Hang on!" The weight of the man shifted, but it wasn't enough. Solomon continued to slip toward the edge of the scaffold, despite my best efforts to fight for balance. My eyes darted around the surface, looking for anything that could help.

A chisel Mataio and Ben used for final adjustments to the sheet metal balanced against the toolbox. I dropped to the scaffold and snatched it with my free hand. As I fell, I cocked back the tool, and with the added force of my fall, thrusted it into the surface. The chisel buried into the mix-concrete only a few centimeters, but it was enough to hold mine and Solomon's weight.

"Ben! Mataio! Grab him!" I yelled at the two men, who were just now getting to their feet.

Some of the adrenaline and shock was wearing off now, and the pain in my hand expanded up my arm. The ripped fibers of bone and muscle screamed for restoration. At the end of our clasped arms, I saw Solomon's panicked eyes staring up at me. His grip twitched and slipped.

Ben rushed over and grabbed at Solomon's wrist, but it was too late.

Solomon's hand slipped, and in the blink of an eye, he was gone. Ben and Mataio screamed as they collapsed beside me, their faces marked with horror.

Fuck! This wasn't supposed to happen, I thought. I knew the spit amplifier was going to cause a shock, but no one was supposed to go over the side. The empty view from the scaffold where Solomon had held on so desperately moments ago now filled with thousands of workers who hadn't seen the fall, carrying on, unperturbed. I knew he was gone, but my mind refused to perceive it, to acknowledge the reality. I'd planned everything to the letter. How could I have known there would be an unexpected drill test?

There was no point in asking questions now—Solomon had paid the price. His body lay face down, arms and legs sprawled out, twisting unnaturally. Workers rushed over to assess the fall, but his lifeless body didn't respond to the poking and prodding. He was dead, all because of me.

The coagulated gel froze against my skin and soothed me before quickly turning into an intense burn, feeling like my hand was being ripped apart. The worksite surgery tent was much cleaner than I'd expected it to be. Maybe someone had finally realized productivity would be higher if they kept the workers alive.

A nurse shifted around the medical equipment in the cramped room until she made it to my bedside. She had a soft face, something you didn't often see on the Continent. Her flustered demeanor further alluded to her trainee status.

"How long?" I asked bluntly.

My voice startled her. "Should only take an hour or two," she said.

The blood vessels in my hands were beginning to repair themselves and delivering much-needed blood to the area. Gradually, the edges around the hole turned from a rotten red to a fleshy pink as the tissue and bone developed.

It was actually incredible to watch it happening. Although my surgery after the cycle crash had been miraculous, watching a hole in my body slowly repairing itself with the help of stimulating gel was a sight to behold.

Yet for all its wonder, the hole served as a reminder of Solomon's death, which I knew would inevitably fade from my mind. He wasn't a friend, family, or even someone I particularly liked, but he was dead because of me. I dreaded the moment when I realized that I'd forgotten him.

The door to the recovery room swung open violently, and a heavyset man walked through with a tox mask draped around his neck. His facial hair was thick and housed what seemed to be crumbs of the day's lunch. He shot a look at the nurse, whose face paled with fear.

"Leave us, please. He has everything he needs, correct?"

The nurse nodded and scampered out of the room. The large man took a seat near the foot of my bed and fired up his personal device, flicking through some photographs of Solomon's dead body and then the hole in the scaffold where we'd been working. From Solomon's description, this was our Section Supervisor.

"Walker, you doing all right?" he asked without breaking his review of the photos.

"Yes, sir."

"Quite an ordeal out there today, and unfortunately not too uncommon."

His eyes lit up, and he tilted his head at a picture showing the inside of the scaffold. Although I was looking at it in reverse, I could tell it was the replacement piece opened up by the blowtorch. The metal hung awkwardly inside, and as the man scrolled to the next photo, a view of the scaffold lining showed discolored black remnants of the fire.

"You know what happens if a torch were to blow through the inner lining of the scaffold?"

"No."

"The scaffold is an integral part of ensuring the drill can function properly and reduce unneeded variance during difficult mining. If the inner scaffolding is damaged, this whole section needs to be replaced." He flipped the photograph around, zooming out to show the large section of scaffolding. "All this would need to be replaced. Weeks of work, Walker."

"I was just trying to protect the replacement metal."

"I know, but you ended up protecting a lot more than a piece of metal."

He stood up and put away his personal device before glaring at me. It seemed hostile, but the pull at his lips gave away his masochistic thoughts.

"Why did you try to protect a piece of metal, Walker?"

Possible answers flooded my mind. This was the moment everything had been leading to, a shot to impress an official, but I couldn't stop thinking about Solomon. His body lying limp at the bottom of the gorge. *Is that what EO looked like during my surgery? They're both gone because of me!*

"I believe in the Design." My lip quivered, an unintentional show of emotion. "I came here to help my city, and I don't know, there was a threat, and I acted."

"It's more than a hole in your hand. You tore your tox suit, you know that, right? Do you understand what that means?"

"Yes."

"Well, that takes a lot of courage and some real dedication to the Design." He let out a laugh. "On your first tour, no less."

"I just want to do the best I can to continue to build up Kaua'i City."

He paced the room, moving his fingers and counting in his head. I held my breath. There wasn't much more I could do to convince him to consider me for relocation to Outpost 378. If this failed, the only option left was stealing an MCV and finding it myself. But if it came to that, it would be almost impossible to get off the Continent alive.

"Walker?" The pacing stopped, his fingers no longer fidgeting. He'd decided. "How would you like to work on a special project?"

My face remained cold and neutral, but the drumbeats of victory rang in my chest. He was sending me to 378.

"I would be honored, sir."

"I thought you might say that. There is a project I think you would be perfect for. You're willing to sacrifice for the Continent and the Design, and that's exactly the type of person we need for this."

"Thank you, sir."

He turned to leave, speaking over his shoulder as he left, "You will be picked up and transported this evening from your outpost."

Before he made it out the door, I sat up. "Sir, can you tell me what happened to Solomon?" It was a question Kilo Walker wouldn't know the answer to, so I needed to ask.

"Who is—" He cut himself off, a sliver of sympathy flashing across his face. "Right. Solomon's body will be cremated and disposed of properly. He was a good man who made a mistake, but the island cities are grateful for his service."

Properly. What a joke. His body would be dumped in the middle of nowhere with all the other bodies from the week and burned until all that was left of them was ashes blowing in the wind.

Everything about this was wrong. I tried at every turn to listen to EO, to mend what was broken and make peace with Kaua'i City, but every step pulled me further into the muck.

Maybe there was no mending what was broken. I wasn't broken. I was made exactly the way this fucking world wanted me made. I had gotten someone killed and ended up with a promotion.

Whatever type of weapon they are building, I'm going to find it. Then I'm going to get EO, and I am NEVER coming back!

CHAPTER 19

I felt every jagged bump from the washboard-like road. Although it was impossible to tell exactly what vehicle we'd been shoved into, thanks to the blindfold, it wasn't an MCV. However, I figured there were about ten or twelve other recruits, courtesy of the distinct murmuring sounds from behind the transport mouthpieces ripping into the fleshy insides of our mouths.

The other passengers were shuffling in their seats, likely reaching the limit of their patience. I used everything I'd ever learned about controlled breathing, pain tolerance, and muscle control to fight back the growing panic in me that had been overcoming my comrades. Within the metal clasps tightened around my wrists, I relaxed my hands and let them rest on the inside of my thighs.

An unsuspecting bump in the road threw each of the passengers against one another. The jolt locked my mouthpiece, further gashing my mouth and leaving a taste of blood. "Fuck!" I tried to speak, but my jaw moved less than a millimeter, sending a blaze of pain into my chin.

A picture of the strict rubber mouthpiece popped into my mind, wrapped around my face like a breathing apparatus for the infirmed. On its own, it didn't seem like it could do much harm, but I should have known better than to speak. Once clamped, the rubber ionized, causing even the smallest movement to result in jarring pain. *Figures!* Only on the Continent would they use something on recruits reserved for murderers and psychopaths.

It took a few moments, but I realized the bump that had lurched the vehicle forward was the wheels transferring from dirt to pavement.

We're here.

Although there weren't many paved roads on the Continent, it would stand to reason that a weapons program at Outpost 378 might require smooth transportation surfaces. Even with my senses dulled, careful whispers in the cabin left me with a hunch that we'd just entered somewhere cut off from the rest of the Continent, somewhere a secret project could thrive.

After gliding along the road for a few minutes, we stopped. A muffled conversation took place between the officials in the cabin and someone outside, but it was too difficult to make out any specifics.

Moments later, the vehicle lurched forward again. I tried to focus, watching the white Rorschach blots on the inside of my eyelids float aimlessly, waiting for our final stop. The door of the transport vehicle screeched open.

"Once you get out, grab onto the person in front of you and follow them. Got it?" I heard a raspy voice order.

Passengers on either side jumped at the official's directives. I nodded my head a few times toward the voice. The muscles in my neck flared from the pain in my mouth, and my legs wobbled as I stood.

Outside the vehicle, my foot grabbed the pavement, and I caught the jumpsuit of the person in front of me. A second later, the back of my own jumpsuit was pulled back at the hands of another passenger.

We walked cautiously, being occasionally prodded by an official to move faster. Each step down the grated staircase clanked until we stepped onto a quieter, more solid surface. Without warning, I bumped into the person in front of me again. A moment later, a clumsy body from behind did the same.

Grunts soon turned to pained groans, and the person I held jerked. A pair of rough hands pulled down my blindfold, then grabbed my mouthpiece and yanked it out, relieving the tension in my jaw, but also delivering a final dose of agony.

White spotlights attached to the ceiling blinded us. I covered my eyes, attempting to give them time to adjust, but I could hardly see anything. After a few moments, the concrete corridor came into focus, and I made out seven other recruits lined up. At first, I couldn't process the bushy hair of the person in front of me, but once I realized, a jolt of fear surged through my body.

"Matagi?" I whispered.

He turned just enough for us to make eye contact before saying, "Bro, I didn't think I was going to see you again."

"No talking." Heads turned as one of the officials screamed down the line.

Another official shoved a heavy bar across the door into the wall, leaving the sound of shrill, scraping metal itching my brain. Once it disappeared, the door slipped open, and the official entered. We followed him in, Matagi and the recruit behind me, letting out shallow breaths with each step.

The room wasn't at all what I'd expected. Chairs sat compressed in imperfect rows, facing a scuffed metal table. Numerous digital maps and blueprints came to life along the walls, much like the ones I'd seen in the security official's office back at Outpost 101.

We sat and waited quietly for directions from the officials. Instead, a woman appeared from behind us, wearing tox suit underclothes and a tox mask draped around her neck. She sported short, black hair with what looked like razor marks on the left side of her head in a circular pattern.

"Welcome to Outpost 378," she said dryly. The confident demeanor wasn't unusual, but she exuded less of the unnecessary bravado of other officials.

"What are you doing here?" I hissed out of the side of my mouth to Matagi.

His eyes drifted before he responded quietly, choking down a lump in his throat. "One of the officials asked if I wanted to work on a special project, and I said yes."

"You shouldn't be here. You're going to get yourself killed."

"I don't—"

The woman cut him off by raising her voice.

"You are here, well, you were selected because you have the requisite skills to support this project, but more importantly, you have shown a deep appreciation for the work we're doing on the Continent."

Her thin eyes scanned the room for the first time, briefly meeting mine before moving on to the next recruit. It only lasted a moment, but in that instant, it seemed like the deep, black pupils penetrated my soul, searching for my true self, finding the answer effortlessly. I hoped she was as naive as the other outpost officials.

The woman dropped her personal device onto the table with abandon and waved her hand over it, instantly materializing blueprints.

"This is what you'll all be working on for the foreseeable future."

The image showed a 3D model of a building you might see in Kaua'i City. It was a tall, rectangular structure with windows reaching thirty or forty stories high and a sturdy foundation that plateaued out.

A residential building? I wondered.

"Construction has already begun. You will all be fitted into various work squads to ensure it's built as soon as possible. This is your contribution to the Speer Project." Several looks shot across the room at the mention of the project title.

A coy smile broke across the woman's face. "None of you have ever heard of the Speer Project, and now that you've joined it, you will never tell an outside soul about it. Work starts now. If you have construction experience, follow Official James. All those with geological experience, follow me."

I thought fast, knowing I couldn't pass for geological support, but construction on a residential building wasn't going to cut it either. I needed something that would get me close to the heart of the weapon. I threw my hand up, bracing for the chance a bullet might tear through my chest a moment later.

"What about security experience?"

A chill fell over the room. If I hadn't known the rank of the woman in charge before, I did now. She'd already started leaving but halted as I spoke, turning her head to look directly at me.

"I wasn't aware we had any security recruits in this shipment."

A part of me wanted to test the woman, but Kilo Walker would never do something like that.

"I'm not actually a security recruit, ma'am." I glanced around anxiously, half playing the part and half regretting the split-second decision. "I have some security experience in Ludo, and I want to do whatever I can to serve Kaua'i City."

She let out a grunt before she looked over at the official on the other side of the room and nodded. Then she left, followed by two recruits from the front row.

Without warning, a hand yanked on my collar, dragging me out of the chair and onto the floor. Instinctually, I wanted to pop up and deliver two quick blows to the man's stomach before sending my knee through his nose, but again, the situation called for restraint.

The security official dragged my limp body through the corridor we'd entered but then stopped about halfway. He placed his hand on the concrete wall. A thin green line lit up around his print, and a whoosh of air came from a slit in the wall. With his free hand, the man opened it further to reveal a blind corridor into the depths of the compound.

With his help, I hobbled to my feet.

"In there?" I asked.

"Yes."

Just inside, the man started to close the door but fluidly pushed my head between the corridor wall and the slab, slamming the door shut on my skull.

I slowly regained consciousness, idly registering a line of blood running down my middle finger and growing into a bubble at the tip until it dropped to the floor. It was a tiny splash in the pool below that must have accumulated while I was unconscious.

A pinching sensation came from plastic restraints coiled around my hands and connected to the back of my metal chair. In front of me sat a man in an unbuttoned, decorated outfit. The medals that chimed against each other were the same ones I'd been awarded: Three Years Lost, Five Years Lost, Eight Years Lost, and so on.

With a serrated blade, he crudely cut a slice from an apple. The juice from the toothy bite dripped down his chin before he wiped it away with the back of his knife-wielding hand.

"Where am I?" I asked. My senses still hadn't completely recalibrated, but it was clear what this was. "Why am I tied up?"

The man stabbed the knife into what remained of the apple and placed it on the ground.

"You asked about joining a security detail, yet you're a construction worker, Mr. Walker. You thought you could just volunteer, and we'd throw a suit on you? Obviously, we have some questions."

"Like what?"

"Why do you want to join security?"

I hesitated, still working to read the man. "I want to help Kaua'i City as more than a construction worker."

"Oh, is that right? A shitty gambler all of a sudden wants to give his life for the city?" His eyes drifted to above my head. I hadn't noticed before, but now I could hear scarcely audible breathing behind me. "Only took him a week. Must be some kind of miracle."

I licked the dried blood on my lip and waited for the arrogant prick to get on with the show.

"Your file said you have some basic training. What's that look like?"

"I fought Lua. I guess I figured if I was being brought onto the project, maybe you could use my skills."

He let out a hefty laugh, rattling his medals. "You think we're fist-fighting on the Continent still? You're hilarious. An old piece of shit like you wins a few fights in the island city, and all of a sudden, you're a fucking draft pick?"

"I just want a chance, sir," I said as humbly as my voice allowed.

His gaze lifted again before he gave a slight nod. Suddenly, there was movement behind me. A powerful arm curved around my neck and constricted.

I struggled in the chair, but it was bolted to the ground. The blood drained from the cut in my hand as I forced harder against the restraints.

"One last question. What are you doing here, Mr. Ressler?"

If the blood running down my hand could freeze, it would have. *Fuck.* The calculated risk of joining a security detail now wrapped around my neck, and my cover had been blown wide open. *Why didn't I just work on the stupid residential building?!*

"It doesn't matter anyway. I will sleep fine whether I know or not," the man said.

Blackness crept into my peripherals. His fading figure stepped directly in front of me and crouched over, his hands on his knees. "We ran a tox screen. You lied when you said it was your first time."

"Fuck you!"

With every ounce of energy, I turned my wrists in the restraints. The plastic cracked under the pressure and gave out.

Before the restraints could hit the ground, I brought a heavy fist around from the right side and slammed it into the man's jaw. Caught off guard, he stumbled back, losing his balance, and crashed to the ground. I threw my hand back and felt around the bristly stubble of the man choking me from behind until I found an eye socket. As soon as it registered, I jammed my bloody left-hand thumb straight into the eye cavity and ripped out what I could.

He let out a terrifying scream and released the tension on my neck immediately. I curled over and dropped from the chair, gasping for air. In the corner of my eye, I saw the security official I had just laid out pull his knife from the half-eaten apple before he scrambled to his feet and charged. I rolled to the right just as he brought the knife down, screeching it across the concrete floor.

Finally getting to my feet, I knew I had a chance. He slashed frantically back and forth. I dropped a shoulder back with each swipe, keeping my hands close to my chest and waiting for a moment's opening. The official's eyes flashed.

His knife swung again, this time aimed at my face, but his inaccuracy gave me just a second to grab his tricep and push him off balance. I struck fast at his kidney with my free hand.

Pain clouded his face as he staggered back. I took a forceful step toward him, but my weak-side knee gave out as a bloody hand grasped my foot before I could throw a punch. The muscular man with the gouged eye lay curled up, with his free hand trying to halt the blood pouring from his socket. Credit to him, through the pain, he mustered enough control to grab my leg and wrestle me down, if only for a moment.

As I rose, shaking off the bloodied man, so did my interrogator, clutching his side before adjusting the grip on his knife. He lunged forward without committing to a full stab, obviously testing my reflexes. We circled each other like boxers in the ring, breaths held tightly as we waited for the first move.

I couldn't think of an advantage to striking first. His weapon would always give him the upper hand if I put him on the defense, but who knew how long I'd have until other security officials showed up?

It was worth the risk, so I rushed forward with open palms, knowing the only chance of getting in a powerful strike relied on me deflecting any reactive knife maneuver. He sliced toward his strong side, aiming for my forearm. But he was too slow. My palm connected with his wrist, stopping the forward momentum and forcing his arm across his body.

This time, I didn't hold back. I drilled my fist into the same spot as before. The sound of cracked ribs pulled a slight smile across my face, and he dropped, gasping for air.

I moved over to his beaten body and lifted my foot before crashing it down on his head. His eyes closed, his body falling limp, but he still drew breath.

"That's the difference between you and me." I hawked whatever spit remained in my mouth at the man. "You'll wake up."

I leaned down to grab the knife, but something else poked out from behind his back. The ice-cold metal of a pistol tingled in my hand. *Cocky.* I felt around his pockets for anything else of use. I reasoned his personal device and tox mask might be helpful, but everything else was dead weight.

My other captor whimpered as he crawled toward the door, leaving a painted trail of crimson behind him. A swift blow to the back of the head left him like his partner. The hairs on my neck triggered at a faint sound emanating from outside the door. A familiar warmth filled my chest, and my heart skipped a couple of beats.

I crept to the door, the pistol outstretched, with the knife held underneath. I reached for the handle, listening intently to garner any indication of who or what was on the other side. The black imprints on my pistol revealed it to be a Kauaʻi City model.

Twelve shots—whatever was on the other side, I needed to make them count. My heart pumped. I tried to focus all my attention and adrenaline on honing my reflexes. In a fluid motion, I unlatched the door and barreled through.

Nothing. The corridor was empty. A clunking sound came from behind the outward-swung door behind me. I pivoted around to get a view, my index finger pressed firmly against the trigger. A set of confused eyes looked back at me.

"EO!"

"Kilo?"

"It *is* you!"

My knife and gun dropped to the floor, and I lunged at him, wrapping my arms around his neck. His warmth was real, a growing heat that calmed my beating heart.

“I’m so sorry. I tried to stop them, but they severed the stem.” I fought back the tears and pulled back to look at him. “I should never have said what I said. I didn’t know if I would ever have the chance to tell you—”

EO looked around the hallway, and for the first time, I realized his arms rested idly at his side.

“Are you okay?” I asked.

“I’m not sure. I think I’m just still coming back.”

“You know who I am?”

“The stubborn, self-isolating, worse-looking version of me?”

“You’re an asshole.” I laughed and squeezed my arms around him again. “I missed you.”

“Where are we?” EO finally hugged me back, but when he pulled away, his eyes still wandered around the corridor. The blank look on his face gradually grew with expression, as if I was watching his emotions regulate in real time.

I tried to answer him, but an alarm blared through the corridor. Flaring red lights replaced the white strobe lights before turning the corridor dark.

“We need to go now. You’ll figure it out.” I picked up the gun and pulled on EO’s arm as he stood transfixed by the battered bodies in the interrogation room.

“What did you—?”

“No time to explain! Let’s go!”

“Did you find out what’s happening on the Continent?”

“I’m trying!” I yelled.

We ran through the maze of corridors, both of us attempting to decipher the mix of signs and rooms. The corridors were absent of any security officials, but they wouldn’t stay that way for long.

Finally, we burst through a door that opened to a staircase. We descended frantically, but the endless flights of stairs seemed to lead to nowhere.

“We need to go lateral,” I said, pulling EO away from another staircase. We burst through the next door to find ourselves outside the compound, looking down through a grated walkway that weaved alongside the exterior of the building.

The cold winds blew against the building, penetrating my unsuitable clothing. Without thinking, I attached the tox mask I had lifted off the official to my jaw and looked at EO. He stood motionless, gaping at the crater below. The view froze my synapses. I couldn't fathom what my eyes registered.

The entirety of the mine circled down in a funnel with a wide base about 500 meters below. It was inexplicable. Rather than thousands of workers accompanying transport vehicles up and down the mine or operating heavy machinery at the base, an entire city stood erect before us. Levels of buildings poked out, complex mazes of walkways and roads connecting each of the towers and levels.

"It's an island city," EO said slowly, his words trailing off.

"It's a Continent City," I responded, matching his awe.

Whatever imbalance EO felt within, he had been shaken back to equilibrium at the sight. And I now realized what I'd been chasing. They weren't building a weapon; they were building something far more dangerous.

CHAPTER 20

It was at least a full minute before either of us strung together a coherent set of words. The wind continued to howl around us as ant-sized people worked far below. The concrete spires only reached halfway up the mine, but sprawling work sites along the walls proved the Designers weren't done yet. But why? What point could there possibly be to building a city on the Continent? No one could live here.

Stories of experimental towns hundreds of years ago were nothing more than failed attempts replaced by the smaller, stable outposts that still protected workers from Carbon Sytride. But even then, they weren't perfect.

I recalled some Designers considering plans for large domes sealing off small towns inside, but those had been scrapped due to the infeasibility of vertical and horizontal expansion.

"This isn't some weird malfunction I'm seeing from coming back, is it?" EO asked.

"No." But I still couldn't accept the reality before us and searched, like EO, for some explanation other than the obvious.

"Kilo, do you see what I see?"

"Yeah. A concrete jungle where they don't grow."

"No. Look at the people there." He pointed to an area of the upper wall in visual proximity, but even through a squint, they were largely indistinguishable. "They aren't wearing tox suits . . . or masks."

It couldn't be. It made no sense.

"Are the Designers purposefully exposing workers on this project? After a couple of days, they'll be dead."

"That would explain why the deaths on the Continent have been abnormal." But the folds on his forehead suggested another theory. "What if—" His eyes shifted as he tried to grab the idea that was formulating. "What if they don't need tox suits?"

"Not possible. The Continent will be contaminated for another 1,000 years at least."

"What about the Helvik Theory? What if it's true?"

"They aren't deep enough. Even if it was possible, they would need to be at least two kilometers down."

EO shifted, scanning the building that supported us. All that was visible was the outpost number, along with a couple of warnings that we'd clearly disregarded.

"Where are we on the Continent?" EO asked.

"It's hard to know for sure, but Outpost 378 should be somewhere just south of the Maui-Kaua'i border." My brow rose in anticipation, questioning where he was going with this.

"Do you have your personal device?"

"I have *a* device." I produced the security official's device.

"Give me voice command and repeat what I say."

I nodded, initiating the program.

"Pull up map type XYT, South America circa 2000," he said. I repeated it word for word.

The virescent home screen that floated above my hands soon turned to a mostly unfamiliar map. The translucent topographical configuration was split into pieces by thin black lines, each encompassing unknown words. I clearly recognized the Continent, but I couldn't figure out what made this map special. With a still finger, EO pointed to the northernmost part of the map and slowly traveled down before he stopped and tapped the spot.

"Here," he said as I drew in closer, trying to pick up what may have been obvious to him but not to me.

"Right here. You see the color? Look at the intensity of that green," EO said. He was right. A soft ocean green turned gradually to deep, dark emerald in a pattern of uneven ripples around the point.

"Are we looking at an organic map?"

"Yes, and this point right here was the densest organic area on the Continent, maybe the world." With two fingers, I grabbed the point on the map and pulled it open, enlarging the area to show a new pattern of topography with a darker range of green within the dark sphere.

"If the concentration of Carbon Sytride here were diluted, the Helvik Theory wouldn't require two kilometers; maybe only a couple hundred meters," EO explained. I released my fingers, and the map snapped back to its wide view.

"If that's true, how long until this area would be habitable near the surface?"

"I don't know, but it definitely wouldn't be a millennium."

The implications were unknowable. With the island cities at each other's throats after the fall of Honolulu City, the value of a livable area on the Continent would be immeasurable. If the other island cities found out about this, it could lead to all-out war, but if Kaua'i kept it secret, they would have something more powerful than any weapon on earth: space.

"How close are we to the border?" I asked.

The search for an exit to the top of Outpost 378 proved challenging, even with EO's help. Surprisingly, the flashing red lights and alarms no longer rang through the compound's hallways. The sight of any person along the endless corridors and staircases still bred panic, but soon turned routine.

People hardly looked at me when we passed by. It was as if everyone working here was living in their own world, a reality unperturbed by passersby. The more people we passed, the sooner a pattern began to emerge: They were broken. The souls of the hopeless, caged by the dreamers. Every pair of hallowed eyes and sunken shoulders confessed the true experience here.

Most were construction workers or engineers, either donning reinforced, polymer tox suits designed for heavy-duty construction or thinner suits with special masks that could connect to a personal device, but even a few security officials passed without a glance. Maybe their souls were slowly succumbing to the weight of the Continent.

We climbed several levels in search of a route to the surface but remained deep underground. From where we'd stood on the catwalk earlier, we were still about twenty levels below a surface exit, and time was running out. The two unconscious security officials I left behind earlier meant there would be an all-out manhunt at this outpost sooner or later, but for now, it seemed like they wanted to keep it quiet and contained to the level we'd been on. If they wanted to find me without notifying the entire complex, it meant we had some time.

"Come on, in here," I whispered.

As we entered the unknown level, I questioned what we would even do when we found the top. It wasn't like a transit service was waiting to take us back to the island city.

We searched each of the closed doors for any signs of something that could help us find our way up top and out of Kaua'i territory.

An insignia of a serpent wrapped around Kaua'i City posted on a glazed door window gave me a slight bit of hope. I pulled EO inside.

In the waiting room, a larger version of the insignia loomed over us from the wall behind an intake desk. The threat was low, but not zero, even with med workers.

"We need to figure out how to get to a vehicle up top. Can you remember if the med staff at 313 ever had transport logs?"

"I'm pretty sure they were kept by med security. You think they'll have them here?" EO's skepticism didn't inject confidence, but it was worth a shot.

I pulled the collar of my torn jacket up as far as it could go, barely hiding the dark marks around my neck. A slight man in scrubs sat behind the unimpressively styled eggshell desk, typing away on an obstructed screen.

"Excuse me, I was sent up from security to get a transport log. Can you help with that?"

The typing continued, but slowly the man distributed his energy between the two tasks.

"Name?" he said in a high-pitched voice.

My brain rattled off names, trying to recall either of the tags on the men left in the interrogation room. *Martens? Manchun?*

"McBride," I replied confidently, but we were screwed if the request needed facial confirmation.

"McBride, McBride, McBride. Here you are." He looked up, his eyes scanning my worn-down profile before looking down again at the screen. Although slight, the twitch of his jaw gave him away.

In a fluid motion, I flipped back my jacket and drew the pistol tucked in my waistband, shoving it in the man's face.

"Easy. I just need to know where the transport vehicles are," I said.

"You aren't getting out of here." His lips pulled up at the corners as if by a puppeteer. "No one leaves the project."

I eyed EO before responding, but he couldn't help.

"What do you mean?"

"No. One. Leaves." The med official lunged for something behind the desk, but I was faster. My finger twitched and sent a bullet tearing through his knee, turning it into a mess of bone, blood, and tissue plastered against the wall. I brought the handle of my pistol down across his head and cut his scream short. *One*. The man dropped to the floor, out cold.

"Kilo. What the—"

"We're leaving," I said. "I'm not losing you again."

I scaled the desk and landed in the med worker's chair. My body cried out for respite.

"What about him?"

I reached under the desk and held down the finger-sized button. "A med team will be here in a minute. You said I'm not a murderer, right?"

He nodded.

On the screen at the desk, mugshots of the unconscious security officials stared back at me with a warning label attached to McBride's work clearance: WARNING: FOUND INJURED AT 11:47 A.M. SUSPECT ARMED AND DANGEROUS.

I waved away the screen and searched for the vehicle manifests. A slew of patient records and reports clogged the database. Even if I knew where to look, it could take hours to find the transport logs.

A patient record caught my eye, not because of who was in it, but because of the terminology. LIFE CONTRACT REFUSAL—TERMINATION COMPLETE. *What the—?* The file opened automatically with a list of worksite progress reports, med treatments, and outpost history information. At the end, a single sentence sent shivers down my spine. SERVICE EVALUATION: REFUSED LIFE CONTRACT. CATEGORIZED FOR IMMEDIATE TERMINATION.

"You see this?" I swallowed.

"They aren't letting them leave," EO said. "Wait, what's that?" He pointed to a hidden notation on the side of the document.

DPM QUALIFICATION: FAIL.

"Designers are giving them DPMs to work here?" I questioned. It took a second to process the connection, but then it clicked. "How can you tell the difference between a replica and a real DPM?"

"I don't know if you can, not just by looking at it," EO answered.

"The replica DPMs we've been seeing in the island cities . . . I don't think they're replicas."

We both stared at the words. DPMs were the most closely guarded single piece of technology in the world, but here they were being used as enticements. I couldn't fathom how important this outpost must be for Designers to allow DPMs out of the ridged clutch of Design City.

The looking glass through which I'd seen our world for so long finally broke, and for the first time, I could see the true reality of what was happening around us. DPMs were leaking into the island cities from the Continent because it was worth building this city at any cost. Every aspect of life was malleable in the Designer's hands. They only needed the impetus. "They are buying a lifetime of servitude in order to tip the balance of power," EO said.

"And they're quietly killing the ones who refuse," I finished for him.

"They're hiding a massive worksite in the death numbers," EO murmured.

My heart palpitated at the thought. "We'll find the vehicle depot, but there's something I have to do first."

"What? What could possibly be more important than getting out of here?"

I brought back the search function, hoping the information would be updated, and typed in a name. "Something you'd want me to do."

A couple of minutes later, we blasted through the med facility door, alarming the downtrodden workers in the hallway. It didn't matter, as the entire security team of this building would be on us in minutes. With a bullet through the knee of a med worker, quiet was no longer an option for the Security Forces. The minute I'd tripped the emergency alert for the office, the alert could no longer be contained to the personnel files.

Taking the stairs two at a time, we made it down three levels until a scanty directory posted beside a door displayed the department locations in this dreadful place.

"Construction facilities," I muttered under my breath. "Maybe he's still there."

"Who?" EO questioned as we picked up the pace once again.

"A friend."

"You don't have friends."

"Fine. Someone who doesn't deserve to die."

A security official turned the corner ahead of us with two of his colleagues in tow. His eyes scanned my beaten body, and he didn't waste any time in firing off a few wild shots.

The drywall around us exploded. I grabbed the corner of the wall and unleashed three bullets toward the men. Before the wisps of smoke from my barrel cleared, we were already sprinting back down the hallway. *Four.*

"It should be up here." We pushed through a set of twin doors. For a moment, they swung back and forth toward their natural equilibrium. I looked around for the sign. *It has to be here.*

"Eight," EO said as he continued, examining the intersecting hallways ahead.

"Eight what?"

"Bullets. You've got eight left."

"I'm counting up, not down," I said.

The doors swung open one more time, just enough for two green laser trackers to sneak through the opening, but the fingers on the triggers weren't fast enough.

The discharge from my pistol echoed through the hallway and sent the swing doors flying open. The bullet drove through, tearing open the shoulder of the security official. In response, a second official unloaded a rapid hail of bullets down the corridor.

"This way!" EO pulled me around the corner as shots screamed by us.

I noticed a familiarity to the hallway, the feel of it, but it was difficult to place. I stopped in my tracks.

"Why are you stopping? Let's go!"

"In here." I attempted to pull open the hallway door, but the handle stiffened under the pressure. Taking a step back, I unleashed a single bullet at the metal frame, leaving only a thin hole in the metal, along with the reverberation of destruction. *Six.*

Inside was the room where Matagi and I'd been briefed by the outpost official earlier today; the empty chairs remained in lazy rows. Maybe it was the door or something about the outside walls, but I'd recognized it, if only faintly.

"We need something on where construction workers were sent."

I waved the personal device across the digital maps and documents on the table. Without them, the desk looked empty, an unremarkable, artificial metal slab.

The device activated several construction plans but didn't produce the in-progress residential building. I bent down to examine the desk drawers. Some were locked, but I yanked open the ones available and peered inside.

"Gotcha. This is the building he'll be working on."

The digital plans of the residential building illuminated, and I transferred them to the desktop.

"Where are you? Where are you?" I muttered.

"Wait, I saw this building." EO leaned in closer. "Yeah. This was right below us on the terrace; you probably missed it because you were looking out at the rest of the city."

Below us? I thought. "How far?"

Completing some quick calculations, he guessed, "Eight levels, maybe?"

"That's where we're going then. The woman in charge wouldn't have wasted any time getting them to work."

I grabbed EO's shoulder and pulled him through the other door into the corridor where I'd been knocked out earlier. A fishy smell lingered inside. Along the corridor lay eight mouthpieces, saliva still glistening on some of them. "There has to be an exit out this way."

As we ran, my eyes tried to keep up with the signage posted. I searched for anything that might lead outside, but all the doors seemed to lead to offices.

I slammed my hand against the concrete wall. We'd run out of runway. I could only assume the dead end had somehow been where they'd brought us in from the transport.

"What now? They're coming," EO said as he steeled himself, watching the corridor.

"Give me a second; I'm thinking."

Scanning the homogenous wall, it clicked. I frantically moved my open palm along the smooth surface. Nothing. I was too close.

I took a step back and positioned myself as if I were entering a doorway. My palm rested firmly against the wall in front of me. Nothing. I moved it slowly, in a small range of motion. Seconds later, a thin, red line illuminated the imprint of my hand, slightly below where I first made contact.

"My only fault is that I'm tall." I couldn't help the smile that crossed my face.

"Shut up, just go."

Through the heavy, block door, a darkened staircase elevated a few meters before the outside light illuminated the path. Cold air engulfed us as soon as we exited the tunnel. We ran along the grated walkway until we hit a staircase and descended. It must have been part of a larger outdoor walkway, but here, a jagged staircase extended up to the surface and then dipped downward, entering the outskirts of the city, several hundred meters below.

I imagined the walkways being an escape for inhabitants of the city, but the officials likely enjoyed the shortcut. For a moment, my curiosity spiked, but some questions would have to be left unanswered. The pulsing wind grew in fervor with each level we descended. The half-erected building now sprouted right below us.

Once we reached the top of the structure, we jumped onto the temporary bridge that edged out and connected with the upper section of the building. Across it, hundreds of recruits were working around the upper levels, sending sparks dying into the air as they welded the metal foundations into place.

"Where's Matagi?" I shouted to one of the recruits.

"Who?" Her reply was lost through the heavy welding gear, but I understood.

I surveyed the building, looking for someone I might recognize from the briefing earlier, but welding gear covered most of the recruits from head to toe.

"What do they look like?" EO asked, following my gaze.

My heart was thrumming, knowing the longer we stood here, the less time we had to get topside.

"Hair! He's got a lot of hair!" I screamed back over the winds and ambient noise.

EO didn't question it and went to work scanning the recruits for anything. He had a way about him, being able to tell when something meant more to me than I even realized. He didn't need to know the kid's name, or why it was important, because he knew *me*.

"Hair! Is that him?" EO pointed to the far side of the building. Most of the person's body was obstructed by the angle, but an unmistakable nest of hair bounced outside the gear.

I didn't answer. In a full sprint, I ran along the scaffolding, around the fragmented building. I grabbed Matagi and ripped him down from a suspended harness.

"Kilo? What're you doin' here?" Matagi said, pulling off the welding helmet.

"We need to leave now." I grabbed him by the arm, almost pulling it out of its socket, and led him back across the bridge.

Bullets fired from above rained down around us and tore through the grated walkway. Without looking, I let loose a couple of shots in the shooter's direction. It bought us a few seconds of cover, and we sped toward the facility, which was buried into the wall of the mine.

I hurried Matagi up the stairs until we reached an entrance we'd passed by earlier. Once inside, he finally broke free.

"Kilo, what's going on? What are we—" he stammered.

I squeezed his shoulders and forced him to focus. "Matagi, if you stay here, you'll never go back to the island cities, and they will kill you."

"What do you—"

"I'm trying to save your life. Now let's go!"

CHAPTER 21

Matagi felt his way through the outpost maze and led us to an elevator. Apparently, the geologists had been taken deeper into the facility to test some of the seismic activity in the region and adjust the building plans accordingly. The construction team wasn't so lucky.

They went directly down to the work site to begin construction on the brand-new residential building, the first of its kind in the outpost. Since Matagi was part of the construction crew, the officials took him and the other recruits through a service elevator to get them working as quickly as possible.

Matagi's trust in me was baffling—he barely knew me, and with no explanation of why, he led us to the elevator. Blind trust like that would probably get him killed someday, but I felt for the kid. Even saw a bit of me in him. He wasn't a clandestine operator; he was just someone that fit the Company's description. He didn't deserve to die in this place.

My erstwhile companion tried to get some answers, but I didn't give him much. There would be time for that on the drive. For now, I needed him to get us topside.

"There it is!" Matagi yelled.

EO and I followed him to the end of an empty corridor, where we found ourselves in front of an old elevator. It required the user to pull up the barred hatch before entering. If that wasn't enough, the rust along the frame told us the elevator was far from a cutting-edge model.

I pulled up the hatch, the crusted metal almost ripping open my hand, and I pressed the service button. A good sign—I didn't expect any officials or security personnel would be using this death trap of their own free will.

The elevator rose to meet us, uttering an ear-splitting screech. Once inside, I searched the array of buttons for anything close to the upper levels. I smashed the "Level One Loading" button, and the elevator creaked as it jolted upward.

Level One would be close enough. Based on the information I procured in the medical office, there weren't any med transports, but they had to transport materials, people, and everything else somehow. The loading dock seemed like as good a place as any.

"What kind of vehicle do we need to get to the border?" My head tilted in EO's direction. His bewildered glance shook me back to reality, and I realized my mistake.

"What?" I turned to see Matagi's confused eyes staring back at me.

"Sorry, I was just talking to myself."

"It didn't sound like that at all. It also didn't look like you were talking to me."

I'd only made this mistake a handful of times in my life. Maybe being alone for a week had broken some of the muscle memory of speaking to EO, or maybe the screwed-up situation had thrown me off. Either way, I'd never found a successful way to explain myself out of this pointed question.

Matagi frowned at me, clearly realizing I didn't have a good answer. "Kilo, you gotta trust me, man. I don't know what is going on, but you told me I'm in danger, and I believe you. I could see it in your eyes the moment I met you—you've used whatever facade works best." He took a deep breath. "But if you want me to keep trusting you, you're gonna have to give me something."

I didn't expect the kid to be so deep. *Maybe I shouldn't have saved him. I'm not looking for a therapist.* I pushed the thought from my mind, afraid there was an element of truth to wishing I could walk away.

It'd always seemed so simple to tell people about EO, but when it came down to it, it was like tearing open my chest and exposing my most vital organ, waiting until it was cut out and sold. The last person I told had to comfort me out of a panic attack. My mind had been convinced the words would kill EO and have me thrown in prison or worse.

He was right, though. To save his life, I needed him to trust me, and there wasn't a better way than to confess to something so unimaginable.

"I have a DPM."

"Fine. Don't tell me."

"It's the truth. His name is EO."

"Kilo—" Matagi's eyes met mine, realization dawning that I was telling the truth.

"A DPM? How . . . I mean . . ."

"It's a long story, but he can help us, or at least he can help me help you."

The elevator screeched to a stop at Level One. I pulled open the hatch cautiously, my other hand cradling the pistol. With the two shots on the walkway, I'd now emptied eight bullets. The last four would need to count.

The loading area only housed a few workers and officials. They were scattered around the open area, loading various vehicles and taking inventory. The heavy breath I'd been holding for the past few minutes released in a cloud of steam. *Finally, a break.*

Vehicles filled the loading area, ranging from light, all-terrain buggies, to heavy, long-range transports, and even a few long-range security vehicles. The rows of vehicles provided just enough cover that we might be able to steal one and slip out.

I surveyed the area, counting seven workers and three security officials. The closest official was balanced against a vehicle a few rows down, his face nuzzled in the neck of a female companion. At the furthest wall, the other two listened to an indiscernible transmission. *Not easy, but doable.*

I led Matagi and EO through the cache of vehicles, looking to EO occasionally to see if he had any helpful updates on the security officials. We finally made it within a few meters of two Panthers, small-sized, long-range transport vehicles. We continued to creep toward the lean, fierce, Cross-Continent Vehicles. I thought back to the few times I'd ridden in Panthers—if they still ran the same, they might just get us out of here.

"Stop," EO said in a monotone.

"What?" I whispered.

"A security vehicle just pulled into the far side of the dock. I can't hear much of what they're saying, but it sounds like a briefing about you."

I popped my head up around the tire of an MCV. The outpost official directed a few of the security officials to different areas of the loading dock. A finger pointed in our direction, followed by two security officials whipping their heads. I retreated to my hiding place.

"Two coming this way. Options?" I asked.

EO's face contorted as he searched through scenarios.

"I could distract them," Matagi answered for him.

"No. That's too dangerous; they'll shoot if they see you."

"But they don't know I'm with you, right? I could say I got lost getting back to my work site. It's my first day."

"No."

"He has a point, Kilo," EO said, his words hanging in the air.

"What? I'm not risking his life."

"I think he can do it."

"I'm not putting him out there. He's not like me!"

"He is *exactly* like you. Let him try."

"What did he say?" Matagi asked.

I tightened my eyes and refused to break the stare with EO. "He said you should try."

Without warning, Matagi stood up and walked toward the oncoming security officials. I grabbed at him weakly, but the fabric of his shirt slipped through my hands. It was too late.

"Excuse me. Excuse me." Matagi's voice carried toward the officials. The two men reactively drew their weapons. Matagi stared down at the heavy assault rifles pointed at his chest before throwing his hands up in the air and pleading for mercy.

Time to go.

The MCVs were high enough off the ground that I was able to spider crawl under one after another until I reached the row of smaller-sized vehicles. Closest to me rested two Panthers, the thick metal grills underneath a slitted windshield.

The lock detached with a quiet click, and the reinforced door slid open. I surveyed the layout surrounding the steering wheel. It was slightly different from what I remembered a decade ago, but close enough to figure out.

The engine roared to life, and I slipped the gearshift into reverse. The wheels spun until they caught the concrete below and yanked the vehicle backward. Free of the other vehicles, I slammed the shifter into first and punched the pedal to the floor, tapping a combination of the buttons on the dash that pushed open the passenger door.

Bullets ricocheted off the angled side of the Panther as I sped down the driving lane toward the exit. The pistol I'd placed comfortably on my thigh now pointed out the open door. I fired off four bullets in quick succession at the frantic security officials, who dove for cover behind a long-range transport truck.

"Twelve," EO said. "You're empty."

With the cover, Matagi broke into a full sprint toward the Panther, directly through the row of vehicles. I locked the emergency brake and pulled the steering wheel hard to the left, sliding the Panther ninety degrees to a full stop.

Our Panther was already moving by the time he leaped in. The haze of bullets closed in from several angles as the security officials emptied everything in their weapons. We sped through the rows of vehicles before I caught a view of the ramp. I jammed the Panther hard left and headed between two parked MCVs toward the light.

The Panther bounced onto the steep ramp leading to the Continent outside. I pressed a button above the shifter, and the stick dropped, letting out an ear-splitting crack from the engine.

"Oh my God, we did it!" Matagi yelled. However, the reflection in the rearview mirror told a different story.

"Not yet." Two long-range security vehicles came into view, gaining speed and following us onto the ramp. As we raced toward the top, I took full advantage of the Panther's extra gear and shoved the stick up and to the right. The front tires of the low-bearing buggy left the ground, and we shot out from the loading bay, angling up off the ground. Rays of sun poured in through the windshield until the front of the Panther dipped back toward the earth. A plume of dust rose behind us as the wide all-terrain tires regained traction and launched us forward.

"Kilo, they have weapons systems," EO yelled. He watched the vehicles behind us leap out from the loading bay and tear through the dust.

"I know. I know."

"What do you know?" Matagi asked frantically, twisting his head to get a glimpse of the SVs behind us.

"DUCK!" I shouted at him. Bullets slammed into the back of the Panther, cracking the reinforced metal frame. Atop the security trucks, men strapped into suspension harnesses unloaded mid-range heavy weapons.

As the vehicles shifted, the men stayed idle; the contraption redirecting any force transferred but not already absorbed. *Shit.* I looked back at the frame breaking away. It'd hold for a while, but with the endless high-caliber ammo in the SVs behind us, we didn't have much time before the gunners wore us down.

"Kilo, you've got to get us to open terrain, or they'll tear us apart," EO warned.

"I'm working on it!"

I yanked on the steering wheel to reposition the vehicle onto the asphalt stretch of road that led away from the outpost. The gusts of wind blowing against us grew louder as we gained speed on the open road. The pavement wouldn't last forever, but hopefully it would give us a chance to outrun them, and enough of a head start to make it to the border.

"The frame won't hold much longer."

"We just need a little more distance," I shot back at EO.

The SVs started to fall behind, with more and more shots failing to connect from the gunner's hellfire.

"Come on," I whispered. I watched the speedometer fight against the vehicle's max speed. "Come on."

A shot hissed into the buggy, breaking through the frame.

"Oh shit!" Matagi yelled.

"More distance . . . just a little more," I said.

Moments later, the SVs finally faded into specks, until only a pair of black dots trailed behind. Even though they had firepower, bullets only went so far against a Panther. I looked over at Matagi and let a small smile break the tense muscles in my face.

"Now we did it," I said.

He laughed and relaxed back in his seat. "If you really did save me from whatever's going on back there, thank you."

"You're welcome." Then I peeked into the back seat to see EO's face deflate.

"Now, can you tell me what was going to kill me?" Matagi added.

"Kilo, they didn't slow; they stopped."

My head whipped around to see the SV specks behind us.

"They're gonna use—" EO didn't finish.

"Matagi, get down!"

The back of the Panther erupted in a collage of metal and reinforced glass. In the same instant, Matagi's chest did the same, splattering viscera across the inside of the windshield. Blood gurgled from his lips as he tried to speak. Both his hands flailed against the spewing river.

"Matagi!"

"Kilo." He tried to grasp my hand, but the lacquer of blood made it impossible.

“Help me.” With only one hand covering the hole, blood poured down his stomach.

“Hang on! You’re going to be okay! We can fix it. We’ll get you to the border!” I screamed. His dilated pupils faded as his head slumped to his shoulder. I pleaded with him, tears clouding my vision, “Matagi? Matagi! Come on!”

“Kilo, he’s gone,” EO whimpered. I looked at him for help, but he sat powerless in his despair.

The air whistled in through the bullet-sized hole in front of Matagi’s limp body, releasing Carbon Sytride into the vehicle. The burnt stench of organic matter from an Old World flooded the vehicle. We were no longer protected by the Helvik Theory. I pulled my tox mask up and strapped it around my face.

“I know what you are thinking, but you can’t go back.”

My fists constricted around the steering wheel as my blood burned white-hot.

“Kilo. You did what you could to save your friend, but we have to get back to the city, or this was all for nothing.”

Fighting back every urge, I closed my eyes and let the Panther tear into the open tundra toward Maui’s Continent territory.

It was a hellish drive, made worse by the decaying body of my friend riding passenger. The burn of my salty tears refused to let me forget. *How could I let this happen? We were clear. One clean, long shot, and he was gone.*

As hard as I fought it, Shipley played devil’s advocate in my head. *I taught you better than that, Kilo. You could have serpentined, put him in a safer position, anything, but you didn’t. You just let your friend die. Same old Kilo, never quite able to escape, and now leaving more bodies in your wake!*

If I had left him in Outpost 378, he’d still be alive, I thought. *He could have had a life, even if he was stuck in that place. I took that from him.*

"It's not your fault," EO responded, as if he'd been listening to my thoughts.

I looked back at his red, puffy eyes. It had been a silent journey for the last two hours until now. There hadn't been anything else to say. They'd killed him, and I'd let it happen.

Ahead in the distance, specks of black in the frozen, white wasteland soon turned into watchtowers spiraling up, guarding the zone that belonged to Maui City. Warning shots scattered the ground around the Panther but failed to deter our acceleration toward the center gate.

"Turn back or you will be fired upon!" a voice screamed from the top of the watchtowers. Ditches in the ground slowed our approach but didn't stop it. The buggy crawled up and down the man-made ravines, stretching the Panther's suspension to the limit. Through the wired fencing that connected the watchtowers, heavily armed security officials ran toward the gate. I punched the accelerator and aimed us at the entrance.

The slitted metal cracked open at the center with the force of the Panther, doing equal parts damage to the gate and our front end. I hit the brakes and brought the Panther to a screeching halt just inside the compound. An oddly constructed outpost sat in front of us, releasing more armed men out into the dirt receiving area. Maui City security officials surrounded the vehicle and slowly constricted around us. I raised my hands to the ceiling of the Panther as a security official opened the driver's side door and dragged me out.

"We have a body," someone yelled from the other side of the Panther.

"Who are you?" A security official jammed his weapon into my ribs.

I wiped some of the dirt from my jacket before raising my arms once again. "My name is Kilohana Ressler. I work for Big City DIIP, and I have information about a secret project in Kauaʻi City territory."

Another official leaned over and whispered in the ear of the woman in front of me, whose rifle was aimed at my chest. I glanced over her shoulder at EO.

"He's saying you're inter-island, so you have to go through Niʻihau."

I shouldn't have expected anything less. There was a dead body in my vehicle, and I claimed to be a foreign agent. But I couldn't let their protocol take me to Niʻihau. Who knew what the Doctor would do to EO if I didn't hold up my end of the bargain?

"What are you doing in Kauaʻi City territory if you're from Big City?" the woman demanded.

"I don't have time to explain everything, but long story short, they're building a city superstructure at Outpost 378. You can't send me to Niʻihau."

She scoffed. "Right. Take him to transport. Let them figure it out."

"No! I'm serious. They're building a city at Outpost 378. Please, listen to me!" Two other security officials grabbed my arms and dragged me away from the Panther. "Dammit, listen to me!"

Others lifted Matagi's body out from the Panther and onto a stretcher. "Please! He was my friend. I tried to save him," I cried.

EO watched them dump the limp remains of my friend over a ridge beyond our sight. We'd made it to Maui City territory, but for what? Matagi had died for nothing, and I wouldn't be able to do a thing about it from Niʻihau.

CHAPTER 22

I watched the waves relentlessly crash over the prison transport through a modest porthole in my cell. Unlike the larger transport ships that brought recruits to the Continent, this one was no match for the ferociousness of the sea. My stomach churned each time the boat rocked and left the taste of yesterday's bread and oats in my mouth.

I pleaded with the ship's crew to review my case or contact someone in Big City, but they ardently refused—it wasn't their problem. Yet they didn't mind resigning me to the quiet hum of the ship's engine.

Although it was small scale compared to the transport vessels, this prisoner ship was still designed with reinforced steel and an energy-dampening lining that reduced the outside noise. The solitude gave me ample time to think about Matagi and Solomon—two bodies left in the muck of the Continent.

Eventually, the dark, mesmerizing waves gave way to the brilliant, clustered lights of the island cities in the distance. We'd arrived. The unmistakable glow of Kaua'i City stood steadfast, the steward of Ni'ihau Island Prison. But Design City remained invisible, hidden behind the layered clouds. Once upon a time, Shipley had offered to take some of us on a tour of the prison; I regretted my disinterest.

"Follow the yellow line. If you deviate from it, you will be shot. Transition personnel will be waiting for you on the dock." The guard watched me through the rusted bars with bloodshot eyes sunken into pale skin and twisted a heavy key.

One step outside proved her threat was authentic. Heavily armed guards waited, positioned strategically along the yellow guiding line, which weaved its way to the exit. EO followed behind as I navigated to the ramp between the ship and Ni'ihau.

The sheer vastness of the prison obscured much of its structure, but I could extrapolate that the single, low-angled, concrete part of the dome covered the entirety of the island, like a massive, monochromatic cobblestone jutting out from the earth, adhering to the natural boundaries of the shoreline. Unlike the island cities, Ni'ihau looked much less terraformed and must've borne more of a resemblance to the island that had existed in the Old World.

Waves crashed against the rocky coastline, spraying salty mist across the dock. A shallow tide of seawater soaked my boots before rushing back over the meager cliff. Stoic prison guards surrounded white-coated men and women, their masks cheap imitations of those worn by the Night Sticks.

There were a few other prisoners on the transport, likely all deserters, and we lined up in front of the welcoming party. The guards assigned each of us a doctor, who led us into the jaws of the prison. Its wide, arched entrance enveloped us into the shadows until flickering lights created a pathway.

As we descended into the heart of the prison, the walls shrunk and screams from inside echoed toward us. A firm shove from a guard supplemented the soft gesture from my doctor, directing me into a cubical room. The only object inside was a thin steel bench. Along the closest gray wall, a wide, two-way mirror concealed any witnesses.

The guard slung two chained cuffs around my wrists, digging them into my soft flesh. A tug proved the cuffs had been fashioned to a chain connected to the floor. There was little give but enough for some movement.

"Your intake coordinator will be with you soon. Do you have any injuries?" The doctor's voice sounded disturbingly like an automated answering machine. I tilted my head to expose the purple and blue ring around my neck.

"Okay, good. Nothing too serious, then. *He* will be with you shortly."

"Wait, this is a misunderstanding. Something's going on at Outpost 378!" Ignoring my plea, she left, and the guard slammed the door behind her. EO paced along the wall.

"Whoever it is, just tell them the whole story. It's not that . . ."

I gave him an incredulous look. Even if I could tell them in a way that made sense, there was little chance the cuffs would come right off and I would be escorted to the next ferry.

The handle on the outside of the door scratched against its sliding mechanism. A foot breached the threshold, belonging to a dark-suited man, colorfully paired with an impeccable vest and necktie. His focused, granite face didn't look up from the floor as he strode into the room. An in-color version of the monochrome-chiseled man from the banner at the Ludo rally met my gaze. A pair of dirty blue eyes pierced through my soul.

"Hello, Kilo," my father said. The fingers on my hands curled over each other reflexively, but there was nothing EO could do.

"You've been persistent in your commission."

I pulled at the chains, sending a loud rattle through the room. The burning in my wrists helped ground me and keep an episode at bay, but I still found myself unable to speak. EO crouched behind me and put his hands on my shoulders. It was hard to tell whether my labored breathing resulted more from anger or fear. Either way, my father saw right through it.

"You must get that fire from me," he said through a thin smile. With a wave toward the wall, the mirror went dark. "I'd imagine you've seen the rara avis of Outpost 378. I never thought it would be *you* to threaten it. A moment of weakness coming back to haunt me."

"You—" I finally mustered the strength to speak, but his raised voice cut me off.

"No, Kilo. You are only speaking to me for one reason. You will answer every one of my questions, and then we will never see each other again." He waited without blinking, watching me like a wolf perched above a sheep. "Go on . . . tell me what you saw out there."

"I'm not telling you anything," I muttered.

He leaned in, looking past me, and whispered in my ear, "I know you think you're entitled to something because I fucked your mother, but that's not how this works. You've probably dreamed about this moment ever since I left you in that horrid alley. Put it out of your head now; you won't get any help from me—no satisfaction, no answers, nothing. Do you understand?"

"I don't want a single thing from you."

He stood back up, reigniting the unbreakable stare I remembered all too well from pieces of a lost childhood.

"Well, that's all right. Maybe if Sandra's life is on the table, you'll be more amenable to such a simple request?"

"Don't you touch her!"

"*I* don't need to do anything. I'm a Designer, Kilo, but in this case, it might be worth the bloodstains. Now, tell me what you saw."

I screamed as I pulled against the chains, forcing every muscle to their absolute constriction. He began pacing and rubbed at his temples. "Fine. I'll just start going down the list. I'll find Ade and the kid, too."

"Fuck!" Anguish ripped through me. EO rushed around the bench and grabbed my hands. What was I supposed to do now?

"It's okay, just tell him. It's not worth them dying over, and we're not dead yet."

My head slumped down, and I released the tension in my arms.

"I saw the city, and I know it's not affected by Carbon Sytride."

"Good. So, you don't know much about it." His tongue wrestled inside his mouth, and the next words came out cautiously. "Who were the Designers on Big City that sent you?"

I thought about it for a second before answering, "Decambra."

"And?" he asked pointedly.

"Designer Makrumbi."

"Designer Makrumbi sent you here?" For the first time, there was a hint of fear in his voice.

"He sent me to Kaua'i DIIP."

"What about the Continent? Did he send you specifically to the Continent?"

"He sent me to the *DIIP*."

He stood there for a moment, watching. I assumed he was determining the opaqueness of my answers, but I couldn't be sure. With two knuckles, he rapped on the door. The door scratched open slightly.

"Give me your personal device," my father ordered the guard outside.

A personal device slid through the opening, which he grabbed and opened frantically as the door slammed back shut. I watched my father lose himself in the projection, typing furiously. The screen was blurry, a static shade of gray fizzling with each interaction. I glanced at EO.

"I can't see anything. The devices are probably masked," he said. I shouldn't have been surprised, but it gnawed at me as seconds turned to minutes. I refused to speak first or ask my father anything. I was willing to answer his questions if it meant saving lives, but I wouldn't give a hint more.

"Did they tell you anything about *the Mountain*?"

"*The Mountain*?" The question caught me off guard. I'd started to lose myself in anger, the pain that had lined my veins all these years.

"Yes, *the Mountain*, did you ever hear those words?"

"What the hell is *the Mountain*?"

"Answer the question, Kilo; did you ever hear it?"

"No, I've never heard of *the Mountain*."

"Fuck!" He hurled the personal device at the mirror, shattering it into pieces. His chest heaved as he fought to regain his composure. With both hands, he stroked back his long gray hair, then gave me an indignant look before storming out of the room. That was it.

Two guards replaced him and removed my cuffs.

"Don't hurt them! Don't fucking hurt them!" My words fell on deaf ears.

The guards grabbed my shoulders, lifted me off the ground, and forced me out of the room. They took me deeper into the facility, passing several more rooms inside which white-coated doctors spoke with the other prisoners from the transport.

The captives' faces were wrought with anger, pleading for freedom. One by one the doors opened behind me in a symphonic rhythm. Doctors exited, followed by guards dragging their prisoners. With each step deeper into the facility, a putrid smell intensified. After a minute of walking, I saw a cable car suspended from a ceiling rail ahead.

The guards pushed me inside, the smell of rotting organic matter reaching its peak. The filthy cable car provided a glimpse into the treatment of prisoners here. The doors slid closed behind me as an automated system came to life, illuminating the decaying food and puke inside. I wasn't excited to experience the rest of it.

I didn't know what to expect when I heard about Niʻihau, but it wasn't this. The stories of prisoners sent here were humane, or at least humane enough for the Designers to get away with it. Now that I had information to save EO and stop an inter-island war, I was on my way to be locked up and left to rot. It was almost funny.

The car sped deep into the belly of the fortress, only to stop unceremoniously after a short ride. The door of the car opened to reveal an empty cell. I stepped over the gap that led to nothing more than a dark abyss and into the cell. The only evidence of life were digital locks on the columns of cells below that blinked a faint green and the pained murmurs from inside.

Inside, a ripped cot, dented metal toilet, and violently scratched mirror were the only amenities provided in my new home. As I looked closer, I noticed a personal device lay atop an unappealing pillow. I fired it up to find that any information was severely restricted. There were some books and other forms of entertainment available, but any access to larger networks was blocked.

"You okay?" EO's voice was warm, but it didn't help.

"Fine. I just want to forget about it. I did what he said."

"I'm sure he won't hurt them; he has no reason to."

My jaw clenched at the words. He wasn't wrong, but my father's power wasn't confined by rationality. He'd sent a bastard son to the Below without hesitation, so what would stop him from hurting a few random people?

A sudden bang sounded from the other side of the wall. Startled, I dropped the PD and took a step back.

"Just another prisoner," EO said.

"Can they hear me?" I asked.

"If you're close enough, maybe." I cozied up to the wall, pressing my face against it before turning and cupping my hands around my mouth.

"Hello?" Silence. Then a flurry of banging on the wall, louder with each strike.

"He can hear you. He just doesn't sound like a talker," EO mused. I tried the other wall, watching my reflection in the mirror.

"Hello?" I waited a few seconds and tried again. "Can you hear me?"

"Yes." The muffled voice sounded hopeless and pained, the voice of a man whose body and soul had been beaten into submission.

"Hi—" I paused, suddenly at a loss for words. "How long have you been here?" The words fell out awkwardly, but they were all I had right now. They were enough to keep him talking.

"I don't know."

EO cocked his head, listening intently.

"What?" I mouthed to him. He motioned for me to keep talking and pressed up against the wall.

"I'm sorry. Where are you from?"

"I can barely remember what it looks like. Who knows if it's even still there?"

"Well, I just got here, so maybe I can tell you."

EO closed his eyes as he processed every memory in his mind, searching for something.

"I'm from Nāpali," the man said, and EO's eyes shot open.

"Kilo! I know who that is!"

"What? Who?" I mouthed again.

"Mo!"

I took a few steps back from the wall and whispered, "Are you sure?"

"Positive."

"But the DIIP records said he was dead. What's he doing here?"

"I guess you need to ask him."

I slammed the wall a couple of times before speaking. "Maurice, is that you?"

The room fell silent as we awaited a response. It didn't come. I knocked on the wall again.

"Mo, I know it's you. It's Kilo." I looked at EO, but he shrugged. I slammed the wall again. "Mo, talk to me!"

No response.

I found it impossible to sleep. Although my body was exhausted and beaten, my brain refused to succumb to unconsciousness. It was punishing me for what I'd done on the Continent. *Maybe I belong here. As long as they feed me and EO can have his books, isn't this exactly what I wanted?*

It comforted me to see EO sleep soundly through the night, although it wasn't really sleep; it was more of a focused stasis. He described it like a daydream, but one that he was in control of, like a human's non-REM sleep, a sort of time dilation. His relaxed face was deceptive. I could never really tell whether he felt happy or fulfilled. He was so good at forced optimism.

Maybe if the Doctor somehow heard where we were, she'd let EO live. There was no point in reversing the work Kilah had done. I couldn't do anything for her now, no matter how much she threatened.

Abegail's frightened face popped into my head. Her small hands curled within Ade's as she cried. The thought constricted my chest. Even if EO lived, I still couldn't give up on Sandra.

I closed my eyes and tried to refocus my thoughts on something less painful. Calculating how many years you lost while on the Continent wasn't an exact science, but you could get close enough. The hole ripped in my tox suit by the spit amplifier had been unsealed for about ten minutes, so three or four years on top of being on the Continent for a week. Add that to the years I'd lost during the past decade, and . . . it was more than forty years of my life cut short.

Another routine pounding interrupted my calculations, but this time, it wasn't from the manic prisoner. The pounding came from Maurice's cell. EO's focus also broke, and we locked eyes, the same thought racing through our minds.

The pounding continued until I leaned up against the wall and knocked back.

"Is that really you, Kilo? If it's you, there is only one way you could know my voice through a solid wall."

"EO," I replied with a smile.

Distorted crying broke out on the other side of the wall. What he must have gone through being in here alone for who knew how long. It was only natural to break.

"It's okay, buddy. It's me. I'm actually a bit surprised you're talking to me at all. The last few times we were together ended in bruises and a couple broken bones."

A booming laugh, exactly like Bless', stopped the cry. "We have a long time to throw shit at each other, but for now it's just nice to talk to someone."

"Mo, what happened?" A couple of seconds passed with no response. "I read a report and talked to Bless. I thought you—"

"Don't say his fucking name!"

For a moment, it didn't feel like there was a wall between us at all. His voice reverberated through my cell. EO eyed me as his face dropped.

"Did he put you in here?"

"My own brother! Sold me out like I was one of his shitty fighters."

The resounding noise of bone slamming against concrete chilled my blood. Then I realized the heavy thumps weren't Maurice banging his fists against the wall; he was banging his head. "He only cared about *the future.*"

"What does that mean?"

"I don't want to talk about it. I want you to tell me what you're going to do to him for me."

I guessed at what might have happened between them, and any way you shaped it, it wasn't good. Any positive feeling I could muster toward Bless melted into air. *How could he do something like this to his own brother?*

A fraction of the anger Maurice must have felt invaded my system. But hurting Bless was unthinkable. Next to EO, he'd been my closest friend, and knowing Mo, he wasn't hoping for me to just slap his brother around a bit.

"Mo, we are both stuck in here, and even if we weren't, I know what you're thinking."

"You never used to be that naive. Big City changed you."

"What are you talking about?"

"This prison wasn't built for Designers, and for all intents and purposes, you're a fucking Designer." The words struck a nerve. A sting from every extremity raced toward my heart, exploding in a ball of fire. *I'm not one of them!*

"You said there'd be time later for the old shit."

"Stop being so sensitive and think about it."

"EO?" I asked.

"This prison wasn't meant to hold someone with a DPM," Maurice answered.

"Shit." As much as I hated to admit it, he was right. Everyone in this building—guards, prisoners, and interrogators—were all the same, but I was different. For as long as I could remember, I'd tried to convince everyone I was the same as them, and even believed it. But if I was honest, the worst part of me had also given me the greatest gift.

"You have any ideas how EO is supposed to help me in here?"

"A couple, but first I need you to promise you'll do what you deep down know you *can* do." The myriad of scenarios left me unsettled. Hopefully, it would be enough to convince him I was willing to do *something*.

"What do you have in mind?"

"Make him hurt past the point of ND."

"So, you want me to torture your brother? I'm not going to do that, but I will beat the shit out of him for you if that's what you really want."

He acquiesced in a grunt.

The room fell quiet for a moment, and I snapped back to reality within the cold walls of our maximum-security prison. For just a moment, it had felt like we were sitting in his house in Nāpali.

Bless and I had always been close, two brothers bound by more than blood. At times, I'd thought all Maurice wanted was for one of us to prove he mattered, too. We were shitty to him, even if we loved him. Things changed and grew more challenging as we got older, but Mo was always my brother. Now, we were talking about the same issues but wishing we were back in that house.

"Make sure you do it on the platform," Maurice finally said.

"Fine. Now tell me how to get out of here?"

"Losing there will be more painful than anything physical anyway." I couldn't see him, but I guessed he had a smile on his face for the first time in forever.

"Mo, come on. Help me."

"The car you came in on, that's how they deliver food. You haven't been here long enough, but it shows up, the car doors open, food gets placed through the slit at the bottom of the cell door, and then the car moves on to the next cell. If you can get the cell door to open from the outside, you can jump on the car and ride it to the end."

"What's at the end?"

"Does it look like I know?"

"Right, sorry. So how do I unlock the door from the inside?"

"Do you remember what it looked like, the outside of the door?" He didn't wait for an answer. "Well, he does, and he can tell you exactly how to do it."

"EO?" My eyes lifted from the spot on the wall I'd been using to picture Mo on the other side. EO turned and moved to the cell door, examining it as if he could see right through.

"You see the keypad, EO? When the car comes by, it auto-connects. You need to create a new input that tells the door to open as if there is a prisoner extraction request."

EO nodded. "I think we can do that. If there's a tray, maybe we can use it to reflect a false signal to the receiver outside, and it will confuse the system."

"What did he say?" Maurice asked.

"He says he thinks we're getting out of here." I couldn't help but feel the tingling of excitement, but it quickly faded. "What about you?"

"You'll come back. Whether or not you care to admit it, there's no way you're going to leave someone you care about in here. Plus, I will sleep tight knowing you're beating the shit out of Bless."

I half grinned, knowing he meant what he said. Maurice wasn't always someone to look up to, but he was tough. He'd survive.

"I won't leave you here. I promise."

CHAPTER 23

A couple of hours passed while we tried to figure out a way to get the personal device to produce specific images. According to EO, each of the code inputs contained Greek symbols. He didn't tell me how he knew, and I didn't ask.

Among the books, photographs, and videos encrypted in the device, there had to be components of our key. EO tried to explain the intricacies of the exterior locking mechanism, but to little effect.

"Basically, there's a digital key, a series of inscriptions set in a specific order and angle to communicate with the mechanism," EO said.

"Like Holo-lotto?"

He sighed and glanced at me with patient eyes. "Not quite that simple. To trigger the door open, we need the specific combination."

I couldn't recall a digital key transferred between the cable-car and the cell door, but EO assured me there had been one. From his description, the key would be a holographic projection of symbols that were then rolled into the correct sequence against the digital receiving pad of the door.

Unfortunately, according to Maurice, the key combination was reset every time the cable car returned to a loading area, but one aspect of the procedure worked in our favor. Each cell in a certain block received the same keys during a cable car run, no matter what it was—food, medical, or prisoner transport. So long as we could get the full door access key and input it before the car returned to a loading bay, we'd be out. There was only one way to do this, and Maurice was the key.

"You ready?"

"Fuck you!" Maurice shouted back.

"So, yes."

With the crack of bone, a paralytic scream resounded from Maurice's cell. I'd said he didn't need to compound fracture it, but he'd insisted on giving us as much time as possible.

"Holy—"

His cries were interrupted by a muffled alarm ringing in his cell. Maurice had estimated thirty seconds before a car showed. The whizzing of the cable car gliding toward us would become audible within fifteen and would be set to open Mo's cell door to transport him to the med center.

This was it. We only had a few moments to cobble together as much information as possible from inside our prison cell. I squished up against the wall, stomach down, with my ear positioned in the crevasse that had been used to deliver food this morning. EO stood directly above me, his hands firmly planted against the wall and his eyes closed in complete focus.

I took a final breath as the cable car whizzed past and its doors slid open. Then silence. My lungs burned, but I refused to breathe, to even allow a thought to permeate the complete blackness in my mind, a blank canvas for EO to work with.

The auto-car connected to Maurice's cell with a beep that pierced my ears amid the tranquility of the cell block. Maurice had agreed to hold in his pain during the moments before he would be taken, and he did so brilliantly.

"I think I got it." EO drew his hands back from the wall, still maintaining focus. The fading sound of the car being drawn away by the complex system of cables meant we were on the clock to put the pieces together.

"Okay. Place the Theta at a 90-degree angle."

I fidgeted with my personal device, pulling up a graphic of the Greek letter Theta and adjusting it appropriately. EO moved his hands in an exotic pattern to draw various symbols in the air with his fingers.

"Omega at 180 degrees . . . no wait . . . reflected along its axis."

I didn't understand the distinction, but I complied.

"Take a Delta and—" He paused, stumped. "Leave it."

"Is that it?"

"I'm not sure. I think so."

A running stopwatch ticked above the sequence as I placed the personal device in a scratched square near the tray opening. 13.78 seconds flashed by. With our original expectation of thirty seconds out the window, we needed to work fast.

My fingers ran frantically across the functions on my device to align each of the symbols equidistant from each other in the correct placement, according to EO's instructions. There was no way of knowing how or whether the proprietors of the prison would be notified once the cell door opened, but either way, this remained our best chance. The cables of a car hissed before another flew by.

"Hurry up. Come on."

Moments later, a flurry of cable cars jolted by, clearly not intending to stop near us. Then one of them came to a halt just outside our door.

"Position," I said. I dropped and sat cross-legged, waiting for the car to shoot the dinner tray into the cell.

"Get ready," EO said.

The silver tray holding food, packaged tightly with cellophane, slid into my lap. I quickly flipped it, with the food intact, and slid it back through the hole, tilting it at as close to a 45-degree angle as I could.

"Up slightly," EO directed. I carefully moved it higher until EO's eyes shot open.

"There!"

"Activate," I said, directing the personal device balanced at my side to open. The hologram emanated from the device, struck the tray dead center, and reflected upward.

"Steady. Steady."

With a click, the door unlatched and receded into the wall. Hardly enough time elapsed for me to drop the tray and retract my hands before the door ripped them clean off. The tray tumbled down the side of the prison wall, hitting the floor at the bottom after a few seconds, the distant clang hinting at the true depth of the prison.

I leaped up and hurtled across the small gap into the cable car just as the doors slammed closed behind me. EO followed, but didn't quite get inside the car before the doors appeared to cut him in half.

It was comical for a moment as his body contorted between the closed doors, his programming unable to make sense of his interaction with the environment. I couldn't help but laugh while his appendages swung violently.

"Can you please do the thing?"

His shout reverberated both inside and outside in a muted echo.

"What thing?"

"Shut up and just do it."

I squeezed my eyes closed, relaxing my muscles, and envisioned EO standing clearly within the cable car. Seconds later, his body stood weightless directly in front of me, his eyes shut and breath slow. Neither of us were exactly sure how it worked, but somewhere in EO's programming, there was a way to reset him when his interaction with the environment malfunctioned.

I completed the scene by focusing on the details: boxes piled high in the corner, jagged rips from where the automated system had pulled out trays of food, the array of buttons perfectly aligned in thematic order, and grafted walls connected to the door system. My eyes opened. There he stood, a matured version of the vision in my head.

"Thank you. Was that so hard?"

"I wanted to enjoy it for a second."

We sat on one of the unopened boxes, our feet suspended above the floor, while the car floated along to our unknown destination. It stopped frequently to eject food into the nearest prisoner cell, each time offering a glimpse of what went on there.

"Once we get the information to the Doctor and find Sandra, we're on the first train back to Big City. I can't do this anymore."

EO didn't respond right away, his face consumed with thought. I could only guess at the narratives running through his mind, but I knew him well enough to feel his reservations.

"What about Maurice?"

"What about him? I'll find out what happened back in Big City and do what I can to get him out, and then *he* can get revenge."

"Kilo—"

"None of this would have happened if we'd left that night. We haven't grown, EO; if anything, I've regressed. I've hurt more people in the past week than in the past year." The emotions tugged at my heart. "I can't be this. I can't be here any longer."

"You can help these people. I know that's not what we came here for, but *you* can."

"I've sacrificed enough!" I practically shouted the words at him.

The cable car stopped abruptly, and my mind warped back to the present. The brief wave of adrenaline washed out like the tide. I peered through the open doors. A cluttered corridor curved into the facility with stacks of similar boxes from inside the cable car lining the walls.

The doors had only been open for a moment before light footsteps from out of sight turned to heavy boots clopping toward us. I looked around the car for any cover but found nothing.

Outside the car, a protruding section stretched along the face of the wall perpendicular to the hallway. I looked to EO, hoping for another way out, but knowing it was the only option.

"Go," EO said. "It's probably going to hurt."

"Thanks."

I clawed my fingers around the metal hinge that couldn't have extended more than an average doorframe and scaled the wall until I was out of sight from anyone in the hallway. Below, my feet dangled above the sea of blinking green lights.

EO stood squarely in the car's doorway, watching the corridor intently. I waited, defenseless, no more than an arm's length away.

The person spoke indistinctly to themselves. Their words became more audible with each step closer until they must have been right around the corner. Then . . . nothing.

I watched EO's eyes follow something in the corridor. The skin covering my fingers felt like it was tearing at the knuckles. My full weight fought to take its pound of flesh. The blood in my fingers rushed to the tips, trying to maintain my grip.

"You okay? She's almost gone." EO said.

Clanking sounds commenced around the corner, and moments later, trays of food flew into the auto-car, only a woman's arms visible from where I hung. My grip started to give, the sweat on my hands making it difficult to keep hold. I pulled my pinky finger and put it over my other fingers in the hope EO would see the signal.

"Just a second. One more. All right, you're good."

I jumped back into the cable car, trying to soften the landing by rolling as I hit the floor, but a stray foot caught on a tray and knocked it to the plated floor with a loud crash. As I burrowed behind some boxes, the faint sound of receding footsteps stopped. EO looked at me before assessing the worker's movement. I dared not breathe.

"She's—" The pause hung in the air. EO eyed the woman, waiting for her to decide. "Leaving."

A huge sigh blew through my lips, and I assessed the damage to my hands. They would bruise, but nothing that wouldn't heal.

A few moments passed before I dared to peek out of the car. The corridor lay empty, save for a few more boxes.

"I think we're in luck," EO said as he crossed over to the corridor.

I followed him as he casually strolled around the bend and up into a larger, seemingly endless hallway. Scattered doors stood closed along the route, leaving an uncomfortable amount of open space beyond the walls. An occasional sign suggested what might be behind the doors, but we pressed forward, looking for an exit.

"This place seems deserted. I assumed it would be crawling with people," I said.

A slightly opened door revealed a barren room. No windows, not even a desk or a chair sat inside. It was almost as if it had never been used.

"What's wrong with this place?"

"I don't know, but right here is where we wanna be." EO motioned to a door, much wider than the others and sealed with an airlock lining.

"Open it."

A burst of cold air whooshed in as the airlock released, and the door creaked open. I forced it inward, taking a step over the threshold, only to hear a crunch beneath my boots. I stepped out onto the makeshift dirt platform elevated above the cliff's edge below.

"Not bad," I said.

"We're not there yet."

I turned back to see EO looking out. The harsh waves lapped up against the rocky coastline that extended along the island. The descent to the water gashed my hands and legs from the craggy terrain. It didn't help that my hands had swollen from the unwanted grip training earlier.

At the base of the island, an inlet beach served as a brief reprieve, the result of years of erosion. I took off my shoes and sat as the coarse sand between my toes mixed with some of the sweat from my feet. I'd always found it profoundly uncomfortable and never understood the Designers' obsession with it.

Even so, my feet sank into the beach. I picked up some sand and poured it out of my funneled hand, spraying it across my legs, when the sand began to shift. It turned from a dark gray to a milky white. Around me, the light shined, burning my skin.

"Pour it like this, sweet boy."

The voice sounded soft and kind, just like my mother's, but this memory didn't feel like mine. A hand wiped away what sand was left on my legs and grasped another handful before letting it waterfall over the side of her palm.

"See?"

The woman's face crested into vision, and my mom's brilliant smile looked down at me. A hand pressed against my back. I turned to see who it belonged to, but the light faded, and the sand burned back to its present charcoal gray.

EO stared off into the ocean. "You know how long the swim is?"

I paused for a moment. "No idea. I just won't think about it."

"Twenty-five kilometers."

"Why would you say that? I was fine." I grabbed a fistful of the dark sand and let it waterfall over the side of my palm like my mother, spreading it across my legs.

"Do you ever remember going to a white sand beach?" I asked, and waited as he searched the sea for an answer.

"Why?"

"I think I just saw something, a memory maybe. It felt real but . . . not mine."

He turned, his head bowed, and his eyes rose to meet mine. "There is something I've been meaning to tell you since I got back. Some things I've held on to for a while, but . . . maybe you need to remember."

"Remember what?" The words involuntarily came out cold. "I trusted you to hide only what you needed to. What haven't you told me?"

His mouth opened to speak. But then I remembered the days I'd spent without him, the words I'd said in the indi-cycle just before we crashed. He deserved better. Behind us, a siren blared, and spotlights sliced through the dawning sky.

"I trust you. You can tell me when we get back if you want to, but I know you love me, and I know everything you do, you do for me," I said.

He provided a shameful nod and looked back out toward the island city. The murky water rose and fell against the cliff of Niʻihau. Lights lustered, just visible in the distance, clouded by the haze. In what world did I ever think it was possible to make the swim back to Kauaʻi City?

I stripped down to my briefs and waded into the sub-sixty-degree water. Shivers ran up my spine as the waves tried to force me back to the island, a voluntary keeper of the prison. I dove through the next wave, popping up after its crash into the tail of white water.

At first, the freezing temperature accelerated my heart rate and delivered a short-lived burst of energy, but as I paddled, minute by minute, my body fought back. A burning in my muscles, accompanied by a need to gasp for air at every chance, stopped me. After a while, I floated aimlessly in the water, hardly feeling the cold anymore.

Without asking EO, I couldn't tell how far I'd come or how long I had been out here. He paddled up next to me, with a similar look of fatigue, a gesture that did nothing to help my aching body. Behind us, Niʻihau had faded, but Kauaʻi City remained in the distance.

"There's no way I make this," I wheezed as the water billowed around me.

"Close your eyes and push through. I will guide you," EO shouted as an enormous wave rolled over us. "Don't give up. I believe in you."

I turned onto my stomach, pointed myself toward the lights, and started paddling, eyes shut tight. I placed every available ounce of focus on the movements—left, right, left, right. It must have worked because EO didn't need to course correct often, and the minutes turned into hours. At one point, I gave in and opened my eyes for a split second to see the growing city ahead, the beacon of lights now clearly visible.

"Close your eyes and swim!" EO shouted.

The current surged close to the city. I fought through the tide with all my remaining energy. I brought my right arm over in a powerful front stroke, and my hand sunk into the sand. I tried to gain purchase, pulling myself out of the water, but the sand melted away like butter in the sun. Another wave crashed behind me, tossing me toward the beach.

The dry sand caught my weakened body, and I finally felt my swollen muscles from the swim. I opened my eyes to see the blurry, towering city above me. Kauaʻi City taunted my near comatose body, but my mind fought to stay awake.

Despite the warm sand beckoning me to stay, I managed to pull myself up to my knees and look at the dividing wall between me and the Kauaʻi arcology.

I'm not done yet.

CHAPTER 24

The sand crunched beneath my feet along the beach toward the island city wall. Based on the direction of Niʻihau, I assumed I'd washed up somewhere between the Kalahani District and Ludo District. A stroke of luck I didn't take lightly.

Maybe I'd judged the Company too soon. If their tunnel to the beach really did exist, I'd gladly tell them everything I found at Outpost 378. I wondered whether the Doctor had found Sandra. At first, I gave it slim odds, but after witnessing the power she had to create Kilo Walker and place him at a specific outpost, maybe I could hope.

Along the walk of the outer wall, EO again became a storyteller in a vain attempt to make the trek easier. But everything had drained my emotional strength. I felt myself boiling over and realized I might burst into an episode at any moment. I wanted to ask about what he knew, what he'd been hiding from me, but I decided against it in my current state. His memories would still be there in a few hours, so we trekked on.

"Hey, is that—" EO didn't finish, instead bolting toward the island city wall. I followed and tracked his gaze to the faded footprints in the sand. As we followed them, the footprints deepened, unaffected by the tide, until they stopped just before the wall.

I looked around, half-expecting to see someone on the beach or at least something watching us, but the island was empty. Even above, the curvature of the wall made it impossible to see any of the Mid-City buildings.

"It has to be around here somewhere, right?" EO asked. I placed my hand against the concrete and felt for any sign of an entrance. Nothing.

"Maybe this isn't the right place?"

Just then, my bare foot caught on something beneath the sand. We looked at each other before I dropped to my knees and started digging. A few centimeters under the sand, a mechanical contraption lay hidden from the world. No one would have known to look for it, even if they'd managed to get outside the island city.

I climbed back to my feet and pressed my foot against the contraption's broadside until it produced a rough, mechanical click. A moment later, the solid concrete wall split and rumbled apart, revealing a narrow pathway. I looked around, uneasy with our solitude. I'd finally witnessed, firsthand, the value of maintaining access to the beaches. This was the only place in the world where your soul was free from the Designers and Carbon Sytride—a different kind of freedom.

EO went first and guided me into the soggy tunnel. Inside, the pathway tightened as it led us into the city, a dark and ominous route back to civilization. The uneven rocks along the path refused to take pity on my feet, and my shoulders caught on the rough walls a few times, leaving a trail of blood behind us.

Finally, an incomplete section of the rocky interior appeared up ahead—a door. EO motioned toward it, and I pressed my ear to its moist, wooden exterior before pushing inward.

EO took a cautious step inside, positioning himself at the entrance to the disheveled room. Piles of clothes sat scattered across the otherwise empty space. I held back my vomit from the soiled, sweat-drenched smell wafting around us.

"What the hell is this place?" EO asked. He bent over to inspect a ripped shirt that lay atop one of the piles. "Oh God."

“What is it?” I asked.

“Let’s go. I think I know where we are.”

Fresher air waited for us outside, but the hallway was riddled with the type of dilapidation you’d only see in certain parts of the Below. Broken furniture and medical equipment were strewn along its length, ending with a sharp turn in the hallway. Each step required precision to ensure the soles of my feet weren’t torn open from the debris hiding in the clutter.

The further into the building we traversed, the more I understood. Faint voices drifted through a pair of nearly unhinged double doors. I noticed empty cloth bags disregarded along the path, stained with brown and red and stamped with an unmistakable logo.

LUDO DESIGN FOOD SUPPLY

“I don’t want to go in there,” I said.

“I wouldn’t blame you, but we don’t have much of a choice.”

I looked down at my blotchy, exposed skin, only the briefs saving me from being bare. Some discoloration from my swim had receded, but knowing what might be in the other room brought a new, internal wave of biting cold.

“How does anyone survive this place?”

I pushed through the doors into a wide hall. Rotten hospital beds were pressed together in uneven rows, holding what could only be described as people a single step from death. On the far side of the room, people dressed in ragged coats and fraying pants huddled together, fighting for scraps out of the Ludo Design food bags.

Even from this distance, I could make out the half-matured pork slab. Parts of its midsection curved inward toward its spine, dripping a brown, greasy equivalent of blood. The fleshy red parts of the hog had already been torn to shreds, and now, these people’s filthy hands dove into the unfinished synthetic meat.

“Who are you?” I hadn’t noticed the man hunched over one of the beds.

He wrestled inside his jacket, but his blood-soaked latex gloves made it challenging to retrieve his pistol.

I threw my hands in the air. "My name's Kilo. I work with the Company." I took another look around at where we stood. "I've never been here before, but if you talk to someone, I'm sure they can explain who I am."

The man's bloodshot eyes and deep creases under his sockets told me more of his state than his drained words: "Tell them yourself."

"Is there someone here I can talk to?"

He placed the gun back in his pocket, ripped off the gloves, and gestured past the huddled groups of people. I watched him put on a clean pair and plunge a scalpel straight into the abdomen of the woman he'd been working on. The shock caused her body to jolt up. She screamed and grabbed at the doctor, begging for more of the pork in a delirious frenzy. Instead, the man stuck an ND inhaler into the woman's nostrils and depressed the cartridge trigger. Her flailing limbs relaxed until she faded back into unconsciousness.

I forced myself to walk past the crippled people in beds, some with scarred-over holes in their throats and others with sewn-up lacerations across their torso. One man's eyes followed me as I passed, his black teeth and tongue trying to speak. His weak hand rose slightly from the bed and pointed toward the floor at the foot of the bed. A half-filled ND inhaler sat wedged between the leg of the bed and the floor. I handed it to him and waited, but the inhaler never made it to his nostrils.

"I—"

"I don't know either," EO finished for me.

The groups of hungry people didn't turn as we passed. I couldn't understand how they could stomach the half-matured slabs of pork. The same stench from the piles of clothes at the entrance didn't seem to affect them.

I thought back to the packaging facility Kamalu and I'd staked out while waiting for Reklov. I'd taken it for granted then, but I wondered who decided which children ate reconstructed, matured pork and which children ate . . . this.

Before I passed the last group, an icy hand grabbed at my rib cage.

"Do you want some?"

A boy, maybe six or seven, held up a piece of the brown meat. His stomach protruded from his body, and the sharp curvature of his collarbones nearly poked through his skin.

I wasn't sure what to say and stood awkwardly, looking into his glassy eyes.

"Tell him he can have it," EO said.

I stumbled over the words. "You can have it."

"Okay, thank you." The boy sat back down alongside a few other children and bit down into the chewy meat.

"Come on. What we can do is get this information to the Company."

I followed EO into the open room at the end of the hall. A woman hunched over a desk, a piece of the red, fleshy pork half-eaten next to her.

"Hey," I said. She didn't respond. "Hey!"

Her body jerked back, and she looked around wildly. "Who the hell—"

"My name's Kilo. I need to talk to your boss."

We waited outside the Company's building, trying not to think too hard about the people inside. The dank alleyway sank between the Company's annexed processing house and a dilapidated apartment complex. Lights glowed in only a few of the windows above. Apparently, electricity was not a luxury *everyone* was afforded, contrary to the Design.

"I heard rumors, but nothing like this," EO said.

"Fuckin' Design."

"You think they'll all die?"

I thought about what incomplete synthetic meats did to the human stomach. "I don't know." Even the thought of it revolted me.

"It's smart, though," EO said.

"What?"

He looked back at the Company's building. "You offer people a way outside the island city but make them walk through addicted, starving, and dying people to reach it. They are stoking hatred for the Designers . . . and offering freedom and breeding radicalism in return."

A hooded figure wrapped around the corner of the alley. "Kilo?"

I tried to see the person's face, but they were still shrouded in the shadows.

"Who's asking?"

"I'm with the Company, and a mutual friend who requested I bring you these." He rummaged around in a satchel strapped to his chest. "Here, I have some clothes for you to blend in."

He pulled out a black hoodie and some cargo pants, along with some worn shoes that looked at least a size too small.

"A mutual friend, huh? And who would that be, someone learned?"

Whoever it was, the clothes were a welcome gift. I still hadn't recovered from the chill of the ocean, so the hoodie and pants brought some feeling back to my legs and chest.

"Yes, sir."

Sir, huh?

"We have a duo-cycle coming."

I grunted in acknowledgment but was still skeptical. I knew the Doctor had worked with the Company to get me to the Continent, but what did they want in return? After all, they'd said their services came at a price.

A few minutes later, the cycle pulled up, and we got in. As we drove through the city, the abnormal presence of red glows in the distance struck me as odd, and I looked to EO for insight. He had none.

"What's with the colors?"

"Things have gotten worse since you left. Restrictions in Ludo are elevated, and the Company has started to fight back." He pointed out the front window. "Ludo protesters are burning anything they can get their hands on before the Night Sticks beat them to death."

I followed the smoke as we traveled under one of the mid-level areas. Instead of a protest being broken up by the Night Sticks, the mid-level was overrun with people. We swerved out of the way of a flaming Designer banner that floated down into our path. My fist tensed, and I braced for my father's face to look down on me, but thankfully this banner belonged to another Designer.

My intrigue turned to consternation as I recalled the district fires of Honolulu City. I remembered the beginnings of it, the small district revolutions that were "under control," and then the fires. The burning glows in the distance were the first step in history repeating itself.

We passed by the diner where EO and I had eaten lunch a week earlier. The hint of bacon and eggs wafted from the revolving door and grabbed at the shriveled pit of acid in my stomach.

Life in the Kamehameha Building had all but ceased. Unlike a week ago, only a few groups of people now walked about the building. My handler must have been right; people of the Ludo Below had enlisted in the war outside.

We followed my handler into the elevator, then jolted upward toward the thirty-seventh floor. The mildew smell of a water-soaked level reminded me of my previous meeting with the Company. Somehow, I was more nervous than before. A shifting balance of power in the Below wasn't anything good, and I intended to tell them something that would change their entire world. If they weren't already angry with their lack of food or medicine, they would be now. Unfortunately, it's the messenger that's often left with a bullet.

My handler banged on the door, shaking the Company's emblem that was fashioned in the middle of the metal entrance. Unlike the first meeting, Fuka threw the door wide open.

"I got him." The handler directed Fuka's attention to me.

"Bring him in then."

A lot had changed since the tense meeting here a week ago. Groups of men and women circled around small desks in various parts of the room, all discussing the projections above their personal devices. The secretive meeting place for the Elders had turned into a full-fledged war room.

The apprehension in the room turned palpable at the sight of us. The quickened speech patterns, shaking legs, and furrowed brows heightened my concern about what we'd just walked into.

"Aloha, Kilo. Through here." A familiar face I couldn't place waved me through into an adjoining room, where an empty chair awaited in the same meeting formation as a week earlier. The shoulder-tattooed Elder who'd run the first meeting was delivering an emotional speech. The faces of the other Elders scrunched with a wave of wrought anger, having eaten up the tattooed man's platitudes, some hyper-fixated critique of the Design that was the fire beneath this revolution.

He ended his rousing and turned to me. "As I was saying, I believe Mr. Ressler will be extremely helpful to our cause."

The man who ushered me in took his seat, his shaved head jogging my memory. He was the one who had been seated at the end of the table, questioning my legitimacy the first time we met. Now, he sat quietly and waited like everyone else in the room to see if there were earnings from their investment.

I recognized all the faces, but a new one supplemented the gathering, one who hadn't attended previously. I recognized her, too. Dr. Amelia Manuma sat stone-faced at the tattooed man's right hand. It took a second to process, then turned obvious. The Doctor wasn't an acquaintance of the Ludo Company; she was a full-fledged leader.

The tattooed Elder gestured with his hand. "Mr. Ressler, please have a seat."

I did as I was told and scanned the room.

"I don't think we properly introduced ourselves last we spoke. I am Masaki, the leader of the anti-Design movement in Kaua'i City, and I believe you already know the Doctor."

"We've met," I responded, the words seething through tight lips.

"The Ludo Company is working toward something bigger, and we have grown to be more than a district gang," he said.

His manic eyes blazed back at me with the room's milky white lights catching on newly formed beads of sweat. I'd seen this look before on the faces of Designers when they thought they'd glimpsed the future. He believed every word, enough to die for it, to sacrifice every person in this room for it. EO didn't understand, but this was it. These people were just like the Designers. They didn't care what happened, as long as a building was built or a tower was burned to the ground. The temperature of my blood rose with each word.

"Kilo, the Designers are on the brink of losing control of Ludo, something that could upend the entire system. But we need an accelerant, something that can get everyone in Ludo climbing the steps to the top of Mid-City."

He took a deep breath. It was clear their plan hinged on my discovery of something big, something like a weapon, something that could be used to ignite people's discontent. *Be careful what you wish for*.

"Did you find the Speer Project, Kilo?"

"Something like that."

"Well? What did you find?"

"How about you tell me what I walked into from the beachhead first?"

A few of the Elders looked at Masaki, clearly unaware of how I'd arrived back to Kaua'i City. Masaki massaged his jaw for a moment before responding, "You know what it is, Kilo. Don't waste our time."

"You're telling me there is nothing more you can do to help those people? There are kids in there!"

"You're not in the other districts or Mid-City, Kilo. Remember that. We're doing what we can, more than the Designers ever would."

"And that's enough?"

His gaze narrowed. "Tell us what you found."

I opened my arms and motioned around the room. "They're building this."

Confused looks covered the faces of the Company's leadership.

"They are building an island city."

Murmurs between members began to cloud the room. I couldn't blame them. A city on the Continent opened up countless strategic opportunities for Kaua'i City, but they didn't even know the worst part. Among the murmurers sat the Doctor, expressionless as her eyes examined my body language with every word.

"That's not all," I forced over the growing voices. "The city they are building isn't affected by Carbon Sytride." The room fell quiet as a mixture of optimism and horror passed over the faces of the Elders.

"That's not possible." Masaki pulled back his hair with both hands, a grimace of distress settling across his face. "I want to talk to Murray or anyone you can get a hold of in Honolulu right now."

An Elder sitting a few seats away froze at the command.

"Right fucking now!"

"I *told* you this guy was full of shit!" an Elder on the far side of the room shouted.

"Were you at Outpost 378? Did you watch innocent people die to bring this information back?"

I stood up, a wave of fiery anger burning low in my gut. The flashes of Matagi's open chest and Solomon's sprawled body on the ground poured gasoline on the growing rage. EO's secrets were the eternal flame.

"The world as you know it is over. You wanna burn this city down, go for it. The Designers will take everyone from Mid-City and move them onto the Continent. You are all worthless in their eyes and delusional for not seeing it. There is no power too great for the Designers to wield against you. You'll be reduced to fragments just like your friends in Honolulu, and they won't bat an eye."

I left the room behind me in a mess of chaos, Masaki attempting to control the other Elders.

But before I made it through the door, the Doctor shouted for me and quickened her pace to catch up with me.

I turned and spat the words at her: "We had a deal, and I'm guessing you didn't find Sandra, so I would like to go back to believing you're a myth."

"You ignorant child." She grabbed my hand, her nails tearing into the skin. "You think this world revolves around you. Who do you think that reminds me of, huh?"

I pulled my hand away and started, "I don't—"

"Shut up and listen. No one in there fully understands what this all means. They care about Ludo, but you and I know that doesn't mean much. I didn't ask to be in this position, I was born into it . . . just like you. So, you understand what your responsibility is to this island city, to the people that live here—I know your DPM does."

"I'm going to find Sandra and go back to Big City. Everything else can burn, freeze, or crumble for all I care."

Her face moved close to mine, almost impaling me with her stare. "I don't believe you."

"I don't care what you believe. I've done my part."

"Kilo, we don't get to choose the price we pay for living in this world. Everyone here is paying for it, and you're no exception." From behind her back, she pulled out a personal device and my Nambu. Her rough hands grabbed mine once again and forced the device and the gun into them. "Sacrifice isn't about giving up what we can; it's giving up what we can't. Go see your friend and see if you don't understand."

CHAPTER 25

My rapping on the door reverberated through the cramped hallways. No answer. Again, I pounded my fist, this time half-expecting other residents of the Coffins to peek out at the commotion.

"Who is it?" A weak voice came from the other side.

"Ade? It's Kilo. Let me in."

The door swung open to reveal a crumpled Ade. Noticeable trails of tears outlined with mascara covered her cheeks. Her oversized pants and thick jacket bore no resemblance to the dressed-up Aloha Alley companion I'd run into a week ago.

She threw herself at me, wrapping her arms tightly around my neck, which I reciprocated with a light hug. Her tears resumed, and her arms squeezed my bones.

"I don't know what to do, Kilo."

"It'll be okay. What happened?"

She backed away, the blood draining from her face. "You don't know?"

For the first time, I scanned Sandra's cluttered apartment. It looked different. Things were missing, but I couldn't inventory what they were. It seemed as though the house had been ransacked a second time, the contents of boxes and dressers untouched before now sprawled across the living area. A scan of the room drew my attention to its center. A box unlike the others sat among the wreckage.

Ade caught my gaze. "Kilo, don't." She grabbed my arm, but it was no use. The box beckoned like an unknown but familiar, unavoidable siren.

EO appeared in front of me, trying to stop my path, but I shoved him aside and bent down above the carefully crafted metallic box, its contents painstakingly protected from any threat. A simple lock consisting of four turning dials, each labeled with the letters of the English alphabet, latched the opening.

"Kilo, stop! Just read the letter. We don't need to see it." Ade waved a single piece of paper with handwritten calligraphy on it. But I knew whatever the note said wouldn't be enough.

The gold dial with silver inscriptions sent chills down my spine. I'd seen this lock often as a child in my father's office in Design City. The dials clicked, and I slowly created a four-letter word with the mechanism—Sofi. My mother's name. My heart stopped for a moment.

The latch released the top of the box, and a wave of putrid air released into the room. As I looked inside, my lungs forgot how to breathe, such a simple mechanism foiled by my anticipatory mind.

At the sight, my throat seized, and my stomach tried to evacuate any remains in my body. I gripped the sides of the box, trying not to lose consciousness. Inside, a decaying heart, bloody and slashed, lay centrally placed above etched words at the bottom of the box. Crudely scratched into the metal, the message read, "A moment of weakness."

My mind flashed back to cold dreams of the truck, of the men arguing aboard it before I received the injection that gave me EO. His face became clear again, the angry, broken features of a powerful man, the same man being burned on banners across the district right now. He'd killed my mother and now, Sandra.

I slammed the box closed, reattaching the latch, and stumbled back to the wall before collapsing to the floor. Ade crawled next to me. She wrapped herself around me, and I let go. I couldn't tell if it was better to have her there with me or be alone, but regardless, the warmth of her embrace helped.

EO's eyes deepened, and he slowly dragged in a ragged breath. He seemed unsure of what to do, of what I needed. He sat with me and held my hand as he broke down with me.

There were no words for a while. We allowed each other to feel what we needed to feel. I relived moments, the closeness with her that seemed unreplicable, but the thoughts of Sandra's demise always crept in. It was too painful, too much to endure. My voice cracked, breaking the silence.

"I didn't leave because I didn't love her."

"I know," Ade and EO whimpered in unison.

Their reassurance didn't feel like enough. My hands felt heavy, as if there was something I should be holding in them but wasn't. I sniffled a few times as I tried to get a hold of my emotions."Does Abegail know?" I asked.

My question triggered panic in Ade's eyes.

"It's okay. I can tell her," I said.

"What do I do? I don't know what to do?" she stammered.

"We need to get you both somewhere safe, somewhere he can't reach you."

"Who?"

I tried to look her in the eyes, but I couldn't. "Someone I can no longer ignore."

"We should take her to Big City. They can stay with us until we figure out something better." EO was right. I contorted my fingers, one on top of the other, and pointed around the room with my eyes. He nodded, stood up, and examined the room.

"I'm going to take you to Big City, and you can stay with me for a while, okay?"

"I don't know how to take care of a kid, Kilo."

"It's okay. I'll help you." I squeezed her tight. There was no answer I could give to make this easier. All I could do was try to convince her that, eventually, things *would* be okay.

"I'll get us some passenger tickets, and we can leave tonight."

Her brow furrowed with angst, but her look soon tempered.

"I just can't believe she's gone," Ade said.

"I know, me either."

I pulled out my personal device and flipped through a few screens until I found the departure times to Big City. A red flash of words prominently shot across the screen.

CAUTION: RESTRICTIONS ARE IN EFFECT ON THIS TRAIN

This made things a bit more challenging, but I could probably still get them through with DIIP clearance.

It really was all crumbling around us. The pacification of the people and the tenuous trust between the cities corroded. As we sat a few feet away from the box containing the unspeakable, our world teetered along an equilibrium, and Ludo was pushing hard for it to tip.

"We can grieve back in Big City, but right now, we need to get out of the Below."

Ade nodded and stood up, extending a hand to pull me up with her. I gave her credit for her strength, and I was happy that she stood with me in the midst of this horror. Even with flushed cheeks and puffy eyes, her warm-hearted nature couldn't be dampened.

"Kilo, you're . . . you need to see this." EO tripped over his words.

I turned to see him staring at something, breathing heavily.

"Grab whatever you can for Abegail. I will help you in a second, and then we'll go see her."

Ade collected some of Abegail's belongings, and I trudged through the mess to EO. A flicker of light caught my eye, and I looked down to see the framed photograph of Sandra partially hidden under the overturned table. I picked it up and handed it to Ade.

"Take this too . . . please."

She stared at the photo the way I had days before, with emotion stirring from a recollection of two intertwined lives.

"Of course," she said, wiping away a tear.

I turned back to EO. His stare was pinpointed on an open cylindrical canister that looked like it should have held cookies or some other treat. Instead, a few off-line credit storage chips, each only capable of holding between five to one hundred credits each, sat at the bottom, but so did something else.

"She was saving up credits?" I whispered, as if talking to myself.

"Seems that way—but look."

I bent down and noticed a small pin among the remaining few credit storage chips. I snatched it up between my fingers and inspected it. An ND pin. Ice ripped through my veins.

At the end of the long piece of metal, a custom knob sat where the head of the pin would normally be, a diamond-encrusted knob. I turned my head to EO. His concerned look confirmed the inconceivable thought.

I put the pin in my pocket, the pressure from my clenched fist screwing it into my skin.

"I'm going to stop them. I'm going to stop them both."

The commotion of the station disoriented me. We fought our way through the hordes of hopeful people looking to escape to Big City. Strobe lights now lined the grand station, and a fortified makeshift checkpoint forced a bottleneck of anxious people. It hadn't been easy, but both Ade and I put on a smile for Abegail.

I stumbled over my words in an attempt to tell her about her mother, but ultimately decided to leave it for another time. I knew the choice was a cop-out, but I convinced myself it could wait—for her own good. Instead, I told her she'd be traveling off-island to be safe.

But we weren't the only ones who recognized the danger looming in Kaua'i City. Red, flashing travel-restriction warnings obscured the once-serene murals covering Central Station's Grand Hall. The other island cities didn't plan to allow Kauaʻi City to ripple through the chain.

It started to make sense in the sea of people why the other cities would restrict travel from Kauaʻi City. The chaos mirrored the footage from Honolulu City days before its collapse. Kauaʻi City hadn't fallen into anarchy yet, but if other districts followed Ludo, it could turn ugly.

A tight-haired, brawny customs agent greeted us with a scowl, and his free hand grasped around his weapon.

"You. Tickets."

A week ago, an authoritative man had sent me on my way with little more than a couple of questions. Now, we would be lucky if the weapon's safety stayed locked. Off to the side, a few Night Sticks stood in reserve, truncheons holstered on their thighs and AAP 445s angled closer to the crowds than the ground.

"Here's mine." I showed him the codes flashing above my personal device. "These two will be traveling with me as diplomatic personnel for DIIP."

The man looked at Ade and then down at Abegail. Her eyes grew wide, and her mouth clamped shut.

"Only you. No unverified passengers. No exceptions."

"Sir, please, there are diplomatic policies in place for this kind of—" I gave my best attempt at civility, but the man cut me off.

"No. Unverified. Passengers." He pushed Ade and Abegail aside and waved forward the person behind us.

EO's sigh coincided with my indignation. As the man attempted to brush me aside, I grabbed hold of his arm, standing firm. Blood rushed to his face as he contracted the muscles along his clavicle. Another agent glanced over for a moment before returning his attention to the family in front of him.

"We're getting on the train. Either you let us through or—"

"Or what?" He grasped my shoulder with his other arm and squeezed.

"When it's time, I want you to get down," I said softly to Abegail as her chin quivered. "It will be okay, but I want you to cover your ears, all right?"

Ade nodded and clasped her hands around the girl's head.

"Enough. Get the fuck out of here," the customs agent said, and shoved me back. I stumbled, catching my balance before grabbing the Nambu from my waistband, and in a fluid motion, drilled one shot after the other into each of the man's feet.

The shots echoed several times throughout the Grand Hall. In a panic, everyone around us dropped to the floor, screaming and patting themselves for damage. With Abegail's ears still covered, Ade dropped to her knees over the little girl's body to protect her from any escalation.

"Come on, let's go." I grabbed Abegail's hand and hoisted her up and out from under Ade. It only took seconds for everyone near our station to see the chink in the armor. Hordes of people, trampling each other, rushed toward the loading platforms. On the far side, Night Sticks wailed away at the closest running families. Something grasped my free hand, and I turned to see Ade sprinting behind me, steps ahead of the mob.

More shots echoed behind in the Grand Hall as I stumbled down the ramp, the massive trains parked, waiting below in perfect rows. Abegail shifted in my arms and pinched my skin, but it wasn't enough to deter my focus.

"What Section?" I threw the question out, not knowing exactly where EO was.

Ade's voice yelled inaudibly, but I heard EO clearly. "Departure seven. Car forty-three, section ten."

The flicker of a malfunctioning train number two rows down read, "Departure seven," and I redirected my momentum. Loud hissing from the far side of the station signaled several trains pulling out.

As we reached the back of our train, flashes of red caught my eye, slowly consuming the lettering on each of the departure signs. One by one, the signs suspended above their corresponding train turned to "DOORS CLOSED." *Shit, Big City isn't taking any chances.*

"Car forty-three, it's right there." EO pointed toward a car only twenty or thirty meters down the platform. I hoisted Abegail up once again, repositioning her to a more comfortable place against my shoulder, and pulled Ade with me. Twenty-five, thirty, thirty-five. The doors whooshed behind us, one by one denying boarding.

"There's forty-three," I yelled. "They're closing! Get inside!"

I threw Abegail onto the top step and ushered Ade behind her. Once inside, she turned to pull me up, but the doors slammed together, separating us. I watched her eyes grow large through the window.

"Kilo!" Steam built up around Ade's hands as she pounded the unflinching glass.

"I'm sorry," I mouthed.

Tears rolled down her face, and I patted the breast pocket of my coat, signaling her to check her own pocket. Her shaking hands pulled out the personal device the Doctor had given me. The device lit up with a DIIP agent badge alongside Kamalu's official DIIP portrait and contact.

"Tell him I sent you," I yelled through the window.

The condensation grew under my palm, aligned with Ade's on the glass.

The train hissed from departure and pulled away into the evening dusk, bound for Big City. I forced down the knot in my throat and hoped to see them again. Somehow, I believed I could make it happen.

A strong arm met my chest as I turned away from the train. EO's clouded eyes leveled with mine. "You don't need to kill Bless," he said. "I know he helped, but this is about your father, all right? Don't forget that."

I tried to focus on my father's image, of him signing the death warrant of thousands, millions of people, but I couldn't help it. The rumination of Bless helping him kill Sandra ate at me like a worm from the inside.

"We're going to Usos first."

CHAPTER 26

We waited in the shadows of the alley, watching the hurried footsteps among the people of Nāpali. If the powder keg in Ludo blew, Nāpali would be next, and there was little anyone could do to stop it.

Across the street, the lights dimmed inside Usos Gym, and the last few patrons trickled out following the climax of the final show. It hadn't taken long to get here from the Inter-Island Train Station, but long enough to stir in the thoughts of what Bless had done to Sandra and Maurice. I played with the ND pin, recalling the countless times I'd seen Bless plunge it into his neck or arm.

He'd been careless, but maybe part of him had a soul. The Bless I knew would never have been so thoughtless. Maybe with his senses elevated, the stimuli were too much to concentrate, and he'd fallen victim to himself. It didn't matter. Enough of a monster had grown inside him to make the brother I knew unrecognizable.

"I think we're good," EO said. I grunted in reply and tried to channel every tangled feeling into fury, something controllable and deadly, but the bubbling pain fought for supremacy.

"Let's go," I said.

I crossed the street, leaving indi-cycles screeching past to avoid hitting me. The club looked the same but now felt foreign. I'd seen it a million times, yet a single element of knowledge had changed that perception forever.

The door shook but refused to open as I pushed and pulled on the handle. I took a step back and unleashed a flurry of bullets at the glass surrounding the metal knob. The reinforced glass soon gave way and shattered. Shards crunched under my boots in the newly acquired entrance.

Faint alarm whistles sounded, but there were no flashing lights and no onslaught of security guards. Bless either wasn't expecting me or just didn't care. The lights appeared dimmer inside, leaving shadowy corners across the arena. The dense ball in the pit of my stomach only grew with each step.

"Kilo, I know what he did, but don't cross the line for him," EO entreated. "Don't lose who you are for revenge."

"We'll see," I whispered.

I fiddled with the trigger of the Nambu, clearing each of the corners until the sand of the fight platform ground beneath my boots. Something tugged at my ears. Beneath the stands, the darkness shifted.

"I guess we both know why you're here, Bruddah." The booming voice projected from the shadows, and Bless strode out onto the platform. His eyes had sunk into his skull as if he hadn't slept in days. "I never wanted to do anything that would hurt you. You're my bruddah."

"Well, your brother by blood is rotting in a prison cell, so forgive me if that doesn't mean much."

I pulled the Nambu up and aimed it at Bless' chest, but the gun shook in my trembling hand. He stood only a few meters away, multiple ND pricks visible on his right arm. More evidence of remnants of a soul, but not enough to hold me back.

"I heard you might have seen him, but I hoped that wasn't true." Bless kicked the sand as he paced. "He deserved what he got. He wasn't on board with what needed to be done and was never grateful for the steps I took to make this place into something."

"What did you do to him?"

"He grew a bit of a conscience, so I had some friends take care of him."

I unloaded two rounds at his feet, spitting up dust around him. "Is that what happened to Sandra? You had some people take care of her?"

Bless' chest bounced with his laugh. "You know exactly who killed Sandra. I was just the fuckin' mule."

The pain bubbled over, breaking through the angry facade I'd tried so hard to craft. A single tear rolled down my cheek and into the sea of sand. "How could you? What happened to you?" I screamed.

"Kilo, Mirella's here—third level." Regardless of EO's warning, the pain overwhelmed me, tears blurring my vision.

"You worked with him. You helped him kill Sandra." I stepped closer and pushed the barrel of the pistol into Bless' sweat-covered forehead. My finger twitched as I tried to force myself to squeeze the trigger.

BANG! A shot from above connected directly with the Nambu, shattering it. I shuttered, blocking some of the flying debris with my arm. Before I could look back, Bless' boot connected squarely with my chest, sending me to the ground. Blood trickled down his face from several open wounds holding fragments of the Nambu.

"It's not that simple, Kilo." Bless took an ND inhaler and ingested a full cartridge. "Men are complicated. I'm not all ambition and not all guilt, but they are both inside me. Because of that, I can only offer you solace through chance."

He pulled a pistol out from behind his back, placed it on the ground, and kicked it across the platform toward the arena stands. "You deserve a chance."

"It's a fair fight, Kilo. Mirella's put her rifle down," EO said. Bless cracked his neck and ripped his shirt off before throwing another inhaler skidding toward my feet.

Fine, let's do this.

I shoved the inhaler up my nose and drew a deep breath. The ND turned from ice to fire in my veins, trickling down through my extremities. The cold air of the Below reacted with the ND and sent tingling across my exposed skin.

A half smile flashed across Bless' face as the drug set in. His lips opened to speak, but I rushed toward him, accelerating fast. I dropped my shoulder and drove it through his chest, lifting him off the ground and onto his back. We slid along the gritty surface, but he managed to regain his leverage. With a powerful thrust, he pushed me aside and rolled away, bouncing upright.

He flexed his broad upper body and angled his arms into a defensive position. The pleasurable shivers of the ND ran up my spine as I mirrored his defensive stance. Bless took a heavy swing, narrowly missing. I found some power in my back foot, took a step forward, and released two sharp punches into his gut.

We traded blows, only blocking a few hits while taking gut-wrenching haymakers. Inflammation quickly grew in my hands, ribs, and shoulder, the earlier week of chaos coming back to haunt me. Thankfully, the ND kicked in and provided hedonic sensations to beat back the pain and allow me to drive forward.

Bless' heavy breathing and increasingly careless punches signaled he hadn't fought in a while, maybe even since he took over the club. EO's muffled yells of encouragement from the side of the platform distracted me for an instant, but an instant was enough. Bless connected a standing kick to the side of my head.

The kick delivered a ringing that consumed my auditory functions and inhibited my balance. I shook my head a few times to clear the cobwebs. Bless took a second, too, and shook off some of the pain from the shrapnel still burrowed in his face.

"Why, man? What is worth all this? You're a killer, a traitor, and a piece of shit, and for what?" My questions forced a break in the fight. We both stood there, chests heaving, and fiery gazes locked on one another.

"You'd never understand. You were fucking born there. You were never one of us."

"You were my brother! Maurice and you were my family!"

"Family? You left! The Continent, Big City, we were just a cushion to brace your fall."

"You're wrong, and you know it. Your family, your father, saved my life, and this is how you repay him for everything he did? This was my home, Bless!"

"You may have thought it was your home, but you lived with EO every day. Every time you fell, he picked you up. You don't understand what it's like for us."

"All this because you don't have a DPM? You selfish bastard."

"You used my dad; I used yours. Now we're even."

I lurched toward him, unleashing everything I had in a two-three-two combo. My final strike connected upward, cracking his jaw and squirting blood out of his mouth. The punch sent him stumbling back and eventually to the ground. It took longer for him to get back up, and it was more than enough time. Without him knowing, I'd shifted the fight toward a spot in the ring that set up my finishing move.

I couldn't tell what tripped the definitive effects of ND, but they washed across me. The ND numbed my body to all its feelings, but my mind remained in control. A forged tool. But I didn't intend to use it. I'd managed to maneuver myself to the far side of the ring and bent down to scoop up the gun Bless had kicked across the sand.

The coarse metal of the fully automatic pistol calmed my breathing. I felt it in my soul, if not against my skin. A look of disgust covered Bless' face as he managed to crawl to his feet. The hammer clicked, and I checked the chamber.

"I'm sorry I left. I'm sorry I was blind as a kid. If it had been different, maybe you wouldn't have turned into this," I said.

"Maybe." Bless spat blood from his mouth.

"You don't get to come back from this, though," I said, raising the pistol at him. With my other hand, I pulled out the ND pin from my pocket and threw it at him. "It was Sandra."

He let out a heavy breath, his legs giving out. "I just brought the box."

"Yeah, but you helped him find her, didn't you?"

He nodded his head, but I wanted an answer.

"Didn't you?" I screamed.

"Like I said, remorse and apathy mix for a cruel cloud of pain, but *you* already know that."

My finger fought with the trigger. I envisioned the bullet ripping through his skull and scattering brain matter across his beloved arena. I forced Maurice's and Sandra's faces into my mind and screamed through gritted teeth. The shot rang out through the building.

A single hole through his neck drained the blood from his body. He clasped his hands around it, just like Matagi had, fighting for his life. The circles grew in his eyes like I'd never seen before.

EO made his way over to the platform. "You know—" he started.

"Yeah."

"Hands up." The shaky voice came from somewhere behind us in the stands.

I turned to see Mirella step out of the dark, gun in hand. She postured powerfully, but her eyes reeked of fear.

"Is he dead?"

"No," I said. Her eyes flinched and looked over to Bless, whose blood was now streaming into the sand.

"Why didn't you kill him?" she asked. The pitch in her voice spiked. Despite clenching every muscle in her body, it sounded like she was about to collapse.

"You didn't work for him because you wanted to, did you?"

The question was rhetorical, but a slight quiver in her lip confirmed it. I knew only too well what Bless was like, even when he wasn't . . . this. Some days, he was your best friend, your confidant, and your cheerleader. Other days, life challenged him, and he made sure you felt the challenges with him. I didn't need Mirella to tell me what she had been through, because I knew.

I lowered my hands, maintaining eye contact as she kept the rifle steady. EO sighed and knelt over Bless' body. His love-hate relationship with Bless always favored hate, but he still had a soft spot for him.

"I don't want him to die, Mirella," I said.

"What do you mean?"

"The hole in his neck leads straight to his cervical spinal cord. I know you have a stasis pack in the back. If we use it now, he'll live."

"But then—"

"Wait long enough so reconstruction surgery won't help, then take him to a hospital. If he can't move his arms or legs, he'll have a harder time hurting people. But you need to go now."

"Okay." The gun dropped. Her tensed muscles relaxed, her eyes locking with mine. I nodded, and she broke into a sprint toward the back rooms of the club.

It took a few minutes to get the stasis pack into position, but eventually, Bless' body lay idle yet alive. She needed to keep him there for six hours before transporting him to the hospital. The doctors would be able to save him, but he would be paralyzed for the rest of his life.

After Mirella finished putting Bless on ice, she let me into his office, which had been turned upside down. The space exhibited the anguish Bless must have been going through the past few hours. I searched through the scattered documents for something.

Bless must have had some kind of evidence linking him to Design City and my father. Twenty or thirty external files sat next to me as I continued to search through anything I could find.

"Did you really see Mo?" Mirella asked.

The question caught me off guard, but I continued to rummage through Bless' office.

"Mm-hmm," I murmured.

"Is he . . . is he okay?"

"He's been better."

Gashes in the walls, flipped tables, and half-hanging swings provided more evidence of Bless' collapse under the weight of what he'd built. Mirella huddled in the corner and watched me for several minutes before she beckoned my attention.

"Here." She threw a hard drive in my direction. I stopped the drive under my angled boot and picked it up.

"What is it?" The weight surprised me. It was much heavier than a normal outsourced data drive. A small engraving on the back tarnished its sleek exterior—a Design City emblem.

"Open it."

I righted one of the flipped tables and placed the drive on it. A twirl of green lights emitted from the tabletop, converging in the center and revealing the contents of the drive. Digital folders appeared in a tree of files, each labeled with years, dates, and locations.

"Is this recruitment data?"

"Yeah, but what you want is right here." She grabbed hold of a small file hidden among the others and expanded it. EO whistled at the sight of the three files that populated the entirety of the digital array.

"He was going up there?"

"Every month. He met with someone regularly to ensure district recruitment from Ludo and Nāpali remained above average. I didn't know everything that was going on, and I'm still not sure I want to know."

"Well, you're going to find out soon enough."

I played with the files, opening and closing them, searching for something specific. EO's and Mirella's eyes bounced around, following my search until, finally, I found it. The words read like a crime story EO would have told: "Modified Blood Markers—Blessman Ta'ala."

"This is how we get up there," I said.

Mirella opened her mouth to reply but paused. "Right, you're talking to your DPM," she said as a hint of rose flushed her cheeks. "You don't look anything like Bless, though."

"Alessia," EO said.

I translated his suggestion for Mirella. "There's someone who can help us with that."

CHAPTER 27

The coarse alley wall of the DIIP building warmed up after a couple hours of leaning against it. I watched the people of Mid-City like I had outside Bless' club, seeing how the knowledge of what was happening in Ludo affected them more and more by the minute. Their laughing and courteous gestures had all but stopped. Their walks and reactions to loud noises or other unusual stimuli heightened. Although our world had been chunked into smaller pieces by the Designers, in this moment, everyone lived on the same island, inextricably connected to the city underneath our feet.

Without my personal device, getting back up to Mid-City had been challenging, but the commotion of unrest in Ludo left some gaps in the access ways between the two cities. Thanks to some help from EO, we slipped through and caught one of the crowded general elevators to the Kaua'i City DIIP building. There we waited.

I tapped a passing pedestrian commuter on the shoulder and asked for the time. A few minutes to six a.m. If Alessia planned on spending time at the DIIP building today, she would show up soon or not at all.

"What are you going to say?" EO asked.

"I don't know. The truth?"

He grunted in response. I cranked my head in his direction and raised an eyebrow. "Sorry. I know that's your thing. I'm worried about you."

"I know. We're together, though, so there's nothing to worry about."

He stared incredulously at me. "In what world?"

"All right, if you get torched again, I'll make sure I go, too. Happy?"

"Not really."

My mind ran through the past twenty hours and stopped at the Ni'ihau beach. I'd completely forgotten about EO's caginess. After the meeting with the Company and finding the box, thoughts of Bless and my father had consumed my mind. But now, in the breath between gasps, I remembered.

"What were you holding back on Ni'ihau?"

The question sent a shift through EO, but he stared fixedly down at his feet. Now, more than anything, I felt curious. "If you need to hold on to it, I understand."

EO dragged out the response. "The dreams you have about the platform and the truck aren't where the story begins. The memory of your mom at the white sand beach happened days before you descended."

"Why don't I remember it? I only remember the platform, saying goodbye."

He sucked in as much air as he could before releasing it with his words. "Something happened when you went home that day, a conversation between your mother and your father. He told her he'd decided to send you to the Below."

"Okay, so what? I assumed that conversation happened at some point."

"The conversation wasn't so simple, Kilo. Your father loved your mother, but—"

"If he loved her, he wouldn't have killed her."

"I . . . he said they would never survive if people found out you were his child, and your mother, she—"

The rumble of a motorcade caught my attention. I craved what EO knew, but it needed to wait. Out of the Designer car stepped several colorfully dressed security guards, each carrying fully automatic weapons. The colors of their clean-cut suits shifted with the runoff water from above. I understood the idea behind Designer fashion, but I'd never grasped how they could look at themselves in the mirror as they dressed.

"There she is." EO pointed at a crowd of guards, which flashed glimpses of a flowing, salmon-colored neon dress between them. Although I possessed Bless' altered blood markers, I didn't intend to take any risks. We needed Alessia.

"I don't want to hear it," I said before letting out a high-pitched whistle tune. The pitch shifted back and forth in an upbeat rhythm, a rhythm to the song Alessia and I had loved as kids. EO's face, tight-lipped, still scrunched as he nodded in sarcastic kudos.

The gang of rainbow-colored Designers stopped, and the guards held back whoever was trying to break from the bubble. Yet Alessia burst through like a child fighting their way out of the womb. Her head whipped around, searching for the sound, until her eyes locked with mine. I slipped back around the corner, out of sight, and waited.

The lavishly dressed woman came around the corner, grabbed hold of me, and crushed me in her embrace. "What are you doing here?"

"It's nice to see you, too. More times in the last couple of weeks than in the past two decades."

"You're supposed to be back in Big City."

"I didn't want to leave without saying goodbye to an old friend."

She pulled away and swiveled her head in search of her entourage. "I've heard rumblings, Kilo."

I didn't know how to explain the past week to her in a way she would understand, but I tried. "I found something . . . on the Continent. The Designers are upsetting the balance between the cities."

"Outpost 378?"

"You knew?" A flash of anger accompanied the question.

"Of course not. I just learned about it today. The Designers are trying to keep a lid on it, but it's spreading like wildfire in the Below. That's why you're here?"

Just as I opened my mouth, Alessia cocked her head, listening. "I will."

"What did your DPM say?" I asked.

"I want you to answer the question first. Why are you here?"

I darted a glance at EO to see him nod in encouragement.

"I need to get into Design City, and then I'm going to stop *him*."

The green in her eyes all but faded, her gaze drifting away and focusing elsewhere. Her face twitched a few times as she listened intently. I wrapped my jacket tighter around my shoulders and waited for her DPM to finish.

"Kilo," she started, her tone hardened, "if I help you and you miss, the global population drops by a fifth by the end of the week. You understand?"

I nodded.

"You need to kill him and check for a pulse."

Her unequivocal response jarred me. I expected her to see the reason for stopping my father, but she didn't sound like herself. It was easy to feel the raw desire and to dream of tearing my father limb from limb, but her words made it real.

"What are you going to do if I kill him?" I asked pointedly.

Her face pulled at the accusation underneath the question. "You wouldn't understand."

"Understand what? That—"

"You came here to use me, Kilo; don't get excited when I take advantage."

"You're just like them, aren't you?"

"I want Kaua'i City to survive! If what I've heard about Outpost 378 is true, you should be thanking me."

"Kilo, you need to do this," EO said simultaneously with her.

I turned, failing to hide the confusion on my face. "Neither of you sees the issues here? Even if he is the worst piece of shit on the planet, blood doesn't wash off, and you . . ." I looked back at Alessia. "*You* don't care what happens as long as you inherit the desk."

"It's not about you anymore," EO said. "This isn't like Bless."

His words overlapped Alessia's. "This is bigger than you. Isn't this what you wanted?"

"I don't know! I have killed him a million times in my head, but . . ." I closed my eyes and massaged my pounding temples.

"I would trade places with you in a heartbeat if I could," EO said. "You don't deserve this, but you're the one here."

Every moment I'd spent wishing to trade places with him, wishing to have it easier, and thoughts of breaking from the shackles of blood and flesh swirled in my mind. But now, the utter pain behind his eyes, asking me to do this, the anguish of not being able to carry my burden reeked from his pores. I wouldn't wish that on anyone.

"Okay. Do the right thing, Alessia. Do what that little girl up top would've done. I'll play my part."

"All right. It'll take me a couple of days to get your blood markers into the system."

"No need." I produced Bless' digital hard drive and showed her the Design symbol. "I just need someone to grease the elevator cables."

She examined the silver block before lighting up her personal device.

"6:14. Meet me at the Gateway at 7:45." Without another word, she turned, the bottom layer of her dress brushing against my leg, and headed back to the DIIP entrance.

Revenge wasn't enough to cross the line. The evidence lay in a stasis pack at Usos. It wouldn't be enough up top, either. I realized the answer to EO's question, to Alessia's concern, to the Doctor's hope. I thought back to the pyramid-filled cemetery. The families of Matagi, Solomon, and Sandra were drops in the bucket of what would come.

Shipley's words echoed in my head from when he relieved me from duty. *You will never kill a man in cold blood. You will never be willing to do what is necessary, even if the scales are unbalanced. You're selfish, and you're weak. You don't know what it means to sacrifice, and you never will. You've never understood that the ultimate sacrifice isn't death; it's living with it.*

It looked like Alessia had been waiting for hours, her arms crossed and eyes dreary, resting on an uncomfortable bench. Her body no longer curved with the flowing work dress. Instead, she wore baggy cargo pants with an oversized jacket, a traditionally unbecoming outfit for a Designer.

I almost forgot what a Designer could look like outside of their audaciously colorful and perfectly tailored garb. Alessia had always been different, though, or at least I'd thought, unenchanted by the idea of Designers. Now, she'd turned to something else, a compromise of two worlds.

"Hey."

"We don't have much time." She motioned to the empty seat on the bench next to her.

We sat across the street from the entrance to the Gateway. Concrete and glass buildings guarded the auspicious elevator building. The Gateway resembled a gold-infused Architecture Building, something that melded together the architecture of both Mid-City and Design City.

"So?" I asked.

"You have the blood markers on you still?"

I produced the hard drive to reassure her. Her eyes darted between the open personal device on her lap and the hard drive. I'd never seen her so on edge. As a kid, she'd always been the fearless one, testing the boundaries of the city and asking questions no one else did.

"All right, good. I'll do all the talking. You just need to pose when they ask."

"Easy enough."

Her facial expression disagreed.

She led me to the crossing bridge down the street. Once on the other side, I picked up the pace to keep up with her. EO followed along, then stepped close to the armed guards and inspected their expressions as we passed through the rotating glass doors.

Inside, the building looked different from what I remembered. In my mind, it was more impressive, the statues larger and the colors more vibrant. It all seemed too real, something that mismatched the narrative of the Designers.

The white tile floors led visitors to a long, marble-covered desk helmed by several white-haired managers dressed in three-piece, off-white suits. As we approached, their leathery faces came into focus, their hair turned from a sleek white to silver with a yellowish tint, and the two oversized elevator doors rested in the obsidian wall behind them.

"Ms. Landrum, I didn't recognize you. Forgive me. Will you be heading up to the city this morning?"

"Yes, thank you, and I will be accompanied by Mr. Ta'ala, here."

The elderly woman fixed her eyeglasses and gave me a once-over. With the snap of a finger, she called over two guards, who each took out circular handheld devices. They waved them along our bodies but found nothing.

A green light accompanied a low pulsating beep before the guard positioned the contraption centimeters from my nose. The device whirred and scanned my blood markers. The scanners looked new, but I remembered them from every time we'd visited Mid-City. This I was prepared for, and thanks to Bless' drive, I wasn't worried.

Alessia's scan finished first, and she turned to watch for the results of mine. When the whirring noise ceased, the guard lowered his device to view the illuminated results.

"Thank you, Mr. Ta'ala."

I nodded while EO snooped around the other side of the desk, squinting at whatever the other managers were working on.

"Well, isn't that nice. Hopefully, your business will be concluded quickly. Right this way, please."

The white-haired woman guided us to the elevator doors and placed her open palm on the wall, soon illuminating a handprint scanner that resembled the one used in Outpost 378. It didn't surprise me now.

"Thank you," Alessia said as the elevator doors opened.

We stood inside for a moment before the doors shut on the woman's displeased stare.

"She was . . . pleasant."

Alessia snickered. "You get used to it. The change in the zero-tolerance policy didn't help their temperament."

The elevator doors opened to a wide walkway covered in vines and encapsulated by a canopy of trees. Luminous rays of gold pierced through it, painting a beautiful pattern of light guiding the way. Design City, just how I'd left it.

Alessia stepped out and into the shade of the concrete dock. It stood alone, an isolated transport depot at the edge of a Design City suburb. At the end of the walkway, I saw a golden dome, and below it, projected signs. Even from this distance, I could make out the directions to each of the districts of Design City.

I tried to take my first step, but my feet refused to detach from the elevator floor, as if my shoes had turned into synthetic cinder blocks. The periphery of my vision swirled, the disorientation of colors shattering my focus.

My heart rose into my throat. I felt Alessia's warm hand interlock through my fingers, and EO's arms squeeze me from behind in a compression hug.

"You're okay. Just walk with us." EO's calming voice helped ease the tension as we passed by a group of Designers waiting for the elevator.

I forced my feet forward, wincing through the turmoil.

"Is he all right?" Someone's voice rippled through my mind.

"Yes. He has a bit of a natural light sensitivity."

I could tell one of the voices was Alessia's, but the other seemed to come from another world. I moved another step, less arduously this time, still without any sense of how far we'd come. In an instant, it seemed like we traveled the distance of the city, and in the next, we were standing still.

The swirling worsened, dampening my senses until I could hardly discern any differences. I struggled to breathe and attempted to force my hands around Alessia's. The gold of the dome consumed my sight, and my vision became a lustrous blindness before . . . black.

"Hey, you with us, Kilo?"

My eyes adjusted like a personal device, slowly pixelating a dynamic image. The wood molding of the room appeared first, followed by the quaint and cozy living room. I sat, sunken into a colorful brocade sofa with Alessia extending a steaming mug toward me.

"Drink this. It will help."

I complied. The hot liquid tasted appalling but streamed down my throat, soothing the pain. "Where are we?" I asked between sips.

"You don't remember?"

The question was rhetorical; how could I forget? Before my descent, I'd spent more time in this house, this home, than anywhere else.

I rendered visions of every part of the house. This three-story, stilted, gray tower held the rooms of my childhood. I stood and made my way to the stairs on wobbly legs.

"I didn't think you would still live here," I said.

The rooms looked different. What once was a kid's play area with toys sprawled within the forest-painted walls had been transformed into a drab white office. Alessia's bedroom, which used to feature a sea-themed bunk bed, now housed a neatly made queen-sized bed and a nightstand riddled with black prescription bottles.

Outside the window, Design City sprawled out like farmland from the Old World, culminating at the skyline with a highly congested set of elevated buildings. I recalled most of the Designers living in houses like Alessia's, modest yet tall. Designers only allowed their suppressed taste for narcissism to shine in the City Center.

I grabbed the frame of the window, feeling the blood drain from my legs before returning moments later. My desire to never step foot up here again had not been unwarranted.

"Kilo?"

"Yeah?"

"We should talk before I leave."

"Leave? Why are you leaving?" I followed her into the office, where her Designer personal device projected into the center of the room.

"I can't be here when you see him. You know that," Alessia said.

"Right." I rubbed the throbbing headache through my temples, but it didn't help.

"If you want to get to your father, you'll need to follow him home from here." She pointed to the floating stadium in between us. "He, along with some of the other senior Designers, will be there at the Design Show today."

"Why can't I just go to his house?" I asked.

"If you want to do this, you need to remember where you are. You won't be able to move freely throughout the city, especially around his buildings."

"Okay, fine. So, once I get through the masturbatory Design Show, I'll just hop in a cycle and say, *Follow that guy*?"

Her eyes tightened, clearly displeased with my lack of precision.

"All right. All right. Use the winner?"

"Exactly. Although they don't technically get to meet with him, they do get a chance to go to the Design buildings after the competition."

"That seems a little conditional," EO chimed in. "You have to get to the competition, then somehow get to the kid after they win, then impersonate your way into one of the most respected buildings on the island city?"

"He's right. This isn't exactly foolproof."

"It's the best you're going to get. Last resort, you can use your real blood markers to say you want to see him, but it's eighty/twenty whether you're shot on sight or buying yourself five minutes before the whole city knows you're there."

I couldn't think of an easier way of getting to him, so I didn't push her.

After all, this was always likely to be a suicide mission, or at the very least, an unnecessarily complicated way to fulfill a masochism I didn't know I had.

She powered down her PD and handed it to me.

"I have another one," she said.

Her designer version looked almost the same as the one I'd owned, but with a fragile glass encasing instead of the typical reinforced casing. It made it possible to see the inner mechanisms of the device and left me in awe of the power and knowledge it contained. I could only guess the Designers enjoyed the feeling.

"Where will you go?" I asked.

"I don't know, probably DIIP. It will look better if I'm there when it happens," she responded.

"Makes sense."

Alessia tilted her head and nodded. "Timeline-wise, I need to leave now." As she reached the door, she turned back. "I'm sorry for what you are going to find up here and what you have to do. Good luck, Kilo."

All I could give her was a halfhearted nod. It was too much to think about right now. I heard the door close on the floor below. The house now belonged to me, if only for a couple of hours.

"So?" I turned to EO.

"It's weird . . . being here." He stared out the window, the city from his memories now something he was experiencing for the first time. I felt happy for him. His disdain for the Designers had always been based on my experiences, so he'd lived here secondhand and firsthand at the same time. Even if this place burned the core of my hatred, he deserved to take it in, to understand it for himself.

I sat with him while he spent some time looking at the city. He asked questions he already knew the answers to, but I indulged him and performed as a tour guide for an inquisitive child. A heavy knock sounded from the front door below and brought us back from the city views. I grabbed reflexively for a weapon that now lay in a hundred pieces at Usos. *Damn it.* I'd been lucky to make it from the Below to Design City without a gun, but I'd taken it for granted that I wouldn't need one up here. My feet barely touched the steps down to the first floor. I snatched a ceramic decor piece from the foyer table and crunched it in my jacket. The muffled noise hadn't alerted whoever had knocked.

I held on tight to a sharp fragment and pressed my ear tightly against the door. The ambient noise of the air conditioning system dampened the sounds outside. I jumped as the knock split through the door again.

"Open the door!"

CHAPTER 28

The strained shout from the other side of the door sounded more like a wheeze. I waved my hand across the motion sensor and dropped the makeshift glass shiv. Outside stood an elderly woman in a clean, kempt outfit. Although she was several inches shorter than me, her presence and confidence made up for it.

"Let's go, Mr. Kilo. You have an event to attend."

"What are you . . . how do you know me?"

She pushed past and strode into the house. "I've known you for a very long time."

I studied her face. The creases around her eyes cut deep into her skin, and her gray widow's peak angled into her forehead. Her left eye twitched slightly, but her dark green irises showed a hint of nurture. It hit me.

"Marie?"

"Well done. Took you long enough." Snorting, she turned and opened a closet door in the living room. Its wood frame unveiled an assortment of carefully sorted, colorful suits.

"You can't go looking like that."

"Wait, what?"

Her expression said, "Are you serious?" presumably to the stupid question, which brought back memories. It wasn't something I thought I would miss, but her disdain for childlike ignorance left a warm ball in my stomach. It took only moments to feel like a ward under her care.

"Do you still work for Alessia?"

"This one will do just fine." She tossed a three-piece soft blue suit at me. "In the cycle in five."

She promptly shuffled past me without answering my question and slammed the door behind her, leaving me with a stupid, boyish smile on my face.

"Did you know it was Marie?" I asked EO.

A coy smile threaded EO's lips as he shrugged. "I deserve some entertainment before this all goes to hell."

The suit fit smaller than what I'd been used to and didn't have much give in the important areas, but it looked nice for a Designer suit. A heavy white vest complemented the coat and pants. One look in the mirror and a Designer stared back at me, save for the general disheveled look above the shoulders. It would do.

The cycle sped off, and we watched an unimaginable number of trees pass by. It struck me as odd. There were trees and landscaped areas around Mid-City and even in the Below, but the trees meant something different here. The lushly lined highways resembled a detailed art display, with every leaf cultivated to evoke a trace of beauty. I closed my eyes and listened for the trees playing rhythmically with the wind. Designers didn't see trees as organic or ecocentric, but as decor.

I opened my eyes to see the floating buildings of the City Center rising in front of us, atop the two- or three-hundred-meter city foundation. A concrete, inverted trapezoidal plateau reached up from the ground of Design City. The once-unassuming square domiciles were now exquisite architectural creations atop the foundation, with the tops of the huddled buildings brushing against the clouds.

The highway rose into a double helix, bending our duo-cycle around the oncoming traffic. From inside the cycle, the optical illusionary road repeatedly weaved around itself until we reached the top of the City Center's plateau. I glanced through the rear window, seeing the infinity pool of green and its towers poking out from beneath it.

In the City Center, buildings lined the streets as if created from a teenager's fever dream. I recognized some of the Designer administration buildings: construction, city design, and transportation, but some appeared to be new or redesigned.

"What's that?" I asked.

"Inter-Island Building. They built it after Honolulu."

My head turned, and my eyes followed the column-encircled building until it disappeared behind us.

"Did things really change up here after?"

"More than you'd think," Marie responded.

"Hmm."

EO watched the buildings fly by, jerking his head each time he saw a new and interesting sight. Part of me wished he'd been able to spend some time here, but that would've required *I* spend time here, which did not strike me as fondly.

After a few minutes of driving deeper into the stilted city, the competition hall appeared from behind a row of Designer buildings, like a colossus waking from obscurity. Its oblong shape rose at its end, much like the City Center that held it. Crowds outside were dwarfed by the solid marble exterior playing canvas to colorful etchings of the generations of Designers. A futile ode to this inbred society and its achievements.

"You'll be dropped on the far side, the only entrance for general Designers; from there, you can find your way."

"Do you know what I'm doing here, Marie?"

Her deteriorating bones cracked as she whipped her head around. "No. But I trust Ms. Alessia." Her eyes dropped, and she reverted to watching the road. "Just like I trusted your mother."

"I didn't know you two were close?"

"Not so much, but soon before you were sent away, she would come to me, and we would talk. Deep down, we both knew there wasn't much to be done beyond some words of comfort."

"And my father?"

She looked in the rearview mirror. "I had my suspicions, and I suppose they were confirmed, but no, I've never met the man."

The cycle slowed to a stop, with crowds of people on either side of the street chaotically attempting to enter the arena. I gave Marie a nod, which she ignored before wishing me good luck.

I jumped out and disappeared into the crowd.

"Kilo, about your mother—" EO said.

"Not right now. We need to get inside before the competition starts. This is our only chance to get to him."

"I know, but Kilo—"

"It's fine. Whatever it is, it can wait."

His shoulders dropped, and he followed me through the crowd. I enjoyed being able to speak freely to EO up here. Somehow, it felt natural. *Maybe Mo and Bless weren't so wrong.* But the thought quickly faded.

Every time I bumped into someone, they extended a warm apology until they saw my face. It didn't matter, though. As long as I didn't bump into someone important, I found catharsis in throwing a shoulder here and there at these walking estates.

A line of escalators at the general entrance dropped off countless dots of people at varying levels of the stadium. I took the one that ascended to the highest level. As I stepped off, the buzz of people inside the building became overwhelming. It was impossible to keep track of the broken conversations about Design jobs, the unrest in the lower cities, or which contestants they thought would win.

The confusing mix of corridors led to the various sections of the stadium covered with holograms of previous winners, their Designs ranging from the practical to the idealistic. The section designation on Alessia's personal device read, “UPPER GREEN ROW 45,” which, after a few minutes of being swept around in the pedestrian traffic, appeared above an arched entrance.

I shuffled past families of Designers before finding my seat on the cushioned bench. EO hunched in front of me, and we looked far below at the tiered stage. In its center, a skeletal scaffold held up a transparent cubic backdrop that seemingly portrayed the same scene from every angle.

Above us, barely visible domed lights at the four corners of the stage focused their beams to the middle of the cube. It looked unassuming now, but if this competition lived up to the hype, the Mixed-Reality stadium would soon come to life.

At the far end, beyond the valley of seats, rose the hierarchical rows of senior Designer seating, culminating in the open-faced boxes soon to be occupied by the heads of divisions.

Based on the unique designs of the boxes, I deduced which sections belonged to which Designers. A box just left of the center was designed with ancient Chinese cultural artwork. The thin, lengthy body of a dragon snaked around the box with its head resting above the central seat and its mouth agape, ready to rain down fire. I recalled the same dragon in my father’s office and his home, a tribute to a story that fueled him.

It wasn’t long before the stadium filled, and a powerful roar among its inhabitants shook the arena as the lights dimmed. A person basking in an aura of stage lights started the show. The excitement around the introduction enveloped the man’s voice, and every sentence he finished was met with uncontrollable applause.

The moment we’d been waiting for soon arrived. The speaker’s voice echoed through the building as he introduced the various Designer section leads. Finally, he introduced the Designer for Island City Protection and Endurance. My father’s name sent a roar through the crowd. I focused on controlling my breathing through gritted teeth. I couldn’t afford an episode.

Far across the stadium, my father’s carefully manicured, shoulder-length white hair swung as he turned to each side of the stadium and gestured to the adoring people. My heart pounded, and the periphery of my vision blurred. I couldn't tell if it was rage, pain, or scars that caused my tunnel vision, but I forced myself to look back at the stage. This wasn't the time to feel *everything*.

A few moments later, the competition started with an intense configuration of lights that followed a young woman from the staging area tunnel out to the stage. Once there, the lights formed a well-designed, Mixed-Reality work garage indistinguishable from the real thing.

Before speaking, she moved deliberately around the stage and grabbed various tools and components. She brought her haul back to a machine that resembled a mix between a crab and an octopus. However, I couldn't determine whether the contraption was substantive or a production of the lights.

Then the arms of the mechanical crab-octopus pushed up its body, crawled over to one side of the stage, and scaled to the top of the scaffolding. Its arms moved organically, each component of metal combining and releasing seamlessly. At this distance, with a little makeup, it may have passed as a real crab-octopus freak of nature.

The lights adapted, swinging around to follow the machine as it ripped apart the stage, holding together two sides of the scaffold with extended arms. Once the machine destroyed the stage, two of its other arms clamped onto the fractured ends of the metal poles.

After a brief pause and a bit of crowd work from the contestant, its widespread arms brought the two sides of the scaffold in close before they leeched together like two powerful magnets. The scaffolding for the stage once again stood steady, a perfect restoration of the structure. The crab-octopus climbed down and took a bow along with its Designer.

The host's voice again boomed from the stage. "A wonderful Design, with specific uses such as underwater transit repair, which fits very nicely into this year's theme of Inter-Island Cooperation."

The host congratulated the young woman and ushered her offstage before the lights dimmed once again. "Our next contestant is one of the most brilliant up-and-coming Designers. His Design is a true work of architectural mastery that may affect Mid-City and the Below for generations to come."

My mind wandered. One exhibition was enough for me. The next three contestants received a gamut of reactions as they presented their architecture designs, transportation conceptions, and one faulty mask upgrade for the Continent. I couldn't help but laugh at the wild misunderstanding and ignorance of the work that took place on the Continent.

Across the stadium, heads in the Designer boxes often turned away from the stage, engaging in more interesting or self-important tasks. Even from this far, I could make out a small group of Designers congregating with broad smiles on their faces, toasting tall glasses and sampling the assortment of catered dishes. They wouldn't have to wait much longer to judge the contestants. I didn't know why I would expect anything less. Design City reflected the world they'd created.

Finally, the last contestant took the stage. Someone could have coughed from the Designer boxes, and every person in the stadium would have heard. Unlike the other contestants, everyone, including the senior Designers, focused intently on the presentation. The boy began with a flowing dance and seemingly became one with the lights. Presentation counted for half the battle with the Designers.

He circled a small box in the center of the stage and waved his arms frantically, coaxing the box to open. He finally kneeled to open it manually, obviously part of his presentation.

BOOM! The stage exploded, sending shrapnel flying into the stands all the way up to the Designer boxes. I ducked, trying to get out of the way of the larger debris, but a needled pain burned into my cheek.

"Where did that come from?" I yelled.

"It was the stage." EO stood in front of me, surveying the damage. "Whatever it was, it wasn't planned."

A red glow from the center of the arena engulfed the stage. Thousands of scared Designers ran for the exits, fighting to hurdle over one another. I stood up, holding steady as several people tried to push past me. They were forced to climb around and resorted to screaming obscenities, but my focus remained on the Designer boxes across the stadium. Security shielded the senior Designers, who were hurried out of the box and huddled into private elevators.

"We're screwed." EO waved his hand in front of me to break my gaze.

"Not necessarily. Come on." I climbed over the rows of seats to the edge of the section and peered down to the benches below, gauging about ten or fifteen meters, but if I landed on the cushioned seats, I didn't expect to break anything.

"You're not serious."

"You see a faster way down?"

I lowered myself over the ledge and let go. My knees buckled, and I rolled off the bench seat. I'd technically been right; nothing broke, but I'd severely underestimated the pain. EO landed with a thud next to me and let out a prolonged groan.

I wanted to smile through the throbbing, seeing him act as if he was in pain for my benefit. "See, not so bad," I lied through a clenched jaw.

We repeated the same painful process four times as we made our way to the ground level. It wasn't much, but somehow, EO's performance each time we jumped made it hurt a little less. By the time we reached the stage, our limbs flared, and we hobbled past the fiery box. It loomed much larger up close, but there wasn't time to look around. We headed toward the congested tunnel that led into the staging area.

The chaos inside matched the energy of the entire stadium. Design Show personnel had partitioned off contestants in their personal staging areas, and Night Sticks stood at the entrance of each contestant area. Beyond, attendees tried to force their way past other guards toward the exits. Tears streamed down the faces of the contestants as their teams tried, and failed, to console them in anxious congregations.

Clearly, no one knew what had caused the explosion, and a mixture of desire to contain and restore consumed those in charge. Among the pandemonium, I recognized an advantageous opportunity.

"Who do you think was going to win?" I asked as EO and I peered into the various contestant rooms.

"Octopus-crab, no doubt."

I scoffed, but based on the presentations I'd paid attention to, he was probably right. It likely didn't matter which one we picked, as long as it wasn't the kid who blew up the place.

The young woman who'd dazzled Design City with the metal crab-octopus monster hid behind her contraption in the furthest room, while someone on her team argued with a Night Stick. I nodded to EO and stepped forward, shouldering one of the Night Sticks. He whipped around and cocked his arm, energizing his truncheon with a crack.

"I'm so sorry, sir. I didn't mean to bump into you." I raised my hands in a supplicatory gesture. "I'm here to tell you they have been cleared to leave the building."

"I don't know who you are, but no one leaves."

I just needed the Night Stick to take a step, but he refused to budge. "Look, you can take it up with whoever's running this shit show; just let these people go. Please."

"I don't think you understand how—" He took a step.

I swept my leg around before his foot could hit the ground. He dropped to the floor with a thud, his truncheon slipping from his grasp. I lunged for it, rolling past another guard into the partitioned room. By the time I grabbed it and stood up, the other guard swung wildly toward my head. The blue sparks exploded as his truncheon collided with mine.

Behind me, EO made his way over to the mechanical crab-octopus and kneeled next to the cowering young woman. I didn't know how close I needed to be for him to get the information, but the closer, the better.

I battled back and continued to play defense. The Night Stick sustained his charges, swinging recklessly with a clear plan to win by beating me to death.

"We're good," EO shouted. "Let's get out of here."

Let's see what this thing can do.

The Night Stick reared up and swung repeatedly. After a few moments of his lashing away, a chance for a shot exposed itself. I stabbed the truncheon into his gut and sent a shockwave through his body armor.

Even with unthinkable voltage, the electricity-dampening technology in the suit reduced the effect to something like touching a cycle battery. Though the small shock gave me just enough time to gain position to swing back. With three quick blows to his arms, I saw the pain grow in his eyes through the narrow slits of his mask.

"Hurry up, Kilo!"

EO motioned toward reinforcements barreling toward us from the arena tunnel. Among them, I noticed a few automatic pistols holstered but unlatched. *Time to go.* I kicked up hard between the man's legs, connecting with the crotch of the suit. Although reinforced, it wasn't padded enough to protect his vulnerability. He grunted and keeled over. I reared back for another powerful swing and connected with the side of his helmet. The electricity, combined with the force of the blow, knocked him off his feet, and his face smashed into the ground.

"Run!" I shouted to everyone in the contestants' room.

With the abrupt exit of an entire contestant team, confusion set in among the other Night Stick guards stationed around the staging area. Two of them suddenly left their station to run after us, sending another contestant team off toward the stadium. Night Sticks cut down people rushing toward the exits as fast as they could, but they couldn't stop everyone. Gunshots rang out behind us.

We sprinted through the double doors into a corridor that led to the back side of the stadium. I briefly turned and launched the truncheon behind us over the crowd of Designers running for their lives. It missed one of our pursuers but forced them to stutter a step.

EO's stupid grin bounced alongside me.

"Shut up," I growled.

Someone in front of us broke through the doors first, opening the tunnel to hundreds of shouting Designers outside. I pushed my way into the crowd and disappeared.

CHAPTER 29

The flashing lights of a motorcade raced by. I caught a glimpse of some senior Designers through the tinted windows of their custom SUVs. It was odd seeing so many large vehicles in Kaua'i City, but social mores didn't always apply to Designers.

The final SUV passed, and I scanned the heavily trafficked street for a suitable target. On the far side, a yellow indi-cycle idled, caught between the sidewalk and the inner lanes of traffic. I crossed through the yielding cycles with EO in tow.

An absentee driver near me gassed her cycle, trying to catch the drift of the motorcade. The cycle slammed into my leg before screeching back to a halt.

"Fuck. That hurt." I slammed my fists against the cycle's hood, denting the metal inward. From inside, the driver produced a few hand gestures that were unbecoming of a Designer, but I didn't have time to teach her that lesson.

I finally made it past the fifth driving lane, grabbed the handle of the yellow indi-cycle, and yanked open the door. "Get out."

The woman said nothing, frozen, with her jaw agape. I leaned in to see whether there were any kids in the back. *None, good.* I grabbed an arm and pulled her out, throwing her onto the ground.

"Sorry," I said, and watched her scamper away into the crowds of people.

I forced the cycle into the growing traffic of escaping Designers.

"Was that necessary?"

"You tell me. How far ahead of us are they?"

EO squinted as he looked through the front window. "Far enough that it's hard to tell, but I can still hear the sirens—"

"Good."

I mounted the curb, sending the cycle shaking on the uneven sidewalk. Frazzled pedestrians leapt out of the way at the sight of our speeding cycle. In another time, the walking path along the city streets would have been serene and inviting. Today, it was flooded with worried Designers.

It was unprecedented in Kaua'i City for an attack on Designers to happen in Design City, let alone the City Center. I debated the chances the presentation had simply malfunctioned, but with the fire fueling the riots below burning hot, my credits were on disruption.

Design City Center buildings flashed by mere meters from our cycle. Although my focus only lasted a few moments before it needed to return to the pedestrian walkway, I caught a closer look at the finishings of the evocative buildings. Cracks in the paint, concrete pieces breaking off the base, and discoloring on the upper levels implied deterioration. The impurities were small, something people who passed every day might not notice, but I did. I found even the smallest contradiction to the ostentatious expectations in my head noticeable. Marie had been right; things had changed.

"You see that?"

"Yeah." EO's brow furrowed, his mind spinning to decipher its meaning. "I wonder—" He cut himself off and refocused on the road ahead of us.

The traffic started to break, and the lights of the motorcade grew stronger in the distance. I swerved the cycle back onto the road and slammed into another vehicle before regaining control and unleashing the engine.

Horns of other drivers blared with each lane we tore through. In the rearview mirror, a couple of cycles tangled up and spun into a Designer building, sending steam billowing up from the crash. I didn't dare look at EO. I wasn't interested in his take on my method of tracking down our target.

“Help me upload the girl’s data.” I placed Alessia’s personal device on the dashboard and booted up the system using the voice function.

“I don’t think the motorcade is going back to their residences,” EO said. Ahead, the lights of the motorcade still flashed, but the sirens stopped. The road opened to the double helix and spiraled down from the City Center. I kept my distance behind a few other cycles, but stayed close enough that any move they made remained visible.

“Diana Masters’ data merge ID 477822,” EO said.

I repeated the words.

The personal device carried out EO’s command, and Diana’s competitor information populated above the device. Now all I needed was to convince someone I’d been the one on that stage, but easier said than done.

After a few minutes, the motorcade took a sharp turn and exited off the spiral road onto a lingering highway headed out into the outskirts of Design City. In the distance, silhouetted buildings stood on the blurred line between the manufactured dirt and the rays of the setting sun. The motorcade headed toward the conglomerate of auxiliary work buildings.

Hundreds of parked cycles, some still with their headlights lit, waited outside the structures. I pulled the cycle off the road and cut the lights. The buildings rose into the sky, a set of six interconnected, stretching maybe half a kilometer along the edge of the island city superstructure. Among them, connecting glass-covered skywalks supported a few Designers hustling back and forth between sections.

I tracked the motorcade vehicles as they broke away from one another and headed for separate buildings. The parked cycles moved out of the way, parting the sea for the senior Designer SUVs.

The SUVs came to a stop, dimmed the lights, and released well-dressed, armed men and women into the golden evening. Now, I just needed to wait and see which building belonged to *him*. I had a hard time making out the faces from our distance, but EO filled in the gaps.

“Is that him?” I asked.

A sturdy man exited one of the cars and faded into a blanket of bodyguards.

"No."

"Well, which one is he?"

"Be patient," EO said. He then pointed a finger toward one of the middle buildings. "There."

I could only see a hint of silvery-white hair before the group of people disappeared into the building. My eyes narrowed, and I watched the SUV depart. A lone security guard blocked the stairway entrance of my father's building. It was time.

Whipping wind rivaling the gusts on the Continent blew back my hair as I approached the security guard. The moment he saw me emerge from the road, he yelled something garbled and aimed the automatic rifle at my chest.

"Easy. I have some information." I motioned inside the building to where my father had disappeared and took the first step of the stairs.

"Senior Designers and their teams only," he said.

"Look, I was a contestant—the autonomous reconstruction design."

The man's eyes remained empty, confused at the combination of words.

"The crab-octopus thing," I said.

Behind the angry blank stare, it finally clicked. But he still held fast, blocking the entrance. I took another cautious step. "I think I know what happened with the last contestant, but I need to speak with one of the leads."

His gaze stayed locked on me as he continued to hold his position, but there was a twitch in his ankle, and he took a step back. I lowered my hands slightly and curled my fingers, one on top of the other, for EO. If there was anything he could give me, now was the time.

"What's your name?" the guard said.

"Blessman Ta'ala." I lowered one of my hands slowly to my front pocket. "I'm just grabbing my personal device to show you who I am."

The guard stiffened, pushing the gun closer to my face. I halted my motion at the click of the safety release. "Knees."

I bent down to my knees and folded my arms behind my head. EO's eyes remained laser-focused on the trigger. The man stepped down and circled around my back. Once he made it back into eyesight, he swung the rifle behind his back and unholstered his sidearm. He bent down and patted both of my front pockets, his tensed face easing when he found them empty.

"Okay, show me your device."

I flicked through the merged information until my DIIP headshot popped into focus. Nothing beyond the headshot belonged to me, but EO had patch-worked Bless and the girl's data well enough to pass. Hopefully, this brute hadn't been paying enough attention to the Design competition because a gender swap would be a bit more difficult to explain.

"Aren't you a little old for the competition?"

"From fourteen to twenty-four. My birthday's next week," I said without hesitation. "I've been working on this forever."

"If you're twenty-four, I'm fourteen," EO said.

The guard's shoulders dropped, and he lowered the gun to a comfortable position. He squinted at the information on my device, and my eyes darted to EO. He chuckled to himself and shifted around the guard, examining him.

"All right. I can take you inside, but you need to go straight to reception, where they will escort you to the appropriate lead."

"Thank you." I coated the words with earnestness. "I believe I can help figure out what happened with the explosion."

We followed the guard up the steps and into the building, where he pulled us into a hallway that extended throughout all six of the Designer auxiliary buildings. The apricot-colored interior matched with a pristine, white marble floor and tan lines interwoven along the walls.

"You need to go upstairs and through the first door. If you don't follow my directions, I'll throw you out personally."

"Yes, sir."

I followed the curved stairs, my hand gliding along the gold banister. As I approached my destination, I continued past and down the hall. I secretly hoped for a directory of some kind, but I didn't anticipate being so lucky.

Although we'd clearly seen commotion among the buildings from the side of the road, it now seemed empty. There were no foyers, no communal areas, and no open offices. Instead, the building was nothing but decorated empty hallways lined with locked office doors.

I inspected each of the doors, looking for anything that might hint at who they belonged to. One after another exhibited intricate murals, hand-carved into the exterior wood. They all told a story, some uplifting and optimistic, others reminiscent of the history that had brought about the island cities. The end of the hall angled toward the back of the building and, if possible, out over the edge of the city.

Dead end. Neither of us found anything that resembled what I could remember of my father's office. The soft orange glow of the sunset peeked through a tinted window at the end of the hall, its light alluring. People all over the island cities would kill for a moment with a sunset. I watched the amber dome head toward its eclipse of the horizon.

A warm arm that wasn't there wrapped around my shoulder and words echoed, opening my heart, but fleeted as I tried to grasp them. My chin quivered only for a moment. *Mom.* I knew this was the closest I would ever be to her again.

"Kilo," EO said softly.

I wiped away the trail of a tear and followed EO's gaze to the cliff edge below. A protracted concrete walkway reached out over the hard-packed ground, far above the layered cities below. The curvature of the building partially obstructed it from view, but it looked like an open entryway connecting the skywalk to an office on the ground floor. The memory hit me.

"It's him." Heat flushed my face, and I rushed for the staircase. "Help me find the right office."

I took the stairs two at a time and broke into a jog, listening to EO's directions from behind. The emptiness of the building still bothered me, but under the circumstances, senior Designers probably forced extraneous personnel to work at the inner-city offices.

"This one," EO said, and pointed across the hall.

The mural carved in marbled wood told a simple story: a voyage of thousands of people escaping to a developing Kaua'i City. But among the tribes of fleeing people swam a lurking dragon.

I slammed open the door's handle, almost tearing it off. I looked around and found no one, but the office contained remnants of a focused man. Multiple devices waited in stasis along the heavy desk between me and the skywalk.

In an instant, everything rushed back. I recalled a vision of the office from before, layered over the top of this current version. A faceless man appeared in my mind, pacing rapidly around the room, wildly throwing his arms around as he commanded the various devices. The soft upholstery of the desk chair tickled my legs, and the warm comfort from a familiar sun massaged my back.

I took a step toward the desk, but a creak from behind forced a reflexive spin toward the door, jarring me back to reality.

"Hello, Kilo."

CHAPTER 30

My father brushed past me with so little regard I might as well not have been there at all. After making himself comfortable behind the desk, he focused on the rotating documents that came to life in his presence.

I'd dreamed of this moment my entire life yet had failed to prepare for standing here in worn and bloodied boots. Ignored.

I tried to open my mouth, but my heart pounded into my throat. His dominance, the unwavering surety of his power, saturated the room. I felt like a child again, *his* child. Although the power he held over the room, over my life, existed as nothing more than a fallacy, his unyielding grasp tightened around my neck.

"Bless' blood markers?" he finally asked, turning to open one of the desk drawers.

I nodded, and he graced me with a look from the corner of his eye.

"Well, have a seat if we're going to talk." He motioned to the vacant chair across from his desk. "Hopefully, you killed him. That's what he deserves after blowing everything up."

"I'll stand." The words wavered despite my best efforts.

"Fine."

"You okay?" EO murmured.

He wrapped his hands around my arm, but I shook my head at him. I couldn't control the swirling in my head, the fire in my gut from Sandra's death, the Continent. Nothing was accessible. My thoughts seemed to smash together like cycles at a mistimed intersection.

"I almost forgot—EO, is it?" My father's eyes drifted until they stared directly at EO, as if he'd been made of flesh and bone. "It's nice to finally meet you. Well, after designing you, I suppose."

"Go fuck yourself." EO spat the words at him.

"I assume he isn't a fan?" my father asked.

"Kilo, he's nothing. Do what you came here to do."

A full row of teeth flashed through his thin smile. "Well?"

I pulverized Alessia's personal device in my hand, leaving shards and blood falling from my fist. The child that had once played in this room, that had crumbled under the weight of an omnipresent power, had died in descension. My mother's hands no longer provided comfort or stability, but I didn't need them. EO's warm grasp pulsated through my skin, sending waves of harmony throughout my body. I let in a deep breath and broke through my petrification.

"You took everything from me. You are single-handedly destroying the lives of hundreds of millions. I'm surprised your face is still capable of smiling."

"Kilo, you may have my blood, but don't act for a second like I ever cared for you. You were nothing more than a release I needed in a moment of weakness, so if you're here for an explanation or some alignment of stars to make sense of it all, you can fuck right off." He reached across his desk toward a button guised within the wood surface. "I don't have time for a grand explanation."

I cut across the office and grabbed his wrist before it reached the button. His torso contorted around the desk, and the small bones cracked under the pressure of my hand. He glared back at me with pain and frustration thundering in his eyes.

"What—" he tried to say.

I shoved him to the floor, hardly needing to exert any energy.

Up close, the wrinkles gouged into his porous skin and the ruined veins in his eyes led to marred yellow eyelids. He'd become a victim of carbon, dust, and time, just like the people who worshipped him.

Underneath the surface of the desk, I felt around for a smooth bump. The hidden compartment dropped down with a click.

"You may not have cared or even thought of me, but I didn't have that luxury." I pulled out the hidden pistol and examined its chrome exterior. "Every single memory of this place brought pain to a ten-year-old kid, but thankfully, a memory or two happened to be useful."

His eyes narrowed, and he pulled himself to his feet, dusting off the five-piece ebony suit and favoring his injured wrist. His restraint surprised me, but a look of impatience grew on his face as I watched him wait for my move. I took a few steps back, holding the gun comfortably, pointed in his direction. I didn't expect a surprise move to be in his repertoire, but I didn't intend to take any chances.

"I don't care about how you did it, what you planned on doing, or even why. All I care about is stopping this world from being destroyed like the last one. That means killing you."

"Destroy? Your mind is small if you think stability was ever in the cards. Since Honolulu—"

"Like I said, I don't care about any of it. What I know is building a city on the Continent, concealing the fact that one of the island cities has control of livable land, is a death sentence for all of them and what remains of our fucking race."

"You're so—"

"No! You and the rest of the senior Designers claim to have built this world as a guarantee of extension, an extension of life, of space, of human ability, but it's only ever been a toy set for families that think their greatest achievement in the history of humanity is building *up*."

I found my arm stiffening with the gun pointed at his chest, my finger pushing the trigger to its absolute limit. A wave of contentment flowed over me as I watched his face change. He looked small, a shell of the demagogue he presented to the world.

"You're going to kill me, Kilo?" He drew himself up, the remaining bravado blazing from his eyes. "Then what? You ended this world the second you told them what you saw. Killing me doesn't change anything."

"Ask your DPM if killing you changes anything. I'd like a more reliable opinion," I spat back.

His tongue roamed his cheeks as he unhinged his jaw. My question hung in the air, weightless.

"He doesn't have a DPM," EO said softly.

I lowered myself into his chair and flicked the gun, motioning for him to sit across from me. Small circles of the cherry wood were now light brown, discolored from where my father's arms had rested for forty years, and the unbothered leather gave way to the rigid cushion within. The chair sent fireworks through my synapses, bringing forward the hazy feelings of grinning in discomfort, sitting here as a child.

"How'd you get it removed?"

"You think it's been removed?" A smile encroached on his face. "I just don't use it."

"What do you mean you don't *use* it?

"There is no need for him."

EO's confused look mirrored the uneasiness in my chest.

"Humor me."

"He's in *there*." A long, bony finger pointed toward a bookshelf lined with several physical copies of books I didn't recognize. "I convinced him to never leave his three-by-three room cemented behind the books."

"Jesus. He's a prisoner."

EO walked over to the case and felt along the lines where it touched the wall.

"You're worse than I thought. It's one thing to do what you did to me, but to torture your own DPM? You're a monster!" I shouted.

"I did what I needed to do." His nostrils flared. "We are the only ones capable of preserving life in this city. The world is no longer unified as it once was, not after Honolulu."

"We?" I pulled back the hammer and checked for a bullet in the chamber. A copper shell stared back at me. I repositioned the sight square between his eyes. "What do you mean *we?*"

"All these years, and you still don't know?"

My eyes darted to EO, pleading for this not to be what he'd hidden from me.

"You really believed your mother was dead all these years? It almost makes me feel sorry for you."

"That's enough!" I screamed. My finger twitched as my blood boiled and swirled. "I don't believe you!"

"I've watched you ever since I sent you down. You can't kill us."

"Can't I?" I inched closer to him, but my voice cracked with the words.

"You kill, but not in cold blood—even if they deserve it. That's why you ran, wasn't it? That's why you left your friends and family, the only girl you ever loved, to start a new life. You weren't strong enough to survive in that world any longer. You have never been willing to sacrifice what matters most to you."

Every muscle in my arm clenched as I tried to force the trigger back, but my finger wouldn't move. The corners of his lips peeled back, his piercing eyes remaining locked with mine.

"I'll kill you. I've wished for your death my whole life."

The internal pressure squeezed around my neck, and blood flushed my face. I tried one last time to blast a hole through his face, even as I wailed in pain.

"You have one thing in your life that you can control. The one thing that is most important to you. You know as well as I do what you give up if you pull that trigger, even if it's me."

The door to the office creaked open, and in stepped a salt-and-pepper-haired woman. Her eyes dazzled a brilliant green in the fading sun, and her skin, although wrinkled, pillowed softly over her wide cheeks.

Through a broad smile, she spoke muted words. My father stood and wrapped his arms around her. In unison, they turned and looked down the barrel of his pistol.

"Hi, sweet boy." The dimples at the end of her bright smile delved into her cheeks in a slightly different place, and the hairline sat unevenly in a foreign path along her brow. The mystery of it sent disorienting memories clashing with reality. But her voice remained a unique, soft pitch that could only belong to her.

"Mom?"

"Yes, Kilo."

I lowered the gun as numbness slowly invaded my system. "How are you . . ."

"It doesn't matter. What matters is you are here with me." She extended a gentle hand. "I know you're angry, but let's just sit and talk."

"No!" The rebuff roared out of my mouth from somewhere deep inside. "He's destroying the island cities. He is building a city on the Continent and doesn't care how many people he has to kill to do it."

A moment passed before the sweet smile on my mother's face faded. "*He* isn't doing all of that, Kilo, *we* are."

"What?"

As the dazed word left my mouth, my father lunged at me, pulling a knife out from behind his back. I whipped the pistol up and pulled the trigger, experiencing the sequence recurrently, milliseconds after it happened. The bullet burrowed into his body, followed by the same bullet a second time, as if I'd fired again. My mind attempted to dissociate me from the experience, creating a psychologically twisted encore.

Blood stains spread across the white vest of his suit, and he collapsed to the floor. My father's fight ended no more valiantly than Bless' with the light fading from his eyes. A life rooted in every inch of the city had extinguished in moments.

Tingling spread down my arm, and I looked to see the dagger lodged in my shoulder. The blade ripped through flesh as I pulled it out. I inspected the gold-encrusted, curved quillons of the weapon for a moment, sensing the prestidigitation it represented, and released it to clatter against the floor.

My mother's expression remained unchanged, but her empty eyes stared at me."I guess we'll never know if you could have killed him in cold blood, if you could pay the debt we all owe this world. No matter, what's important is that you can't kill *me*." She threw her hands in the air, defenselessly.

"What?" I asked again, not knowing what else to say.

"Kilo, you cannot be this naive . . . my *son* cannot be this naive."

"Mom, I . . ."

Her eyes stirred, and eyebrows lowered as if she were talking to a suffering animal. "I know I should be sorry, Kilo, but how can I be?"

The words sounded as though they had been pre-recorded, overdubbed by someone I didn't recognize. But the decades of longing that had grown for my mother congested my chest.

"This world was never broken. It was Designed as an imperfect perfection. Unfortunately, the cracks have grown into fissures and we . . ." She paused as she looked down at my father's body resting in its bath of growing blood. "*I* will make it into something that works."

"I'm so sorry," EO said. His head bowed, eyes welling with tears. "I thought I was doing the right thing. I was trying to protect you."

My face had lost all its feeling. Inside, the war raged, reconciling who the woman standing before me was—the words or the memory. The real and fabricated imprints on my mind overpowered the reality.

"How are you . . ." I started again.

"All this time and EO never told you?" My mother's words scratched at my chest. The last minute failed to be anything short of paralytic. My father lay dead at my feet, and my living, breathing mother now taunted me as EO rued the secrets he'd held for so long, expunging the pain with quiet lamentations. *What is this? How could I have been so wrong about everything?* The city being built on the Continent hadn't been conducted by a man but by a couple, the same couple who had sent their only child to the Below for a shot at exaltation.

"Mom, I have to stop this, please."

"Kilo, the moment I accepted a job at your father's office and ascended from Mid-City, this all became inevitable."

"I can't let this happen. You can put an end to all of it," I pleaded.

"The plans are in motion. The other island cities don't stand a chance—they have nowhere to go."

"But if they learn about Outpost 378, it will just be a reproduction of the fall."

"And? A whole world burned like a forest to create something better, but it wasn't an event. The fall of the Old World was a step in a cycle . . . I helped your father understand that."

"I won't let you destroy Kaua'i City like he destroyed me."

The thin smile on her face widened ever so slightly. "Kilo, we made that decision together. *I* traded your life for this, and I have never once regretted it. Your father and I have changed the world, not destroyed it." She lowered a hand in offering, the same hand that had once poured sand along my leg as a child. "You can have what you want if you want it. You don't care about all of this."

"That's not true. I've always cared. A part of me bent but didn't break." I tried to pull the pistol up, but its ineffable weight thwarted my attempt. "People died to get me here. They cared about what happened. I won't let you continue to build that city."

"You can't, Kilo. I know that, and so do you. As long as I am breathing, there isn't a way to stop the Continent City."

"Kilo, look at me. You are the strongest person I've ever met," EO said soothingly. I glanced at him. Pools of tears gathered beneath his eyes as he stepped into view. "I never wanted you to have to do this, to go deeper down the path they sent you, but this isn't just about you anymore. Kilo, I love you, but you have to do this."

The gun fought to leave my grip, but I wrenched it with every ounce of desire left and aimed at the pair of deep green eyes. She didn't even flinch. With a coy smile, she dropped her other hand and switched her focus to the minibar. The auburn drink she poured into her glass flowed without the slightest tremble.

"For what it's worth, it was your father's idea to kill Sandra," she said.

The final rays of a vanishing sun broke through the outer doorway, basking the room in its warm glow. My mother rapped against the door twice with the silver Designer ring around her middle finger.

"Come now, don't you want to know what's happening in Big City? What *the Mountain* is? How I found breathable air on the Continent?" A sip of her drink went down effortlessly before she took a breath. "Knowledge and a relationship with your mother are the only things you can ask for now."

I turned to EO. "Put your hand on my shoulder."

"What?"

"Just do it."

EO's light, warm touch sent chills tearing down my spine. My mother was right, I couldn't do it. Not alone.

The bullet fractured through the glass, sending its contents spraying around her. My mother grabbed her stomach with both hands as the blood oozed through her fingers. Her knees thumped to the bloodstained floor as she fought to stay upright.

I walked around the desk, the smoke still steaming from the barrel. The whites of her eyes disappeared as if the darkness from inside had already consumed whatever soul lingered. She tried to say my name through a gurgle, spilling blood onto her chest. For a moment, she reached out a blood-soaked palm before returning it to cover the open hole.

"It doesn't matter what happens to me. I understand now. The only worthy sacrifice is that which you value most. My soul . . . I choose to give it to you."

The second shot tore through her face, jerking her head back and splattering an artistic fan of blood across the minibar and onto the wall. Her body collapsed, now bathing in a pool of gore and alcohol.

I hyperventilated uncontrollably at the sight. I tried to refocus on my extremities, but I couldn't. My hands, my feet, and my arms had all gone numb, and now my mind refused to fight back. The gun crashed to the floor, and I spun to see EO, one step away. The floor reached up to me as the effects of my neural pathways immobilized me. A moment or two passed before I felt EO's chest press against my back.

"I got you, Kilo." EO's arms forked under my own. "Come on, let me help you get out of here."

I hung on to EO's shoulders and climbed to my feet, as if it were possible for him to carry my weight. I didn't dare look back as he led me outside.

The fresh breeze left my exposed skin tingling as I locked the office door behind us. EO helped me stumble along the skywalk high above the city. With each step, my legs bore the burden I knew EO wished he could help carry, and eventually we made it to the end. We sat down at the edge, our legs floating in the dusk sky. A blur of steel and concrete gradually sloped down below us.

"I will always be here for you, Kilo. I won't let this end you."

The streaks of clouds scarcely moved across the sky. I thought of trying to reach for them, hoping they might help me float away to some uninhabited island.

I let out a primal scream, unleashing every ounce of pain still residing within me, nearly ripping the strained skin of my cheeks to shreds. In the distance, the lights of the island cities grew brighter with the melting away of the sun. Only the vision of Abegail and Ade safe in my apartment brought a moment of calm amid the deconstruction of my soul.

Darkness swept through my cells, the oxygen in my blood attempting to disperse it, to fight life back into me, but my body succumbed. In an instant, I felt it . . . the remnants of myself fleeting, as if my soul had been numbed by ND. The tears had dried. Now, nothing more remained beyond the salt-laden trails along my cheeks.

Wood splintered behind us as someone tried to rip through the skywalk door. I closed my eyes and felt the wind rush against my face as I imagined myself falling into the depths of the island city. Then I opened them, allowing the comforting vision to fade into dust.

"What do we do?" I asked weakly.

"We save as many people as we can. We fight so this world doesn't destroy itself. We make sure your sacrifice wasn't in vain." EO's eyes filled with a testament of hope and continued to fight back the clouds of agony in my eyes. "We do what we can."

He didn't need to explain to me what it meant, what it would be. I knew.

ABOUT THE AUTHOR

Scott T. Miller is an author, researcher, and educator. He received his PhD in Global and International Education from the University of Hawai'i at Manoa and recently moved from Oahu to California to work in education. Scott adores science fiction and at every opportunity is writing, reading, and watching science fiction stories. Captivated by the alluring possibilities of science fiction and dystopias, Scott has a deep reverence for stories that explore the outer reaches of human capabilities and dysfunction and has been influenced by the immense wake of authors such as Philip K. Dick and Richard K. Morgan. Scott lives in Fresno, CA, with his wife, Bell, and dogs Hiro and Pebble.